ROGUE STAR: NEW WORLDS

(1st Edition)

by Jasper T. Scott

JasperTscott.com
@JasperTscott

Cover Art by Tom Edwards
TomEdwardsDesign.com

TABLE OF CONTENTS

AUTHOR'S CONTENT RATING: R

Intended Audience: 16+
Swearing: Occasional
Sex: None
Violence: Moderate

Author's Guarantee: If you find anything you consider inappropriate for this rating, please e-mail me at JasperTscott@gmail.com and I will either remove the content or change the rating accordingly.

ACKNOWLEDGMENTS

This book comes to you in its presently-polished form thanks in large part to a fantastic team of editors, proofreaders, and advance readers. A big thank you goes out to my editors Aaron Sikes and Dave Cantrell, and to my proofreader, Ian Jedlica. In addition to this fine team, at least twenty advance readers provided substantial feedback on early drafts of this book. You guys are amazing! My heartfelt thanks goes out to: Bill Lents, Chase Hanes, Daniel Eloff, Dara McLain, Davis Shellabarger, Harry Huyler, Ian Seccombe, Jeff Belshaw, Joseph Kane, Karl Keip, Karol Ross, LeRoy West, Lisa Garber, Mary Kastle, Mary Whitehead, Michael Madsen, Pat Ingram, Paul Burch, Raymond Burt, Rob Dobozy, Rose Getch, Shane Haylock, Victor Biedrycki, Wade Whitaker, William Dellaway, and William Schmidt.

In addition to all of these people, I owe a big thank you to my wife for her unending support, and finally—many thanks to the Muse.

To those who dare,
And to those who dream.
To everyone who's stronger than they seem.
—Jasper Scott

*"Believe in me / I know you've waited for so long /
Believe in me / Sometimes the weak become the strong."*
—STAIND, Believe

DRAMATIS PERSONAE

Main Characters

Logan Willis

Katherine "Kate" Willis

Rachel Willis

Alexander "Alex" Willis

Richard Greenhouse

Akron Massey

OneZero

Secondary Characters

Mayor Parker

Celine Hartford

Harry Hartford

Ivan

Lucky

Minor Characters

President-General Nelson

Major Davis

General Hall

Dr. Robert "Bobby" Beck

Dexter "Dex"

Alice

The Overseer

Lobot

The Hive

PREVIOUSLY IN THE ROGUE STAR SERIES

At the beginning of Rogue Star: Frozen Earth, Richard Greenhouse discovers a rogue star on the outskirts of the solar system moving at over five hundred miles per second.

Ten years later, his brother-in-law, Logan Willis, is fired from his job as executive editor at Harper Collins. He rides the train home early and stumbles in on his wife having an affair with one of the neighbors. He checks into a hotel and wakes up to a call from his wife. She's frantic. She tells him that scientists have detected some kind of signal from space and that it's headed straight for Earth. People think it's aliens. She asks him to come home. Some kids were driving down the street throwing beer bottles at houses and shooting guns in the air. Logan flicks on the TV and sees the headline at the bottom—

BREAKING NEWS

ALIEN SIGNALS DETECTED NEAR EARTH, SOURCE MOVING TOWARD US

Logan rushes home, watches on the TV with his family as the president holds a press conference to discuss the recent findings. She assures the public that the radio signals scientists detected are a natural phenomena coming from a previously-undiscovered celestial body—a cold, dead rogue star that she insists will pose no threat to Earth.

Reassured by this news, Logan goes downstairs to sleep on the couch; then he gets a call from his crazy brother-in-law. Richard insists the president was lying and that the rogue star, which he discovered ten years ago, is going to drag Earth away from the sun, causing massive tidal waves, and plunging us into a new ice age. He says that he's been part of a massive cover-up for the past ten years, and that he couldn't say anything because the government threatened to kill Kate, the kids, and even Logan if he told anyone. He invites Logan and his family to join him in a shelter that he's prepared outside San Antonio, Texas.

Logan dismisses Richard's warnings as the ravings of a drunken conspiracy theorist—he's cried wolf plenty of times in the past, and usually with a bottle in his hand.

Three weeks later, the news breaks that Richard is right, and the world plunges into chaos. Logan and his family rush to get on a flight to San Antonio and join Richard in his shelter.

At the airport they encounter a man in a

cowboy hat named Bill who seems far too interested in where they're headed. Peering over Logan's shoulder, the man manages to read Richard's address off Logan's laptop. Soon after the Willis family arrives at Richard's shelter, we learn that 'Cowboy Bill' has followed them there. Cowboy Bill sneaks into the shelter while Logan is out looking for his son, Alex, who ran off to be with a girl he met, Celine Hartford. Cowboy Bill shoots Richard and holds Logan's wife and daughter hostage in the shelter.

A deadly firefight ensues as Logan returns with his son. They manage to chase Cowboy Bill off. Kate calls 911, and Richard is rushed to the nearest hospital.

Soon after his recovery, we learn that Richard has been studying the radio waves coming from the rogue star. His pattern-matching algorithm has found a match. The signals are structured; aliens really are coming to Earth.

Richard plans to share his findings with the SETI institute in California; he's going to fly there tomorrow. After being attacked by Cowboy Bill, no one wants to stay behind, so Logan and his family decide to go with.

At the airport Richard is in the process of contacting an old acquaintance via e-mail: Akron

Massey, the billionaire behind a decades-long project to colonize Mars. The rockets haven't launched yet, but they will soon, and Richard is hoping that his discovery of intelligent alien life will be enough to impress Akron and earn him a seat aboard one of those rockets. He hopes to abandon Earth before everything goes to hell.

Akron Massey surprises Richard by replying almost immediately and inviting him to his mansion in Bel Air. Richard asks if the Willis family can go with, and soon they're all flying down on Massey's private jet.

In Bel Air they meet Massey and talk over breakfast. He learns about Richard's discovery and promptly asks him to keep it quiet. Things are bad enough without adding aliens to the mix. He wants to get Richard to join him at a private underwater shelter called Haven that he built in the Gulf of Mexico. There Akron has already gathered together a thousand of the brightest minds he could find. He planned to ride out the apocalypse with them in safety and rebuild after the dust cleared. Now, together they'll study the alien signals in secret and see what else they can learn before they share the news and start a new wave of global panic.

Massey invites Logan and his family to join

him in his shelter, too, but not yet. First Richard must help him convince his ex-wife that the aliens a bad news, and Earth is a lost cause. Akron wants her to join the Mars Colony mission with him and their two grown sons. At that point, Haven will have four extra beds and an empty luxury suite — more than enough for Logan's family and Richard to share.

The Willis family and Richard fly back to San Antonio. Richard goes back to his shelter with the others in order to pack his bags. Upon their arrival, they discover that Cowboy Bill broke into their shelter. He ambushes them with a gun, and a life-and-death struggle ensues. With all of them at gunpoint, we finally learn why Cowboy Bill was after them — he was one of the men hired to watch Logan and his family in case Richard tried to go to the press with what he knew about the danger posed by the rogue star. Alexander surprises Cowboy Bill, and the main characters gang up on him, taking him down together and ultimately killing him. They bury him beneath the woodpile rather than call the authorities.

Richard shows Logan and Kate how everything works in his shelter and then leaves for Akron Massey's underwater colony, promising to call them on the ham radio when it's time for them to join him.

Ten months go by. Logan and his family haven't heard from Richard. It's just seven days before the rogue star is scheduled to arrive! He should have contacted them by now. The world is becoming increasingly chaotic and dangerous. And then the aliens arrive. They turn out to be machines. They give us an ultimatum: we have to evacuate all of the land around the equator, or else. A global war against the aliens erupts.

Alexander runs out to save his girlfriend, Celine Hartford. Logan is forced to chase after him, and he's confronted with the invading aliens. Narrowly escaping with his life, he finds his son in the Hartford family's basement. They flee the house together and join Logan's family in Richard's shelter.

The next day Logan's wife, Kate, overhears on the radio that the fighting is over. The invading alien machines, nicknamed *Screechers* for how they sound when they speak, won by destroying major cities around the world with next-generation weapons of mass destruction. Now they've begun escorting everyone north.

Logan insists that they should leave, too. Harry Hartford, Celine's father, thinks they should stay and hide in the shelter, but Logan points out that it's just a matter of time before the Screechers find them. Then he mentions Haven and suggests they go looking for Akron Massey at the launch facility outside Memphis where the Mars project is scheduled to launch. If they can find Akron before the rockets take off, they might be able to learn the way to Haven. There'll be no safer place to hide from the Screechers and the cold than Akron's private under water colony.

Convinced by Logan's reasoning, Harry leads the way back to his house so that they can gather fuel and supplies for the trip. In the process, they encounter a fugitive Screecher, one that looks remarkably *human.* Harry shoots at it with a shotgun, but Logan stops him before he can put any more slugs in its armor. The robot stuns Harry, and then tries to communicate with Logan by drawing pictures with its lasers. The machine manages to communicate its desire to protect them. Logan nicknames it OneZero and insists on taking it back to the shelter to meet the others—despite Harry's protests. OneZero's reception is frosty, but she doesn't seem hostile. She'll ride in the back of Logan's truck.

The Willis family and Hartford family leave the shelter in separate vehicles and join the hordes of people headed north. Screechers flank the highways, escorting the masses.

Hours later they reach the Screechers' border at 35 degrees north and enter the town of Norman, just below Oklahoma City. There they pull into a strip mall parking lot to sleep for the night. They run into trouble while trying to find parking, and an armed confrontation results in the death of an antagonistic motorist. Soldiers come to investigate, confiscate the Willis's and Hardford's weapons, and offer a military escort in the morning to help them reach Memphis. They're headed that way, too. The President of the United States is planning to join the Mars colonists, and she's rallying soldiers to defend her at the launch facility.

After a long journey, the characters finally reach Memphis. Along the way they learn that OneZero can cloak herself, a fact which came in handy to hide her from army patrols. Then, with the help of a Spanish-learning program on Logan's laptop, they manage to teach OneZero Spanish. Alexander knows a little, so now they can more or less communicate. The characters spend the night pitching tents on the roof of a famous hotel in Memphis. In the morning they see rockets launching. They're too late. The Mars mission has left. But not long after that, they realize that only some of the rockets have launched; there's a chance that Akron is still on the ground.

They make their way to the launch facility and instruct OneZero to use her cloaking ability to find Akron and communicate their need to see him. Something gets lost in the translation and OneZero mistakenly abducts Akron from the launch facility. Hundreds of soldiers are in pursuit.

Thinking fast, Logan decides to go with it and hold Akron hostage. They flee to the Screechers' border, where they find the Screechers building a wall to keep us out. OneZero helps them steal an alien aircraft, and they use it to fly down to New Orleans and find the submarine Akron used to leave Haven. The Screechers catch up to them in New Orleans and it's a race to reach the submarine. The rogue star is close, and it blots out the sun. The tide is rising swiftly. They don't have much time. They reach the submarine and pile in, but Alexander and the Hartfords get swept over the dock by a wave just before they can reach the submarine. There's a massive tidal wave coming. Akron is forced to take the sub down and abandon them.

Logan and Kate watch, helpless, as a Screecher aircraft snatches their son and the Hartford family out of the water, whisking them away to parts unknown just before the tidal wave hits.

On the way to Haven, Akron and OneZero are able to communicate with each other in Spanish. We learn that the mechanical Screechers used to be biological lifeforms—four different species of them, including humans who were abducted long ago from Earth by a race of aliens called the Primordials. The Screechers' homeworld was ripped away from its sun and captured by the Rogue Star. The Screechers have spent many thousands of years crossing the void between stars, periodically evacuating their dark, frozen planet to more habitable locations. Those evacuees, including the ones who came to Earth, want to transfer their consciousness back to biological bodies. That is why they kicked us out of the equatorial regions. They don't want to freeze to death anymore than we do.

In Haven, Logan, Kate, and their daughter Rachel are reunited with Kate's brother, Richard. There he explains what he learned about the aliens from their signals. They were trying to communicate to us that they were coming, and that their world would be captured by our sun—and it was, along with several others that orbit the same dark gas giant together. The rogue star skipped out of our solar system, leaving them behind.

The Screechers are here to stay, and the ones

who came to Earth might only be the first wave in a much larger invasion.

Somehow, Logan needs to go back out there to find his son and bring him to Haven before it's too late.

PART 1 - HAVEN

CHAPTER 1

I sat at a booth in the Coral Cafe. It was after three in the morning, and I was the only one in sight. I wrapped my hands around a steaming mug of sleepy-time tea and peered into the fathomless black depths beyond the glass dome of the restaurant. A ghostly reflection peered back at me, illuminated by the pale silver light radiating from the jellyfish-shaped light fixture hanging over my booth. It took a moment for me to recognize the face staring back at me as my own.

"You look like hell, Logan," I mumbled to myself. My cheeks were craggy with pockmarks from bits of glass and shrapnel—injuries sustained during the Screechers' invasion. I'd grown a thick, vaguely-trimmed black beard, partly out of neglect, and partly to conceal some of the damage.

There were two haunted black holes where my eyes should have been. Puffy bags and dark circles hung underneath. I looked like I'd aged a decade in the six months since coming to Haven. I felt like it too.

Not getting enough sleep wasn't helping matters. My family and I were among the privileged few who got to live here in Akron Massey's private shelter: Haven Colony, the eye in a gathering storm of invading aliens and plunging global temperatures. The rogue star had come and gone. It had dragged Earth out to an orbit a hundred and twenty-four million miles from the Sun. A thirty-one million mile detour that caused massive tidal waves and arctic conditions in the higher latitudes as the planet was pulled in its wake. Somehow we had survived it all: the invading alien machines we called *Screechers*, other refugees trying to kill us, the frigid weather, and even the rising tides as we fled New Orleans in a leaky submersible bound for Haven. Now, six months later, with all of that behind us, we should have been resting easy. The trouble was, something—or rather, *someone*—was missing. Alex, my teenage son, wasn't here.

A flashback tore through my mind's eye: me watching from the conning tower of Akron

Massey's submarine as Alex and his girlfriend, Celine Hartford, leaned over a wooden dock to help her parents climb back up. Instead, they got swept in by the next wave, and Akron Massey took us down before I could go after them. Minutes later I watched on the periscope as a hovering Screecher disk reached into the water with tentacle-like arms and carried my son, his girlfriend, and her family away to parts unknown.

I winced as a painful knot constricted my throat, and a deep ache radiated in my chest. I rubbed tired, scratchy eyes and squeezed my hands into fists.

Six months. *Six.* I couldn't believe that we'd been trapped in here with Alex out there for half a *year* already. We were lounging in an underwater paradise of good food, warmth, running water, and working lights, while he was probably struggling just to survive—*if* he even was alive.

A painful lump rose in my throat and tears welled up in my eyes. *No.* I couldn't give up hope. Not until I knew for sure what had happened to Alex. The Screechers weren't hell-bent on exterminating us, so they wouldn't have killed Alex or the Hartfords. They'd probably just deported them like they had with everyone else. So long as we respected their borders at thirty-five degrees north and thirty-five degrees south, we were free to share the planet with them. Unfortunately, that left the human population of Earth out in the cold, forced to share dwindling resources with untold millions of displaced refugees.

I'd only seen the first few days of the Exodus as the Screechers drove everyone North, but by now all of Mexico and Central America had probably been emptied into the northern states as well. How many people were there in Mexico and Central America? A hundred million? Two hundred million? My bet was on the higher number. Even six months didn't seem like enough time to relocate that many people, but maybe the Screechers had spent that time mass-producing more of their flying, disc-shaped aircraft.

Two hundred million refugees... all of them freezing, homeless, hungry, and *desperate*....

They were going to tear apart what was left of the United States in a mad frenzy to survive. They'd probably already done that. It seemed impossible for Alex to have survived through such chaos, and yet I couldn't bring myself to believe otherwise.

"There you are," a familiar voice said. I heard slippers slapping the glass floor of the restaurant.

Colorful fish darted about in the aquarium beneath our feet, scraping their glass ceiling as if desperate to get out. I knew just how they felt. Haven was like an aquarium for humans.

"You should be asleep," I said, nodding to my wife as she approached.

"So should you," she said, covering a yawn as she slid into the booth beside me.

I scooted closer to the glass dome to make space and shivered as I entered a pocket of colder air. The water had chilled the atmosphere around the glass. Did that mean the temperature in the Gulf was already dropping? Kate laid her head in my lap, and I draped an arm over her, absently stroking her long brown hair and staring into the inky black depths beyond our aquarium.

"What if you go talk to the mayor tomorrow?" Kate asked.

"He'll just say no again."

Kate's head left my lap, and her gaze swept up to mine, eyes hard and flashing. "So convince him! Wasn't that your job? Convincing people to publish their books with you? It's the same thing, except now you're convincing someone to let you save your son's life."

I hesitated, another objection caught in my throat. I'd already begged and pleaded with the mayor enough. Repeating myself wasn't going to change anything.

"We could take one of the submarines. The Screechers won't see us under the water."

"Parker's not afraid that they'll see the submarine. He's afraid that they'll see us and wonder how we magically appeared in the middle of their territory. Or worse, that the Screechers will jump straight to interrogating us and find out all about Haven."

"They don't know our language," Kate said.

"They *didn't* know it. That was six months ago. OneZero learned conversational Spanish in a few hours, and she learned English faster than the scientists here could build a curriculum to teach her. How long do you think it took the rest of her people to learn our languages?"

"Maybe they didn't want to," Kate suggested.

I arched an eyebrow at her and frowned.

"We can't just give up, Logan!"

"I'm not giving up," I said quietly.

"So what are you doing?"

"Trying to think of a different way to get out of here."

"And?"

I raised my cup of tea for a sip—and grimaced. It was cold. Setting it back down, I sighed and rubbed my eyes once more. "I'm still thinking."

"Well while you're busy *thinking,* our son could be killed!"

"And you think that's my fault?" I demanded.

Kate's blue eyes blazed at me, and her lips trembled. Something crumbled as I held her gaze, and tears slipped down her cheeks. To my surprise she collapsed into my arms, sobbing.

She wasn't really angry at me. I held her and buried my face in her hair. "He'll be okay," I whispered. "Don't forget, Alex was the one who saved us from that psycho in San Antonio. He knows how to handle a gun."

"So do soldiers!" Kate withdrew and wiped her eyes on her sleeves. "Knowing how to use a gun doesn't prevent you from getting killed by one."

I winced. I shouldn't have reminded her of the real danger out there. The real danger wasn't from the cold or the Screechers. It was from the people— millions upon millions of desperate, hungry, homeless people who were willing to do anything to survive.

I pulled Kate into another embrace. "He'll be okay."

She jumped in my arms and sucked in a sudden breath. I was just about to ask what was wrong when I heard the hollow *thunk* of something heavy hitting the glass dome behind me.

"Logan!" Kate screamed. She scrambled out of the booth and stood shaking a finger at something outside. "What *is* that?"

I turned to look, and it was my turn to jump. A nightmarish creature like nothing I had ever seen was silhouetted in the silvery glow of the cafe's light fixtures.

The jaws of the creature were broad and easily big enough to swallow a great white shark whole. Hundreds of needle-sharp teeth as long as my forearm protruded from the upper and lower jaws. The head was bumpy and armored like a crustacean. Four-jointed, crab-like legs radiated from the monstrous head. Each one terminated in a sucking pink mouth dilating against the glass, and four triangular mandibles crusted with teeth were splayed around each of those orifices.

"What the hell is that?" Kate asked again, her voice rising sharply.

As I watched, the creature released the glass and its jointed arms reared back. Instinctively I scuttled out of the booth and stumbled away.

All four legs snapped out—*thunk!* Muffled squealing noises reached my ears as sharp teeth ground against the smooth surface.

Before I could decide what I was looking at, the creature released the glass again, and this time it swam away. I glimpsed a long, armored body and a hairy mass of tentacles trailing from its underside.

"I'll tell you what it's not," I said slowly, blinking into the swirling black depths where that monster had been just a moment ago. "It's not from Earth."

CHAPTER 2

"That's impossible," Akron Massey said slowly.

Kate and I shook our heads. We stood in the living room of the private quarters we shared with the billionaire. An artificial fireplace crackled beneath a large flat screen TV (now only good for watching pre-recorded programs). High ceilings soared above our heads to a circular balcony that gave access to the four bunk rooms upstairs. Our daughter was still sound asleep in one of those rooms.

Akron sat on a plush white couch in front of the fireplace while Kate's brother, Richard, lounged in one of two matching armchairs. He'd swiveled his chair to face a big, curving rectangular window. It was the middle of the night, and that window was as black as the TV screen.

"I know what I saw," Kate said.

Akron frowned and scratched the side of his jaw.

"Something that big will have shown up on sonar," Richard said, still staring out into the black water.

"Definitely," I agreed.

"So why hasn't anyone called to tell me about it?" Akron asked.

"Maybe they didn't want to wake you," Kate suggested.

Akron's brow furrowed, and his eyes pinched into slits.

I suspected another reason. "Mayor Parker took over running Haven after you left. You're probably not privy to command-level information anymore. You should try contacting the control room."

Akron lifted his chin and gazed at some distant point on the domed-glass ceiling of the habitat module. "Alice, contact the control room."

"Calling control room," Haven's computer replied in a pleasant female voice that rippled out from hidden speakers.

"Second Officer Martin speaking. Go ahead, Mr. Massey."

Massey spoke to the ceiling once more. "I have a report from two of my guests... they both say they saw something strange in the water outside the Coral Cafe about half an hour ago. Can you confirm?"

"That's affirmative, Massey. Sonar logged a large blip around oh three thirty."

I watched Massey's eyebrows dart up. He visibly hesitated before inquiring further. "Any ideas what that blip might have been?"

"Nothing concrete, sir. Best guess is a whale—sperm or humpback. Whatever it was, it was about seventy feet long."

"A whale," Massey repeated in an amused voice.

"Yes, sir."

"Thank you, Officer Martin. Massey out."

His gaze came back down from the ceiling, finding ours with eyebrows raised and a faint smile on his lips.

"It wasn't a whale," I said.

"It's the middle of the night. The water is dark. The light from the cafe would barely penetrate five meters. With so many barriers to visibility, it's easy to see things that aren't there. A whale would explain the size of what you saw."

"Sperm and humpback whales don't grow to seventy feet," Richard said, as he swiveled his chair away from the window.

Akron's eyes darted to Richard and back to us. "Okay, I'll humor you. If it wasn't a whale, what was it?"

"I don't know," Kate said.

"Something the Screechers brought with them," I suggested.

"A seventy-foot long *alien* sea monster," Akron replied in a droll voice. "Assuming one of the Screechers' rockets would even get off the ground with something that big—along with the tank full of water it would take to transport such a monster—why would they want to bring it to Earth?"

"Maybe it's a pet," I suggested, matching Akron's droll tone.

Akron smirked. "I'm going back to bed." He rose from the couch and started to leave.

A high-pitched scream split the night, and Kate's eyes flew wide. "Rachel!"

We both ran for the curving stairwell leading up to the second-floor balcony. As my feet hit the first step, I heard a door opening, followed by the tiny thunder of approaching footsteps.

"Daddy, daddy!" Rachel said, skidding to a stop at the top of the stairs. "There's a monster looking through my window!"

Kate and I traded glances, then vaulted up the

stairs. Rachel wrapped her arms around my legs as soon as I reached the second floor. "It's okay, Rach," I said, stroking her hair. "You're safe. It can't get in."

"What did you see?" Kate asked.

Rachel shook her head but said nothing.

"Let's go take a look," Akron said, brushing by us at the top of the stairs. We hurried after him. As soon as he reached Rachel's room, he froze in the entrance. He'd seen it. We piled up behind him, peering over his shoulders at the monster floating outside Rachel's window. Her nightlight was barely enough to illuminate the creature's silhouette, but it clearly highlighted the sucking pink mouths of the four, jointed arms that radiated from the monster's head.

"Still think it's a whale?" I asked.

"No," Akron replied in an awed whisper.

CHAPTER 3

"**W**hen our world was dragged away by the rogue star, we took pains to preserve its flora and fauna so that one day we could restore the planet, or transform another one like it."

I couldn't believe what OneZero had just said. She stood in front of the two-way mirror, staring at us as if she could see straight through, which she probably could.

Wesley Parker, the mayor of Haven, leaned forward in his chair and spoke into the intercom. "What do you mean by *preserve*, OneZero? How many different creatures from each species did you save?"

"All of them, and none of them."

The mayor made an irritated noise in the back of his throat. "Do you think this is a game? If you ever want to get out of there, you'll answer my questions without prevaricating!"

OneZero's gleaming metal head canted to one side. "What is prevaricating?"

"Just answer the damn question!"

OneZero gave no reply. "I have answered all of your questions honestly to this point, and yet you have still not released me. What do I gain from answering you now?"

"I could have you dismantled and your parts studied in a lab!"

"Your threats only serve to underscore the importance of making this a fair exchange. I'll answer your questions, and I'll even agree to work with your scientists to develop new technologies, but I want my freedom first."

Mayor Parker began tapping his foot, his knee bouncing with restless energy.

"I can't release her. She could sabotage this facility and kill us all. Or worse, she could call in the Screechers and get us all captured."

"She saved our lives," I said. "More than once."

"*Your* lives. And that could have been a means to an end," Parker said.

"Not this end," I replied. "When she met us she had no way of knowing we'd end up here. She didn't even know about Haven."

"Spies don't always have a specific goal.

Sometimes they're just sent to blend in, make friends, and study the enemy."

"She killed several of her own people, and they tried to kill her. I don't think that was all part of some elaborate cover."

"Maybe they didn't know about her mission, and maybe the Screechers don't mind the collateral damage."

"Well?" OneZero prompted. "I'm waiting."

I threw up my hands. "This is absurd. The Screechers have nothing to gain by infiltrating us. We're the underdogs, the losers. Our technology is far behind theirs, and they've already proven that they can beat us in a straight fight. What could they possibly learn from us that would be of any use?"

"Something," Parker said. "Something important. I'm telling you, OneZero is bad news, and I won't have her running around loose in Haven."

"Assign a 24-hour guard to watch her," Akron suggested.

Mayor Parker snorted. "She could incapacitate a whole platoon of Marines. A few security guards with harpoon guns aren't going to stop her."

"She's offering to share their technology with us," Akron said. "She could be an asset. Give her a chance to prove herself."

"Or to betray us?" Parker asked. "Didn't she abduct you from Starcast's launch facility? You'd be on your way to Mars with your family right now if it weren't for her."

"That was a misunderstanding."

"Or maybe that's what she led you to believe."

I sighed. "What are we doing here, then? She's not going to tell us anything else unless you let her go, so we may as well go back to bed."

"Put her under house arrest in my quarters," Akron suggested. "Let her out under supervision and under controlled circumstances. If you give her freedom little by little you should be able to mitigate the risks."

Mayor Parker regarded Akron with a frown, scratching his shiny bald scalp as he considered the idea. With a sigh he turned around and punched the intercom. "Here's what I'm prepared to offer. You'll share quarters with Akron Massey and the Willis family. You'll be under guard, and we'll only let you out under strict supervision—and that's contingent on your cooperation. You have to answer all of our questions and help us in any way you can. Does that sound acceptable to you?"

A dim light flickered through OneZero's eyes that reminded me of the blinking red hard drive light on an old PC. "I accept," she said.

"Good. I'll arrange for your escort. In the meantime, as a show of good faith, I would appreciate it if you'd clarify the current situation. How is it possible that there's a 70-foot alien sea monster outside?"

"We digitized all of the life on our world, including ourselves, with the hope of resurrecting it again someday. Now that we have found a habitable world with the right characteristics, we are doing just that."

"There's no way a 70-foot creature grew from an egg to an adult in just six months," Mayor Parker said.

"We have ways of manipulating normal growth cycles," OneZero replied. "It won't take long before the process is complete."

I traded a worried look with Kate's brother, Richard.

"What process?" Mayor Parker asked.

"You would call it terraforming, but that is a misnomer, since we are not trying to make your planet more like Earth. Quite the opposite. Apart from its atmosphere, size, and elemental composition, the world you knew will soon be gone."

CHAPTER 4

The Following Morning
—October 29th, 2032—

I woke up at the tail end of an unsettling nightmare about running through an alien jungle with shadowy monsters chasing after me.

I sat up. The sheets fell away, and I shivered. The other side of the bed was empty. Rachel had been too scared to sleep by herself, and our bed was too small for three, so Kate had agreed to spend the night in her room. My eyes tracked to the window. It was light out now. Rays of sunlight flickered through the water, illuminating silvery schools of fish. The tops of the habitat modules were only ten meters below the surface, so there was plenty of light to see by.

Thankfully, there was no sign of the alien monster we'd seen last night. Akron had assured us that despite its size, there was no way for it to do any damage to Haven. The colony's seven hundred plus spherical modules were far too strong to succumb to brute force, even by a creature as large as the one we'd seen. Scuba divers would have to be careful while performing maintenance and repairs, but otherwise the appearance of alien sea monsters was a curiosity, not a problem. Thankfully, the facility was still brand-new and not likely to suffer any equipment failures in the near future.

I climbed out of bed and found my pair of fuzzy white slippers with *Haven* stitched into the heels with bold black thread. The lights slowly rose in brightness as the facility detected my movement. The illumination began with warm golden hues to approximate a sunrise, but I knew that it would slowly intensify over the next few minutes to a crisp white approximation of daylight. According to Akron, these were 'full spectrum lights,' providing all the necessary exposure for optimum human functioning.

"Good morning, Mr. Willis," Haven's computer said.

"Good morning, Alice," I replied through a yawn as I shuffled to the bathroom.

"It is Tuesday, October 29th. The time is nine

thirteen. There is a breakfast buffet in the Sky Dome until eleven. My logs show that you switched off your alarm, but it is my duty to remind you that you are late for your mechanical engineering class."

I slid open the door to the bathroom and began stripping out of my pajamas. "I know, but thank you for the reminder, Alice."

"You are most welcome."

Naked now, I stared at my craggy, bearded face in the mirror. Long, tangled black hair cascaded to my shoulders. I looked like a bum, or possibly a Rasta. Not combing my hair properly had resulted in an unintentional set of dreadlocks. I wondered if I should finally shave. After that, I could get my hair cut in the salon on the lower decks of the Market.

But I was late for class. Cleaning up could wait. I went to the shower and used a touchscreen display to set the water temperature to a perfect 104 degrees, and then turned the rainfall shower head on. I waited a few seconds for the water to reach the right temperature, and then pulled the glass door open and stepped into the steamy shower. It always surprised me that there was no detectable smell to the water. It was all recycled from toilets and drains, with a desalination module providing a slow trickle of fresh water to restore whatever traces couldn't be recovered.

Hot water poured over my head, dragging a curtain of long hair into my eyes. Water dripped from my beard, pattering over my toes.

"Alice—" I said through the hot, steamy spray.

"Yes, Logan?"

"Are my wife and daughter up yet?"

"Yes, they have already showered, and they are busy getting dressed. Would you like me to relay a message to them?"

For the umpteenth time, I marveled that Haven's AI could actually carry on a meaningful conversation. I'd heard rumors of such technology for years before the shit had hit the fan with the rogue star and the arrival of the Screechers— virtual assistants that could make phone calls and book appointments, or even take calls and relay them like a secretary, but I'd never actually seen the technology in action until I'd come here.

"Yes, please," I said. "Tell them to wait for me in the living room. I'll be out in a minute."

"Of course." There came a brief pause, followed by, "Your wife would like me to remind you to shave the mop off your face and comb your hair."

I smiled at Kate's hypocrisy. Her legs were

busy growing a forest. It seemed only fair to suggest a trade.

"Alice, tell her that I'll shave when she do—"

The bathroom plunged into pitch blackness. My eyes widened, and I blinked rapidly in an effort to see through the gloom. Pale, flickering blue light seeped in from the bedroom. The water ran ice cold. I yelped and jumped into the shower door in my hurry to get away. Dim red lights snapped on.

"Alice! What's going on?"

"We appear to have lost power."

"I can see that, but why?"

"I do not know, Logan."

"Shut off the shower, please."

Rain stopped falling from the shower head, and I shivered, partly from the cold, and partly from apprehension over whatever had just happened. The only way we could experience a blackout was if something had happened to the solar array floating on the surface, or else to the thick cables that tethered it to Haven. Either way it was bad news. The solar array and its cables were built to survive a hurricane, so what could possibly have cut off the power?

The answer seemed obvious to me. This was no act of God. It had to be deliberate, and that could mean only one thing: the Screechers had found us.

CHAPTER 5

We all congregated in the living room in front of the fireplace. Rather than crackling with its usually reassuring warmth, the electric fireplace was dark and cold in the crimson gloom of Haven's emergency lights.

Mayor Parker's voice boomed out over the room's intercom speakers. "Citizens of Haven, this is Mayor Parker from the control room. There has been an unanticipated problem with the solar array, and we have activated emergency power-saving protocols to preserve the charge in our batteries until the problem is resolved. Please be patient and remain calm while we work to fix the problem. Thank you."

"Well, that was vague," I said.

"What could it be?" Kate asked.

"I'll tell you what it is," I said. "The Screechers are invading."

Richard frowned, as did Akron. Kate's eyes widened in horror, and Rachel reached for my hand. We all stared at one another in silence for a moment.

Servos whirred, and metal feet *clunked* as OneZero walked over from where she'd spent the night standing like a coat rack beside the door. "I do not believe that is the case."

Akron arched an eyebrow and jerked his chin at her. "Why not?"

"If my people had found Haven, they would not cut the power. They would simply sink it."

Apprehension twisted in my gut. "Why wouldn't they evacuate us and take us to the border like they did with everyone else?"

OneZero shook her gleaming metal head. "No, we can't swim—we're too heavy—and we didn't bring any submersibles. Getting the people out of Haven would require us to create new vehicles, and I doubt anyone will want to wait that long to deal with the threat posed by this facility."

"Threat?" I echoed. "We don't even have any weapons!"

"That's not exactly true," Akron said. "We have plenty of weapons stored in the armory."

I rounded on Akron. "Then why are your guards all armed with harpoon guns?"

"We don't use firearms inside for obvious reasons."

I turned back to OneZero with a frown. "Even so. Your people turned our biggest cities into craters and obliterated our air force with those flying discs. They can't possibly be scared of a few rifles and handguns."

OneZero shook her head. "For all they know this is a military installation harboring hundreds or thousands of nuclear missiles."

Richard began nodding with that. "Maybe they took out the power so that we can't fire any of those imaginary missiles."

OneZero's head turned to him. "Then why haven't they sunk the facility?"

Akron blew out a breath and headed for the door. "All this speculation is pointless. Parker knows something he's not telling us, and I'm going to find out what that is."

"I'm coming with you," I said.

"Me, too," Richard added.

I nodded to my wife. "Kate, stay here with Rachel and OneZero. Rach, go with your mother." I released her hand and gave her a gentle shove in Kate's direction.

"No, I'm staying with you!" she said and locked her arms around my legs.

Jasper T. Scott

Kate came closer and placed a hand on my arm. "What if they attack and Haven starts flooding with water? We'd better stick together."

I frowned, hesitating, but gave in with another nod. She was right.

We caught up with Akron just as the front door slid open to reveal the pair of security guards standing outside—OneZero's babysitters.

Clanking footsteps followed us to the door, and both guards turned to address the threat. One of them was young with short, carrot-red hair and rakish good looks, while the other was middle-aged and balding with glasses.

"I should also accompany you," OneZero explained. "If my people are here, I might be able to convince them to spare you."

Akron regarded her with a knitted brow. "I thought you said the Screechers aren't responsible for the power failure."

"I said I do not *believe* they are, but it is still a possibility."

Akron grunted. "All right, let's go."

"Sir—" The red-haired guard stepped in front of him to bar the way. "The Screecher is not authorized to leave your quarters."

"These are extenuating circumstances, officer," Akron replied. "She may be able to help us solve the problem."

"I'm sorry, but I still need authorization to let her go."

Akron sighed and reached into his black sports jacket—

His hand came out with a small 9mm handgun. "Step aside."

The young guard's eyes widened at the sight of the weapon, and he froze, while his middle-aged partner raised the harpoon gun to his shoulder and took aim. "Drop the gun, sir!"

"You first, Seth," Akron replied.

The balding man's eyes widened behind his glasses at the sound of his name.

"You forget, *I* built this facility, and *I* invited you to join me here. We're not strangers; if anything we're more like family. Akron's eyes pinched into thin slits and his gaze swept to the red-haired guard. "Neal Masters, right?"

The young man nodded.

"You both trusted me enough to place your lives and the lives of your families in my care, so trust me again now. OneZero is not the enemy, and she's not trying to kill us, but her people are, and if you don't let her help us, they might just get it right."

Seth lowered his harpoon gun, and Neal

stepped aside. Akron put his gun back inside his jacket. "If you need an excuse to give to Parker or the Security Chief, tell them the truth: I pulled a gun on you."

"Yes, sir," Neal said."

CHAPTER 6

"That's the view from cameras on the oil rig above us," Mayor Parker said, leaning over the shoulder of a middle-aged man sitting at the control room's security station.

Richard, Akron, and I stood on the other side of the security station, peering at the screen, while Kate and Rachel were waiting outside the control room with OneZero, just around the corner and out of sight of the security guards. Akron wanted to see what was going on before trying to convince Mayor Parker to let OneZero into a secured area.

"What are those things?" Richard asked.

There were thousands of glossy, black-skinned sea creatures, bobbing impossibly on *top* of the water. In between those glossy black bodies I caught a glimmer of an explanation for their gravity-defying act—an equally black sheet that stretched clear across the water from one oil rig to the next. It was the solar array that served all of Haven's electrical needs, but right now these creatures were using it as a giant air mattress.

"Maybe they're sea lions," I suggested. I recalled having read somewhere that sea lions will climb onto boats to sunbathe, often sinking them in the process.

"No," Richard replied. "There aren't any in the Gulf of Mexico."

"Maybe they're migrating because of the changing weather patterns," Akron suggested.

Mayor Parker shook his head. "They're not sea lions. Zoom in for us please, Officer Brogan."

The technician manning the security station did as he was told and the camera zoomed in on a section of the solar array directly below the oil rig. Individual creatures came into better view, revealing that each of them had *eight* muscular legs with webbed feet. Their bodies were sleek like an actual sea lion or a seal, but they had eerie white eyes, and broad jaws full of shark-like teeth. Two funnel-shaped ears dangled on flexible stalks from the sides of their heads. They looked like some kind of cross between actual sea lions and spiders, or maybe spiders and sharks. The editor in me decided on spider-sharks.

"What the hell...?" Richard trailed off, shaking

his head.

"My sentiments exactly," Mayor Parker replied. "We already checked our databases. No one's found anything even remotely like them. This is a new species."

"Another alien species," Akron said.

"That seems to be the case, yes," Parker replied. "I hate to admit it, but it would be good if we could get OneZero up here to see what she knows about these creatures before we attempt to clear them off the solar array."

"I'll go get her," Akron said, already on his way to the door.

I followed him there. He placed his palm against a panel beside the door to open it, and we strode down a curving polycarbonate corridor, surrounded by water and glittering schools of fish. I caught a glimpse of a large shadow lurking at the furthest extent of visibility and hoped it wasn't the monster we'd seen last night. Maybe it hadn't been such a good idea to leave Kate and Rachel out here in a plastic tube surrounded by alien sea monsters.

We rounded the curving corridor to a broader section with benches on both sides. Kate and Rachel were sitting on one of them, and Kate was pointing to a rippling wall of colorful yellow and blue fish.

"Where's OneZero?" Akron asked, looking around quickly.

"Sitting over there," Kate said, turning to point to the empty row of benches on the opposite side of the corridor.

"Where?" I asked.

A frown creased Kate's brow, and she slowly shook her head. "She was right there a second ago...."

"OneZero!" Akron called out sharply.

No reply came.

"Where did she go?" Kate asked.

"Maybe she's hiding," I suggested.

Akron sighed. "Parker is not going to like this." Turning to my wife, he added, "What happened? You were supposed to be watching her."

To be fair we hadn't made that very clear when we'd left her and Rachel here with OneZero. Akron had whispered a vague suggestion that she keep an eye on the robot before we'd continued on to the control room.

"I *was* watching her," Kate said. "I only turned my back for a few seconds."

"She must have cloaked herself," I said, remembering how she could make herself disappear in plain sight.

"Can't you find her with Haven's sensors?" Kate asked.

Akron snorted. "The surveillance and smart systems are based on cameras and motion detection, both of which are defeated by whatever technology is making her invisible. As long as she's quiet, she could stay hidden aboard this facility indefinitely. This is one of the reasons I didn't argue to have her released sooner."

"So why did you?" I asked, my tone curious rather than accusing.

"After six months of good behavior, locked up in the brig, I guess I thought she deserved a chance to prove herself. And her promise of cooperation seemed worth the risk. If we could learn to adapt Screecher technology, it would go a long way to putting us on an even footing with them."

I grimaced. "Well, it seems like she baited us with that."

"And Parker is going to blame me for whatever she does next," Akron replied.

"You're making it sound like she has an agenda," Kate said. "Remember, she saved our lives."

"Not mine," Akron said. "She put *my* life in jeopardy to save all of you."

"Because she's our friend!" Rachel said. "She

doesn't like you."

"How do you know that?" Akron asked.

"She said you think you're too smart, and that makes you dumb."

Akron smiled wryly. "Is that so?"

"Yes."

"Maybe she doesn't want smart people around her because they'll figure out what she's really up to."

I frowned. "Now you're calling the rest of us dumb."

Akron hesitated. "Not dumb... naive. OneZero is still an unknown quantity, and her loyalty to you and your family is largely unexplained."

"I saved her from Harry when we met."

"And yet she helped Harry just as much as she helped you. That doesn't strike you as odd?"

I found myself suddenly at a loss for words.

"Come on," Akron said. "We'd better get back to the control room and tell Parker the bad news."

CHAPTER 7

I hurried back to the control room with Akron to deliver the bad news.

"What do you mean she's *missing?*" Mayor Parker demanded. "She broke out of your quarters? Why haven't the guards I posted called it in?"

Akron explained how he'd pulled a gun on them and left Kate to watch OneZero just outside the control room; then he went on to describe her cloaking capabilities. Parker's eyes and nostrils flared, and he waved a hand to cut Akron off. "You're just telling me about this *now?*" he thundered. "If I had known that she could do that, I never would have agreed to let her out of the brig! I could have you arrested for this!"

"Perhaps," Akron said quietly. "But I think you'll find that I'm better to have as an ally than an enemy. Everyone here owes me their lives, including you, and gratitude runs deep—for some, anyway."

Parker snorted and shook his head, but I noticed that he didn't threaten Akron any further. "What are you doing with a gun, anyway? It's illegal to use firearms in Haven. *You* were the one who established that law."

Akron nodded agreeably. "That's a fair point, but let's discuss that later. Right now we have bigger concerns than the contents of my pockets."

Parker visibly ground his teeth. "Very well." He turned and nodded to First Officer Brogan at the security station. "Post guards around sensitive areas and send out teams to search for that robot. Make sure they understand that it's invisible to the naked eye. They'll have to get creative to find it."

"Yes, sir," Brogan replied. He issued a station-wide alert over the intercom to be on the lookout for OneZero, and then contacted Sergeant Peterson, Haven's chief of security, to explain the situation and relay Mayor Parker's orders.

"Officer Brogan, our men are nearing the target area!" someone in the control room announced.

"Copy that," Brogan replied, and I watched as he toggled between different camera views from his station. The one he chose was mounted at the back of an orange lifeboat. Four people in black wetsuits and diving gear sat inside. All four of them were holding automatic rifles. A fifth person's hands could be seen passing in and out of view as he steered an outboard motor at the back of the boat. From the way the camera was moving, I realized that he must be wearing the camera on his head.

"Does this feed have audio?" Mayor Parker asked.

"Yes, sir," Brogan replied and stabbed a button on his console.

A flurry of sounds came streaming into the control room. Heads turned as officers looked up from various stations around the room. I heard the roar of the outboard motor resonating, the prow of the boat slapping on the water as it skipped over swells, men shouting to each other over the noise, and a distant wailing of animal sounds that were somewhere between a wolf's howl and a lion's roar.

"Here we go!" one of the men in the boat said just as the boat jumped over another swell. Hundreds of gleaming black spider-sharks appeared on the horizon. A few seconds later the boat began to slow.

"On my mark, we shoot over their heads! Not at them!" the man at the back said. *"We just want to*

scare them, not piss them off."

"*Copy that, sir,*" another man said.

The outboard engine shut off, leaving the lifeboat to drift on in relative silence with its momentum. Water slapped the sides of the boat, sloshing up and over. It glided to a stop within about a hundred feet of the nearest spider-shark. They looked a lot bigger from here than they had from the camera at the top of the oil rig.

"*Take aim!*"

"You should have sent a helicopter," Richard whispered.

"We didn't want to risk showing up on the Screechers' radar," Parker explained. "It's bad enough that we had to send a dinghy."

"*Fire!*"

Bullets rattled out, and the distant roaring of the alien creatures grew to a maddening volume. They dived off the solar array by the dozen.

"*It's working! Keep it up!*" One of the men yelled.

"You need to get them out of there right now," Richard said. "They're going to go after the boat."

"No, they're not," Parker scoffed. "Look, they're disappearing into the water. They're running away. The sound is scaring them off."

As the thunderous roar of weapons fire

continued rattling through the control room, my skin crawled with an awful creeping sense that Richard was right.

The men in the boat took a break from firing to reload their rifles. Wisps of gun smoke swirled between them.

"Do you hear that?" Akron asked.

"Hear what?" Parker replied.

A *whooshing* sound came rippling over the room's speakers, barely audible above the sound of waves lapping the sides of the boat, but rising swiftly in volume as it approached.

"They can't hear it," Richard said. "They're wearing earplugs."

The *whooshing* sound became thunderous, and a shadow passed over the men in the boat. Some kind of translucent snake wrapped around the man at the prow and plucked him right out of the boat.

"Woah!" The man at the back ducked reflexively and looked up at a massive bird with four glittering wings that flashed with rainbow-colored reflections.

It looked like a giant dragonfly. The body was flat, translucent, and tapered at the back to a whip-like tail that was wrapped around the man from the boat. He screamed as the monster soared, carrying him swiftly higher. The men in the boat looked on in shocked silence, shielding their eyes from the sun as that beast carried the man ever higher into the sky. It was headed straight for the upper levels of the nearest oil rig.

"Shoot it down!" the man at the back said, even as he raised a rifle to his shoulder and sighted down the scope. He squeezed off a three-round burst, and the shimmering bird went tumbling from the sky, wings glittering as it fell. The man wrapped up in its tail fell at least fifteen meters to the water, hitting with a visible splash.

"Shit!"

The boat motor screamed at a high pitch, and the dinghy leapt forward, skipping over the waves to reach the point where the man had fallen.

As they drew near, the volume of the motor dropped to an idling rumble, and the boat slowed once more. The water thrashed violently with darting black shapes.

"They're going ape-shit!" One of the men said, leaning over the side of the boat. "Fuck! They're eating him!"

The man at the back leaned over for a better look, and the camera revealed that the water was red with blood. *"Weapons free! Kill the bastards!"* he screamed and squeezed off rattling bursts into the water.

Parker hurriedly leaned over the First Officer's shoulder to scream into the mic. "Don't shoot, you idiots!"

But it was too late. An eight-legged black monster leapt out of the water and landed in the boat, knocking three men flat, and sending a fourth over the side with an abbreviated scream. Bloody jaws gaped open, and the man at the back whipped his rifle up for a point-blank burst. Bullets tore chunks out of the monster's glossy black hide with meaty *thwups*, revealing pale white flesh underneath. The spider-shark threw its head back with a shrilling roar and then lunged. The camera vanished in darkness. A muffled scream died in a gurgle, and suddenly wet crunching sounds were all we could hear. Flashes of light stole in through jagged rows of teeth, revealing sticky red chunks sloshing in a river of blood down a furry, mushroom-white tongue.

My stomach flipped, and I looked away with a grimace.

CHAPTER 8

"We're going to have to send in the helicopters, after all," I said.

Mayor Parker blew out a breath. "We can't."

"Why not?" I asked. "If we're fast we can minimize the risk of Screechers detecting them."

"That's not the only problem," Akron replied. "Shooting them from above adds the additional concern of punching holes through the solar array with any bullets that miss their mark. Not to mention, we won't solve our problem by reducing those creatures to a dead weight that will have to be removed manually."

"Then what are we going to do? We can't just sit here in the dark forever. Without power we can't grow fresh food or desalinate and recycle water, and I'm guessing we won't last long like that."

"Not to mention we'll run out of air without

the CO_2 scrubbers," Richard said.

"Water will run out first," Akron replied. "Even if we strictly ration showers and toilet flushing, we'll only last about ten days before all of the water in the reservoirs ends up in the recyclers."

"Assuming there's still enough power to run the pumps, you mean," Richard said. "Without that, we won't even be able to get the water out of the reservoirs to use it."

Akron nodded to the first officer. "What's the efficiency of the solar array right now? Those alien..."

"Spider-sharks?" I suggested.

Akron arched an eyebrow at me before continuing. "They can't be blocking every available inch of the array."

"We're down to just under ten percent. It's enough to power select systems like the lights and pumps, but not enough to run the heaters, UV lamps, air scrubbers, desalinization plants, or water recyclers."

"So we've got what we've got for air, water, and food," Richard said.

"And in the worst case, we have ten days to evacuate," Mayor Parker concluded, rubbing his jaw. "That's not enough time."

"It is if we start evacuating everyone to the nearest shoreline," Akron replied. "We have four subs. Each one can carry twenty passengers. A round-trip to New Orleans takes about ten hours. Add two for boarding and refueling and we can move a hundred and sixty people per day. We have nine hundred and seventy-six people on board, so that means—"

"Nine hundred and seventy-one," First Officer Brogan interrupted as he spun his chair away from the security station. He was a big man with dense black stubble on his cheeks, and dark eyes lurking beneath the brim of a classic white captain's hat— turned pink in the crimson gloom of Haven's emergency lights. "We just lost five."

A heavy silence fell as we remembered the men who'd died trying to scare off monsters squatting on our power source.

Richard was the first to break that silence. "At that rate we could get everyone to shore in about six days."

All eyes turned to him.

"Six days to evacuate, and we have ten," I said.

"Good," Mayor Parker said. "That gives us four days to solve the problem and fix the array. I'm confident that we can do that."

"Richard and I can put a team together to

brainstorm solutions," Akron said. "In the meantime you'd better implement water rationing."

"Try to make sure your solutions don't involve sending more men to their deaths," Parker replied.

"Is there anything I can do?" I asked, glancing between the mayor and Akron.

"Don't flush any toilets," Akron replied.

"And find OneZero," Parker added.

* * *

I found Kate and Rachel right where Akron and I had left them, sitting on a bench in the corridor outside the control room.

"So?" Kate asked as I stopped beside them. "You still haven't told us what's going on."

I took a deep breath and sat down to relate the bad news.

Kate's brow knitted, and she slowly shook her head. "You think it will come to that? Evacuating Haven?"

"I hope not."

"Well, at least we'll be able to go look for Alex."

I considered that as I peered into the gloomy blue depths beyond the corridor. "The plan was to find him and bring him here, to safety, not for all of us to join him in the chaos out there. Even if we find him, we won't be in any position to help."

"At least we'll be together," Kate said. "We'll find a way to survive."

I arched an eyebrow at her. "We'll be competing with a few hundred million other people for dwindling resources in an increasingly hostile environment."

Kate's eyes narrowed to slits. "What are you saying? You don't think Alex survived?"

Rachel peered around her mother's shoulder, watching me with big eyes.

I flashed a smile for her benefit and shook my head. "I didn't say that. Anyway, we're getting ahead of ourselves. They'll fix this, and then I'll find a way to get out of here and go look for Alex."

Kate nodded slowly. She reached for my hand and gave it a quick squeeze. "I know you will."

"We should go get some food. What time is it?"

"I'm not wearing a watch," Kate replied.

"Me neither," Rachel added.

"Hopefully the Sky Dome is still serving breakfast." I lifted my eyes to the ceiling and spotted the glossy eye of a surveillance camera. It was mounted on a central beam that ran along the ceiling to brace the curving polycarbonate walls. "Alice? Are you there?"

Silence answered my query. Haven's AI was yet another power-hungry system that had been taken offline.

"I guess we'll have to go there and find out for ourselves," Kate said.

We got up from the bench and walked down the corridor together. I held my wife's hand on one side, and my daughter's on the other, watching colorful streams of fish scrolling by the transparent walls, and keeping an eye out for any giant sea monsters that could threaten the integrity of the corridor. I still didn't fully believe Akron's assurances that the monster we'd seen last night wasn't a threat to Haven.

We walked on, heading for the nearest bank of elevators. The corridor was about two miles long, and it ran all the way around Haven, branching off at right angles to provide access to the modules on this level. There were ten different levels of seventy-two modules, five descending below the command level, and five rising above. Each level was arranged in a circular configuration inside of a matching ring-shaped corridor just like this one.

I looked up and saw the shadowy outlines of the level above us. Through the inner wall of the ring the nearest bank of elevators appeared — three transparent tubes disappearing above and below us into the hazy blue depths. Haven had nine banks of elevators in all, eight around the rings and one in the center next to the facility's only stairwell. That meant we had to walk about a quarter of a mile to get from one set of elevators to the other, but since the control room was situated in the middle of two such junctions we only had to walk for about a minute to reach the nearest one.

I hit the call button, but it didn't light up. I frowned. That was odd. The elevators had been working when we'd come down from the upper levels earlier. I looked up and noticed that the floor-counter displays at the top of the elevators were dark. "Looks like they shut down the elevators," I said. The mayor was probably looking for additional ways to save power in an attempt to prioritize key systems.

"We'll have to use the stairs," Kate said.

We walked on a bit further until we came to a numbered door with a glowing sign that read: *Hydroponics*. I waved my hand and the door trundled open at half its usual speed. At least we didn't have to crank it open.

On the other side of the door we continued down a raised catwalk that crossed through half a dozen interconnected hydroponics modules. The air inside of them was fresh and humid. I peered over the railings and saw stack upon stack of leafy green vegetables. I winced and shook my head at the thought of them all wilting and dying.

Here and there hydroponics engineers tended to their crops in spite of the power outage. They probably thought the power would be restored soon. Hopefully it would, but I knew better. Even when the men in the boat had fired their rifles to scare off that colony of spider-sharks, they'd only succeeded in scaring the ones closest to the edge, and by now they were probably back to sun tanning on our solar array. I had a bad feeling they had claimed it for their breeding grounds, and if that was the case, we were going to have to kill them all to get them off. There had to be at least a thousand of them out there, and while we had just as many people in here, I doubted we had enough dinghies to put more than fifty on the water. It had only taken one of those spider-sharks to take out four heavily-armed security officers. With those odds we stood to lose in a straight fight.

I hoped Akron's team could come up with a better idea than slaughtering the beasts. If not, maybe we really would have to evacuate everyone to the shore—and that wasn't a comforting solution. We'd already encountered leviathan sea monsters, giant dragonflies, and whole colonies of spider-like sharks. What horrors would be waiting for us on the land? I wasn't sure I wanted to know the answer.

CHAPTER 9

There was still plenty of food in the Sky Dome when we arrived, but it was all cold. The inside of the dome should have been blazing with a vivid illusion of sky and wide-open fields, hence the name of the restaurant—Sky Dome. Instead, the dome was a blank and shiny black that shone with an angry light in the pulsing crimson glow of Haven's emergency lights.

When we finished our breakfast, we filed out with a trickle of other latecomers and walked by row upon row of serving counters with cold, half-empty serving trays of food. Those leftovers were all going to spoil without power to refrigerate them.

We returned to the stairwell and started climbing. Akron's habitat module was located on the uppermost level of Haven. The color of the water around the curving windows in the stairwell became progressively lighter as we ascended, and we began to see more and more sea creatures. As we neared the top, an eight-legged spider-shark darted through a nearby school of fish, using its broad jaws to scoop up dozens in one bite. I pointed to the creature as an example of what was camping on our solar array.

"They look dangerous," Kate said.

"They are," I replied between gasps for air as we reached the landing at the top of the stairs. Kate and Rachel were similarly winded. I took a moment to lean on the railing and catch my breath. We'd climbed just five levels, but that was the equivalent of ten or fifteen floors due to the height and separation of each level.

Once we'd recovered, I turned and waved one of three doors on the landing open and led my family down another corridor, this one lined with rectangular windows and numbered doors leading to various habitat modules. The residents' names were listed beside each door. We came to one with a golden *1*, and the names of Akron Massey and his family listed. Even after six months, Akron hadn't removed the names of his two adult sons or their mother, nor had he thought to add any of my family's names to the list. I wondered if that was a subtle reminder that we were to blame for separating him from his family. Akron had been on his way to Mars with them and the other colonists when we'd accidentally ordered OneZero to *abduct* him from Starcast's launch facility outside Memphis.

I waved the door to Massey's habitat open, and we walked in. Kate went to sit on the living room couch with Rachel. I joined them in the armchair beside the couch and rubbed tired, aching eyes. I felt the beginnings of a headache encroaching. The pulsing red emergency lights probably weren't helping matters.

"I'm bored," Rachel said.

I couldn't blame her. I felt at a loose end myself. We couldn't do anything to help with the present crisis, and without power we couldn't distract ourselves with a movie or an old season of some TV series. Kate and I couldn't even continue with our studies—courses designed to make us productive members of Haven's society—and likewise, Rachel couldn't do any of her homework.

I thought about using my e-reader to read a book, but I was between books, and the station's digital library would be offline along with all the other non-essential systems.

"What if they don't find a way to fix this?" Kate asked.

"Then the mayor will evacuate everyone to the shore," I replied.

"It won't take long for the Screechers to find us if he does that."

"No, it won't," I agreed. "But they'll just take us north and drop us on the other side of their border. Maybe they'll drop us close to where they left Alex, and we can start our search."

"Maybe," Kate said.

"I bet OneZero could help us get the power back," Rachel put in.

I smiled ruefully at her. "Maybe, but she's not here."

"Yes, she is. She's right over there—"

Rachel pointed to a shadowy corner of the dining room, and I turned to see a shimmering silhouette standing wraith-like behind an artificial plant.

"OneZero?" I asked, blinking in shock.

The silhouette solidified and she stepped out from behind the plant with a muffled *thunking* of metal feet. "Yes, Logan?"

I jumped out of my chair. "What are you doing? Everyone is looking for you!"

"Please do not tell them where I am."

I shook my head, incredulous. "Why are you hiding in the first place?"

"Because I want something, and this is the only way to get it."

My brow furrowed. "What do you want?"

A light flickered through OneZero's dark eyes. "To go home."

* * *

"Home?" I asked.

"To my world."

"I don't understand.... I thought your people came here because Earth is more habitable than your world."

"It is. For biological lifeforms. I am a robot, and I no longer wish to become human."

"So you had a change of heart."

"I do not agree with what my people have done. I would not be able to live with myself knowing that my life came at the cost of so many others. I would rather stay a machine forever than steal someone else's home."

I smiled faintly. OneZero had a good heart. The more I spoke to this machine, the more I liked her. "That's very noble of you, OneZero, but how does hiding here help you to go home?"

"The first step is to escape Haven," she replied.

"You're invisible. Escaping shouldn't be hard,"

I said.

"Not hard," OneZero agreed, "but I do not know how to operate your submarines, and I cannot swim."

"So you need someone to go with you, or at least to send you on your way."

"Ideally, yes."

Kate butted in, stealing what I was about to say next: "Hiding from the authorities isn't going to convince anyone to help you."

I nodded. "If anything you've only made them more suspicious. Even Akron was voicing doubts about you, and he argued for your release yesterday."

"I have to hide, because if I don't, Mr. Parker will make me help him bring the power back, and I will get nothing in return. If I wait until he is out of options, then I will be in a position to bargain for what I want."

I gaped at her. "You're going to wait until you have more leverage."

"Yes," OneZero replied.

I shook my head. "People could die while we're busy exploring other options. We've already lost five men."

"We have?" Kate asked, blinking wide eyes at me.

"If they're lost, we should send people looking for them," Rachel suggested.

I grimaced, realizing that I'd run my mouth off without thinking. I didn't want Rachel to know that people were getting eaten alive out there. Fortunately she'd taken my meaning literally.

As for OneZero's self-serving plan, a nagging suspicion had formed in the back of my mind about that. I got up and walked around the couch to address her more directly.

"How do you know what's going on with the power? You weren't in the control room when we learned what was happening."

"No, but I was listening when you told Kate about it afterward."

I blinked, realizing that OneZero had probably never left the bench where Kate had last seen her. She'd simply made herself invisible and waited, hiding right under our noses the whole time. In fact... the door to Massey's habitat wasn't programmed to open for her, so for her to have entered Massey's quarters and hidden behind that plant, she must have followed us in.

"OneZero," I said slowly, shaking my head.

"Yes, Logan?"

"You can't wait until the last minute to solve this problem. People are going to die."

"If I don't wait, the mayor will not grant my request."

"Get him to guarantee that he'll help you before you do anything," I suggested.

"He could lie."

I shook my head. "I'll hold him to his word, and so will Akron. Besides, I have a similar request to make. I'm going with you when you leave."

"You cannot come to my world, Logan. It is too cold, and there are no longer any provisions for biological life forms. You would have to become a machine."

I shook my head. "No, I'm not going to your world. I'm going to look for my son and bring him back here."

OneZero's eyes lit up with a bright flash of comprehension. "You are going to find Alex."

"Yes. The mayor will have to let both of us go if he wants to restore the power. I won't settle for anything less."

"Thank you, Logan. You are a good friend." OneZero took a few halting steps forward and folded me into an awkward, rigid hug.

I smiled and hugged her back. Her metal body was ice-cold to the touch, but I forced myself to hold on as long as she did.

OneZero stepped back, and took me by

complete surprise with what she said next. "I know your pain. I have children, too."

"You do?"

"Yes."

"How..." I trailed off, wondering how robots reproduce.

"Many, many years ago, before I became this." She hefted her metal arms by way of indication.

"Where are they now?" Kate asked.

A dim, flickering light entered OneZero's gaze. "Dead."

"I'm so sorry," Kate said. "I can't imagine..."

"Don't be. I have them with me, and one day I will bring them back."

My brow furrowed at that, and I wondered why she hadn't already done so. Digital death was erasure, but if OneZero had their data with her, then surely it would be a simple matter to restore them in new robotic bodies.

"Why haven't you brought them back yet?" Kate asked before I could.

"They made bad friends, and even worse enemies. Legally, they must be pardoned before they can be resurrected. That is the other reason I must return home. My world is divided into two political groups. The one in power, and the one that tried to overthrow them many years ago. My son and daughter were both a part of that rebellion, and they died fighting it. Now that the majority of the ruling party has left to invade your world, there is a chance for the other party to take control through non-violent means."

"You mean by democratic means?" I asked.

"Yes, and if the minority comes to power, many thousands of dead freedom fighters will be pardoned and brought back to life, including my children."

I nodded along with that. It was reassuring to learn that OneZero's allegiance actually made some sense. She had sided with us out of contempt for the Screechers' ruling political power. They'd killed her children and made it illegal to bring them back. There was something about that which didn't add up, however.

"If the ones who invaded were responsible for killing your children and branding them as criminals, then why did you come here with them?" I asked, shaking my head.

"Because I had hoped that in the chaos and confusion of invading and colonizing Earth I would have a chance to resurrect my children without anyone noticing."

"But you changed your mind about that after you got here."

"Living in the land that my people stole would make me and my children just as guilty as the ones who stole it."

Again, I couldn't help but respect OneZero for taking such a moral stand. There were plenty of groups throughout history who had done just the opposite—even my own ancestors, who'd been among the English settlers that came and stole America from the tribes who'd originally lived there.

"Well then, let's try to get you home so that you can join the revolution." I had to admit, the possibility of a rebellion among OneZero's people gave me hope. If the Screechers began fighting each other, it could only be good for us.

OneZero nodded, and her eyes brightened. "I will be in your debt if you can help me do so."

CHAPTER 10

"This is blackmail," Mayor Parker said, watching OneZero carefully. The pair of guards who'd escorted us into the control room were aiming their harpoon guns at her—but spearing her with a couple of metal poles wouldn't be enough to stop her.

"It's not blackmail. It's a simple trade," I replied. "OneZero didn't cause the power crisis. She's not the source of the threat, and therefore, she's under no obligation to help us resolve it."

"She might not have caused it personally, but her people did," Parker said. "If I let her go, how do I know that she won't lead her people straight to us? Down here she's cut off. There's no way for her to send a message without at least getting to the surface first." Mayor Parker slowly shook his head. "I won't compromise the security of this facility."

Richard sighed. "It's already compromised. I don't see anyone else offering a simple solution. We can't clear the solar array without risking irreparable damage to it, and the only way to avoid risking more lives is to use the helicopters, but that puts us at risk of discovery the same as if you release OneZero."

"I'll go with them," Akron put in.

Mayor Parker frowned. "Is that supposed to convince me? You designed this facility. No one knows it like you do. You're an asset down here—not someone I want to be rid of."

"I have a plan to stay hidden," Akron said.

"Oh? And what's that?"

"We take a submarine all the way up the Mississippi until we clear the Screechers' border at Memphis."

First Mate Brogan swiveled his chair to face us. "You'd never make it. North of Baton Rouge, the depth of the Mississippi varies wildly. Our submarines have a diameter of ten feet, and that's if you don't count the conning tower. You'd need at least that much depth to play with all the way to Memphis. You'll run aground on a sandbar long before you get there."

"So what do you suggest?" Akron asked.

"If you want to avoid detection by staying

underwater, your best bet is to go around the Florida Peninsula and up the east coast."

"That will put us a long way from Memphis," I said.

"Why do you have to go there?" Mayor Parker asked.

"Because that's where my son will be," I said. "As the crow flies, it's due north of New Orleans, where the Screechers picked him up."

Mayor Parker pressed his lips into a thin line. "As much as I sympathize with your situation, Mr. Willis, I think it's time you accept the reality of the matter: your son is dead."

I flinched at that pronouncement.

"You need to focus on the family you still have. Your daughter, for example." Before I could reply, he went on, "*If* I agree to let OneZero go, she will have to travel up the east coast as Mr. Brogan recommended. And if you two are a package deal, then you'll just have to find your own way to Memphis from there."

"I also need to get to Memphis," Akron said. "So we can travel together."

"What for?" the mayor asked.

"I need to get to Starcast's launch facility. In storage there's a prototype of the rockets we used for the Mars Mission. If I can make a few adjustments and improvements, it should be enough to get me to *my* family on Mars."

OneZero's eyes brightened at that. "I have new terms."

"*What?*" Mayor Parker exploded. "I haven't even accepted this deal, and you're already trying to bargain for more?"

"These terms do not involve you or Haven," she replied. "They involve Mr. Massey. Finding a way to leave Haven is just the first step. In order for me to return home I will also need a vehicle to get me there." She turned to Akron. "I will help you get to Memphis, if you will help me get home. If your rocket can reach the planet you call Mars, then perhaps it could also be used to reach my world?"

"That depends..." Akron said slowly. "I'd have to know how far away your world is, how fast it's moving, its trajectory... there's a lot of calculations that would need to be made before I could make such a promise."

"I can help with that," Richard said. "Get me to a place with working Internet and I can use my credentials to access data from the James Webb Space Telescope. Failing that, I can try to contact some of my old colleagues to see what they know. Someone has to have been tracking the new planets in our solar system. I'll help... if you let me go to Mars with you."

Akron snorted. "Sure, why not? What's one extra mouth to feed in a colony with strict population controls?"

"So that's a yes?"

"That's a—I guess I don't have a choice," Akron replied, frowning. "But I suppose you have proven your worth over the past eighteen months."

I glared at Richard. "You'd leave your family behind?"

He offered me an apologetic look. "Logan, you and Kate have each other, and the kids, but I don't have anyone."

"You have us, too," I said.

"It's not the same, and besides, this is the chance of a lifetime! You can't blame me for taking it."

But I did blame him.

"What do you say, Mr. Massey?" OneZero prompted.

"Assuming it's possible to reach your world with my rocket, you are free to use it for that purpose, but only *after* I use it to reach Mars."

"Then we have a deal," OneZero replied. "And you, Mr. Parker?"

Mayor Parker's eyes roved around the room,

taking in all of us. "I don't even know who I'm negotiating with anymore."

"With me," OneZero said. "I'll solve your problem, if you let me leave with the others. They will help me to go home in exchange for my help in getting them safely to Memphis."

Mayor Parker appeared to be considering the deal. Reaching up to straighten his glasses, he nodded to OneZero. "If you can figure out a way to get those creatures off our solar array *and* make sure that they won't come back, then I'll let you go."

"All of us?" I pressed.

"Yes, all of you," he replied, waving impatiently at me. "Well, Screecher?"

"I accept your terms," OneZero replied.

"How are you going to get rid of them?" Richard asked, his eyes pinching together with curiosity.

OneZero replied with a deep, thrumming howl that made my entire body vibrate. It was both the saddest and eeriest sound I'd ever heard.

"What the hell was that?" Mayor Parker asked.

"The mating call of one of their natural predators."

"There's a creature that *eats* spider-sharks?" I asked.

"Yes," OneZero replied.

"And that sound will scare them off?"

"Yes."

Mayor Parker turned to Akron. "How do we use that?"

"We could set up buoys around the array with speakers set to blast out that sound periodically." Akron replied. "If it works as OneZero says it does, then it should be enough to scare them off and keep them off."

"Let's get to it, then!" the mayor said, clapping his hands.

Heads bobbed in agreement, including mine, and I let out a deep sigh. My whole body hunched with that exhalation, and a world of tension suddenly left my muscles. It felt like I'd been holding that breath for the past six months. *Finally,* I had a way to get out of Haven and go looking for my son. I couldn't wait to tell Kate the good news.

CHAPTER 11

One Day Later
—October 30th, 2032—

The following morning I stood in the corridor outside a brightly-lit airlock, hugging my wife and daughter goodbye.

"I love you," I whispered into Kate's hair. She nodded against my shoulder, and sniffled loudly in my ear—a sound I could hear clearly now that Kate had helped me to tie my hair up in a *man bun*. I'd debated cutting it and shaving, but more hair meant more insulation against the cold.

"I love you more," Kate replied.

We kissed each other goodbye, oblivious to our daughter hugging our legs, and to the constant flow of people walking in and out of the airlock, loading supplies into our submarine. The mayor hadn't come to see us off, but at least he was sticking to his word and letting us go.

"I wanna go with you," Rachel said, tugging on my arm to get my attention. Letting go of Kate, I dropped to my haunches in front of Rachel and gripped her by her shoulders. "You can't, Rachie."

Her lower lip popped out, and her eyes narrowed. "Why not?"

"Because it's dangerous."

"Then you shouldn't go."

"But what about your brother? He's out there somewhere. I have to go so that I can find him."

"What if you can't? You don't even know where he is!"

I hesitated. I'd spent the past twelve hours since OneZero had solved Haven's power troubles trying to avoid thinking about that very problem. Finding Alex was my own life-sized version of Where's Waldo, and it was complicated dramatically by the fact that he'd been out there wandering around for six months already. It might be reasonable to assume that he'd started out somewhere south of Memphis, but he could be literally anywhere by now.

"I have to try," I said, as much to convince myself as Rachel.

She shook her head, tears springing to her eyes. "Don't go."

"Hey," I pulled her into a hug. "It's okay. I'm going to be fine. I've got OneZero with me, remember?"

Clanking footsteps approached at the mention of her name. "I will make sure no harm comes to your father," OneZero said.

I withdrew and wiped Rachel's tears away with my thumbs. She was sniffling quietly, her whole body shuddering with barely-restrained sobs.

OneZero placed a metal hand on her shoulder. "Do you trust me, Rachel?"

"Yes."

"Then do not be afraid."

Rachel nodded, and I straightened on creaking legs. Kate's eyes found mine. She was biting her lower lip, looking torn. She wanted to go with me, but we'd talked at length about that the night before. Someone had to stay and look after Rachel. And besides that, it would be easier for me to find Alex if I didn't have to worry about them.

"How long will you be gone?"

I blew out a breath and shook my head. "It's impossible to say. It's going to take four days to travel up the coast. From there, hopefully there's enough infrastructure left for us to find an easy way to Memphis. Akron is going to try to charter a flight. Failing that he'll buy or rent a car. It could take as much as a week just to get there, and then I'll have to start retracing our steps to all the places where Alex might have decided to go and wait for us. There's no way to know how long that will take." I didn't add that I was also planning to go out on foot, starting from the Screechers' border south of Memphis. I had to put myself in Alex's shoes. He and the Hartford family would have arrived at night, half frozen to death, desperate for warmth and shelter. They wouldn't have gone far. If I was lucky, even now, six months later, they'd still be somewhere close to where they'd started out.

Kate nodded quickly and brushed away a tear. "Okay."

"Time to go!"

I turned to see Richard standing behind me. He swept in and gave Kate a hug. "You're in good hands, Katsup," he said, and she smiled with the use of his childhood nickname for her. "There's no safer place on Earth than where you are right now."

"I know," she said, fresh tears welling in her eyes. She withdrew and punched him in the arm.

"Ow," he said, rubbing the spot. "What was that for?"

"For leaving us."

"Kate, it's Mars! It's a dream come true. Even if this planet wasn't crawling with alien robots, I'd still want to go."

"I know," she said, nodding quickly, "And you should go, but I'm still going to miss you, you big idiot."

"Hey who knows, maybe we'll figure out how the Screechers' rockets work and we can set up an interplanetary shuttle or something."

Kate smiled wanly at that.

I gave Rachel one last hug and kissed her on the top of the head. "I love you," I said in a hoarse whisper.

"I love you, too, Daddy," she replied. "Come home soon."

"Everyone ready over here?" Akron asked, walking out of the airlock.

"Yeah," I said in a raspy voice.

The four of us marched into the airlock, and Richard and I turned to wave goodbye. Akron had no one to say goodbye to, so he went straight to the ladder in the center of the airlock and climbed into our submarine.

"I'll be back before you know it!" I shouted just before one of Haven's security guards shut the hatch behind us. Kate nodded and blew a kiss to me through the transparent porthole in the upper portion of the hatch. I winked and blew one back. Rachel was struggling to break free of her mother's grasp, and I could hear my daughter's muffled protests even through the heavy metal door. I caught her eye and shook my head. At that she stopped fighting to pout instead, and I smiled. Rachel began waving vigorously, her arm blurring along with my eyes. I waved back and blew another kiss.

"Come on, Logan," Richard said, pulling me away gently. "We've got to shut the inner hatch."

I wiped my eyes and followed him down the ladder into the submarine. He waited for me to get down and then climbed partway back up the ladder to shut the hatch behind us. OneZero was already seated beside Akron, both of them having skipped our maudlin last goodbyes.

All but the front two rows of the sub's seats had been folded flat so that our white plastic crates of supplies could be strapped down on top of them. Richard and I went to sit across the aisle from each other, directly behind Akron and OneZero.

"Let's hope we don't spring any leaks this time," Akron said with a grin.

It took a second for me to remember what he

meant. On our way to Haven our sub had taken a beating from tidal waves and had sprung a leak. Not in the mood for his morbid sense of humor, I laid my head back against my seat and shut my eyes.

A horrible sinking feeling settled into my stomach, and for the first time, I wondered if I was doing the right thing. This was a fool's errand, and I was its fool.

I opened my eyes to find the hatch to the cockpit open and Akron sitting in its only seat. Muffled thunking noises sounded through the hull, and I felt the submarine break free of Haven. A deep thrumming noise began, and a mild acceleration pushed me into my seat. I glanced out the porthole beside me and watched as the bright shining beacon that was Haven began slipping away. Broad blue windows glowed with light and life. I saw my wife and daughter standing at one of them—Rachel still waving goodbye.

My lips quirked into a painful smile, and I waved back, desperately hoping that they could see.

PART 2 - BRAVING THE NEW WORLD

CHAPTER 12

I sat staring out the porthole beside me, still trying to decide if I'd done the right thing. In the midst of that internal debate, I was also trying to spot any alien monsters lurking in the water around us. Spider-sharks weren't worrisome, but the crab-like leviathan that had hunted us outside the Coral Cafe was a terrifying prospect. Akron had said that one of them couldn't possibly damage Haven, but what about a submarine?

I looked away, back to the fore and found myself staring at the back of Akron's head. He sat on the seat in front of me, working on a tablet he had balanced on his lap.

"How long is it going to take to reach wherever we're headed?" I asked.

Akron twisted around to look at me. "Pamlico Sound, and it should take four to five days. Once we're in the sound, we'll sail up to Washington and find a place to drop the anchor."

"Washington?" I asked, shocked that he would even suggest we visit that blast crater.

"Not DC," Akron said. "Washington, North Carolina."

"Oh." I'd never heard of it, but that made a lot more sense. "That's the closest place we can go?"

Akron nodded. "It's sitting just past thirty-five degrees North where the Screechers' border is."

I nodded and laid my head back against the seat with a grimace. Four to five days sharing cramped, dank quarters. I felt claustrophobic just thinking about it.

"What's your plan to find Alex?" Richard interrupted.

I cracked my eyes open, to stare at the softly-lit beige interior of the submarine. "I'll start at the border below Memphis, and put myself in his shoes. Hopefully I'll be able to figure out where he went from there."

"That will never work," Akron said.

"The odds of success are poor," OneZero agreed.

"You have a better idea?" I snapped, my eyes flicking between them.

"Maybe," Akron replied. "Join us at the launch facility. If there's still Internet, and if Alex is smart,

— 101 —

he'll have found access to it somewhere along the way. We have to hope that he's sent you an e-mail or some kind of message."

"That's a lot of ifs," I pointed out.

"It's worth a shot," Akron replied.

"Trusting that the Internet is still functioning is a long shot," I said. "For all we know there's nothing but a wasteland to the north and everyone's out there rubbing sticks together."

"For our sakes, I hope not," Akron said quietly.

I laid my head back and shut my eyes again, trying to ease my fears with deep, controlled breaths. Exhaustion came swirling in, and I reclined my chair, turning it into a bed. Soon I felt my thoughts sliding away into darkness. I saw Alex lying in a ditch, buried in a snowdrift, his frozen hand reaching for help that never came.

Accusing voices whispered all around me: *this is your fault. You left him behind. You should have made Akron turn the submarine around.*

And then suddenly it was six months ago, and we were on our way to Haven.

"Turn around," I told Akron.

He smiled. "No."

I grabbed him by his jacket and shook him. "Turn the sub around!"

His head bobbed agreeably. "No."

I punched him in the face and blood smeared his lips, but his grin never wavered.

"He's dead, and it's all your fault," Akron laughed.

An animal noise escaped my lips, and I knocked him flat, throwing punch after punch until his nose exploded and spouted dark rivers of blood.

"You can't blame me, Logan," he giggled, spitting blood.

A snaked began hissing, and metallic ping-pong balls bounced around the cabin, leaving silvery jets of water in their wake.

"We're taking on water!" Richard said. He sounded far away, but approaching fast. I could hear his feet thumping on the rubbery floor, followed by—"Logan, wake up!"

Someone was shaking me.

I blinked awake and looked up at Richard with bleary eyes. His face was carved with worry.

"What's wrong?"

"We're leaking. There's already six inches of water in the bathroom!"

I sat up in a hurry and turned to see the door to the cockpit open and Akron inside, busy at the controls.

"Any luck?" Richard called up to him.

"The drain pump isn't going to be enough. We have to fix those leaks!"

"Leaks?" I asked. "You mean there's more than one?"

Richard gave me an incredulous look and gestured to the flattened rows of seats behind us. I twisted around to see thin jets of water misting into the cabin in what had to be at least a hundred different places. There was already an inch of water on the floor, sloshing in rippling waves toward the bathrooms at the back.

"How long have we been leaking?" I asked.

"Only a few minutes," Richard replied.

I gaped at him. At that rate we'd be up to our chins in just a couple of hours.

CHAPTER 13

"Can we fix the hull?" OneZero asked.

"I don't know," Akron replied. "There's a lot of leaks."

Even after we'd surfaced to reduce the water pressure outside, water was still pouring in.

"If we can't fix the damage, we'll have to go back to Haven," I said, watching as Akron tried to stop one of the leaks with his thumb.

OneZero had helped us to peel back the white and beige paneling inside the sub to reveal the drab, gray hull underneath, exposing dozens of leaks just like the one Akron was holding with his thumb. The air inside the sub was thick with shifting curtains of mist. Water ran in rivulets down the portholes and walls. Even my clothes were damp.

"We'll never make it back," Akron replied.

"How long was I asleep?"

"Four hours," Richard replied.

I turned to see him standing behind me, checking a smaller, pinhole-sized leak on the other side of the submarine. He was frowning at his hands and rubbing his fingertips together.

"What is it?" I asked.

"Dust. Looks like metal. It's all around this leak."

I shook my head. "What does that mean?"

"Same thing here," Akron added, holding up his hands to reveal that they were sparkling with silvery particles.

"Is someone going to explain what's going on?"

"This isn't normal wear-and-tear," Richard said. "Someone deliberately drilled holes in this submarine—from the inside."

"What? Who would..." I trailed off as the answer came to me. "The mayor."

"Parker didn't want us to leave," Akron added, scowling. "Damn it! I wondered why he didn't put up a bigger fight to keep us there. He decided to sabotage our submarine instead."

"But, if he drilled holes before we left, then why didn't we notice the leaks earlier?" I asked.

"He obviously didn't drill all the way through," Akron replied. "He drilled just deep enough that it would take some time for the water to push its way in, long enough to make sure that we couldn't turn around and take another sub." Akron pushed by me and ran to the back of the submarine, splashing our crates of supplies as he went. I hoped they were waterproof.

Akron yanked open a storage compartment and produced a briefcase-sized rectangular box. He came back and opened the case on top of one of the storage crates.

I walked over for a better look. There were several black rolls of flexible material inside the case, along with two yellow tubes of something called *Life Calk*. "A patch kit," I guessed.

"Yeah," Akron confirmed, frowning deeply as he studied the contents of the case.

"What's the problem?"

Richard came over to join us.

"The problem is," Akron began, "at least one of us will have to go outside to apply the patches."

"What about the alien creatures out there?" I asked.

"We don't have a choice," Richard added.

"And that's not the only problem," Akron said. "We don't have enough patches and caulk for all the leaks."

"We don't have to stop all of the leaks,"

OneZero said. "We just have to slow them down enough so that we can get to shore."

"Get to *shore?*" Richard echoed. "In the middle of Screecher territory?"

"They will not harm us," OneZero replied. "I can keep you safe."

Richard's brow wrinkled. "Haven is closer."

"We can figure out where to go *after* we patch the hull," Akron said. "Logan, I need you to watch the sonar and warn me if anything is coming."

"I don't know how to read sonar," I said.

"I do," Richard replied.

"Then Richard, *you* watch the sonar, and Logan, you guide me to the leaks through the portholes."

I nodded.

"What can I do?" OneZero asked, a flicker of light stealing through her gleaming black eyes.

Akron studied her for a moment. "You can help Logan pinpoint the leaks."

"It will be dangerous in the water. I should go out instead."

I frowned. "I thought you couldn't swim?"

"I can't," OneZero replied, "but I *am* waterproof, and I can adhere to the hull." She illustrated by pushing her palms together slowly. When they came within six inches of each other they suddenly snapped together with a metallic *clank*.

"Electro-magnets," Akron said. "All right, change of plans. You're coming with me. Two of us will work faster than one."

"Not if you get eaten," OneZero replied.

Akron smiled tightly. "That's why you'll be there to watch my back." He pointed to the patch kit. "Come on. I'd better show you how to fix a leak."

* * *

I directed OneZero and Akron to one leak after another through a combination of frantic waving and pointing. So far the system was working. We'd patched almost a dozen leaks already. There were at least as many still misting into the cabin, but we'd fixed the worst ones first, and now our situation was much less urgent.

While I waited for OneZero and Akron to finish patching the next two leaks, I scanned the water for threats. The shimmering blue water quickly turned black as I peered down. It was easy to imagine shapeless monsters cruising through those hazy depths. Each time I thought I spotted something, I called it out to Richard, and each time he reported that there was nothing on sonar.

Another flicker of movement caught my eye. I waited for it to resolve into something more tangible, not wanting to call out yet another false alarm.

But this time I heard Richard shout out a warning over the comms. "Akron, I've got something *big* on sonar, and it's headed straight for you."

My eyes skipped about, searching for some sign of what Richard had seen, but there was nothing. I heard Richard talking with Akron over the comms, but I could only hear his side of the conversation.

"I don't... hang on..." he said. "It's right below us. Fifty meters down... forty... thirty! Akron, get back inside now!"

My gaze snapped to the cockpit where Richard was sitting, then back to the porthole, wondering what I could do. For lack of any better ideas, I ran to the rear airlock and peered out the window in the inner hatch, waiting to see Akron and OneZero return to the flooded chamber.

I heard hurried *thumping* noises coming through the hull just above my head—probably OneZero crawling around.

"Come on... get back here!" I muttered to

myself.

Just then a loud *thump* tore through the hull, and the deck went spinning out from under my feet. I went flying and hit the ceiling. Dirty water poured over me with wet slapping and sloshing sounds, as if poured from a giant bucket. I spluttered and gasped, and then fell back down, this time landing on top of the slick white crates that contained all of our supplies.

I lay there, winded, with the submarine rocking under me, but thankfully no longer rolling. I heard Richard cursing from the cockpit amidst a loud roaring noise that sounded like... water. Cold dread slid into my stomach. This wasn't the high-pitched hiss of the pinhole-sized leaks we had yet to patch, it was the throaty roar of a broken water main.

Adrenaline singing in my veins, I pushed off the crates to see an angry white torrent of water gushing in and turning the few inches already pooled on the deck into a whirlpool of white froth and dirty foam.

CHAPTER 14

I jumped off the floor and cast about desperately for something that might stop or slow the water gushing through the ragged tear in the side of our hull. Richard came splashing through from the cockpit.

"Shit! We have to get out of here!" He had to yell to be heard over the thundering roar of water pouring in.

"And go where?" I shouted back. "We're in the middle of open water!"

I heard the groaning roar of pumps starting up in the airlock behind me. Spinning around, I saw that the outer hatch was shut, and Akron was inside with OneZero. The water swiftly fell away from the circular window in the inner hatch. Moments later I heard Akron turning the wheel to open the hatch, and I stepped aside to make space. He struggled to push the hatch open with all the water swirling around inside the cabin. It was halfway up to my knees already.

Akron pulled off his diver's mask and gaped at the gushing tear in the side of the submarine. "We have to abandon the submarine before we start to sink."

"There has to be something else we can do," I insisted.

OneZero brushed by us and went to examine the leak.

"There isn't!" Akron said, yelling to be heard over the roaring water. "We already used up all the patches in the kit, and none of them were big enough for that! There's an inflatable life raft in the conning tower, behind the cargo netting at the top of the ladder. I'll need your help to deploy it." Akron went wading down the aisle to the ladder, kicking up waves as he went.

I started after him. Richard stood beside OneZero on the far side of the ladder, both of them watching like idiots as water poured in. I reached the ladder and waited for Akron to climb it. "Come on! We have to go!" But neither of them reacted to what I'd said. Thinking they hadn't heard, I waded over and grabbed Richard's arm to get his attention. "Hey! Did you hear me? We have to—"

The deck skipped sideways and we flew into

the wall. My head slammed into the plastic interior, and my ears rang with the impact. Despite that, I heard a splash, and turned to see both Richard and Akron sitting in the aisle, submerged up to their chests in the frothing water. OneZero remained where she'd been standing, unmoved by the impact. Waves sloshed back and forth, rebounding off the walls and making peaks in the aisle that nearly washed right over Akron's and Richard's heads.

"What was that?" Akron asked as he pulled himself to his feet.

"That monster is back!" Richard replied.

"And you want us to go out there?" I demanded. "Are you crazy? How long are we going to last in an inflatable dinghy against whatever the hell is hitting us?"

Before Akron could reply, OneZero half turned away from the gash in the side of the submarine, and I noticed glittering silver streams flowing from her fingertips to the damaged hull. "You'll have to outrun it," she said.

"Outrun it?" Akron asked. "We're sinking!"

"Not for long," OneZero replied, "but I can't promise that I'll be able to seal another leak like this one. It would be best if we didn't take any more damage."

Akron gaped at her, only now noticing whatever OneZero was doing. "If you can seal that leak, then why the hell didn't you do that before?"

"Akron!" Richard snapped. "Get us out of here! We can ask questions later."

He snapped into motion, wading toward the cockpit and disappearing through the open door. A moment later, I heard the engines thrum to life, and the submarine leapt forward. I grabbed the nearest supply crate to keep from falling over as the deck angled sharply down.

Diving in a leaky sub—that didn't seem like a good idea, but I guessed that we couldn't go as fast if we stayed on the surface. Besides, at this rate, we wouldn't be leaking for long: whatever OneZero was doing, it was sealing the gash in the hull at an unbelievable rate. The water coming into the cabin had slowed from a gushing roar to a high-pitched hiss. Seconds later, it became a misty whistling that harmonized with the other pinhole-sized leaks... and then it stopped altogether. The gleaming streams flowing from OneZero's fingertips thinned to thready strands of gossamer and then vanished like wisps of smoke.

Richard and I stared at the silvery patch of metal where the leak had been, then at OneZero, and back to the leak. It looked like it was moving, as if millions of metal ants were milling around there. As I watched, sparkling clouds fell away from the hull and sank into the water sloshing around our legs like handfuls of sand. I was speechless.

"You want to explain whatever the hell you just did?" Richard said, jerking his chin to the freshly-sealed rent in the side of the submarine.

"You're welcome," OneZero replied.

"Oh no—" Richard wagged his finger at her. "—you're not getting off that easy."

Akron came splashing back from the cockpit. "It's stopped following us," he said.

I breathed a sigh of relief and took a moment to look around and take stock of our situation. The leaks looked to be mostly under control. There were still at least a dozen places where I could see or hear water hissing in, but we'd patched the worst of it.

"OneZero," Akron said slowly. "Why didn't you just fix the leaks like that in the first place?"

"My self-repair nanites are not meant to operate outside of my body for long. When I project them like that their power cells become depleted very quickly, and after that they cannot be recovered."

"Nanites?" I asked. "You mean micromachines?"

"Not microscopic, but small, yes. They are what I use to repair my systems and components when I suffer damage. Now I've used them all and I won't be able to repair myself if something happens. That is why I didn't want to use them to fix the smaller leaks. They did not seem serious enough to warrant compromising my future safety and survival."

I began nodding slowly. "That's what I saw falling away like sand?"

"Yes. They ran out of power."

"Well, it worked," Richard said, running a hand over the smooth silver splotch where OneZero's nanites had repaired the hull. His hand came away glittering with silvery dust. *Metal dust,* just like what we'd found around the holes that had been drilled into the hull. The air grew still and sharp with silent accusations.

"OneZero... what is this?" Richard asked as he held his palm out for everyone to see the gleaming metallic residue clinging to it.

CHAPTER 15

OneZero cocked her head, as if confused by Richard's question. "What do you mean? I just told you what it is." She pointed to the metallic dust clinging to his palm. "They are nanites."

"Really?" Akron asked. "Because it looks exactly like what we found around the original leaks that we patched together."

"Are you suggesting that *I* caused them? You saw me. I never left my seat since we came aboard."

"*You* wouldn't have to," Richard replied.

"The metallic filings produced by a drill may *look* the same as depleted nanites, but if you had a sample of each, and a microscope to examine them, you'd be able to tell the difference immediately."

"Unfortunately, we don't have a microscope," Akron replied.

"Then you're just going to have to trust me. I

did not sabotage this vessel. Why would I? And if I had, why would I risk my life to help you repair it? Both now by using up my nanites, and earlier, by joining you in the water."

"She's right," I said, shaking my head. "That doesn't make any sense. Let's not start pointing fingers at each other. We still have a long way to go, and we're going to need OneZero's help to get there."

Akron frowned, but Richard appeared to relax. "So do we press on or go back?"

Akron appeared to consider that. "If we go back, and Parker is the one who sabotaged the submarine, then he might do something worse the second time. We can't continue with our original plan, because we're still leaking, and those patches won't hold forever."

"Then..." I trailed off shaking my head.

Akron turned to OneZero. "You mentioned earlier that if we went to the shore you could keep us safe. What did you mean by that?"

"If we can find a city populated by my people, they will help us."

"*Your* people?" I asked. "Aren't they all your people? Or do you mean that they'll help us by deporting us to the other side of their border?"

"No, I'm speaking about *my* people as defined

by our shared ideology. They are a subset of the four races that came to Earth."

"What ideology is that?" Akron asked.

"I believe you would call it pacifism," she said.

"So you're not the only one who disagreed with the invasion?" I asked.

"No, there were many others. By now they will have built their own cities. If we can find them, they will help us get to the border safely."

"Why didn't you mention this before?" Akron asked, his eyes pinching to suspicious slits.

"Because the mayor would not have let us go if he knew that we intended to make contact with my people. He would have seen it as too risky. And it *will* be risky. If the supremacists find us, they may decide to kill us."

I blinked in shock. "Why wouldn't they just take us to the border like they did the last time?"

"Many months have passed since your people were expelled from our territory. The assumption now will be that anyone who remains could be a terrorist. Furthermore, the supremacists will want to keep human-Screecher bloodlines pure now that they are being transferred to biological bodies. In order to do that, they can no longer afford to be lenient on natives who violate our borders."

"I see," Akron replied. "So most Screechers

will shoot us on sight, and yet you're sure that your people—*the pacifists*—will want to help us instead."

"Yes."

"How do we stop the war-mongers from finding us first?" Richard asked.

"Hide in one of your old cities. The Screechers will have given them over to the assemblers to strip for materials."

"The who?" Richard asked.

I remembered the flying, cicada-sized Screechers that I'd seen at the border disassembling a temporary wall of piled cars and using the materials to build a more permanent barrier behind it.

OneZero gave a more technical description to Richard, and then added, "The assemblers have limited awareness. They won't report our whereabouts if they see us, and for our own safety they're only programmed to go after inanimate objects."

Akron ran a hand along a dense crop of stubble growing on his jaw. "So you're suggesting that we go to the ruins of our nearest city and wait until you find the pacifists?"

"Exactly."

Akron turned to us. "What if she's lying?"

"To what end?" I asked.

"I don't know, to expose Haven. Maybe that's what she's been after from the start."

"There's no way she knew about Haven back then," I said.

"Are you sure she couldn't have overheard you talking about it?" Akron replied.

My brow tensed in an angry knot. I'd been asked that question before, soon after we'd first arrived at Haven. My answer was the same now as it had been then. "I'm sure."

"I should mention," OneZero began, "that I wouldn't need to physically deliver you to the Screechers to reveal Haven's location. You took this submarine to the surface to fix the leaks. At that point I could have easily transmitted a message to my people."

"She's right," Richard replied. "Water interferes with radio signals. She's spent the entire time since leaving for Haven with us too far underwater to get any signals out, but now there's nothing to stop her from calling home."

"Except that we're still a long way from the coast," Akron pointed out. "You'd need a very powerful transmitter to get a signal that far. Besides, technically she's still trapped in a metal tube surrounded by water. We're closer to the surface, but only the conning tower is exposed. There are still plenty of barriers to getting a clear signal out, but once we reach the shore that will change. That would also explain why OneZero might have wanted to drill holes in the sub. To force us to shore."

Unease crawled into my gut with those facts laid out. Richard looked equally troubled. I'd left my wife and daughter in Haven, thinking they'd be safer there. If OneZero was planning to reveal their location, they could be in serious trouble.

OneZero made a noise that sounded like an electronic version of a sigh. "If my goal is to expose Haven, then why don't I just kill you all and jump out the hatch to send a signal? Or, if you think I can't reach anyone from here, consider that I could simply threaten your lives and force you to go to shore. I wouldn't need to drill holes, or waste time trying to convince you with lies about a group of pacifists that might want to help you."

Relief spread through me with those arguments. If OneZero were our enemy, there were a lot of easier ways to deliver us to the Screechers.

"She makes some good points," Richard said.

"Yes..." Akron mused, as if he were still trying to think of a way to redeem his theory.

"Do not be afraid," OneZero said. "If for no

other reason, you should trust me because I need you to get home."

"What about your people, the pacifists?" I asked. "They must have rockets that could take you home, too."

"Yes, but that does not mean that they will do so. In your society, is help freely given to anyone who asks, regardless of the cost?"

Akron shook his head. "No, people have to provide adequate compensation for goods and services."

"It is that way in my society as well. Some things are freely given, such as food, shelter, and energy, but others must be earned. I do not have the resources to buy a ticket home, but I can help you in exchange for a ride aboard your rocket."

"Let's say I believe you," Akron replied. "That just raises a new question: why would your people help us get to Memphis? We have nothing to offer them in exchange."

"I believe there is something that they would like in return."

"Such as?"

"The pacifists are pariahs. After their refusal to help with the invasion, I am certain that has only become an even greater concern. They are in danger of being eliminated by the supremacists who did all the work. You could offer my people asylum."

A wary look contorted Akron's face. "I have no authority to offer them anything."

"You were close with your people's leader, were you not?"

Akron blinked in shock. "How do you know that?"

"I have ears. I listen."

"Even so, she's on Mars now. I don't know who the new president is, or if there even is one."

"But if there is someone in charge, you could use your influence to speak to them on our behalf. We could offer our help in exchange for asylum."

"What kind of help?" Richard asked.

"You need help to survive in the cold, and we have the technologies to help you do that."

"That sounds like an interesting proposal," Akron said. "But I'm sure you don't speak for your people, just as I don't speak for mine."

"And yet you can imagine that your people would be interested in such an arrangement. I can also imagine that mine would be."

"And you'll need to talk to them to confirm that."

"Yes."

"Now we definitely have to head for the

shore," Richard said.

I felt some of Richard's excitement seeping through me. This could be the answer to all of our problems.

"So what are we waiting for?" I asked. "Let's get to shore and start the negotiations."

CHAPTER 16

The closest city was Tampa, Florida, and *close* meant almost four hundred miles away. At a top speed of eighteen knots we'd be there in just over eighteen hours.

Now, an hour after patching the hull, the drain pumps had taken care of all of the water sloshing around on the deck, and we'd changed out of our wet clothes with what we'd packed into our supply crates. Unfortunately we could only get so dry with water still misting in from the pinhole leaks we'd been unable to patch.

Water glistened on every surface, and beaded in my beard and hair, running in tiny rivers down my bright blue jacket. It was water-resistant, so at least my shirt was relatively dry underneath.

We passed the time in a thick, uneasy silence. We'd placed a lot of faith in OneZero's good intentions. No matter how many times she'd proved herself so far, it was still unsettling to have so little control over our own fates. I kept trying to think of some overarching plan or sinister plot that I could ascribe to her, but nothing made sense. If she'd drilled the holes in the sub, then why fix them? And as she'd pointed out, why bother? As soon as the sub surfaced, she could have easily exposed Haven.

I thought back to when she'd first decided to cast her lot in with my family and the Hartfords, on our way north from San Antonio. Why us? We weren't special or particularly influential in any way—just two families headed north to get away from the invasion. Why not hitch a ride with someone else? And why had she been on the run in the first place? I realized how little I really knew about this friendly alien, and that just unsettled me further.

"OneZero..." I began.

"Yes, Logan?"

"Why did you join us that night, when we met in the Hartfords' house?"

"Because I didn't want to be forced to kill anyone else."

"Anyone *else?*" Richard echoed.

OneZero took a moment to reply, as if gathering the courage to speak, or recalling something painful—maybe both.

"We had just captured a military base not far from where you found me.... It was easy to shoot people who were shooting back. Even though we were the invaders, you were always the ones who fired first.

"Once we finished clearing out the soldiers at the base, we had to search the buildings and round up any survivors. I came across a woman and two small children. She screamed and shot at me with a small weapon. I shot back before I even realized what I was doing. Her children watched her die. They were small. Helpless. They cried and screamed for their mother to come back, and when she didn't, one of them came and beat me with his fists, as if those tiny hammers could accomplish what countless bullets had not.

"My unit leader arrived and ordered me to take them to the nearest transport for relocation. I had to pry them away from their mother's corpse, and carry them. They struggled and cried the whole way. The transport pilot was forced to stun them to fasten their restraints. Afterward, I watched that transport hover up and streak away, and I imagined those children being kicked out into the snow and left to fend for themselves.

"That was when I realized that I was on the

wrong side. And so I fled before I could be ordered to help clear another engagement area."

There was a lump in my throat that wouldn't let me speak. Richard and Akron must have been in similar condition, because neither of them spoke either.

Eventually OneZero broke the silence. "I am trying to make up for what I have done, but if you cannot believe that, then perhaps it would be best if you turn the submarine around and return me to Haven's brig. It is where I belong."

"No," Akron said in a hoarse voice, shaking his head. "Thank you for sharing that. I haven't personally done anything like what you did, but I've never been forced to fight for my country either. Those who have can probably relate to the story you just told. Conflict is never black and white. There are victims on all sides, and you're not the one who ordered this invasion. I think I can speak for all of us when I say that this actually helps me to trust you more, not less."

I nodded. "I agree. It makes you seem more human."

"Technically, I *am* human," OneZero replied. "Or I was once, a long time ago."

"And you've just reminded us about that," Akron said.

"Thank you for your... understanding," OneZero replied, her eyes flickering with a dim light. "I am no longer capable of crying," she said. "But I am perfectly capable of experiencing the same degrees of sadness and regret. That is why I wanted to join you, Logan. I had a debt to pay. I still do, and if I can help you find your son before I leave, I will."

I cleared my throat and nodded to her. "Thank you."

CHAPTER 17

Seventeen Hours Later
—October 31st, 2032—

We slept fitfully through the night in our damp, foul-smelling metal coffin. Akron divided the time into rotating four-hour watches in which we took turns looking for blips on sonar and alerts from the autopilot—as well as signs that one of our hull patches might be about to fail. Despite our newfound sense of kinship and trust in OneZero, we didn't assign a watch to her. If she noticed that as a sign of lingering suspicions, she didn't ask about it.

We all stayed up through the last four-hour watch to reach Tampa, crowded like sardines into the cockpit. Akron cut our forward thrust as we entered Tampa Bay so that I could deploy the periscope.

"We've reached periscope depth," Akron said as soon as we stopped rising. "What's it look like above us?"

"Uhh, give me a second..." I began deploying the periscope—something Akron had showed me how to do when I took over for him at the end of the first watch—and rotated the camera up. Bright bands of sunlight danced in web-like structures on the surface. I ached for a glimpse of the sun, of real sky and the far-off line of the horizon...

"Well?" Akron prompted.

"I can't see any debris..." No, that wasn't true. Those scrolling bands of light were broken by plenty of oddly-shaped shadows. "There's some debris floating around us, but nothing directly above."

"More debris," Richard said. "The tidal surge was at least a hundred and thirty feet. That's enough to level most of the coast. A lot of debris will have been dragged out into the bay when the water receded."

"And still be there six months later?" I countered.

"Maybe."

Akron muttered a curse, then said, "Pop the periscope out for a better look."

I deployed the periscope the rest of the way to

the surface. It burst free, and my spirits soared with the sight of blue sky, and the dazzling orange eye of the rising sun flickering through the cables of the aptly-named Sunshine Skyway Bridge. I couldn't believe it was still standing, but Richard had said something about the center of it being higher than the tidal surge.

Then I noticed something and horror took the place of my elation. There was no water between us and the bow-shaped rise of that bridge. Or rather, there didn't *appear* to be. A nearly solid island of debris stretched all the way there, covering the mouth of Tampa Bay like urban lily pads that bobbed and twitched endlessly in the death throes of an entire coastline. I gasped.

"What is it?" Akron asked.

Not waiting for my reply, he pulled me away from the periscope and took a look for himself.

He was silent for long seconds. When I blinked my eyes, I could still see the afterimage of the debris: floating rooftops, pink and yellow tufts of insulation sticking out like bits of cotton candy, overturned boats, beams and planks of wood stacked like broken sticks. If there was that much debris floating on the surface of the bay, how much had sunk to the bottom?

"This is not good," Akron said slowly, still

peering into the periscope. "I don't know how we can get through all of that."

"The debris will be backed up around the bridge," Richard said. "If we can get through, there's a good chance the water will be clearer on the other side."

Akron stepped away from the periscope. "*If* we can get through."

I wondered about other options. "Maybe we could sail up or down the coast and look for a better place to go ashore?"

"No." Akron shook his head. "I picked the Tampa Bay for a reason. The coast around it is littered with keys, islands, swamps, and wetlands for hundreds of miles in both directions. We could spend days looking for a better place, and I don't think we can trust those patches on the hull to last a second longer than they have to."

"Then let's try," Richard said. "We just have to navigate the channel between the pillars in the center of the bridge. After that, we stay close to the surface, but not too close, and go as far as we can. We just have to find one spot that's safe to surface and then deploy the lifeboat from there."

"We could have a long way to row," Akron said.

"Better that than have to spend another minute

in this leaky coffin."

Akron snorted and jerked his chin to me. "What do you think?"

"Let's do it," I said.

Akron pressed his face to the padded eyepieces of the periscope once more. I watched as he made adjustments with dials and the handlebar-like grips. At last he stepped away from the apparatus and went to sit in the pilot's chair.

"I think I can do it," he said. "The gap between the pillars is pretty wide."

The submarine's engines thrummed to life, and I rocked back on my heels as we started forward.

"I'm surprised that the bridge survived," I said.

"It didn't," Akron replied. "Or not all of it, anyway. It used to be over four miles long. The only part still standing is the center."

Neither Richard nor I had anything to say to that. We didn't want to do anything to disturb Akron's concentration. From this distance, just a slight miscalculation was all it would take for us to slam into one of those massive pillars instead of cruising safely between them. I kept an eye on the sonar display, hoping that it would tell him if we were getting too close.

"Here we go..." Akron breathed. He made

slight adjustments with his joystick and turned on the exterior lights, illuminating a swath of murky water around the bubble-shaped cockpit. A few drab brown fish darted through our field of vision, but thankfully no pillars or sunken debris.

Then a ghostly outline appeared off to our right. I pointed to it just as it resolved into a gray pillar of concrete, sweeping in fast. We were going to hit it.

"Akron!"

"I see it," he gritted out, kicking the joystick to the left and sending us stumbling into the side of the cockpit.

I watched out the side of the canopy as we cruised harmlessly by with a few feet to spare.

"We're through," Akron breathed.

"Now we just have to navigate the bay," Richard replied. "Try to stay as close to the surface as you can. We don't know how much debris may have sunk to the bottom."

Akron nodded slowly, his attention fixed on the controls and the murky water. Dark bits of organic debris drifted in the submarine's external lamps like clumps of ash. Dark shadows swirled at the farthest edges of visibility, motionless and drifting, others darting in between.

"Are those dead bodies...?" I trailed off, horror

surging inside of me as I leaned forward for a better look.

"Akron," Richard added in a quiet voice.

"I know," he replied.

The engines changed pitch as we slowed to a crawl. A moment later, those sunken shadows snapped into better focus—

Dead fish. Tens of thousands of them. I let out a sigh. "I thought those were people."

"Why are they all dead?" Akron asked. He didn't stop the sub. This wasn't the kind of debris that could cause us trouble, although it did cut our visibility dramatically. We cruised on through, dead fish thumping against the canopy and the hull.

"Probably contamination or dropping temperatures," Richard suggested, just as an eight-legged black monster darted through the cloud of dead fish, stirring them to life.

"Whatever killed the fish, it doesn't seem to affect the marine life the Screechers are breeding," I said.

"No, *they* appear to be thriving," Richard replied.

"That's going to present a problem for us," Akron said. "We've already seen that those things are aggressive. If they see us out there rowing a lifeboat to shore..."

OneZero interrupted with a deep, thrumming howl.

"She'll scare them off," I said.

"Let's hope so," Akron replied.

It had become impossible to see through the dead swarms of fish. Spider-sharks flitted here and there, enjoying the sushi buffet.

"Why aren't they floating to the surface?" Richard asked, glancing up.

I followed his gaze, seeing nothing but more of the same. "Maybe they're holding each other down." I shook my head, dismissing the question. "Akron, we're blind. You'd better—"

A sharp metallic shriek reverberated through the hull, and Richard and I stumbled into the back of Akron's chair as the submarine jerked to a stop, dead in the water. We all froze, listening for the sound of water gushing in. Thankfully, the only sounds we heard were the straining of the engines and the hissing of old leaks.

Akron hauled back on the throttle.

"What did we hit?" Richard asked.

The pitch of the engines increased, and I blinked in shock. I thought Akron had stopped the engines. "What are you doing?" I demanded.

"I'm trying to reverse out," he replied. He

waggled the joystick back and forth, and I felt the sub pivoting in place. "It's not working. We're wedged on something."

"Try diving, or going up," Richard suggested.

The straining of the engines ceased, and I heard pumps rumbling to life as Akron followed that advice, but still, nothing happened. After a minute of that, Akron twisted around in his seat, his face lined with worry. "We're stuck."

I glanced up through the canopy again, seeing nothing. "How far are we from the surface?"

"Maybe a dozen feet."

"So we can't deploy the life raft?" Richard asked.

Akron shook his head.

Dread gathered like a storm in the pit of my stomach. We'd have to swim out through one of the airlocks, but the water was crawling with spider-sharks.

"How far are we from the shore?" I asked.

"Two or three miles."

"We'll never be able to swim that far," Richard said. "Even if we could, we'd get eaten long before we made it."

"And don't forget—I cannot swim," OneZero added from the open door behind us.

I turned to look at her, having momentarily

forgotten she was there. I imagined our bloated corpses joining the fish in the water, alien sharks ripping off pieces as they darted by...

CHAPTER 18

"**W**ell?" Akron asked as OneZero came back into the sub from the airlock. She was dripping wet, but looked to be in one piece. None of the alien sharks had tried to take a bite out of her.

OneZero shook her head. "We appear to be lodged between two interlocking sets of debris. I would need proper tools to cut us free."

"Tools such as?" I asked.

"An underwater saw," Akron suggested.

"Do we have one?"

"Not here. Back at Haven there's plenty."

"And you didn't think to pack one?" Richard asked.

Akron shook his head. "How was I supposed to know that something like this would happen?"

Richard threw up his hands. "Maybe because the entire gulf coast is bound to be littered with debris?"

"This isn't helping," I said. "We need to find a solution. Any ideas?"

Akron let out a slow breath and tore his eyes away from Richard. "There's enough scuba gear for all of us, and waterproof duffel bags to take supplies with us."

"What about OneZero?" I asked. "She'll sink."

Akron studied her. "We could make her float. Strap on enough life vests and she'll bob right up."

"And what about those monsters out there?" Richard asked.

"I believe I can scare them off with the mating calls of their predators," OneZero replied.

"But how are they going to hear you if they're underwater?" Richard asked.

"The sound will propagate through the water better than through the air," OneZero replied.

"True, but will it be loud enough?"

"Yes, but my speakers don't work underwater. We'll need to get to the surface first."

"What about the swim?" I asked. "You said it could be a few miles to the shore."

"And we'll be carrying heavy bags of supplies on our backs, right?" Richard added, looking troubled.

Of the three of us, he was the most obviously out of shape, his belly pushing his jacket out well past his chest.

"There's nothing we can do about that," Akron replied.

"We could strap on our own life vests," I suggested.

Akron nodded. "That will help."

"I don't know..." Richard trailed off.

"You have another idea?" Akron asked.

Richard's silence answered for him.

"Then we'd better start packing." Akron walked down the aisle to a floor-to-ceiling cabinet. He yanked it open and withdrew the first duffel bag. "Here," he said, handing it to me. "Pack dry, warm clothes, shoes, then food and water."

"What about guns?" Richard asked.

"That too."

I studied the bag in my hands. "It doesn't look big enough for a rifle."

"It is if we field strip it first," Richard said, accepting another bag from Akron.

"Field strip?" I asked.

"Disassemble."

"You know how to do that? And reassemble it?" Akron asked.

"Sure, for an AR-15."

"Then get started. Logan and I will take sidearms."

I nodded along with that. It would be less weight to swim with.

We each went to our supply crates and began packing dry clothes, weather-proof jackets, gloves, and black knitted stocking caps. The bags filled up fast. When it came to boots, I only had the pair I was wearing, and they were still wet. I took them off and wrapped them in a plastic bag before stuffing them into the duffel bag. Akron passed a rifle and two boxes of ammo to Richard, and he got started with the disassembly; then he passed me a 9mm Beretta and another two boxes of ammo.

I wrapped the ammo in double plastic bags and stuffed it into my pack. Then I checked the gun, making sure the safety was on. I pressed the button to eject the magazine and slowly pulled back the slide to make sure the chamber was empty. A random misfire would be a stupid way to die. Seeing the chamber was clear, I re-inserted the magazine and packed the gun between my boots and jacket.

Last of all I packed six bottles of water, a dozen protein bars, a butane barbecue lighter, a can-opener, and four cans of chili. When done, Akron showed me how to roll the top of the bag down to make a watertight seal. I tested the weight and grimaced. It had to be at least forty pounds.

Swimming with the bag would be hard.

When we finished packing, we stripped to our underwear and put on our wetsuits. Akron and Richard helped OneZero put on a life vest and then used duct tape to strap two more around each of her limbs. We put on our own vests next, followed by oxygen tanks, masks, diving headlamps, and flippers.

We crowded into the airlock with all of our gear, and Akron shut the hatch behind us.

"Ready?" he asked, his hand resting on the red lever that would flood the chamber.

Richard and I nodded.

"Regulators in," Akron added. "Make sure they're right-side up."

I closed my lips around the rubber mouthpiece to form a seal. I tried breathing a few times just to make sure it was working. Air flowed freely in and out of my lungs and the apparatus. I gave a thumbs-up and nodded once more. Richard did the same, and then Akron put in his own regulator and flooded the airlock.

Muddy-looking water came swirling in around our feet, rising fast. It felt cold and wet even through my neoprene suit. My heart began pounding at the thought of what awaited us out in the bay. Of all the ways to die, being eaten alive by an alien shark had to be one of the worst.

As the water reached our waists, my duffel bag grew lighter. Maybe carrying it wouldn't be so hard after all. Moments later the water was up to our chins. Despite the weight of my gear and supplies, the life vest buoyed me up easily. We had to push off the ceiling with our hands to keep from bumping our heads.

The water scrolled up past our masks, and Akron squeezed by us to reach the outer hatch. I turned to see OneZero plastered to the ceiling of the airlock thanks to all the life vests we'd strapped to her.

Akron turned the wheel on the outer hatch and then pushed it open. Black water greeted us. We turned on our diving headlamps, illuminating a solid wall of dead fish. We hesitated there, our headlamps sweeping to check for signs of the spider-sharks we'd seen earlier.

My heart beat so fast that I felt dizzy. It didn't help that this was my first time scuba diving. What if my regulator got knocked out? Or if I couldn't tell which way was up and ended up diving to the bottom instead of up to the surface?

Akron glanced over his shoulder and gave us a thumbs up before swimming out and vanishing in the swirling clouds of fish. OneZero went next, followed by Richard. Realizing I was the last to leave the airlock, I pushed my fears aside and swam after them. As soon as I left the airlock I began rocketing to the surface. Dead fish crowded to all sides, streaking past me. *Twelve feet.* That's how far Akron had said we were from the surface. The water lightened steadily as I rose; then my head broke free, and water ran in rivulets down my mask. I saw the others bobbing around me on a blanket of dead, floating fish. Debris rose like islands around us, replete with eight-legged black monsters sprawled out and basking in the sun.

I pulled my mouthpiece out and slowly swam over to Akron. "What if they see us?" I whispered, my eyes on a nearby mound of debris with three spider-sharks lying on it.

Akron shook his head but said nothing.

"Shit!" Richard hissed, whispering too sharply and splashing loudly in the water. "Something just brushed my leg."

One of the creatures raised its massive head to look at us with staring white eyes. It gave an audible snort, and then let out a howling roar before diving into the water. The other two got up next, making sad echoes of that sound, and jumped in after the first. OneZero let out a thrumming howl that sputtered, sounding pathetically soft in the open air. That noise wouldn't have scared a mouse.

"Swim!" Akron yelled.

CHAPTER 19

We swam like our lives depended on it. Water splashed around us like a cannonade. The dead fish made it hard to swim, and made it feel like something was constantly moving around my legs. I hoped they'd shield us from the spider-sharks.

Akron led the way to a mess of wooden planks, mixed up with bits of roofing, siding, and insulation. All of it was piled around a cabin cruiser floating right-side-up and miraculously intact. There weren't any spider-sharks on board—at least not that I could see—probably because debris shaded the deck of the cruise. Spider-sharks liked the sun. OneZero brought up the rear, howling and sputtering to scare them off.

Akron reached the debris and waded through. Yanking off his flippers and tossing them up into the boat, he then pulled himself up a gleaming metal ladder hanging off the back. I took it as a good sign that nothing bit his head off when he climbed in. I reached the ladder next, took off my flippers, and went up on shaking legs. We both helped Richard up, and then set down our bags and began taking off our diving gear while we waited for OneZero to catch up. As soon as I removed my mask, the stench of rotten fish made me double over and gag.

"That's bad!" I hissed.

"And I was thinking we could cook some of those fish if we made it to shore," Akron said, holding his sleeve to his nose.

I straightened and shivered. The cold air was already biting through my wetsuit.

"I can't believe we made it," Richard said just as OneZero reached the ladder and grabbed one of the rungs.

"They must be stuffed from eating all those fish," Akron replied.

OneZero pulled herself halfway out of the water, her speakers still spluttering with that mournful howling sound—

And then she vanished, sucked under in an instant. "OneZero!" I yelled, leaning over the back of the cabin cruiser to stare into the frothing green water. One of the life vests she'd been wearing bobbed to the surface, shredded and torn.

"Shut up!" Akron hissed.

I turned to find him fumbling to open his bag. Digging through it, he withdrew his Beretta, and pulled back on the slide to chamber a round.

We stood frozen in the back of the cabin cruiser, our eyes scanning the water, ears cocked for the slightest splash.

"She's gone," Richard whispered after several minutes had passed.

Akron shook his head, peering over the back of the boat with me. A flurry of bubbles mushroomed on the surface, followed by silence, and then another much larger bubble.

"Robots don't have air inside of them, do they?" I asked.

"What else would they have?" Akron replied.

"Then they must have cracked her open." My shoulders slumped, and a lump rose in my throat, taking me by surprise.

"We need to find a way to shore," Akron said, stepping away from the sides. I watched him and absently studied our surroundings. The cabin cruiser was listing to one side from the nest of debris leaning on top. If we could get the debris off, and if the motor still had gas in it and still worked, maybe we could use this cruiser to get us to shore.

But that seemed like one too many ifs. *Don't boats like this have a key-based ignition?* The odds of finding that key in the ignition in addition to all of the aforementioned strokes of luck would be the equivalent of winning the lottery.

"We can't swim the rest of the way," Richard whispered, backing away from the sides of the boat.

"No," Akron agreed, studying a metal rack mounted on the wall beside the door leading into the boat's interior.

Richard turned and shone his diving lamp through that door. He cautiously approached the darkened space. There could be anything hiding in there. But if there were something, surely with all the noise we'd been making it would have crawled out to get us by now. More likely we'd find discarded supplies, maybe even a life raft. Drawn by blind curiosity and impossible hopes, I walked barefoot across the deck to reach the open door.

The inside of the cabin was a mess. A wooden beam poked in through a broken acrylic window. The deck was strewn with clothes, cutlery, broken beer bottles, fishing poles, bottles of water, bits of debris, and dented cans of food. I walked in, careful to avoid the glinting shards of glass, and began looking around for something we could use.

The cans of food and bottles of water caught my eye. Provisions. Maybe this had been someone's getaway boat? That might explain how it had survived. It fled before the tidal wave hit. I checked the cans—caviar, sardines, artichokes... snacks, not real food. If this had been used as a getaway boat, little to no forethought had gone into stocking it with supplies.

"Find anything useful?"

I looked up to see Akron silhouetted in the open doorway, and I shook my head. "Not yet."

Richard was sitting on a torn vinyl bench seat, hugging himself to stay warm, his head laid back against the wall, his eyes wide and staring in shock. "Even if we get to shore, what are we going to do without OneZero?" he asked. "You heard what she said about the supremacists shooting us on sight."

"One problem at a time," Akron replied. "Come take a look at this. I might have an idea of how to get us to shore."

I stood up, and Richard glanced at him. "Such as?" he asked.

A thump on the underside of the boat interrupted us.

"What was that?" I asked.

Another thump came, followed by a splash.

Akron turned, his gun tracking, but I ran past him to see what had made that splash.

"Logan, wait!" Akron said.

A hairy yellow and red creature was climbing up the ladder. It was OneZero, covered in entrails and seaweed. She was missing an arm, and holding a big fleshy white chunk of something in her remaining hand. She jumped into the boat.

I ran straight up to her and crushed her into an awkward hug. "You made it," I said.

She dropped the mound of flesh at my feet with a noisy *splat* and returned my hug. "I am not easy to chew," she replied.

"What happened?" Akron asked as I withdrew.

Speakers sputtered to life and she replied in a watery voice: "One of them took me down and tried to swallow me whole. I got stuck halfway down its throat, so I reached in and ripped out its heart." OneZero nodded to the pale mound of oozing flesh on the deck.

Akron smiled crookedly. "Good job."

I looked to him. "You said you have an idea for how we could get to shore?"

"Yes." He waved me over. "Come take a look at this."

I saw the metal rack he'd been examining

earlier. There was a white rectangular case strapped into it.

"What's that?" I asked, even as I read the faded blue lettering on the package. My eyes grazed the first word, a brand—*SEAGO*—followed by the most beautiful word I'd ever read: *LIFERAFT.*

CHAPTER 20

"It's self-inflating," Akron explained. "Similar to the one in the submarine."

"How are we going to move it?" Richard asked.

"There are paddles inside," Akron said.

I couldn't believe our luck.

"There is one catch."

My excitement stalled. "And that is?"

"It's a four-man life raft."

My brow furrowed, and I gestured to the others. "We're four."

"Yes, but OneZero weighs as much as two men, and she has plenty of sharp edges that could pop the raft."

The ragged shoulder where her arm had been torn away provided more than enough sharp edges all by itself.

"We can't leave her," I said, shaking my head.

"No, we can't, but we can't afford to have her in the raft with us, either. We'll have to tow her along with a life buoy."

"You saw what those things did to her," I said, shaking my head. "She'll never make it."

"I have a theory about that," OneZero said before Akron could reply. "I believe our movement, specifically the noise we made by swimming, was what attracted them. If I stayed very still, they likely would not notice. They have very poor sight."

"We'll still be dragging you," I said. "That's movement."

"But it won't make a lot of noise," Richard said.

"Exactly," OneZero replied.

"And what about our paddles?" I asked.

"We paddle softly," Akron said, nodding to himself. "We'll have to risk it. Help me get the raft out."

Akron set his gun down on the deck and worked to loosen the nylon straps securing the raft. He opened the metal cage that held it, and we carried it out together. It was heavy, but between the two of us we managed. We set it down to study the faded instructions on the case. Akron pulled out a nylon rope trailing from inside. After pulling out a few loops of length, Akron tied the end around the back railing of the deck. That done, he nodded to me. "Now we have to throw it in."

"Throw it in?" I asked.

"That's how it works."

I frowned, but decided to take his word for it. We lifted the plastic case and carried it to the back of the boat.

"On three," Akron said, and we began swinging the case back and forth. "One, two... three."

It hit the water with a loud splash, and I cringed, expecting to see our only hope of getting to shore sucked under by a spider-shark.

When nothing happened, I let out a breath, and Akron gave a firm tug on the line. To my amazement, the white case sprang open and a bright orange life raft emerged, rapidly inflating itself into a square pyramid that looked like a floating tent. There was a floating yellow ladder facing us with an orange block of text above it that read: *BOARDING.*

Akron grabbed an orange life buoy off one of the boat railings and handed it to OneZero. "Put it around your waist," he said.

She stepped inside it, sliding the ring over her life jacket-wrapped legs. Akron took one end of the rope attached to the lifebuoy and tied it around his waist, then went to recover his gun and duffel bag from the deck.

"I'll go first," he said, while slipping the gun into the bag. He rolled down the top to seal it, and then slung the bag over his shoulder.

"Be careful," Richard warned.

Akron used the rope to reel in the life raft until it was bumping up against the back of the boat. He handed the line to me. "Hold it steady."

I nodded, and watched as Akron stepped onto the boat's ladder and then straight into the raft. Grabbing the line, he waved me over next. I grabbed my bag, but hesitated at the sight of my diving mask, headlamp, and flippers lying discarded on the deck beside Akron's and Richard's.

"You won't need them," Akron said.

"We hope," I replied, and tossed the items to him one after another. When I was done, I climbed down into the raft. Richard went next, rocking the raft with his greater weight as he climbed in. Akron pushed us away from the boat and waved to OneZero. She began lowering herself into the water. The lifebuoy floated up around her chest and got stuck there. Akron still had the rope tied around his waist, but now he loosened it and tied it around a ring hook dangling inside the raft. After that, he cast about, looking for something.

"What is it?" I asked.

"The emergency pack... it has the paddles."

I looked back to the boat. "We didn't leave it, did we?"

"No, it's in here," Akron replied, still searching for it. "There." He reached into an orange pouch that looked far too small to contain any oars—

And pulled out two bright yellow paddles about half the length of my forearm—the ends only, with no poles attached. He handed one to me, and then pulled out a short blue pole hidden inside the yellow blade of his paddle. The entire thing couldn't have measured more than a foot and a half. I slowly pulled the pole out of my own paddle.

"You're joking."

"I'm afraid not," Akron replied. He removed another item from the emergency pack. A knife.

"Careful with that," Richard said.

He nodded, and used the knife to cut the rope still securing us to the boat. Picking up his paddle, he turned to me. "Ready?"

"I guess."

We leaned over the side and used the paddles like beavers' tails. It was agonizingly slow going. It took us several minutes just to get twenty feet, and my arms were already aching from the effort. Having to drag OneZero behind us wasn't making it any easier.

"This is going to take forever," I said, sitting back on my haunches to catch my breath.

Akron withdrew, frowning. "These rafts obviously weren't built for maneuvering."

"What's the point of that?" Richard asked.

"No one expects to be able to row to shore from the middle of the ocean. They rely on emergency beacons instead."

Richard snorted. "Well, what the hell do we do now?"

OneZero raised her hand and waved to us, then she reeled herself in and grabbed the side of the raft. "Allow me." She began kicking, and we made slow but steady forward progress, with the added advantage that she wouldn't suffer fatigue.

"I thought you said movement attracted the sharks?" Richard asked.

"It does," OneZero replied. "And I couldn't scare them off with water in my speakers, but now..."

A deep, thrumming howl issued from the grille where a human mouth would be. It was as loud as a siren, and much more impressive than what I remembered during our initial scramble from the submarine to the boat.

"They dried out," I realized, relief swelling in my chest.

"Yes," OneZero replied between howls; then she added, "I cannot see what's ahead. I need someone to guide me."

I looked to the opposite side of the tent-like canopy above us. There was no way to see through it. Another oversight.

Akron scooted over with the knife he'd used to cut the rope earlier and sliced a window in the canvas. As that flap fell open, I saw that we were headed straight for a mountain of debris that was crawling with dozens of spider-sharks.

"Left!" Akron cried, and a dozen shiny black heads jerked up at once. Funnel-shaped ears rotated toward us and jaws yawned open.

CHAPTER 21

OneZero increased the volume of her howling until it was painful to listen to. Spider-sharks dived off their island of debris and into the water. I watched them without blinking, afraid that they were headed toward us.

But we sailed right by their island without incident. I looked out the back of the raft at OneZero's churning legs—our very own outboard motor. I kept expecting to see her sucked under by a shark, but nothing happened, and we made steady progress toward the coast.

Akron periodically called out directions to guide her between the floating mounds of roofs and wooden beams. We floated right over some of the partially submerged wooden beams and roofing, and each time I winced, expecting something to rip open the bottom of the raft.

That didn't happen either, and to my relief, the

debris actually began to thin out. The coastline emerged, a confusing jumble of shapes and colors with a handful of tall buildings still rising in the distance.

"Is that Tampa?" I asked.

"No, I think that's St. Petersburg," Akron replied. "Or what's left of it."

I watched the city resolve into greater and greater detail over the next hour of our approach. It looked like it had been bombed. The only structures still standing were the tallest ones, which I'd seen from a distance, and even they looked like empty shells ready for demolition. I couldn't see a clear street or an empty space anywhere, just piles and piles of waste and ruin.

The remains of what might have been a harbor emerged ahead of us, and Akron guided us in. I recognized a piece of an airplane's wing, and grimaced. Had it been shot down during the invasion, or dragged out with the tide?

The floating ruins became denser again as we drew near to the shore. Akron did his best to get us through, aiming for a jutting peninsula and a collapsing group of two and four-story buildings.

"We need a safe place to wait while OneZero looks for her people," Akron said, shouting to be heard over her incessant howling. After more than an hour of it, I was sure that sound had to be coming from *inside* my head.

Akron pointed to the tallest of the collapsing structures on the peninsula—a building that was just four stories high. "Somewhere in there should do," he said.

It amazed me that such short buildings had survived the tidal surge as well as they had.

We came within a dozen feet of the shore and could go no further for all of the debris. "This is our stop," Akron said, picking up his duffel bag and getting ready to jump in.

I hesitated at the thought of diving in again, but picked up my bag and followed him out through the hole he'd cut in the canopy. We splashed into the water one after another, held afloat by our life jackets. Akron led the way, swimming and pushing through floating beams, roofing, and insulation. After just a few seconds of that, we were able to climb up and walk the rest of the way to shore.

"I can't believe we made it," Richard breathed as we walked down a pile of nested wooden beams on the other side of a slumping metal railing around the water's edge.

"We wouldn't have made it if it weren't for her," I said, my eyes on OneZero as she walked down behind us.

"You are welcome, Logan."

Chilled from our brief swim and the long trip to shore in our wetsuits, we hurriedly stripped out of them and dressed in dry clothes from our duffel bags. When finished, we sat and ate a meal of protein bars and bottled water from our rations, while OneZero kept watch.

A cold breeze blew across the debris-strewn peninsula. I shivered with the lingering chill of the water, but I was warm enough now in my weather-proof coat. Seagulls cawed in the distance, reminding me of simpler times and lulling me into a more relaxed state. Exhaustion weighted my eyelids and adrenaline left my system in a rush. Suddenly my whole body began to ache like one giant bruise.

"We'd better get moving before something sees us," Akron said, groaning with his own collection of injuries as he pushed to his feet. "Get out your guns," he said, and produced a Beretta from his bag.

I did the same, and Richard began pulling out pieces of the AR-15 he'd stuffed into his bag.

"Some assembly required," he said.

"How long?" Akron asked.

"Two minutes, tops."

"Do it," Akron replied.

He and I watched our surroundings carefully, with our Berettas at the ready while Richard re-assembled his rifle.

"All set," he said, jumping up and loading a round with a noisy clatter of the charging handle.

Akron nodded. "Let's go."

We grabbed our half-empty bags and started toward the most pristine building in sight. I counted three ragged, collapsing concrete floors above the pillars on the ground floor, and pieced together what was left of the sign above the broken entrance: KNIGHT OCEANOGRAPHIC RESEARCH CENTER

We headed for the missing doors. Moldering office furniture and chunks of concrete clogged the entrance along with what was left of a fallen palm tree festooned with dead brown fronds. Part of the second floor had collapsed, creating a ramp that we could climb. Akron led the way up, using his free hand to grab handholds of jutting rebar and concrete.

"Looks like this floor is mostly intact," he said from the top of the ramp.

Suddenly OneZero bolted past me, almost sending me rolling to the bottom. I looked up to see her grab Akron roughly.

"Hey! What—"

The rest of what he said was muffled by the metal hand she'd wrapped around his mouth. I reached the top of the ramp just in time to see why.

A pair of large black shadows were skulking around the second floor, no more than fifteen feet away.

CHAPTER 22

None of us dared to move. The two creatures nosing through the rubble came closer to the light, and I saw them in greater detail: long flat snouts, four thick legs, and bumpy, armored gray hides. Long, whip-like tails lashed the air restlessly. Big feet with long claws crunched in the rubble. They inched ever closer, but for some reason they didn't seem to spot us. The nearest one came to within just a few feet of us, lifted its snout, and sucked in a rattling breath through two holes where its eyes should have been. Large cone-shaped structures that might have been ears sprouted to either side of its head. I watched the creature turn its head first one way, then the other, its ears dilating and expanding as it did so.

The creature took a step toward me, sniffing the air in rattling snorts. Ear cones rotated toward me and expanded to megaphone-sizes. My hand tightened on the grip of my Beretta, and I aimed for one of those ears. OneZero bent down and picked up a chunk of concrete. She threw it over the side of the second floor, and it shattered noisily on the ground below.

Both creatures' heads whipped toward the sound. The one closest to us made a clicking noise, and then they both bounded after the piece of debris, spraying rubble in all directions. They leapt out of the building, sailing through open air and landing easily with their legs bent and tails flicking.

"Run!" OneZero whispered. She led the way, racing down what might have been a hallway between offices before the tidal surge. We ran after her; our feet like thunder, crunching through broken glass and splintered wood... but we were followed by loud snorting, clicking, and the skittering of claws.

Glancing back, I saw the two monsters come bounding up the ramp we'd been standing on a moment ago. Richard was just a few paces behind me. I turned back to the fore and ran faster.

We reached the end of the hallway and piled through an old metal door hanging off one hinge. I bounced off the far wall and Richard slammed into me from behind. OneZero shut the door and planted her back against it. "Get to the roof!" she ordered.

We were standing in the crumbling remains of a stairwell. Broken windows and cracked walls let in slivers of light. Akron began vaulting up the stairs, but before Richard or I could react, a loud bang sounded from the door as one of the monsters rammed into it. OneZero lost a few precious inches, her metal feet digging furrows in the concrete. Three-clawed hands appeared, reaching around the blue metal door, followed by a snorting snout full of glistening teeth. Furious clicking and snarling sounds issued from behind the door.

"Go!" OneZero said. "I can't hold them for long." Her feet were still sliding on the landing.

I launched myself up the stairs after Akron with Richard close behind. We flew up one flight, and then another, taking the stairs two and three at a time. By the time we reached the third floor, the door OneZero was holding burst open with a loud boom, followed by the sound of crunching debris and noisy clicking. Gunfire rattled out as OneZero used the integrated weapons in her arm. High-pitched squeals followed, and then came the sounds of a struggle. The gunfire grew silent.

"Keep going!" Akron called down to us. We hit the fourth-floor landing, and I heard skittering claws racing up behind us. I blinked the spots from my eyes, and shook my head, feeling like I was about to pass out. Richard launched himself past me, wheezing like a chain-smoker.

Struggling on, I glanced back and saw a big shadow bounding toward me. A sharp jolt of adrenaline surged inside of me, and in the next instant I collided with Richard. We stumbled and fell through an open door into the light and scrambled out onto the rooftop. Akron slammed the door shut behind us with a *boom*. A loud impact followed, and I saw the rusty metal at the bottom of the door bulge out toward us, followed by the sound of frantic scratching and snorting.

A gleaming claw poked through a rusty patch in the door, and tore a hole wide enough for a whole foot to slip through. Metal shrieked as the creature peeled it back.

"They're coming through the door!" Richard screamed.

Akron fired into the hole, three times in quick succession, drawing more pig-like squeals from the monster on the other side, but the clawed foot reappeared, followed by a second one. I dug through my bag and pulled out my gun, firing into the hole with Akron. Several bullets plinked off the door, while others hit their mark, but those scrabbling feet didn't withdraw, and the hole kept getting wider. It grew large enough for a dog to climb through. Richard joined in with the heavier cracks of his AR-15, but even the rifle wasn't enough to force the monster back.

"We're just pissing it off!" I yelled over the ringing in my ears. We stopped firing, and I whirled around, looking for somewhere else to run.

But there was nowhere to go. We were four stories up, and the only way down was blocked by two hungry, bullet-proof monsters.

CHAPTER 23

A whole head and snapping jaws popped through the widening hole in the bottom of the door.

It was wriggling through the hole. Akron, Richard, and I fired until our guns were empty. The monster squealed in time to each gunshot, and thin white lines of blood trickled out, but it showed no signs of stopping.

"What is it made of? Kevlar?" Akron shook his gun and pulled the trigger a few times more as if there might be another bullet lodged in the chamber.

"Shit!" Richard said, backing away and shaking his head.

I spun around to see that he'd backed all the way to a crumbling waist-high wall around the roof. A flicker of movement caught my eye, and a familiar form wrapped in yellow and orange life vests crawled over that wall like a spider.

I couldn't believe it. Somehow OneZero had made it. She waved us over, pointing to something over the side of the roof.

Akron and I didn't need any convincing. We sprinted to reach her.

OneZero was pointing to the twisted remains of a tunnel-bridge that spanned the gap between our building and the one beside it. It was at least a twelve-foot drop to reach the cracked concrete roof of that bridge. If we weren't careful we'd break our legs in the fall.

"You need to jump," OneZero said.

Akron was already straddling the wall. He tucked his empty Beretta into the waistband of his jeans, and climbed the rest of the way over. I did the same with my gun and I hurried to follow.

"Go!" OneZero prompted. "I'll try to slow them down."

Akron jumped, landing hard on the roof of the bridge and falling to his knees. I jumped down beside him a second later. Sharp pains shot through my ankles and the arches of my feet. My knees buckled, and I fell over with a grunt. Struggling to get up, I found that my knees and ankles hurt, but otherwise there was no serious damage.

Richard came sailing down next, and the bridge shivered with the greater weight of his impact. He cried out in agony and I saw him rolling on the roof, clutching his ankle.

"Is it broken?" Akron asked.

Before Richard could answer, we heard a flurry of skittering feet and snapping jaws. Our heads jerked up to see OneZero wrestling one-handed with a monster. She fired into one of its ears, and it shrilled in pain, withdrawing to let the other one have a turn. OneZero sent it sailing over the roof, and it landed with a loud *crunch* on an overturned car three floors below. The first one returned, jaws snapping once more, and it swallowed her arm all the way up to the shoulder. Then came the muffled reports of more gunshots, and the creature slumped, sliding off her arm and out of sight. OneZero climbed over the wall and landed easily beside us.

I ran to check on Richard, sparing a glance at OneZero as I went. "I thought you were out of bullets—or dead."

"What made you think that?" OneZero asked in a whisper, cocking her head at us.

"We heard when you stopped firing," Akron whispered back.

"I stopped firing because they pushed me over

the railing and I fell two floors to the bottom of the stairwell," OneZero said quietly.

Richard groaned, drawing our attention back to him. His teeth were gritted and his eyes pinched shut. I rolled up his jeans to find a bloody bone poking through his lower shins. It wasn't his ankle that had broken.

"How bad is it?" Richard panted.

"Bad." I turned to let Akron see.

He muttered a curse under his breath and shook his head. "We won't be going anywhere now."

"I can ride on OneZero's back."

"It would be better if you all stayed here while I go for help," OneZero replied. "I can't guarantee your safety if we run into more Stalkers. They can't smell me, and if I am quiet, they'll never know I'm there."

"Stay *here?*" Akron echoed softly. "Where?" He gestured to indicate our surroundings. I looked around, anxiously checking for signs of another monster. Empty black window frames glared at us from the buildings to either side of the bridge, but it was impossible to discern any details within. "There could be more of them on that side," Akron whispered, pointing to the other building.

"I'll scout ahead and come back once I find a

safe place for you to hide," OneZero replied.

"Those monsters clawed through a metal door," I said, shaking my head. "Where are we going to find that's safe?"

OneZero placed a finger to her lips. "Leave that to me." She strode soundlessly by us, heading for the gaping darkness on the other side of the bridge.

CHAPTER 24

It didn't take long for OneZero to find a place for us to hide. One of the broken windows on the other side of the bridge led us into the remains of an old classroom. A twisted mess of desks and chairs were piled against the open doorway, no doubt carried there by the receding flood waters. The door was long gone, and we could see vaguely through the gaps between rusty chair and table legs. Akron and I had crawled in through the broken window, carrying Richard between us, and now we were sitting on the rubble-strewn floor with our backs to the far wall so that we could see if anything tried to crawl in after us.

Silence ached between the cold, lonely gusts of the wind that whistled past the broken window. OneZero had told us to be as quiet as we could, so we'd spent the last hour staring blankly out the window while Richard chewed on the leather strap of his AR-15 to manage the pain of his broken leg. Akron and I sat watching the window with our Berettas. We'd reloaded them from the cases of spare ammo in our bags—not that 9mm rounds seemed to do anything to Stalkers.

Akron set down his gun and reached into his bag to produce a rectangular object. A bright screen sprang to life, and I realized that it was the tablet I'd seen him using in the sub. For a moment I was afraid that the light of the screen might attract attention, but then I remembered that Stalkers were blind. He opened a notepad application and typed something into it before passing it to me.

I read the message. *We should try to block the window with something. How about that chalkboard?*

I typed a reply. *You mean the two halves of it? There's nothing we can do to secure them, and it won't be enough to stop something from coming in. I'd rather be able to see if something is coming, wouldn't you?*

Akron read over my shoulder with a frown. I raised my eyebrows in question. He gave in with a nod and picked up his gun again. Not ready to dive back into isolation, I typed something else.

Where are they coming from? All those creatures. They must have factories churning them out somewhere.

Akron took the tablet back and set his gun down once more. This time I read over his shoulder. *The better question is why? Why churn out millions of apex predators when you're planning to become biological lifeforms again? I can't speak for all of the Screecher species, but the human ones like OneZero would be just as vulnerable to Stalkers and spider-sharks as we are.*

Akron passed the tablet back, and I wrote: *Maybe they're using them to hunt down human remnants, or to purge Earth's other native populations, or*

A sound interrupted me, and my fingers froze over the tablet's touch keyboard. Horror gripped my insides in a vice. It sounded like...

Akron took the tablet from me and typed: *Is that a baby crying?*

I glanced at my brother-in-law. Richard had his hand on the charging handle of the AR-15. He appeared to be in the process of chambering a round, but he'd frozen halfway through the act.

I took the tablet from Akron and typed: *How is that possible? No one could have survived the flood. Much less a baby.*

Akron typed back, *It's been six months. Someone might have come here afterward to hide in the rubble.*

With a baby? I added to the bottom of the crowded notepad.

More sounds stole our attention, coming from

the hallway beyond the beaver's dam of debris blocking our door—rubble crunching under padded feet, and soft clicking noises. The Stalkers were here, drawn by the baby's cries. Snorting and heavy breathing followed as they inhaled the scent of their prey....

I prayed for the mother or father or whoever was with that child to do something to muffle the sound, but what could they do? Short of smothering it, there was no way to shut a baby up. It was probably just hungry, and now it was going to become food for something else.

I had to do something. Jumping to my feet, I pulled back the slide on my Beretta and yelled at the top of my lungs: "Hey! Over here!"

A loud snort followed, and the crunching footsteps in the hallway stopped.

"What have you done?" Richard hissed, spitting out the rifle strap and hefting the weapon to his shoulder.

The baby's wails had stopped, as if only now realizing the danger it was in. Too late for us.

I heard Stalkers snorting and snuffling at the twisted pile of desks and chairs blocking the door, and hoped they wouldn't try to push through. Metal legs shrieked as the debris skidded along the floor, then stopped. The snorting sounds left the door, and I let out a quiet breath.

Akron pointed with his gun to the open window we'd climbed through. An adjacent classroom also looked out over the roof of the tunnel-bridge we'd crossed to get here. If there was a way into that adjacent room, the Stalkers could crawl out onto the bridge and in through our window.

My heart pounded out the seconds as we waited. At least a minute passed, and nothing happened. I let myself hope the monsters had forgotten about us.

But then two dark shapes crawled out onto the roof of the bridge. They lifted their long, broad snouts and sucked in rattling breaths to sample the air. Their heads swept back and forth, snorting and clicking softly as if conversing among themselves.

Richard took aim with his rifle, Akron and I with our Berettas. Richard's higher-powered weapon might stand a chance of punching through their armored hides, but that was still an untested theory.

One of the Stalkers turned our way and flowed down into the room like a passing shadow; then the baby started crying again, and I saw the second Stalker go creeping back the way it had come. I had to stop it.

Richard caught my eye and shook his head, but it was too late. My mind was already made up.

The Stalker in our room lifted his head to sniff the air, cone ears swiveling....

"Now!" I said, and fired my Beretta straight into the monster's left ear.

CHAPTER 25

All three of us fired on the Stalker. It took the initial barrage of bullets, staggering and shrieking with the heavier impacts of Richard's AR-15. White lines of alien blood drooled to the floor; then the Stalker recovered and bounded toward us, heading straight for Richard. Akron ran in, wielding the severed top of a desk. He swung it into the side of the Stalker's head just as its snapping jaws were about to rip Richard's injured leg off. The desk connected with a solid *thwup*, sending the monster reeling. I fired into the side of its head as it recovered. Akron dropped the desk and produced his Beretta from the waistband of his jeans, joining my salvo. The Stalker ran at Akron, and he fell over with an *oomph*. Jaws snapped shut around his thigh, and he screamed. I fired until my gun was empty, and Richard struggled to clear a jam. Akron had dropped his gun somewhere along the way, and he was struggling with his gloved hands to free his leg from the monsters jaws. Black blood leaked between the Stalker's glistening teeth.

Richard managed to drag himself over and angle the barrel of his rifle up until it was pointing directly into one of the creature's funnel-shaped ears. He pulled the trigger, and it collapsed on top of Akron with one of its back legs kicking spasmodically.

Akron said something that I could barely hear over the ringing in my ears. Richard and I struggled to pry open the dead creature's jaws and free his thigh. We strained and heaved, but it was no use. The Stalker's muscles had contracted in death, and there was no brain left to tell them to release. This gave a whole new meaning to a death-grip. I sat back on my haunches, gasping for air. My ears were ringing, and they felt like they were stuffed with cotton, so I didn't even notice that something was wrong until I saw the terrified look on Akron's face.

I whirled around to see the second Stalker creeping up behind us, its legs bent and tail swishing the air like a lion's.

The Stalker froze, we froze, and then I recovered my weapon and saw that the slide was locked open. Dull dread filled my gut. I was out of ammo. The monster's jaws sprang open, and it leapt toward me. I threw my hands up and fell over backward. Richard repeatedly fired with a noisy roar that I could barely hear over the pounding of my heart. A shadow passed over me, and hot rancid breath filled my nostrils—

And then a thunderous *boom* that I felt more than heard rumbled through the walls and floor, and the Stalker exploded in a wash of hot, foul-smelling gore.

I sat up and scuttled away, spitting out bitter alien blood.

"What—" Before I could even form that question I saw the Screecher disc hovering outside our window. OneZero jumped down from a landing ramp and ran toward us. At least I hoped it was OneZero.

"Are you okay, Logan?" she whispered as she crouched beside me.

"Yes, but Akron isn't." I pointed to him, and OneZero pried the Stalker's jaws away from his thigh one-handed, snapping bones in the process.

Stumbling to my feet, I leaned over him and whispered, "Akron."

But his eyes were shut, his head slumped to one side. I checked his pulse, pressing two fingers to his neck. His skin skipped lightly against my fingertips. "He's alive," I said, "but we need to stop the bleeding." I cast about for something we could use.

"Here," Richard said, already ahead of me. He'd taken his jacket and shirt off, and passed the latter to OneZero.

She and I used it to wrap Akron's thigh. He groaned softly in his sleep as we tied the shirt around his leg, and OneZero uttered a crackle of static that might have been a sigh.

"We need to get him to a bio factory."

I nodded quickly, assuming that was the Screecher equivalent of a hospital. "I'll grab his arms; you get his legs."

Glass, stone, and wood crunched underfoot as we carried Akron between us to the open window and out across the roof of the bridge to the waiting Screecher aircraft. We carried Akron up the landing ramp. A humanoid model Screecher greeted us at the top. I studied it worriedly.

"He's on our side," OneZero said before I could ask.

The robot made a characteristic Screeching sound, and then to my surprise, it *spoke* to me in perfect English. "I will take him from here. Go get your other friend."

Setting Akron down, OneZero and I ran back

down the ramp and across the bridge to Richard.

"You're back," he said in a fading, dream-like whisper, reminding me that Akron wasn't the only one in need of medical attention.

We hoisted Richard up between us, draping his arms over our shoulders. I took the side of Richard's broken leg, and he helped us by limping along with his good leg. Halfway back to the window, a familiar wailing stopped me cold.

The baby. I'd forgotten all about the cause of our troubles. At least my plan to distract the Stalkers had kept it from getting eaten.

"We can't leave that baby here," I said.

"Help Richard inside the transport. I'll get the child," OneZero replied.

She left Richard's side and he leaned more heavily on me in response. I struggled with him to the window, cursing and breathing hard. Getting him up and over the open windowsill proved to be impossible. "Come on, help me, Richard!" I hissed through gritted teeth as I struggled to drag him through by his arm.

"I'm thrying," he slurred, but he was barely conscious. The confrontation with the Stalkers had taken all the strength he had left, leaving him floppier than an old-fashioned rag-doll.

Using my back, I managed to drag Richard

onto the roof just as OneZero climbed out of the adjacent window.

OneZero held a yowling, shrieking creature up by the scruff of its neck and said, "I found the baby." It was hissing and pawing at the air as it struggled to break free of her iron grip.

I blinked in horror and disbelief at the sight of it. I'd risked all of our lives to save a cat.

CHAPTER 26

Besides OneZero, the only other Screecher on board the disc-shaped aircraft was the one I'd already met. Accommodations on board were uncomfortable at best. We had to stand against the curving inner wall of the disc, strapped into unyielding metal restraints that pinned us in place. The outer wall of the aircraft was transparent from the inside, allowing for a perfect view of the devastated Florida coast—miles and miles of rubble and bulldozed trees as far as the eye could see. It was beyond anything I could have imagined. I almost envied Akron that he wasn't conscious to see it.

The cat we'd saved sauntered up to us. It was a black and silver striped tabby cat with green eyes. It rubbed up against me, arching its back and mewing for attention. I'd always been a dog person so I had no idea that a hungry cat could sound just like a crying baby. The cat made another sound approximating a human infant, and I grimaced, hoping my mistake hadn't cost Akron his life. I glanced to my right and saw him slumping against his restraints. Richard's shirt was soaked with blood where we'd tied it around Akron's thigh. His chin touched his chest as he hung from the clamps around his wrists. His hands had turned white from the lack of circulation.

"OneZero—" I called. I couldn't see her, but I knew she was in the cockpit just around the circumference of the disc from us. "Akron's not looking very well," I said. "Could you release his restraints?"

"We're almost there!" she called back. "If I release him now, and he hits his head on the way down, his leg will be the least of his problems."

I frowned at that, but didn't argue any further. OneZero said we had to be strapped in for our own safety—a concern which apparently didn't apply to the feline busy smacking me with its tail. A twinge of doubt formed in my mind: what if the pacifist sympathizers had lied to OneZero, and we were now prisoners on our way to an interrogation?

As we flew away from the coast, I saw tall spires dotting the hazy line of the horizon and frowned, squinting for a better look. They didn't look like the remains of our cities. The height and shape of them was too regular, as if they'd been stamped onto the horizon, or rolled off the conveyor belt of a giant mass-production line.

"Wow..." I whistled softly. "The Screechers have been busy."

When Richard offered no reply, I turned to look at him. Seeing the pinched expression on his face, and how pale and waxy he looked, I realized that he wasn't doing much better than Akron.

"We're almost there," I said, repeating OneZero's assurances as if they were my own.

He nodded stiffly.

To my relief, a moment later the disc slowed down. The world turned around us as the aircraft rotated, and one of those mass-produced skyscrapers swept in for a close-up. A high, circular ring ran around the central spire. That spire must have been hundreds of stories high, and it was blurred by a buzzing black cloud of... *birds?* Below us, I could see that the gap between the spire and the ring was at least a quarter-mile across, and filled with a bright green garden. A gleaming transparent roof spanned the quarter-mile from the ring to the spire, making that garden the biggest greenhouse I'd ever seen. Below that, thin, translucent strands that gleamed like gossamer ran from the ring to the spire in random crisscrossing patterns. Beyond the ring long glass corridors ran along the ground like the spokes of a wheel to glass domes with more green, growing gardens inside. Here and there between the domes, tall, cylindrical exhausts belched steam or smoke into the sky, hinting at underground facilities.

Before I could discern anything else, our disc dropped from the sky, and I became weightless. The cat flew up past my nose with a startled *WREAOOOW!* And slashed my cheek open with its flailing paws. My stomach lurched and my body pulled up against my restraints. Momentum pressed me back against the inner wall of the aircraft as we slowed down, and my vision took on a red-tinged hue as blood rushed to my head. A pounding headache began slamming the insides of my skull. And then I felt all of the same things in reverse as my momentum squashed me into the floor. The cat smacked into my feet with another shriek, but I didn't get a chance to see if it was okay, because all the blood left my head, and I blacked out.

We'd landed on the rooftop of the ring around the central spire. There were dozens, if not hundreds more disc-craft parked in the immediate vicinity. The entire rooftop of the ring must have had enough space for at least a thousand of them. The sheer scale of the complex made my head spin. It wasn't as big as one of our cities, but it had sprung up in just six months, and the ring around the spire must have had a diameter of a mile or more. It was like the entire financial district of Manhattan with all of its buildings had been crammed together and wrapped in a tight circle. Of course now those buildings were sediment at the bottom of a water-filled crater.

OneZero came striding around from the cockpit with the pilot, and the two of them began unfastening our restraints, starting with Akron. I heard and saw the disc's landing ramp groaning open before us, and squinted as the glare of actual daylight blinded me. The seemingly transparent outer walls of the disc were part of a wrap-around digital display that was much darker than the real world.

I felt something rubbing against my legs and was relieved to see that the cat had survived. OneZero let the pilot take Akron and said something to him in their screeching language. The pilot replied in kind and carried him down the ramp, draped limply over his arms like a giant sack of potatoes.

"Hey, where's he taking him?" I asked as

OneZero opened my wrist clamps with one hand.

"To the bio factory. Don't worry. He's in good hands."

OneZero finished by opening my ankle clamps and then did the same for Richard. He leaned heavily on her as she released him, limping on his good leg.

"We need to take Richard there, too, before his infection has a chance to set in."

"My infection?" Richard asked in a shivery voice.

I looked sharply at him. "You've got a fever."

"He's several degrees too warm," OneZero replied.

"I just thought it was c-cold. I gave my shirt to A-Akron..."

"You're still wearing a jacket," I said, shaking my head.

"Come," OneZero urged, walking with Richard toward the open ramp. "It will not take long to fix his leg and clear the infection. After that, I will show you to your quarters."

"What about Akron?" I asked, following OneZero out. Remembering the cat, I stopped at the top of the ramp and beckoned to it. "Come boy—or girl. We've got to go." The cat mewed once and then darted after me. It kept pace beside me as I walked down the ramp to the roof. A cold, gusting wind blasted over the roof, clawing noisily at my jacket.

"Akron's condition is more complicated," OneZero explained as that gust of wind faded. "He was bitten by a Stalker."

"So?" Another frigid gust of wind interrupted and I stuffed my hands in my pockets. Were we still in Florida?

OneZero led us to a square platform with bright yellow railings around it. I could see the rooftop milling with more humanoid Screechers. Between them I also noticed the four-legged ones with their six articulated arms branching out of their backs and their round, glossy heads. We stopped in the middle of the platform, and it dropped down automatically.

"Stalker saliva contains a potent neurotoxin," OneZero explained as the gusting wind faded into the distance and the whirring of the elevator platform took its place. "Right now Akron is paralyzed, but soon even his autonomous functions will cease, followed by his brain."

"What do you mean his *brain* will cease?"

OneZero looked at me. "I mean that he will be brain dead if we don't counteract the toxins soon."

CHAPTER 27

The elevator platform we'd stepped onto seemed to go down for ages. When it finally stopped and broad doors slid open for us, a horrid, cloying smell assaulted my nose.

"What *is* that?" I asked as we stepped out into a bright white corridor.

"The bio factory," OneZero explained. She helped Richard down the corridor, and I followed them out with my lucky feline friend. A muffled *thump* shattered the silence in the corridor, and the cat hissed and hid behind my legs. I risked reaching down to pick it up. To my surprise it let me. Turning to look, I saw a pair of humanoid Screechers walking out of another elevator, followed by an actual human woman and two familiar-looking four-legged monsters. They made clicking sounds as they padded toward us. I froze in horror. The pair of Stalkers wore some kind of saddles on their backs to support a glossy black orb above their front set of shoulders, and behind that, a familiar set of six articulated metal limbs, presently folded against their sides to save space.

"What..." I trailed off, not understanding yet. Were they pets of some kind? My eyes flicked to the human woman walking between the Stalkers, and to the pair of humanoid Screechers walking ahead of her. Was the human a prisoner?

Long, dark hair framed a perfect porcelain face. Bright golden eyes settled on me, widening slightly. She let out a horrible screeching sound, but her lips never moved. The procession stopped, and all five of them looked at me.

The woman's lips flattened into a pretty frown. "That creature is not permitted in the bio factory," she said, her words brittle and cracking like ice.

The Stalkers began clicking ominously amongst themselves, and I heard rapid, clanking footsteps racing up behind me. A rigid hand grasped my shoulder, and I turned to see OneZero standing there.

"I will not allow it to enter any secure areas," OneZero said.

"Be sure that it doesn't," the woman replied, and with that, the entire procession continued past us.

"Stay close," OneZero said.

"I thought you said these are the friendly Screechers?"

"They are, but some are friendlier than others."

"Were those Stalkers?" I asked.

"Female Stalkers, yes."

"What's the difference?"

"Intelligence."

I frowned, and OneZero's eyes brightened. I absently stroked the cat in my arms, and it purred contentedly. "What were they wearing on their backs?"

"Upgrades that enable them to see and manipulate tools," OneZero replied.

I nodded and my gaze strayed to watch as those creatures walked around a corner and out of sight. Suddenly realizing that Richard was missing, I turned back to OneZero and asked, "Where's—"

"He's with one of the engineers."

"The *engineers?*"

OneZero nodded down the hall in the direction that those five Screechers had gone. "I'll show you. This way."

* * *

I peered through a transparent floor into what

appeared to be an operating theater. An entirely mechanical Stalker worked under bright lights, tending to Richard's broken leg. He lay motionless on a gleaming metal operating table, apparently sedated. Each of the Stalker's six articulated arms tapered to thin, dexterous sets of six digits that operated with extreme precision. Those three pairs of arms functioned together as a one-man surgical team. The Stalker simultaneously set Richard's leg, removed broken fragments of bone, cut away dead skin, and cleaned the wound. My stomach turned at the sight of glistening white bone, bloody muscle, and yellow fat, but I was too fascinated to look away. The Stalker sprayed the break in Richard's bone with something.

"What's she doing?" I asked.

"Repairing the bone."

"You can do that?"

"Are you surprised?"

"I suppose not."

The cat in my arms meowed loudly and struggled to break free, reminding me that it was hungry. So was I. "How much longer is this going to take?"

"Just a few more minutes," OneZero replied.

"Good. If we don't get something to eat soon, I'm afraid this cat is going to run off and get eaten by a Stalker." Thinking I should give it a name, I lifted it up and checked its sex. It was a she. "You're a lucky girl," I said, absently stroking her once more. "Lucky." I nodded to myself. "That seems like a good fit."

"Perhaps, but she was not *lucky* for Akron."

"No," I replied.

We waited a few more minutes, until the robot surgeon had stitched Richard's leg shut. It sprayed the wound with something, and the ragged line of stitches disappeared, replaced by a fresh line of pink skin.

"Come," OneZero said. "He'll be awake soon."

We returned to the corridor, and OneZero led us to a nearby elevator. She went in, but told me to wait with Lucky. Minutes later, she re-emerged with Richard. He was awake, smiling, and walking without even the slightest limp.

"That was fast," I said.

"I feel like I have a brand-new leg," he replied, beaming at me.

I nodded, smiling tightly back. Instead of feeling awed I felt threatened. This entire, six-month-old city was a living testament to how technologically advanced the Screechers were. The fact that they hadn't decided to wipe us out entirely when they'd invaded was the only thing that had saved us, but what would happen if they ever changed their minds? An alliance with these pacifists seemed more crucial than ever, but was asylum all they really wanted, and could we trust them?

"I see you brought the cat," Richard said, pulling me out of my thoughts.

"Lucky," I replied.

"Of course she is," he said, smiling and stroking her back. His gaze drifted to OneZero. "Where's Akron?"

OneZero hesitated. "His condition is more delicate than yours was. It will take a few hours to restore him to normal functioning."

"I see," Richard replied.

"In the meantime, you mentioned something about food?" I asked.

OneZero's eyes brightened. "Yes, of course. This way."

She led us to yet another elevator. The doors parted and we walked in. It was a glass cylinder running through a glass tube. As it went up, initially we saw a vast chamber filled with steaming vats of white, pink, and green liquids. Next came bright white chambers lined with blue tanks full of floating biological specimens, and then several floors of machinery and what might have been a data center of some kind. At last we broke free of the windowless subterranean chambers and emerged racing up the inside of the ring-building. Green gardens soared between the ring and the central spire. The glistening gossamer threads that I'd seen from above were everywhere, taut and slicing between the trees at alternating angles. Below, I saw walkways lined with colorful grasses and flowering plants. Meandering groups of Screechers populated those paths, seeming no larger than ants from our height.

I looked up as we crested the treetops and saw the central spire soaring into the sky. Balconies girded the tower like the tiered seats of a stadium, each of them draped with greenery and flowering plants, while misty threads of water trickled between them, sending sparkling, shifting curtains of spray billowing through the gardens.

Buzzing black clouds of insects, or possibly Screecher assemblers, zipped through the air above the trees, joined by even larger winged creatures. One of them swooped past the elevator, revealing broad, leathery black wings that spanned at least nine feet.

"What do you think?" OneZero asked.

"Wow," was all Richard said.

I just shook my head. It was hard to put my

reaction into words, and those that did come to mind didn't form sentences: harmony, light, Eden, utopia...

The elevator stopped, and I followed OneZero in a daze. Before I realized it, I found myself standing on air. I flinched and leapt back, banging into the elevator doors, which had slid shut behind me. Lucky hissed, clinging to my jacket with her claws and baring her fangs as she peered down.

Richard joined her, staring open-mouthed into the abyss. He balanced on tiptoes on the narrow band of solid ground that ran in front of the elevator doors. His arms were splayed out to his sides, hands scrabbling for purchase. He was a man on a ledge.

OneZero turned to us, floating impossibly in mid-air. An electronic hissing noise issued from her speaker grille. Laughter.

"Don't worry. You won't fall." She stomped on the floor with a muffled thud.

I took a hesitant step forward, trying not to look down, but doing so anyway. Another garden lay below, a jungle surrounded by rocky cliffs, balconies, windows, and thundering waterfalls that tumbled at least five floors into shimmering green pools below. Light poured through a glass ceiling overhead. Blue sky and fluffy clouds soared above.

We were at the top of the ring-building. I looked to one side at a curving wall of solid glass that faced the garden I'd been admiring on the way up. A draft came in from those windows, and a dark avian creature soared in for a landing on long, bony legs. Wings folded, skinny arms appeared, and the creature strode swiftly past us. That wall wasn't made of glass; it didn't exist. This was not a kid friendly place.

I sucked in a deep, calming breath, and dozens of appetizing food smells hit me at once. The floor was lined with tables populated by biological Screechers—the humans sat on chairs, the avians on high, branching stools, and the Stalkers on padded floor mats.

"Let's go find a place to sit," OneZero said, weaving a path between the occupied tables. Richard reluctantly followed us across the transparent floor, cursing the whole way. I kept my eyes level, not daring to look down again.

As we crossed the dining hall, I got a closer look at the avian Screechers. Their bodies were leathery and black like their wings, and they weren't much bigger than Lucky with their wings folded. Rather than beaks, I saw broad, expressive faces with startlingly human features. Six long white fangs protruded from serrated lips and colorful pairs of eyes watched me beneath bony, ridged brows. Small, delicate-looking arms and hands with three opposable fingers held glistening white bones covered in the roasted flesh of some animal. Thin legs with over-sized feet wrapped around the branching arms of their stools, and a second set of wings flared out where a bird's tail feather's would have been.

I felt the humans watching me, too. When I looked back at them, a chill ran down my spine. Their faces were too beautiful and too perfect, their postures too erect, and their expressions too blank—as if they'd all been botoxed. These were robots in human suits, unused to controlling all the muscles in their new bodies.

I felt dangerously out of place, like a homeless bum strolling through a private country club. And that wasn't far from the truth: I looked the part with my overgrown beard and hair, and I'd been homeless ever since I'd packed my family up and left our home in New Jersey. That felt like a lifetime ago now. I wondered if our house was still standing. If it was, it would probably be crowded with starving refugees and buried under a mountain of snow.

OneZero stopped at an empty table with two chairs. Lucky leapt out of my arms and onto the table where she restlessly paced back and forth with her tail erect and her hair standing on end.

Richard and I sat down while OneZero went to the occupants of an adjacent table. She screeched something at them—to which the human sitting there nodded—and then she dragged over an empty chair. She sat down in that chair and regarded us steadily.

"So, what would you like to eat?"

"How about a hamburger and fries?" I asked.

"That can be arranged."

"You're joking."

"No."

I had to see this.

"Make that two!" Richard added.

OneZero inclined her head to him, but she just sat there, staring at us. I wondered if we were supposed to go and place the orders ourselves. I glanced around, looking for a place to do that. The walls were lined with green and bluish-green plants, dark rocks, and trickling water features. Dark holes ran around the circumference of the chamber near the ceiling.

I saw something come flying out of one of those holes with a rectangular white container underneath. It was the Screecher equivalent of a drone, and not far off in design. Four rotors kept the gleaming silver craft aloft as it zipped over our heads and deposited its package in the center of a nearby table. The package unfolded itself, flattening on the table to reveal individual containers of food with transparent lids. Humans, dog-like Stalkers, and Avian Screechers reached for those meals and began digging into them with noisy eating sounds. Only the humans used utensils.

Dinner conversations were sparse and shrill, conducted in the Screechers' binary language. That seemed odd to me, considering that biological creatures should have had trouble making those sounds; then I remembered that the woman I'd run into in the bio factory hadn't moved her lips until she'd begun speaking English. They had to be using technology of some kind. But when and how did that Screecher learn English? Or perhaps the better question was *why*. I had so many questions and so few answers, but right now the most important one pertained to food.

"How do we order our food?" I asked.

"I've already done so," OneZero replied.

I nodded slowly, thinking she must have placed the order digitally. "What about Lucky?"

"I ordered a fillet of fish for her."

"Oh. Thanks..." I trailed off, looking around

— 210 —

once more.

"You are curious," OneZero said.

"Oh yeah," Richard replied for me.

"Feel free to ask questions. I'll answer them as best I can."

"Why is everyone still speaking in binary?" Richard asked.

"Why not?"

I shook my head. "The woman I ran into in the factory spoke English."

"The other species can't vocalize your languages. Only humans can."

"Okay, but *why* does she speak English? I get that your language is still useful among your people, but why bother learning Earth's languages if all the native humans have been evacuated?"

OneZero hesitated.

Lucky sat down between us, mewling pitifully and forcing me to peer around her. "What aren't you telling us?"

"We're learning English because we're preparing to cross the border—the human models, at least."

"But..." I shook my head. "You already spoke to your people about us giving them asylum? There's no way you could have made contact with our government yet. Learning our languages is a bit premature, don't you think?"

Richard's gaze sharpened. "Unless they've already been granted asylum."

"They have," OneZero confirmed. "Your government is currently sheltering hundreds of thousands of my people, and there are thousands more crossing the border every day."

CHAPTER 28

I gaped at OneZero. "We've already agreed to harbor your people? When did you learn that?"

"As soon as I found this city. I went to the *Overseer* to suggest we form an alliance with the natives, and he told me that we already have one."

"The Overseer?" I asked.

"The *Skyling* who runs *Verity*."

I frowned. "If you want us to understand you, you're going to have to stop using new words."

"*Skyling* is the nearest translation for what we call the avian Screechers. Verity is the name of this city, and the nearest English equivalent of the word we use for ourselves is the *Collective*, not Screechers."

"Do you have a name for individual members?" I asked.

"How about a Collectivist?" OneZero suggested.

"I suppose that works."

A buzzing drone interrupted our conversation, landing in the middle of our table. Lucky leapt into my lap to get away from it. The drone left a white package and buzzed away. The package unfolded slowly, revealing two steamy containers with what looked like a burger and fries inside, three sealed beverage cups, and another container with Lucky's fillet of fish. Lucky jumped back onto the table and began nosing around the food. I helped her open hers and she immediately began gobbling the fish.

Richard took the container with his burger, as did I, and we opened them to find exactly what we'd ordered—a burger and fries. "How..." I trailed off, picking up the burger and turning it over in my hands. It even had a yellow square of cheese drooping over the edges, and what looked to be lettuce and tomato creeping out around the bun.

"We print our food from various types of liquid and semi-liquid nutrient pastes. Then we flavor and texture the individual components to create any variety of meals. Some of it is grown fresh, however. The bun, for example, is a type of fungus, browned and injected with flavorings to make it taste similar to your bread. The meat patty is a protein slurry grown in a vat and then layered and cooked in a... is something wrong?"

OneZero must have noticed my expression. "Stop," I said. "You're ruining it. I don't want to know."

"Very well. I hope the meal will be to your satisfaction. I had to provide the recipes myself based on a food encyclopedia I studied while learning English at Haven."

I lifted the burger to my lips with juices running down my fingers. It looked and smelled about right. My mouth began to water, and I took a hesitant bite.

New and familiar flavors exploded in my mouth. I inhaled the burger and then moved onto the fries.

"How was it?" OneZero asked.

"Close enough," Richard grunted.

I nodded, amazed that she had been able to approximate the flavors from abstract texts without having a sense of taste.

"This entire meal was printed?" Richard asked while picking through his fries.

"Apart from the bun, yes."

I opened my beverage cup to find it filled with cold water, and I gulped until it was dry. Remembering Lucky, I found a covered bowl with more water inside, and pushed it in front of the cat.

She stopped licking her paws and lapped the water greedily.

I looked away, back to OneZero. "I thought I saw the Skylings eating legs of... some kind of animal."

"A printed approximation. They are carnivores like your feline friend, and they prefer their meals to resemble pieces of an animal."

"So the fish Lucky ate was printed, too?"

"Yes, a white protein paste printed in a flaked structure."

"Impressive," I replied. "How sustainable is it to feed people like that?"

"We can supply enough food to feed a thousand people with a bio factory that spans just one acre of land."

I blinked in shock. "*One* acre to feed a thousand? That technology could do a lot of good for humanity. One of our primary concerns right now has to be growing enough food to feed everyone."

"That is one of the problems we are helping your people resolve. The biggest challenge is teaching you how to safely harness natural reserves of antimatter, but for now we will supply the necessary—"

"*Natural* reserves?" Richard interrupted.

"What are you talking about? If there were any naturally occurring antimatter it would annihilate itself on contact with... well, anything."

"Antimatter is everywhere around us," OneZero replied, swiping her arm through the air as if to capture some of it.

"Again, that's not possible," Richard replied.

"No? While I was locked up in Haven, your scientists came to me with various problems to solve, representing the gaps in their knowledge. I didn't cooperate, because I planned to use my knowledge to bargain for freedom, but I did learn where your people's knowledge begins and ends. You know that black holes generate antimatter, but you have never been able to create and sustain one long enough to generate useful quantities of it."

My knowledge of physics was somewhat limited, but I knew what antimatter was, and how incredibly hard it was to produce.

Richard looked to be enthralled. "I'm assuming the Collective has made better progress," he said.

"Yes. Antimatter powers everything from our lights to the power cells inside of me. There's a black hole underneath each of our cities that generates it."

I gazed down through the transparent floor between my feet and imagined a swirling black vortex drawing us into oblivion. "How do you keep it from sucking us in? Or the entire Earth for that matter?"

Richard waved a hand at me. "Those are misconceptions. Artificial black holes can't do that. They're too small. One of them would have to grow more massive than the Earth itself to pose a meaningful threat, and it would take forever to do that."

"Exactly," OneZero replied. "And we are careful not to feed them past a certain point."

Richard had a greedy gleam in his eyes that made me think he was about to ask a thousand other questions, but I cut him off just as he was sucking in a breath to ask the first.

"When can we hitch a ride to the border? I assume you broached that topic with the Overseer?"

Richard shot me an accusing frown, but OneZero replied, "I did. We can leave with the next group of emigrants tomorrow morning. If you are finished eating, I can show you to your quarters."

I pushed out my chair and picked Lucky up. She settled into my arms, purring contentedly. "Let's go," I said.

* * *

We were assigned a spacious two-floor apartment that looked like it had been designed with humans in mind. Richard and I retreated to our rooms to shower in en suite bathrooms. I eagerly stripped out of my stiff, sweat-starched clothes and hurried into the bathroom where I found exotic versions of a shower, tub, toilet, and sink.

Taking a few minutes to figure out how to use the toilet, I then went to the shower. It was nature-themed, with sloping, textured rock walls and a rippled floor that looked like sand. I couldn't see any kind of faucet, but there was a black circle that might have been a sensor, and the entire ceiling was pocked with pin-sized jets. I waved a hand inside the shower, and water rained down from the ceiling. The water was warm, but not hot enough for my liking. Still, it was a lot better than the smelly, alien shark-infested waters of Tampa Bay. I stepped in and felt my tension melt away with the kneading lines of water. I cast about for the soap, but there wasn't any.

Then I noticed the suds forming on my skin. Some kind of soap had been mixed with the water. Just as I was starting to relax and enjoy the shower, the water shut off.

"Hey!" I glared at the ceiling and waved my hand in front of the sensor.

OneZero came in. "Is something wrong?"

"It just stopped!"

"Because you are clean."

"Yeah, but..."

OneZero pointed to a shelf with folded white squares on it, and then disappeared. *Towels?* I stepped from the shower, accompanied by on a cloud of steam. Those towels were actually something approximating terrycloth robes. I pulled the robe on and walked into my bedroom. Concealed lights bloomed to a dim golden hue as I entered the room. Lucky was asleep on one of the pillows at the top of a couch-like bed. A fresh set of clothes lay on the bottom—a loosely-woven green shirt and brown pants. I debated getting out of the robe, but it was too comfortable. Spying slippers and shoes at the foot of the bed, I went for the slippers. They were soft and cozy, but too big. To my amazement, they shrank around my feet as I began to walk in them.

Stepping into the hallway, I saw that it was lined with garden-facing windows on one side and more bedrooms on the other. I walked down to the living room and found it empty.

A warm breeze blew in, and hushed voices drew my gaze out the windows to the balcony. I spotted Richard floating in a small, steaming infinity pool that overlooked the gardens below. In keeping with the nature theme of everything else, the Jacuzzi looked to be cut from actual rocks, draped with hanging plants. Water trickled down a small cliff to one side of the pool.

I walked outside. "Hey," I said to announce myself as I went to the transparent railing running along the balcony. We were three floors above the ground, giving me a nice view of the illuminated gardens below. Overhead the sky had darkened to pastel blues and pinks. Here in the shadowy lower levels of the city, night had already fallen. The inner wall of the ring-building curved around to both sides in a glittering sea of lights. The air was fresh and humid, honeyed with the strange fragrances of alien blossoms. A warm breeze blew, slicing through my robe, and I let out a slow breath.

Golden lanterns traced out pathways in the gardens, while green ones illuminated soaring trees. Blue lights limned the water features and pools.

"This is like a five-star resort," I said.

"I assume that means it is to your liking,"

OneZero replied.

"Are you kidding?" I turned to her with eyebrows raised.

"I never want to leave," Richard added with a blissful sigh. "You Screechers—"

"Collectivists."

"Yeah, that—you sure know how to live."

My brow furrowed at that, and I walked over to the steaming pool where Richard floated. Catching a glimpse of his naked backside, I grimaced and looked away. I scooped my hand through the water. It was hot. I was tempted to take off my robe and join him, but I couldn't. Maybe it was the idea of enjoying myself here while my son froze in some hell hole north of the border... but no, that wasn't entirely it. This place was seductive, and I wanted to keep a clear head. Something about these pacifists didn't ring true.

I looked to OneZero. "Your people have gone to a lot of trouble to build a life for themselves here. Why leave and start all over again?"

"Not everyone is leaving. Not yet. Only the humans."

"Yeah, but still—are you really in that much danger from your own people?"

"We have lived a long time, so if we see trouble coming ten or even a hundred years from now, we don't wait until it is upon us to act. My people will need sanctuary when the supremacists turn on us. They are going to prepare that place now, while there's still time to do so."

OneZero gestured with her only arm to indicate our surroundings. "But it is not all about mitigating the risks to ourselves. It's also about making amends. Could you enjoy all of this knowing how many people died to make it possible? And also knowing that the people who died were members of your own species?"

"That's why only the humans are leaving," I guessed. "You feel a greater sense of kinship. It makes you feel the guilt over displacing us more keenly than the others."

"Partly, yes," OneZero replied.

Our conversation lapsed, and Richard filled the silence with one of his own questions. "What about Dark Matter?"

"Dark Matter?" OneZero echoed.

"You know what it is, don't you?"

She was silent for a long moment.

Richard gave her an exasperated look. "Is that information proprietary, or are you busy scanning some kind of encyclopedic database to refresh your memory?"

"Sorry, neither. Actually, I was checking on

Akron's status. He's been released, but there were complications."

A heavy weight settled in my gut, and my brow tensed. I had drawn the Stalkers to us in order to save a cat. It wasn't an empty victory, but hardly a fair trade if it had left Akron permanently disabled or otherwise impaired.

"What kind of complications?" I asked.

"The toxins made it to his brain. I'm told that we were able to map and rebuild most of the dead tissue, but there will be gaps in his memory."

"Permanent gaps?" I asked.

"I'm afraid so, yes."

"How bad is it?" I asked. "Will he still recognize us?"

Richard gave us a troubled look. "What about Mars? If he doesn't remember what needs to be done to re-engineer the prototype, we're never going to get there."

"We'll find out how much he remembers soon. I requested that he be brought here directly. He should arrive any minute now."

* * *

I stood there looking at a man that I recognized, but no longer knew. Gaps in his memory? More like chasms. Akron had just expressed a desire to go to Chicago rather than Memphis.

"You don't remember why we're going to Memphis?" I asked.

Akron stared blankly at me. "It would help if you reminded me."

Richard and I traded worried glances. He spoke first. "You wanted to build a rocket to get to Mars from the prototype at Starcast's launch facility. That's why."

"Why Chicago?" I asked.

"It's the current seat of government. We can do more to help from there."

"How do you know that?"

OneZero put in, "We filled some of the gaps, remember? My people have been in league with your government since the rebirth of your new nation, approximately four months ago. We know much about its inner workings as a result."

Akron nodded along with that, smiling to put us at ease.

That smile did everything but put me at ease. Deep suspicions curled in the pit of my stomach. The Screechers knew the inner workings of our government, and Akron no longer wanted to get to Mars. What the hell had they done to him?

"What about your family?" I asked.

"My family?" Akron echoed, still smiling.

"Shit," Richard muttered. "He doesn't remember."

"We can discuss where to go in the morning," OneZero added quickly. "Right now, Akron needs to wash up and rest." She turned him by his shoulders and started in the direction of the hallway where the bedrooms were.

"What about my son!" I called after them. "You promised you'd help me find him!" I called after her. If we went to Chicago, I'd probably never find him.

"And I will help you," OneZero called back.

I watched them go, feeling betrayed. Something was going on here. I could practically smell it. These Screechers had a hidden agenda, and in spite of all that she'd done for my family over the past many months, OneZero was somehow a part of it.

"I'm going back to the Jacuzzi," Richard said.

Suddenly our luxury accommodations felt like a prison. I'd been right to keep my guard up. I glanced at the door. Maybe it felt like a prison because it was one.

There was only one way to find out. I started toward the door, determined to break it down if I had to.

CHAPTER 29

To my surprise, the door handle turned easily. I got stuck trying to figure out how to work the elevators, so I went looking for a stairwell instead.

The stairs were right beside the elevators. All of this was so familiar—showers, toilets, stairs, elevators, doors with handles that turned—it was almost like the Screechers had somehow studied our civilization and copied the parts that made sense to them. I'd expected something more alien.

I hurried down the stairs in my slippers and terrycloth-like robe, struggling to keep it from flying open. I wished I'd opted to wear the clothes and shoes OneZero had left in my bedroom.

At the bottom of the stairwell, I walked down a short hallway and through a set of glass doors to one of the garden paths. Trickling groups of Human and Stalker-model Screechers ambled along ahead—mostly the biological versions. I set a brisk pace, passing strangers by the dozen and drawing curious glances. I kept my eyes fixed dead ahead to avoid questions about my strange attire.

Golden pools of light beamed down from spherical lanterns that seemed to hover to either side of the path. Green-lit trees soared, some of them familiar, others exotic. A dark blue stream appeared bubbling beside me. Black specks of alien insects flitted through garden lights. I didn't know where I was going, or what I was looking for, but something told me that it was important to push the boundaries of this place and see how these 'friendly' Screechers would react.

No one had tried to stop me so far, but that just meant that I hadn't stuck my nose in the right place yet.

After about ten minutes, the base of the central spire appeared, glittering between shadowy curtains of greenery. I walked straight up to the spire and saw that the bottom lay open on all sides—some kind of a courtyard? Four massive support structures curved up from the corners, reminding me of the Eiffel Tower. A bitter flash of resentment coursed through me with that.

Paris was a nothing but a crater, just like New York and Washington DC. That was a helpful reminder that I had good reason to be skeptical of the Screechers' good intentions. Akron had been skeptical, too, but now he was probably Team Screecher.

Winded by my brisk pace, I slowed down as I passed into the open chamber at the bottom of the spire. In the center of the floor lay a bloated, translucent blob that might have been some Screecher's idea of art. I walked up to it and stood in the shadows beside a railing that ran around the sculpture, preventing me from reaching it. Translucent cables, like the ones crisscrossing through the garden, sliced down from a shadowy ceiling, connecting to the blob on all sides. They spoke to some purpose beyond aesthetic.

I peered at it, trying to decide what it might be. A flicker of movement entered my periphery, and I turned to see a handsome human man a few inches taller than myself standing in a pool of light beside me. He had wavy dark hair and sharp features that filled his face with shadows. Bright green eyes sparkled. He nodded to the sculpture and screeched something at me, but his lips didn't move. Speaker grilles peeked out of his voluminous clothes, and I realized that was how they could still speak binary.

I stood in the shadows, so this Screecher might have mistaken me for one of his own. Stepping into the light to resolve the misunderstanding, I said, "I'm sorry. I don't speak Screech—" But stopped myself before I could complete that slur.

"You're one of the visitors," the man said, switching to English.

"Yes," I replied, surprised that he had heard about us.

He pointed to the sculpture, and said, "Do you know what that is?"

"Art?"

The man's cheeks dimpled in a grin. "It's the heart of the city."

"Well, I guess it *is* in the center...."

"No, I mean that it pumps the city's blood. How do you think all of this was built?" He gestured with upraised palms. "Who maintains it and runs it?"

I arched an eyebrow at the translucent blob, but as I looked at it once more, I realized that it was moving subtly—expanding and contracting rhythmically, as if...

"It's *alive?*"

"Shhh," the stranger said. "Of course it's alive. It's the consciousness behind the smallest members of the Collective."

"The assemblers?"

"I have not heard them called that before, but

that is a fair description of them, yes... the *assemblers*. This creature wields them like an army, just as it once wielded their biological counterparts."

"A hive mind," I said.

"Exactly. Those cables you see are like nerves, connecting the mind to the rest of the city and transmitting its thoughts into action. Even thicker cables run between our cities, connecting all of the hive minds to each other. Together they are one, but also many, and all of them slaves. We engineered them and their children, the assemblers, to serve our purposes."

"Slaves?" I asked. "I thought the Stalkers were the lowest on the totem pole of your society?"

"The totem pole?"

I tried a more literal approach. "I thought the Stalkers were the least-revered members of your society?"

"They are, but they have much more freedom. The assemblers will never be free. We rely on them far too much for that."

Losing interest, I switched topics. "Are you going to cross the border?"

"Tomorrow, yes. Why?"

"Is it true that your people are trying to help mine?"

"We already have. Why do you ask? Did someone say otherwise?"

"No." I shook my head. "I just wanted to be sure."

"Then rest easy, Logan."

My gaze sharpened. "How do you know my name?"

"Your names and faces were publicized ahead of your arrival to prevent any unfortunate misunderstandings."

"You mean so that none of you would kill us?"

"Yes."

I was taken aback by his candor. "Then your people are not as friendly and peace-loving as they claim."

The man shook his head. "You must understand that any natives found wandering around our cities without permission or explanation would almost certainly be terrorists seeking to achieve violent ends. There have been incidents. Being a pacifist does not make one stupid, and prevention is the cure when it comes to terrorism."

I snorted. "You're the invaders who took our homes, and we're the *terrorists?* Under the circumstances, I don't think you can blame us if we've tried to smuggle bombs into your cities."

"I agree, and that is why I am leaving to join the reparation efforts."

The same song and dance as OneZero—they wanted to make amends. So far her story matched his. "What's your name?"

"Deon is the human name that I was given."

"Well, Deon... thank you. You've put my mind at ease enough that I think I might actually get some sleep tonight."

Deon inclined his head to me. "I am glad that I could help. It was nice to meet you, Logan."

"Likewise."

I hurried back down the pathway, retracing my steps to the outer ring of the city. I hoped I was remembering the way correctly. If not, I could end up spending the entire night wandering around looking for my room. I didn't even know what number it was—not that the glowing symbols on the door were recognizable as numbers to me.

I reached the stairwell that I'd come down earlier, and struggled to picture the door to our apartment as I climbed the stairs. I vaguely recalled two vertical lines followed by a horizontal one and another vertical—a binary code of some kind.

When I reached the third landing in the stairwell, I stopped to catch my breath and placed a hand on the wall to steady myself.

Something tickled my hand, and I absently scratched at it. The feeling turned to a crawling sensation that ran down my arm. I flinched and swiped at it. A black crawling thing the size of a cicada hit the floor with a metallic clatter.

I watched it take flight with a buzzing sound and crawl into a groove in the wall, disappearing from sight. One of the assemblers. I remembered seeing similar grooves in the walls throughout the city. Was that where the assemblers lived?

Imagining the walls crawling with metal beetles didn't make the thought of sleeping here anymore appealing. I shivered and hurried out onto the third floor. The hallway was busier than I'd left it, with biological Screechers going in and out of rooms on both sides.

Upon reaching the room with the right sequence of symbols, I tried the handle. It turned and the door swung open. I half-expected to find an angry Stalker on the other side, but instead I saw a familiar, two-story living area, stairs curving up to additional bedrooms, a hallway leading to the ones we'd occupied, and Richard's head bobbing in the hot pool on the balcony.

I considered going out there to tell him about my encounter with Deon, but I was too tired. It could wait until morning.

I turned and started down the hall to my room. Along the way I heard muffled voices—Akron's and OneZero's. Curious, I stopped and placed my ear to the door that the voices were coming from.

"...'t tell them the truth," Akron said.

"They *trust* me," OneZero said.

"And you feel guilty for hiding things? Don't. There's too much at stake. And don't forget about your children. You still have to earn the right to bring them back."

"I haven't forgotten," OneZero said.

"Good. You should go get that arm fixed while we're sleeping."

"You don't need to sleep anymore."

"No, but I do need to keep up appearances. They still think I'm Akron."

"I hinted otherwise," OneZero said.

"You shouldn't be hinting at all."

"What about you? You're making them suspicious by saying you want to go to Chicago instead of Memphis."

"We need to speak with the president," Akron said.

"The real Akron would be more concerned with getting to Mars to be reunited with his family. Besides, the Overseer wants to get people on Mars. We could make the president come to us in

Memphis."

"Yes, perhaps we could, but it is not your place to question me. Don't forget, I am in charge of this operation. Now go get yourself fixed up. You're going to need that arm."

"Of course."

Clanking footsteps approached the door; I flew down the corridor to my room, yanked open the door and eased it shut. Leaning heavily against the door, I tried to get my breathing under control and hoped OneZero hadn't detected me in some way.

My whole body jumped in time to each heartbeat. The sound of heavy metal footsteps receded down the hall, and I blew out a breath that I hadn't realized I was holding. My body sagged as some of the tension left my muscles, and my legs began to shake. I'd been *right* to distrust them!

Why had they been speaking in English rather than their language? Maybe Akron hadn't been wearing the device he needed to speak in binary. Whatever the case, I was grateful for that lapse. My thoughts tracked back through everything that I'd heard, committing it to memory so that I could tell Richard. One line stuck out in my mind: *they still think I'm Akron.* But if he wasn't Akron, then who was he? A Screecher?

If they could steal our bodies, then we were

going to have to be careful around them. My thoughts jumped to Richard, and I remembered him lying on that steel table while a Stalker fixed his leg.

His words echoed through my head: "I never want to leave." And my eyes widened as I realized that he could be one of them, too.

Something brushed my leg, and I flinched with a fresh jolt of adrenaline. Glancing down, I saw Lucky slow-dancing with my leg. She meowed as I picked her up and kissed the top of her head. "It's just you and me now, Lucky."

PART 3 - WORLDS COLLIDE

CHAPTER 30

—November 1st, 2032—

I slept fitfully through the night, waking periodically to check that no Screechers had crept in to watch me sleep—or otherwise mess with me. Of course, there was no way to be sure that they hadn't, since they could cloak and hide in plain sight. Remembering that each time I woke up made it harder and harder to get back to sleep.

At some point I gave up trying and sat up. Looking out the room's only window, I saw rosy light filtering down to the garden below. It was morning.

I peeled the covers back and went to the bathroom for a shower. It ended too soon just like before. This time, rather than a robe, I found a towel to dry myself and then dressed in the loose green shirt and brown pants OneZero had laid out the day before.

OneZero. The conversation between her and Akron last night came flooding back, and suddenly I was afraid to leave my room. I hesitated with my hand on the door handle. What if they turned me into a Screecher like Akron? I'd never see my family again, never even have a chance to look for Alex.

But I couldn't afford to reveal my suspicions. That would be a fast track to Akron's fate. I was going to have to be very careful from this point on.

"Come on, Lucky," I said. "It's time for breakfast."

She hopped off the bed and stretched. I opened the door and walked down the window-lined hallway with Lucky padding along behind me. Noticing the position of the windows, I absently wondered how my bedroom could have one if it was situated *behind* the inner rim of the complex. The window I'd spent the night watching must have been a digital display of some kind.

I found OneZero and Akron in the living room already up and waiting. My steps faltered seeing them. Akron sat on a plush gray and white sofa, while OneZero stood at the balcony windows, watching the diffuse morning light sifting through mist-clouded gardens.

"Good morning," Akron said.

I nodded and smiled, forcing myself to sit on the chair beside the couch.

"Where's Richard?" I asked.

"Still sleeping, I believe," OneZero replied.

Hopefully that meant he was still human.

"You repaired your arm," I commented, even though I already knew about it.

"Yes."

"When do we leave for the border?" I asked.

"Soon."

My eyes tracked to Akron, and I frowned. "Still planning to go to Chicago?"

"No..." He trailed off, and his gaze wandered from mine. His eyes seemed to drift out of focus. "I forgot about my family on Mars."

"But you remember them now?" I asked, trying to keep the suspicion out of my voice.

"Yes, I remember," Akron said. His eyes drifted back to mine, and a tight smile curved his lips.

I smiled back and nodded to OneZero. "I'll go wake Richard." Standing up from the couch, I went back down the hall to his room. Knocking first, I tried the door handle. It turned easily, and I opened it to find my brother-in-law lying on his stomach and snoring, one arm dangling over the side of his couch-like bed. It was an encouraging sight. Still human, after all.

"Wake up," I said, shaking him by a hairy shoulder.

He snorted and pushed off the bed, blinking bleary eyes at me.

My better judgment stopped me from blurting out what I'd heard. "It's time to get up. The faster we get ready, the faster we can go."

"What's the hurry?"

I shot him a dark look. "Your nephew? Alex?"

"Right, yeah, sorry." He sat up, revealing his hairy chest and belly, and yawned into his hands. "I'm up."

Back in the living room, I tried to pretend normalcy while Richard showered and got dressed. Anger made small talk stick in my throat. The temptation to confront OneZero and Akron clawed inside of me, but that would be dangerous and stupid. I needed to wait until I had the upper hand, until I'd found Alex, and was surrounded by *my* people.

Maybe a trip to Chicago wouldn't be a bad idea after all. If I could get to see the new president, or someone *close* to the president, maybe I could convince them to stop the influx of human Screechers before they accomplished whatever it was that they were planning.

Richard came walking down the hall, dressed in a loose green shirt and brown pants like mine and Akron's. His over-long, thinning brown hair was pasted to his head like spaghetti, and his unkempt beard clung to his jaw like a living thing. I wasn't the only one in need of some grooming.

"Ready?" I asked, standing up quickly.

"Let's go get some breakfast," Richard replied.

OneZero took us to the same dining area as before. I noticed that Akron stepped out onto the transparent floor without missing a beat, while Richard and I both hesitated, and Lucky latched on to my shirt—her claws pricking painfully through to my chest.

I ordered a familiar breakfast of scrambled eggs, bacon, toast, and orange juice. Once again, to my surprise it all looked and tasted very close to the real thing. I wondered if this food really was printed from pastes and powders, or if OneZero had lied about that, and they were secretly harboring chickens and pigs in the subterranean levels of the city. If they could print whole colonies of spider-sharks, they could certainly get into producing our native species of livestock.

After breakfast we went straight back to our quarters, and found our old clothes waiting for us in our rooms—patched, and cleaned, along with the waterproof duffel bags of supplies that we'd brought from Haven. In our rush to get to safety, we'd forgotten the bags in the ruins of the marine research center. I dug through my bag and found my Beretta and what was left of the box of ammo.

"It's much colder up north," OneZero explained, standing in the open doorway to my room. "You'll need to change back into your clothes."

But I was still wondering how they'd recovered our bags. "How did you..."

"I sent someone back to look for your things," she explained.

"I'm ready," Richard said, appearing in the doorway behind OneZero.

"Logan isn't," OneZero replied.

"I will be." I stripped out of the Screechers' clothes and pulled mine on as fast as I could. The sooner we got out of here, the better and safer I'd feel. Zipping up my coat, I pulled on the winter gloves and the black hat that I'd packed in my duffel bag before leaving the submarine. That done, I turned to OneZero and nodded. "Let's go."

CHAPTER 31

OneZero led us out onto the roof and into a waiting Screecher disc. Our duffel bags and Richard's rifle were taken and stowed in hidden compartments in the floor; then we were forced to stand again, clamped in place by our wrists and ankles just like before. This time at least we weren't the only ones. Human-Screechers joined us on both sides, filling every available gap around the inner circumference of the disc.

Lucky was left to wander freely once more, but she stayed close to my legs. Remembering how she'd been thrown around on our way down for a landing the last time, I called out to OneZero, asking her to make sure the pilot was more careful with his maneuvers.

She called back, "I'll see what I can do."

I laid my head against the inner wall of the disc and waited for the craft to take off. Anxiety crawled in my veins. The sooner we crossed the border and got away from these perfectly-crafted alien humans with their unknown agenda, the better. Whatever they were up to, OneZero was obviously in on it. I still couldn't believe that she'd fooled me all this time. She'd never seemed to have an agenda before. Were there signs that I had missed?

The submarine. My eyes widened with the recollection of how we'd found metal filings around the holes in the hull—filings that looked just like the nanites she'd used to repair it later. If it weren't for that damage, we never would have entered Screecher territory; we'd have sailed up the east coast and been none the wiser about these supposedly friendly, human-Screecher collaborators.

OneZero must have been the one to sabotage the submarine. She'd deliberately forced us ashore in enemy territory so that we could meet the collaborators. But why? What had come of it?

Akron was one of them now, and I'd overheard him and OneZero talking about getting their people on Mars. Maybe that was the reason.

But Akron's conversion to a Screecher was at least partly my fault. The Stalker venom had gone to his brain and given the Screechers an excuse to go poking around in there. Or at least, that's what OneZero had told me. Maybe they would have found an excuse to convert him even if he hadn't been bitten by a Stalker.

The wall behind me began shivering as the rotor in the center of the disc sped up and the aircraft lifted off.

"Is everything all right?" Akron asked.

I glanced at him and forced a smile. "Just worried about my son."

"Your son?"

"He's missing... somewhere up north."

"Ah. I understand. You'll be able to look for him soon. Do you have any idea where to start?"

I frowned. "The Internet? That was your idea, remember?"

"No, I'm afraid I don't remember," Akron replied.

"It doesn't bother you?" I asked. "The gaps in your memory?"

He shrugged. "They don't feel like gaps. I still feel like myself."

I bet you do.

"That probably has something to do with the parts that the Collective filled in," Richard said.

"Yes," Akron agreed.

Under any other circumstances I'd be

— 248 —

apologizing for what happened to Akron, but this didn't feel like my fault anymore.

Snow-covered plains scrolled by below, interrupted by the soaring, slate gray specters of Screecher cities. Lucky waltzed up to the transparent inner wall of the disc and sat down to watch it all go by, as if looking down on her kingdom.

"OneZero?" I called.

Clanking footsteps approached, and she came walking around the circumference of the disc. "Yes, Logan?"

"How long before we reach Memphis?"

"Half an hour, but we won't be going directly there."

"We won't?"

She shook her head. "We can't be seen to cross the border. That would raise too many questions on both sides. Right now our support for the human natives is a well-kept secret, and it must stay that way."

Interesting. "So how are we going to get across?"

"We've dug tunnels from several cities near the border. One of them is close to Memphis."

"And seeing people popping out of those tunnels like prairie dogs isn't going to attract attention?"

OneZero shook her head. "Don't worry. I'm sure that there are provisions to maintain secrecy at the available exits."

OneZero walked back around the disc to the cockpit, her footsteps clanking noisily, and I wondered why she was the only non-biological Screecher on board. If their presence north of the border were a secret, surely her appearance would be counter-productive to that.

I frowned and shook my head. There were so many things I didn't understand: hidden agendas, lies... familiar faces harboring alien minds. I looked to Richard and studied him, wondering again if he was still himself. Akron was influential. He had ties to Mars and the old government. It made sense that they'd convert him. But Richard?

Richard caught me staring at him. "Why are you looking at me like that?"

I innocently arched my eyebrows at him. "Like what?"

"Like I just grew a pair of horns."

I scrambled to come up with an excuse. "Are you still planning to run away to Mars and leave us behind?"

Richard frowned. "I don't know. If the Screechers are helping us as much as they say they are, then maybe I should stay and lend a hand as well. It's going to be a whole new world when their technologies finish spreading."

"Yeah." I nodded along with that. "A whole new world." *And a whole new* species *when they finish replacing us.*

CHAPTER 32

We landed on the roof of another Screecher city, just like the one we'd left, with a familiar ring-shaped mega-structure encircling a towering central spire. I guessed that architecture wasn't a celebrated art form among Screechers. We all crowded down the landing ramp and onto an elevator platform. I caught a glimpse of a familiar, sharp-angled face. It was the man I'd met last night.

Deon saw me and nodded in greeting.

The elevator platform dropped swiftly, and I held Lucky close, like a child clutching a teddy bear. All these too-pretty plastic-faced human robots bumping shoulders with us made me feel very uneasy. Richard was all smiles, blissfully ignorant of the danger they represented. This was the new, improved version of humanity. *Out with the humans, in with the Screechers.*

After a minute, the elevator slowed to a stop, and the doors opened to reveal a long, dimly-lit corridor with rough brown walls curving away to either side. A set of tracks lay in front of us with a sleek glass and metal train waiting.

Everyone piled out, bumping and brushing by me. I glanced at Richard, and he flashed a grin.

"And I thought we were going to have to walk." He strode out with his AR-15 rifle slung over one shoulder and his duffel bag over the other.

I wondered if we were allowed to carry weapons to put our minds at ease. I felt for the hard edges of my Beretta through the smooth fabric of my waterproof bag. It was there, right where it was supposed to be. No one had tried to confiscate it. These collaborators were obviously going to great lengths to make us trust them.

A pity it's all a crock, I thought.

OneZero stood by the open doors of the train, waving people through. Lucky squirmed out of my hands, but I lunged after her and grabbed her before she got away. Lucky hissed at me, and I scowled back. I was warming up to cats, but they were annoyingly hard to keep track of. Dogs were far easier to control.

I wondered if Screecher-humans saw us that

way: easy to control.

Rows of seats flanked an aisle in the middle, much like the inside of an airplane or a bus. I took a window seat for myself and Lucky.

Richard sat down beside us, unslinging his rifle so he could lean on the butt like a cane as he looked around. "It's amazing how all of this feels so familiar. I guess because it's made for humans. A chair is a chair, right? What else are you going to do with it?"

"What about the elevators, showers, toilets, couches, beds... or public transportation?" I asked. "You're saying there's no other possible configuration for any of it?"

Deon came and sat in the empty seat beside Richard. "Do you mind?" he asked.

"Go ahead," Richard said.

A frown sprang to my lips, and I jerked my chin at Deon. "Why do so many of your designs mimic our own?" I asked.

"Some of it was already invented when the Primordials abducted us from Earth and took us to Cardinal. Other designs evolved out of necessity or coincidence to be similar to what you are used to."

"Cardinal?" I asked.

"Our world. It's a rough—"

"Translation. Got it."

"Don't be rude," Richard said, elbowing me in the ribs.

"Sorry. I didn't sleep well."

"I'm sorry to hear that," Deon said, his green eyes pinching slightly. "I had thought I put your mind at ease after our talk last night."

"You did," I said, picking my words carefully. "But it's still hard to sleep in a strange bed."

Deon inclined his head at that and looked away. I glanced around and noticed a clear aisle. Everyone had taken their seats. OneZero and Akron were seated right behind us.

The train jerked into motion and began gliding forward almost soundlessly. Lights flickered and flashed by as we picked up speed.

I spent the trip in silence, looking sleepy and clinging to the excuse that I hadn't slept well. It was true enough, anyway. I'd barely managed to sleep at all after what I'd learned. Richard spent the time asking Deon and OneZero questions about science on topics that I didn't know about, but his inquiries were all met with deflections and secrecy.

"So, basically you can't tell me anything," Richard said.

"I am sorry," OneZero replied. "Our knowledge must be spread carefully, and under tightly controlled circumstances. That is part of our agreement with your government. It is both for your safety and ours."

Richard didn't look happy with that explanation. Who could blame him? It sounded like a good excuse for the Screechers to keep their technology to themselves. Either they were only pretending to help, or they were making sure we stayed dependent on them.

The train ride lasted about ten minutes.

"End of the line?" I asked, twisting around to find OneZero as the train glided to a stop.

"Yes, Logan."

Doors slid open and Screecher-humans rose from their seats in unison. They formed an orderly line in the aisle and trickled out. Richard followed Deon out into the aisle, but I remained seated—my silent protest to this new invasion. I noticed that none of the aliens had brought any luggage, and they were wearing jackets, but not gloves or any kind of headgear.

I was still wondering about that as the train emptied and OneZero beckoned to me from the doors. "Are you planning to go back?" she asked.

I shook my head and got up with a sigh. "Just tired," I explained with a wan smile and walked past her.

"Do you need a stimulant before we go? We

have a long walk ahead."

"A stimulant?" I asked. "Like what?"

"It can be administered as an injection, or in a beverage if you prefer."

"You mean like coffee?"

"It can be flavored to approximate coffee if you like."

I frowned. "No, that's okay. Let's get going. I'll be fine."

OneZero nodded and walked by us, following the others to a utilitarian elevator platform with yellow railings, just like the one we'd ridden down before boarding the train.

"*I* could use some coffee," Richard said belatedly.

I shot him a look. "We've delayed enough. It's time to find Alex."

"What's with you this morning?"

"Nothing. I didn't sleep."

Richard's eyes narrowed, and he held my gaze for an uncomfortably long moment. "Well, make sure you get your beauty rest tonight."

We joined about two dozen others on the elevator platform. Hardly an invasion, but if the train ran around the clock, it could transport several thousand Screechers across the border every day, and according to OneZero, more than one city had tunnels crossing the border. I grimaced and shook my head. It wasn't bad enough that the Screechers had deported millions into the Northern States, swelling our population well past the point of sustainability—now they'd added themselves to the problem.

The elevator stopped and opened to a familiar-looking garden. A ring-shaped mega-structure curved around to both sides, lined with balconies, and a spire shot up from the center, ending abruptly at the same height as the outer ring. A bright blue sky shone between the spire and the ring, forcing me to shield my eyes as I peered up at it.

"I thought you said your presence had to remain a secret," I said, slowly shaking my head as the occupants of the elevator trickled out. Lucky squirmed in my arms, trying to break free. This probably looked to her like a good place to stay.

Richard and I started to follow the others out, but OneZero stopped us with an arm across each of our chests. "We're not getting out here."

"We're not?" Richard asked.

"We're still underground."

"But I can see the sky," I said.

"That's an illusion. Plants need sunlight to grow, and even artificial sunlight has to come from something. We could have used lamps, but this is more pleasing to look at, wouldn't you agree?"

The elevator doors slid shut once more, and the platform started rising again, quickly picking up speed. I looked up into a seemingly-endless elevator shaft. Lights from passing floors flashed by around us, flickering like the strobe lights in a club. We reached the top, and the elevator doors opened into a snow-covered forest with shafts of real (hopefully real) sunlight flickering down. Ice sparkled on slumping tree branches. Cold air swept around me as I walked out, trudging through more than a foot of snow. My nostrils stuck together as I inhaled, and my breath turned to clouds as I breathed out again. Lucky meowed her disgust and nuzzled into my jacket, for once not trying to escape. I unzipped my jacket and tucked her inside.

"It's freezing!" Richard said, blowing into his hands, and then digging into his duffel bag for his gloves.

Spinning in a slow circle, I searched for some sign of the city we'd been in a moment ago, but I couldn't even find the elevator shaft we'd just walked out of.

"How... where's the city?"

"I told you, it's underground," OneZero

replied.

"All of it?"

OneZero cocked her head. "How else would you suggest we hide it?"

"But... what about the elevator!" Shaking my head, I stalked back the way I'd come.

"Logan—"

My foot hooked under something, and I fell. Lucky wriggled free of my coat and landed on her feet just before my head smashed into something with a hollow metallic *boom*.

"What..." Blinking stars and shaking myself out of a daze, I pushed off a smooth, icy surface, only to find that my hands were planted against thin air, like a mime trying to find his way out of a box.

"It's cloaked, Logan," OneZero said, and pulled me to my feet.

Of course it was. I turned to see what I'd tripped over. A bare, frozen arm stuck out of the snow, bent at the elbow, and black with frostbite. Lucky stood there sniffing the arm, too light to sink all the way through the snow.

Goosebumps curdled my flesh as the scene around me snapped into focus: dark, tangled shapes littered the forest floor—bodies sticking out of the snow, frozen stiff. I noticed that none of them wore adequate winter clothing and realized that these were deportees. Alex's face flashed through my mind, black with frostbite, his hair white with clumps of snow. I shook my head to clear the image. A cold suspicion shivered down my spine. Had all of these people frozen to death, or was their proximity to the Screecher city more than just a coincidence?

I rounded on OneZero and jabbed a finger at her. "Did you kill these people?"

Dim light flickered through her eyes and she took a step back, as if shocked by the accusation. "No, Logan."

I wasn't buying it. I fell on my hands and knees beside the one I'd tripped over and began digging the body out, hunting for proof.

"What are you doing?" OneZero asked.

Not bothering to waste my breath on a reply, I kept digging. Once the body was exposed, I found it—a dark, blood-crusted hole in the man's gray t-shirt. I pointed to it, too angry to care about the consequences.

"Then why is there a bullet hole in this man's side?"

CHAPTER 33

Richard looked pale. "OneZero?" he asked in a quiet voice.

But the Screecher was looking at me. "I assume by *did you do this,* you mean my people. I've never been here before, but I can already tell you that the bullets we use would not produce such a tiny hole. That man was shot by one of your people, either military or police."

"And I'm supposed to take your word for that? You just said you were never here, so how would you know?"

A weapon barrel sprang up out of OneZero's arm, and I flinched at the sight of it. This was it. I'd pushed too far.

The barrel flashed with a muted *plip,* and a cloud of foul-smelling steam exploded in front of me. I looked down, expecting to see my stomach ripped open and guts hanging out. Instead, I saw a steaming hole the size of my fist punched straight through the frozen body I'd uncovered.

"Now do you believe me?" OneZero asked.

Shaking, I slowly rose to my feet. "Why would we shoot our own people?"

"Because they're not your people. Look at him."

Akron stepped forward and studied the dead body. "He's from a different ethnic group."

"Mexican," I supplied. "But that doesn't mean he wasn't American."

OneZero shrugged. "Your nation has a history of hostility toward non-Caucasian groups."

"So we killed them because they're not Caucasians?" I gestured to the field of frozen, snow-covered bodies littered across the forest floor.

"I don't know any more than you do, Logan. I can only make reasonable deductions based on the evidence."

"We should get going," Richard said, hugging his shoulders and glancing around. "Do you have any idea which way to go to reach the launch facility?"

OneZero didn't reply. She stared at the body I'd uncovered, watching as Lucky licked the wound she'd blasted through it.

I scowled and picked up the cat, tucking her back into my jacket. She meowed in protest, but seemed grateful to share our body heat.

"OneZero? Akron? We are still going to Starcast, right?" Richard prompted.

"That way," they said in unison, pointing in the same direction.

I shivered with that subtle reminder of Akron's transformation, but pasted a smile on my face and followed them through the trees, doing my best not to step on the dead. OneZero blazed a trail through fallen trees and bushes with a combination of brute force and humming bursts from green-tinged lasers concealed inside her torso. The frozen bodies were everywhere, and before long they blurred back into the scenery.

After about twenty minutes of that, we reached the apparent mouth of a snow-covered trail and a wooden sign that read VILLAGE CREEK STATE PARK.

Soon after, we came to an empty parking lot, and then a road. Surprisingly, the road had been plowed and tire tracks sliced through a recent dusting of snow on both sides.

"Life goes on," Richard said with a sigh. "Thank God."

"Thank our allies," Akron said.

I shot him a dark look. I wasn't particularly

religious and I knew Richard wasn't either, but that statement got my hackles up all the same. Had this Screecher impostor just elevated his people to god-like status? Or was he simply expressing an atheistic worldview? I hoped for the latter.

Trying to mask my reaction, I looked away and said, "What we need now is a car."

And just like that, as though a genie had granted my wish, I saw running lights winking through the trees and heard the distant rumble of an engine.

I looked to OneZero, wondering how she planned to explain her presence. "Maybe you should..."

I trailed off as she faded to a translucent shimmer on the air, and then vanished altogether. Her voice whispered out of the emptiness, reminding me that she was just cloaked from view, not actually missing: "Make them stop."

I handed Lucky to Richard. He pulled back, wide-eyed, and Lucky hissed. "Hey there..." he said.

I walked out into the middle of the road and flagged the vehicle down, my arms windmilling above my head. It began to slow, and I saw that it was a pick-up truck. Perfect for OneZero to hop in the back without being noticed.

The truck stopped when it was still fifty feet away. Doors swung open, and people ducked out. I saw sunlight glancing off weapons as they poked around the doors, followed by:

"Drop your bags and weapons and walk toward us with your hands above your heads, or we'll shoot!"

CHAPTER 34

Richard handed Lucky back to me, and we did as they asked, dropping our bags in the snow. Richard laid his rifle on top of his bag to keep snow from getting into the barrel, and then raised his hands. I only raised one, since the other was holding Lucky. We walked slowly toward the vehicle—a dirty white pickup that blended well with the scenery. My eyes never strayed from the two men aiming guns at us from behind the doors.

Not a good situation. I reassured myself that OneZero was the ace up our sleeves, although, I had mixed feelings about that. Maybe it would be better if these people spotted her and gunned her down. Then again, they'd probably lose that fight, and even if they won it—we'd probably be next. I glanced behind me to check for some sign of OneZero. Nothing. Not even an extra set of footsteps in the snow. She was good.

"Eyes to the front!" the driver of the truck said.

We drew near enough to see them peeking at us through the windows of the truck's open doors.

"That's far enough. Let's see your passbands," the driver said.

"Passbands?" I called back, shaking my head.

"They're illegals! Shoot them!" the other one said.

"Hold your fire, Dex!" the driver snapped. "Where are you from?"

I hesitated. "New Jersey."

"Pasadena, California," Richard added. "But more recently San Antonio."

Akron said nothing.

"And him?"

I turned to look at Akron. He probably didn't even remember where he was from. I recalled visiting his mansion in LA and said for him, "Los Angeles."

"Can't he talk?" the driver asked.

"Hey, I recognize that guy!" Dex said, slowly straightening into view. "That's Akron Massey! He's that billionaire that ran away to Mars with the president!"

"So what's he doing here, genius? Get back under cover, Dex."

"It's true. I am Akron Massey. I was...

abducted before I could leave for Mars."

I frowned. At least he remembered that much. How much of the real Akron was still in there?

The driver snorted. "Serves you right if it's true. Where have you been all this time that you don't even have a passband?"

"We've been in Massey's shelter," I said.

"A shelter. That sounds nice. So why'd you leave?"

"To look for my son. He didn't make it to the shelter."

"All three of you?"

I pointed to Richard. "He's my brother-in-law."

"And the rich asshole? You expect me to believe he decided to help you out of the goodness of his heart?"

"Our shelter was compromised," Akron said. "We had no choice but to leave."

"Illegals found you, did they."

"Yes," Akron said, playing along.

I frowned and shook my head. "Now what? Or are you just going to point those guns at us until we freeze to death?"

"Dex, search them and then go get their stuff. I'll cover you."

"Roger that."

The one named Dex came out, his boots crunching in the snow. He covered us with a hunting rifle as he walked around the door. I wondered if he was going to search us with his rifle dangling within easy reach, but he laid it down on the hood of the truck.

I got a better look at him while he searched Akron and Richard. He had a thick blonde beard and a mean look in his pale blue eyes. He had to be around thirty years old, wearing fuzzy red gloves with the tip of the trigger finger on the right hand cut off, and a matching red parka lined with sable-colored fur.

He searched me last. As he bent to pat down my legs, Lucky lashed out, slashing his cheek open.

"Fuck!" Dex clapped a hand to his cheek, and his red glove came away redder than before. I smiled, Lucky hissed, and Dex retreated to get his gun. For a minute I feared he would get revenge by shooting Lucky, but he stalked off to get our gear instead. A moment later he returned wearing our duffel bags and Richard's AR-15 in addition to his own rifle.

"Nice hardware," Dex said, covering us with both weapons as he returned to cover behind the passenger's side door.

"What'd you find, Dexter?" the driver asked as

Dex rifled through our bags in the back seat of their truck.

"Not much... spare clothes, bottled water, cans of food, and snacks, but I also found two Berettas and this rifle—he patted the barrel. "And spare ammo."

"Ditch the guns, but take the bullets out in case these morons get any bright ideas."

"But—"

"Forget it. We can't use them."

"We could sell them for more than a kilobyte each!"

"They're not registered, Dex! The bytes won't do us any good if we get killed for trafficking. We'll keep the ammo. That's the best we can do."

My arm was getting tired from holding it up. Lucky squirmed and almost broke free, so I dropped my tired arm and used it to hold her properly.

I heard Dexter muttering about the wasted opportunity as he ejected the magazine in Richard's rifle and opened the bolt to clear the chamber. He deftly caught the round as it came out and placed it in his pocket.

"Excuse me," I said.

"What?" the driver snapped.

"You're really going to rob us? Don't do this. I

have a family, and I need to find my son."

"You're unregistered, so there's no crime in stealing. We could shoot you, too, but that would be a waste of bullets."

"Unregistered?" Richard asked.

The driver sighed and straightened. He stayed behind the door, but we could see him clearly through the window now. He had a shaggy gray and white beard, long, stringy gray hair, and honey brown eyes set in two deep pockets of wrinkles—laugh lines from a happier time. He tapped the bright blue band on his wrist. "If you aren't actually illegals, then you need to get one of these. A passband. Without it, I'm the least of your problems. You could get shot by a passing drone, a cop, or a guardsman. It's open season on illegals."

"But we're not illegals! We're American citizens!"

"Then you'd better prove it, and fast."

"How?"

"Go to the nearest registration center."

"Could you help us get to a registration center?" I asked.

"What would I get out of it?"

"I'm a billionaire," Akron said.

"Past tense, buddy. Your companies all went bust, or else the government runs them now.

Besides, no one uses dollars anymore. It's all bartering. If you're lucky enough to get a job, then you can earn bytes for your trouble and go right back to living the American dream, but for most of us, that dream is just a puff of smoke."

"Bytes?" I asked.

The driver tapped his blue wristband again. "Bits and bytes. Dollars and cents. There's eight bits to a byte instead of a hundred cents to a dollar, and there's a thousand bytes in a kilobyte, and a million in a megabyte. Ten bytes will buy you a haircut and a shave, or a hot meal, but since none of you even has a wristband, I'm guessing you're all dead broke."

Richard and I traded glances. Neither of us knew what to say to that.

"Well, as much as I'd like to stay and chat, we'd better be on our way. Nice doing business with you."

"Wait!" Richard said, as Dexter and the driver got into their truck. He pointed at Akron. "He owns Starcast! He has a mansion in LA! There's got to be something left that we could trade you for a ride."

The driver revved the engine and rolled by us with the window down. "The government owns Starcast, and LA is nothing but rubble. Tough luck guys."

Richard and I watched our ride rumble off, our jaws hanging open, and eyes wide.

"Do you want me to go after them?" OneZero asked quietly.

"And do what?" I replied.

"I could take their vehicle by force."

"Are you suggesting that you kill them for it?" I asked, not bothering to hide the suspicion in my voice.

"I can incapacitate them without killing them," OneZero replied.

"Do it," Akron replied.

A gust of wind hit me, accompanied by the sound of thundering footfalls. A few moments later I saw the driver's door of the truck fly open for no apparent reason. The driver sailed out and rolled a few dozen times in the snow before coming to rest. He didn't try to get back up. I heard Dexter shouting; then a gun went off, and he flew out, too, with the same result. The truck couldn't have been going faster than thirty miles per hour, but that was more than fast enough to seriously injure someone thrown from it.

The driver's door slammed shut and the brake lights blazed to life; then it reversed down the road and rolled to a stop beside us. The driver's side door popped open; a shimmering silhouette jumped out with a heavy *clunk*. OneZero remained hidden, but she'd made herself visible enough that we could see where she was.

"We'd better go before they recover," Richard said, heading for the driver's seat that OneZero had vacated. It was an old, rusting F150, off-white and filthy with slush. I could see yellow stuffing bleeding out of the driver's seat. Even in that condition, the vehicle was probably priceless.

I spared a glance at the two men who'd just robbed us, whom we'd robbed back, and wondered if there wasn't some other way. Maybe we could tie them up and give them their vehicle back after we got to where we needed to go. Just leaving them there, face down in the snow would make us no better than they are. What if they died out here? But for all I knew they were already dead. I only had OneZero's word that she'd incapacitated rather than killed them. Throwing them from a moving vehicle seemed like a random way to accomplish that goal. Yet more proof that OneZero, Akron, and their people were not as benign and peaceful as they claimed to be.

"I'm not going anywhere," I said. Lucky meowed loudly at that, but I couldn't tell if it was in agreement or complaint.

"Logan..." Richard trailed off with a frown. He already sat behind the wheel.

"I mean it. Not unless we take them with us and return their vehicle after we're done with it."

"You're welcome to stay here," Akron said as he hopped in beside Richard.

I felt a rigid hand on my shoulder, and turned to see OneZero's shimmering silhouette. "Don't forget about your son," she said.

"Get your hand off me," I replied.

The weight left my shoulder.

"OneZero, we need to go," Akron said.

"One minute. Logan, please get in the truck."

I narrowed my eyes at her. "No. Not unless we take them with us."

"OneZero..." Akron sighed. "We're wasting time."

"Logan get in the damn truck before they wake up!" Richard said. "They're still armed. Besides, taking them with us could be dangerous. What are we going to use to tie them up? We don't have rope."

"We'll find something," I insisted.

"We're wasting gas," Akron added.

"They could be helpful," OneZero said. "They know how things work on this side of the border. For one thing, they know where you need to go to get registered."

No one said anything for a few seconds. "Fine, but we'll need to disarm them and find a way to restrain them," Akron said.

"That will not be a problem," OneZero replied, and then she vanished in a shimmering blur.

CHAPTER 35

We found duct tape behind the truck's back seats, and we used it to tie up the two men who'd robbed us. We left their mouths free so they could talk and hopefully provide useful insight about what we were driving into. I was forced to sit beside them, because it had been my idea to bring them along, while Lucky perched on the storage compartment between the two front seats. OneZero hunkered down in the back of the pickup, once again utterly invisible, watching for trouble through the back window. We'd left it open a crack so that she could hear us and intervene if our prisoners tried anything.

"I don't know how you pulled us out of that truck—" the driver said. His cheeks were scraped and crusted with blood where he'd rubbed his skin off on the snow and pavement. "—but you won't get away with this. All you've done is sealed your fate. You're all as good as dead."

"You want to explain that?" Richard asked, looking up from the road to glance in the rear-view mirror.

"It's simple. When a squad of guardsmen see that you're not wearing passbands, and we're the ones who are tied up, they're going to blow your brains out."

"Shit," Richard muttered.

"You see?" Akron said. "Bringing them was a bad idea. We should ditch them while we still have a chance."

Dexter's eyes flew wide, and the other man's mouth pinched into a bloodless line. "Wait," he said. "If you cut us free—"

"No," Akron replied.

I grimaced, not seeing any way out of this. "There has to be a way to make you cooperate with us," I said.

"They'll say anything to get us to release them," Akron said, shaking his head.

"He's right, Logan," Richard added.

I blew out a breath.

"Look, we can help you," the driver said, using his shoulder to scratch an itch in his shaggy gray beard.

But Akron was right. We couldn't trust

anything they said now. "What if you give us your wristbands?"

"That won't do..." the driver trailed off suddenly, as if a thought had occurred to him. "Actually, that's not a bad idea."

"But there's only two bands and three of us," Akron pointed out. "Besides, any device that holds a person's life savings *and* their passport will have measures against theft. For all we know tampering with them will trigger a tracking beacon that brings the authorities straight to us."

The former driver's eyes pinched into slits, and I realized that somehow Akron had guessed exactly what would happen. "I thought you said you've been in a shelter for the past six months."

"I have," Akron replied.

Richard glanced at him with a furrowed brow, obviously picking up on the slip as well. He probably thought it was just another *gap* that the Screechers had filled, but I knew better. Akron had already been briefed by the Screechers who'd sent him on this mission, and he knew exactly what was going on north of the border.

The former driver of the truck spoke again, "Look, guardsmen patrol the entrances and exits of every major city. The only way you can do this is to cut us free and give us our truck back. Then we'll take you for registration and spin that story about you all being locked in a shelter for the last six months. You get registered, and we get to keep our vehicle. Everybody wins."

"You robbed us and implied you would have killed us if you could have spared the bullets," I said. "How can we trust you now?"

"I was exaggerating, damn it! Look at me. You think I'm a stone cold killer? I'm a history professor—at least I was before the shit hit the fan."

I looked at the man, noticed the deeply-carved laugh lines around his haunted brown eyes. The shaggy beard that might have concealed a kind face. "What's your name?"

"Dr. Robert Beck, but now everyone just calls me Bobby." He nodded and gestured to Dexter with his duct-taped wrists. "Dexter is my son-in-law."

I nodded. "Nice to meet you, Bobby. I'm Logan. That's Richard in the driver's seat, and you already know Akron."

"I'm starting to," Bobby replied, staring at the back of Akron's head.

"We can't trust them to keep their word," Akron said. "They had a chance to help us, and they passed it up."

Bobby snorted. "Once an entitled asshole, always an entitled asshole. Listen, shit-for-brains, if you think anyone helps each other out for free anymore, you're in for a rude awakening. The only ones who've survived this long are the ones who are willing to do whatever it takes to survive. That means you look out for you and yours, and that's it. You can't blame me for sticking with a winning strategy."

Akron glared at him. "Maybe not, but then you can't blame me for being just as self-oriented. What's stopping us from turning ourselves in at the nearest roadblock without you? We'll get sent for processing either way."

Bobby didn't seem to have an answer for that, but I could see the wheels turning inside his head.

"You'll have to show the registration of this vehicle. It's not registered to any of you, so they'll assume it's stolen. That could get you into some real trouble."

"Could it?" Akron asked. "We could claim that we found the car abandoned, or that the previous owners were killed by illegals and we took the vehicle to flee the scene before we fell victim to them, too."

Again, Bobby hesitated. "That's—"

"Don't try to change your story now," Akron

replied, looking back over his shoulder to fix Bobby with a hard look. "You're dead weight. Worse, by your own admission, you could get us killed if you're found tied up as captives in your own vehicle."

Bobby gritted his teeth, but said nothing.

"Richard, stop the truck," Akron said.

I wracked my brain, trying to think of a way to salvage the situation, some way to cling to my molehill of moral high ground, but I couldn't think of anything.

"Richard?" Akron pressed. The truck ground to a halt, snow crunching under the tires. "Thank you." He looked at me. "Logan, get them out."

Bobby shot me an imploring look, his brown eyes wide. "You took our guns," he said. "If you leave us here with no protection and no supplies, we won't last long. Call it what you want, but this is murder."

"Logan! If you don't get them out, I will," Akron said.

"Wait," I replied.

Akron sighed. "We don't have time for this!"

"Just hang on! Everyone has to wear those bands on their wrists, right?"

Bobby nodded slowly; his brow furrowed as he tried to guess where I was going with that.

I went on, "They contain your ID, a system of payment, and they can be used to track your whereabouts."

"Yes..."

"So am I right to assume that we're dealing with some kind of police state?"

"More of a military dictatorship, but you could say that, yeah," Bobby replied.

I went on, "You mentioned that there's no consequences for stealing from us if we don't have those bands, but what happens when someone commits a crime against a registered citizen?"

A light of understanding dawned in Bobby's eyes, and he began nodding. "That depends... murder will get you the death penalty."

"What about stealing a car?"

"The same," Bobby said, but he hesitated slightly before saying it.

"That's a lie," Akron replied.

"Is it?" I countered. "I wouldn't cast myself on the mercy of a totalitarian regime, if I were you. Bobby and Dexter will report us to the authorities, and after that it won't matter if we're registered or not; we'll have to answer for stealing their vehicle."

"They could report us whether we cut them free or not," Akron said.

A cold knot of dread cinched my throat shut.

Knowing what Akron was, I could guess where he was headed with that reasoning. Apparently Bobby and Dexter could, too. They'd both paled to match the snow-covered scenery. "Our passbands will report it if something happens to us," Dexter said.

"It's true," Bobby added. "They track our vitals."

"If they can do that, then they can be used to call for help, and you would have done that by now."

"If our hands were free..." Bobby said, wiggling his fingers and straining against his duct tape bonds.

"We're not killing anyone," I said.

"Did I say we were?" Akron replied. "We need to ditch them here. We'll reach the authorities before they do, and we'll report them first. Their crimes will trump ours."

"What crimes?" Bobby demanded. "We haven't done any—"

"Thing wrong?" Akron finished for him, glancing back at him with a slow grin. "Then why are there three unregistered weapons under the back seat, packed in right beside your own? You're illegal arms dealers."

"What? That's a lie!"

"Good luck proving it," Akron replied. "Richard? Logan appears to have lost touch with common sense. Would you get these criminals out of our truck, please?"

Richard opened his door and jumped down. Cold air swirled in through the open door, and I shivered. Richard opened Bobby's door and dragged him out.

"Hands off!" Bobby said, and promptly fell over when Richard let him go. His wrists and ankles were still bound with duct tape. Richard reached in for Dexter. He struggled, but Richard heaved and sent him tumbling out beside his father-in-law.

"At least cut them free," I said.

Richard jerked his chin at me. "You want to help?"

I nodded stiffly and slid out along the back seat.

Bobby and Dexter were lying on their backs in the snow, glaring at us. Bobby held his hands up, waiting for us to cut his bonds, but Richard shook his head. "Not happening. I'll free your ankles, but your hands stay tied." He reached into the driver's side door for a hunting knife we'd found on Dexter when we'd searched him and Bobby. Richard bent down to slice Bobby's ankles free with the knife. I saw a dark gleam enter Bobby's eyes, and hurried to pin his legs.

I was too late. A boot kicked up and caught Richard under the chin. His jaw snapped shut, and he fell over backward, dropping the knife. Bobby lunged for it, wriggling like a worm and rolling away from me in the same instant. Somehow he managed to grab the knife even though his hands were taped behind his back, and then he was up on his feet and slicing his wrists free. That done, he took a fighter's stance, low and crouching with the knife in a reverse grip. He squared off to face me and Richard. "Who's going first?"

I froze. The guns were just a few feet away, under the back seat... my gaze wandered to the open door. I could see the barrel of Richard's AR-15 sticking out. Before I could so much as twitch in that direction, Dexter's legs swept mine out, and I went down like a ton of bricks. I landed on top of Dexter. He grunted and crunched up his body like a coiled spring, butting heads with me.

Stars exploded inside my head. I stumbled to my feet, swaying like a tall reed in a storm and struggling to shake myself out of a daze. In the span of those few seconds, Bobby lunged for Richard, Dexter scuttled away, and I looked up to see the hunting knife pressed against Richard's throat.

"Now—" Bobby said, his eyes smiling tightly as his gaze flicked from me to Akron and back. "—you're going to give us our truck back or your friend is going to have a set of gills where his throat used to be."

CHAPTER 36

"Get out of the car!" Bobby demanded.

Akron made no move to obey that order. For that matter, neither did Lucky.

"OneZero?" Akron asked mildly.

"One-what?" Bobby asked.

The truck's suspension released with a creaking sound as she jumped out. Her feet touched the road, and crunching footsteps followed.

Bobby's eyes darted about, searching for the source of those sounds. "Who..." The knife shivered against Richard's throat, drawing a bright bead of blood. "Stop where you are, or I'll kill him!"

The footsteps ceased, and Bobby's brow furrowed in confusion. A split second later they widened in shock and he collapsed in a heap. Richard recoiled from him with a yelp, and I saw that there were a pair of metal rods sticking out of Bobby's back with bright blue forks of electricity arcing between them.

OneZero had stunned him. Dexter, still bound hand and foot, managed to scuttle away. His eyes were like two golf balls inside his head. "How the hell are you doing—"

A pair of gleaming metal rods appeared sticking out of his chest, and every muscle in his body misfired at once. His eyes rolled up in his head, and he collapsed on the snowy street. He and Bobby lay there, twitching and jittering with periodic pulses of electricity.

"Good. Now let's get out of here," Akron said.

OneZero's voice drifted out of thin air. "We cannot leave. Bobby called the authorities. I can detect the tracking signal coming from his band."

"Can't you shut it off?" Akron demanded.

"I could, but the authorities may decide to investigate anyway—especially when they notice their bands are reporting erratic vital signs."

Akron made an irritated noise, and Richard sighed.

I frowned. This was a mess, and it was all my fault for trying to do the right thing. I shook my head. "So what do we do?"

"Restrain Bobby again," Akron suggested.

"OneZero?"

I saw a roll of duct tape come floating out of the car and she went to work with it, wrapping Bobby's ankles and wrists with it once more.

Akron got out of the truck and walked around for a look. "Good. Now we need to remove the stunners."

The metal poles were yanked away and they vanished into thin air, likely concealed in one of OneZero's storage compartments.

When Bobby and Dexter regained control of their muscles, Bobby wriggled around like a worm to get himself into a sitting position. His head turned, eyes casting about for whoever we'd been speaking to. "Who's OneZero and where is he?"

Akron affected a puzzled look. "Who?"

Bobby scowled back, then his eyes drifted to the back of his truck. "There's another one of you, hiding back there. He tased us."

Akron slowly shook his head. "I don't know what you're talking about."

"Whatever. You're dead now. The authorities will shoot you when we tell them what you did."

Akron's brow furrowed and he planted a hand on his chest. "They'll shoot the famous Akron Massey? A trusted public figure?"

"Trusted! You ran away to Mars!" Bobby said.

"Then why am I here? I had a change of heart."

Bobby gaped at him. "You said you were abducted."

"No, I don't believe so."

"You assaulted us!"

"In self-defense."

Bobby's eyes narrowed.

Akron nodded to Richard. "Tape their mouths shut. We don't want them confusing the authorities when they arrive."

Richard found the roll of duct tape where OneZero had left it in the snow, and went to recover the bowie knife that had been pressed to his throat a moment ago.

"Fuck you!" Dexter said, snapping his jaws as Richard taped them shut.

Bobby was next, but he just glared silently at us. Akron recovered the two Berettas from under the back seat. He wiped the first one off carefully with the shirt under his jacket, removing any fingerprints we might have left on the weapon, and then he threw it in the snow, close to Bobby, but still far enough away that he couldn't reach the weapon. I began to understand what he was planning, but the evidence was all circumstantial and our word against theirs—with the added complication that they were registered citizens and we weren't.

Akron began wiping down the second Beretta. When he was done, I expected him to toss it in the snow beside Dexter, but instead he aimed it at me.

I blinked in shock. "What are you doing?"

"Supporting our story."

The weapon went off with a bang, and white-hot fire tore through my shoulder. I collapsed, screaming and rolling around in the snow.

CHAPTER 37

I lay on the road, turning the trampled snow red. Richard was on his knees beside me, applying pressure to the wound with a spare shirt from one of our bags.

"You fucking shot him!" Richard said. "Are you insane?"

Akron passed in and out of my cloudy view, taking our bags out of the truck.

"Who else would I shoot?" he said. "You? Myself? It's his fault we're in this mess to begin with, so it's only fair that he be the one to solve the problem."

I had to grit my teeth to keep from crying out in pain.

"I don't think he hit anything critical," Richard said. "It's just a flesh wound."

"In my good shoulder," I groaned.

"Your what?"

"My GOOD shoulder!"

Understanding crept into Richard's eyes. I'd been shot in the shoulder already, during the Screechers' initial invasion. Now I'd have two bum shoulders plagued with phantom shooting pains and the burning reminder of permanent nerve damage.

Darkness crept in at the edges of my vision, and I shivered violently.

"Stay with me, Logan..." Richard pleaded.

My eyes were sinking shut, my teeth chattering from the cold. Blood loss was obviously taking its toll. I lapsed into a blissful sleep and awoke to the sound of unfamiliar voices.

My eyes sprang open to see Richard still leaning over me, still pressing down on the white-hot hole in my shoulder. My head felt like it was stuffed with cotton. I tried to sit up, but Richard held me down. He glanced at me. "You're awake."

"What's going on?"

He shook his head and looked away. I rolled my head to that side and saw no less than six soldiers standing around the pickup truck. All of them were wearing bulky jackets and pants with gray and green camo patterns. Shiny black boots rose halfway up their shins, and black ski masks covered everything but their eyes. Two of them were speaking with Akron while he stroked Lucky's fur, looking the picture of innocence. Another two soldiers searched the vehicle.

"Found them!" one said, holding up Richard's AR-15 in one hand, and a hunting rifle in the other.

"Are they registered?" one of the soldiers speaking with Akron asked.

A flashlight snapped on, shining in the back of the vehicle. "The AR-15 isn't, but the .22 and the .308 are."

"The two Berettas aren't registered either," someone else added.

"It's just like I told you," Akron explained, still stroking Lucky.

Traitor, I thought. I was bleeding out in the snow, and she'd already found a new master. This was why I'm a dog person.

"Maybe you'd better tell me again," the soldier standing next to Akron said.

"We flagged this pickup down for a ride to the nearest registration center, and these two guys came out pointing guns at us. They took our things, but while one of them was patting us down, he let his guard down, and Richard managed to steal that knife." Akron pointed to the bowie knife. It was tucked safely into the soldier's belt. "Logan got shot during the struggle, but we managed to force them to drop their weapons by threatening the leader. Then we tied them up. After that, we activated the panic button on one of their passbands and waited here for you to arrive."

"Good thing you did. This situation could easily have implicated you as the guilty parties if you hadn't. You mentioned you were hiding in a shelter until recently? Whereabouts?"

"Back that way—" Akron pointed to the distant line of trees back the way we'd come. "In Village Creek Park."

The soldier frowned and shielded his eyes. "Long way from here?"

"Maybe a ten-mile hike," Akron replied.

"I'll take your word for it." He turned and signaled to a few of the others. "Take care of those two."

"What do you mean take care of them?" I asked, but my voice was a thready whisper from the pain. "Richard?" I croaked in a more urgent tone as I saw two of the six soldiers moving toward Dexter and Bobby. Their rifles swept up, and the two duct-taped men began struggling in earnest. Muffled protests leaked out around their duct-taped mouths. "Shit. Richard, they're going to—"

Two gunshots split the wintry air, and echoed away into silence. Dexter and Bobby both lay still with spreading crimson halos seeping out into the snow.

I couldn't believe it. They'd just executed those men. These soldiers were judge, jury, and executioner all wrapped into one, and all they needed to justify their actions was the circumstantial evidence Akron had trumped up to implicate Bobby and Dexter as arms dealers. They dragged the bodies to the side of the road, leaving bright red trails of blood in their wake, and then proceeded to steal their jackets, gloves, and boots.

Two more soldiers came over. One of them took over for Richard, zipped open my jacket and examined my shoulder.

"It's a flesh wound. You'll live." He tied the blood-soaked shirt Richard had been using around my shoulder like a tourniquet, and then the soldiers hoisted me up, and shoveled the three of us into the backseat of the dirty white pickup. The two soldiers who'd helped me climbed in front, while the other four went back to a waiting Humvee, carrying their haul of winter clothes and guns between them.

As the pickup began rumbling down the road after the Humvee, I stared out the window; my eyes skipped from the blood-stained snow to Bobby's and Dexter's motionless bodies, still unable to believe what I'd just witnessed. This was not the America that I remembered.

There was no sign of OneZero, but I had a feeling that she was hiding in the back of the pickup.

"So... Akron Massey, huh?" the soldier in the passenger's seat said.

"That's right."

"I'm surprised you didn't go to Mars. Sure as hell beats this frozen wasteland."

"I wouldn't be too sure," Akron replied. "Mars is much colder, and you can't breathe the air."

The soldier snorted. "Yeah, but I bet no one's killing each other up there."

Akron shrugged. "I certainly hope not."

I wanted to say something about that, to accuse the soldiers who'd just murdered two men in front of my eyes without any kind of due process, but I didn't have the strength for lengthy arguments. "Where are you taking us?" I asked instead.

"For registration."

"Where's that?" Richard asked before I could.

"West Memphis is the closest, so we'll take you there. I don't suppose any of you have documents to prove citizenship?"

"No," I shook my head.

"Do I need them?" Akron asked.

"Not really, because everyone knows you. But your two friends are nobodies."

"What if I vouch for them?"

"That would help, but it's not enough. We can look up their names and other personal info in the system. If we get a hit, that might be enough. If not... do either of you have any registered relatives?"

That was when it hit me. All this time I'd been trying to come up with a way to find my son, and I'd completely overlooked the significance of the passbands. "Yes!" I said. "My son. His nephew."

"Great. Then all you'll need is a blood test to confirm what we have on file for him."

My heart was practically leaping out of my chest with excitement. Of course, I assumed that Alex had managed to find a way to get registered. He hadn't had any documents with him either. Who had he had to vouch for him? The Hartfords? They were in the same boat. And Alex wouldn't have had any relatives to corroborate *his* citizenship. Fear raced like fire through my veins. If he hadn't found a way to get registered, what were the odds that he'd survived this long?

Bobby's voice echoed through my head: *It's open season on illegals.*

CHAPTER 38

West Memphis was surprisingly neat and orderly. There weren't many signs of change besides the dirty, trampled slush, the lack of cars, and the unusual quantity of pedestrians trudging along both sides of the streets. Those streets also crawled with armed patrols made up of former soldiers—now *guardsmen*—and police, so I suspected that had something to do with the lack of chaos.

The guardsmen driving our vehicle dropped me at the nearest hospital where harried-looking nurses dumped me into a rickety wheelchair. Richard promised to look after Lucky for me, to which she hissed, and I smiled. They'd come to an understanding.

I watched the guardsmen drive Richard and Akron away, hoping they wouldn't run into any trouble getting registered. Despite the fact that I wanted Akron to be revealed for what he really was, we needed his help right now. If Alex wasn't registered, Akron vouching for us might be our only chance of getting passbands.

A nurse wheeled me into a cold, dirty-looking room with flickering fluorescent lights and at least thirty people. They were crammed shoulder to shoulder, sitting on the floor or lying in the handful of beds. Another nurse physically removed someone from one of those beds so that I could lie there. The man yelped and cursed at her in Spanish before slumping into a shadowy corner. I wanted to argue about my preferential treatment, but didn't have the strength. The nurse put me on an IV to restore lost fluids and then she took a sample of my blood.

"For registration purposes," she explained, and then disappeared through the open door. A pair of soldiers in army fatigues stood guarding that door in case I or anyone else tried to run.

I lifted my head to look around. Moaning, sobbing men, women, and children surrounded me. Most of them wore bloody improvised bandages like my own, while a few others seemed to have more mysterious ailments. There were no nurses or doctors administering to them. Was this a waiting room for the ER?

Then I noticed their skin color and remembered how the one who'd been evicted from my bed had spoken in Spanish. These were Mexicans or Central Americans displaced from their homes by the Screechers.

Somehow these people had avoided being slaughtered like the ones we'd found in the woods, but given the lack of attention they were getting here, I had a bad feeling that this room had been reserved for them to crawl into a corner and die.

I let out a sigh and rocked my head in disgust on a foul-smelling pillow.

The nurse returned to clean and dress my wound, but rather than prep me for stitches, she simply applied a bandage.

"Hey," I said. "When am I going to get stitched up?"

"When you have a passband," the nurse replied, flourishing her own. "We don't waste valuable resources on illegals." She looked up suddenly, as if she'd just realized that she was surrounded by them. But everyone was too distracted by their private miseries to worry about her.

"And you think that's okay?" I asked.

"Two hundred million descended on us in one month, plus a hundred million of our own. If we hadn't discriminated, we all would have died. We had to draw the line somewhere."

"I can see that," I replied, glancing around. "What if I die before your system decides to give me a passband?"

"Then that's natural selection doing its work. You've got an IV, a clean bandage, and a bed. I'm sorry, but it's the best I can do, and it's more than most *unregistereds* get." A bitter frown pulled the corners of her mouth down, and she turned to leave.

"Can I at least get something for the pain?"

"Don't push your luck," the nurse replied, and with that, she turned and left the room.

I spent a lifetime waiting, sweating through my clothes while enduring waves of agony and biting back screams. Eventually I got tired of being patient and lifted my spinning head to catch the eye of one of the soldiers at the door. "Hey! Can one of you go find out about the status of my registration?"

"Shut up," the soldier snapped.

My head fell back to the pillow, and I endured another measureless span of time, listening to the pitiful sounds of the wounded. Glancing around the room to distract myself, I noticed a young girl, maybe seven years old. Her tear-streaked cheeks were gaunt from starvation, and her eyes were a dull, hopeless shade of brown. Her arm had swollen to the size of one of her legs, black and purple—obviously badly broken.

Hot tears stung my eyes at the sight of her, and I stumbled out of bed, dragging my IV stand behind me. As I approached, a woman beside her looked up. From her appearance I guessed she was the girl's mother, but it was hard to be sure. There were bald patches where her hair had fallen out, her cheeks were sucked even farther into her mouth than her daughter's, and her eyes looked like there was nothing left to hold them inside her head. I felt suddenly nauseous as I stood swaying in front of them, but that could have been my own injuries taking their toll.

"Take the bed. Please."

The mother's eyes flickered with a feeble light. She gave me a fleeting, toothless smile that looked like it might break her face—and in some way it did, by splitting open her recently-scabbed lips. The pair of them struggled to their feet and shuffled over to the bed that I'd vacated. I sunk to the floor, watching as the mother helped her daughter up with withered, trembling arms.

Dozens more gaunt and staring faces surrounded me, assaulting my eyes and stabbing me with guilt. I remembered the field of frozen bodies in the forest, and wondered if they were the lucky ones. At least they hadn't suffered like this.

Tears slipped silently down my cheeks, pattering my jeans and making muddy puddles on the floor.

This is the new holocaust, I thought.

An indeterminate amount of time passed. Nurses came and went, periodically coming to clasp yellow bands around people's wrists before wheeling them out. Those people burst into tears, but I couldn't tell if it was from joy or terror.

Then *my* nurse came back, and clasped a yellow band around the wrist of the girl with the broken arm—around her good arm. The mother burst into tears and hugged the nurse. I winced as I watched that, afraid that the woman might crumble to dust. The nurse didn't return that hug, possibly afraid of the same thing.

"Don't thank me," was all she said. "Thank your sponsor."

Sponsor? The yellow bands must be charity cases. Maybe there was hope for this new world after all.

"Logan!"

I looked up at the sound of my name and saw Richard striding in. Akron was right behind him.

They each wore a bright blue band on their wrist. Richard held out another one as he stopped in front of me.

"We've found Alex," he said. "He's okay."

A dam broke inside of me, and I sobbed shamelessly like the mother of the girl now being wheeled out of the room.

"Logan?" Richard asked, dropping to his haunches in front of me, his brow pinched with concern. "Is something wrong?"

I wiped my eyes with my good arm and flashed a shaky smile. "No. I'm fine. Let's get my shoulder stitched up so I can go see him."

CHAPTER 39

"**W**here is he?" I asked Richard while the nurse scanned my passband using a cell phone with a shattered screen.

"His address is registered to a suburb outside Memphis," Richard replied. "Police can track him through his passband, so it won't be hard to find him once you're fit to travel."

I grinned at that. Police states were good for something.

"Hmmm," the nurse said.

"What's wrong?"

She turned her phone so I could see. I only had 500 bytes to my name. I guessed that was a default starting point for newly-registered citizens.

"Not enough?" I asked.

She frowned and shook her head. "Not even close. You'll have to go through the free clinic. You're a Blue, so you'll get bumped ahead of the

Yellows, but there's another Blue in the OR right now, so you'll have to wait here a little while longer."

Yellows, Blues? I realized she was talking about the color of our passbands. "Where's the free clinic?" I asked.

"How much longer?" Akron added.

"It's in this wing," the nurse said, replying to me first; then she looked up at Akron and added, "Fifteen minutes, an hour... I can find out for you if you like."

"Don't bother." Akron held out his wrist. "Scan my band."

The nurse hesitated, then did as he asked, passing her cell phone close to his wrist. A new figure appeared, a number with eight zeroes. The nurse blinked and tapped her damaged phone, scanning and re-scanning Akron's passband. "There must something wrong with this thing...." she muttered.

I gaped at Akron. "You're still rich. Filthy rich."

He smiled wanly at me, as if he didn't want to brag, but I saw the smug curve to his lips. Somehow the Screechers had known that Akron's wealth hadn't evaporated. They hadn't chosen him by accident.

"My companies all went bankrupt, with the exception of one, Solnet, which actually appreciated. With the electrical grid down and overburdened in a million different places, solar roof tiles, power walls, and solar panels became very popular items—not to mention electric cars."

"So the government didn't seize it."

"They seized a lot of different companies, including Starcast, by buying up their stock and taking them private, but that was in order to prevent key industries from going bankrupt. Solnet was never in danger of going bankrupt."

"He's still a billionaire," Richard said. "And he's probably the richest man in the world right now. Solnet's market cap is sitting at two hundred billion bytes."

My head swam with the implications of that, or maybe it was the pain. This was bad: a *Screecher* was now the richest man in the world. I had no idea what they were planning besides getting Screechers on Mars, but I had to tell someone, and soon.

My nurse was gaping up at Akron right along with me, but she recovered and her jaw snapped shut. "Well, then," she said, standing up and stepping behind my wheelchair. "Let's get you stitched up, Mr. Willis."

* * *

The stitching was done by a doctor, with another nurse assisting. The bullet had torn a deep trench in my shoulder, and I had to endure the procedure with only a local anesthetic. It wasn't enough, or perhaps they didn't use enough, because at some point in the process I passed out.

When I woke up, I was in a plush room with a couch to my left and a large flatscreen TV on the wall in front of me. To my right lay a bathroom, an armchair, and a window. Fat snowflakes danced down from a darkening gray sky to snow-covered streets and rooftops below.

I tried to sit up, but my muscles didn't want to obey. I was still too out of it, but at least the blinding pain in my shoulder had been reduced to a dull ache. An IV line trailed from my wrist, and wires ran from my chest to a machine behind my left ear that beeped in time to my heart.

I felt sleepy, but rested and calm. My clothes were draped over the arm of the couch, cleaned and pressed, the bloodstains mostly gone.

Feeling around beneath the heavy weight of the covers, I felt a hospital gown, and vaguely recalled two nurses helping me change before surgery. Enjoying the warmth of the covers, I realized that I'd been given an electric blanket. This was a far cry from the waiting room where illegals were forced to sit shoulder to shoulder on a dirty floor in the hopes of getting a yellow band and free treatment.

The door creaked open, and a nurse came in wheeling a trolley with a food tray on top. My stomach growled, and I tried again to sit up again. A stabbing pain shot through my shoulder, and I slumped back down.

"Don't try to move too much, Mr. Willis. I'll help you up to a seated position."

Moments later, I was seated and using my good arm to shovel beef stew on a bed of steaming rice into my mouth. The doctor came in next and explained that the stitched would degrade on their own after a few weeks. He asked to see how I was doing, but my mouth was full so I could only nod and smile.

He left the room followed by the nurse. She left saying that I should touch a button on the side of my bed if I needed anything.

Then I was alone with my food and my thoughts, wondering where Richard and Akron were and whether Alex was okay. And where was Lucky? Not that I expected she'd be allowed into a hospital.

I found myself staring into the blank black square of the television while I finished my meal. Wondering if it worked, I found the TV remote clipped to the side of my bed and touched the power button.

A bald man with a deeply-lined face and a square jaw appeared. He stood behind a lectern in a dark blue uniform with medals pinned all over it and stars gleaming on his epaulets. Behind him was a placard that read: *The Presidential Palace, Chicago,* and to one side, some new version of the American flag, stretched taut rather than hanging limply from a brass pole. The stars on the flag were familiar, but now they were the same sky-blue as the passband on my wrist. The rest of the flag was white with a flaming eagle rising out of a black mound of... ash? A phoenix rising from the ashes?

The sound on the TV was muted, but I was too distracted to hunt for the volume buttons. In the top corner I read *LIVE* and the time, 4:32 PM. At the bottom, a bar of text read—PRESIDENT-GENERAL NELSON.

Finding nothing else to catch my interest I raised the volume. "...in these dark times. The Department of Housing and Urban Development is building thousands of shelters and housing complexes across the country, and we are registering more and more refugees through sponsorship programs every day. Crime is the lowest it's been since the Collapse, and employment is on the rise with new jobs being created every day. We have risen from the ashes of defeat, and we will continue to rise until we are back on top and Unity is the most powerful country in the world. Until then, remember, security is freedom." The president saluted and walked off the stage amidst the flashing of cameras.

Security is freedom? Unity? The TV switched to a scene with a pair of news anchors sitting in a newsroom behind a desk that sported a *UNN* logo on the front.

A knock sounded on my door, drawing my gaze away from the screen. Richard stepped in, followed by Akron, and I muted the TV. The news anchors were busy singing the praises of Unity and President-General Nelson, so I didn't think I'd miss much. UNN was obviously a government-run news agency.

"You look a lot better," Richard said, stopping beside my bed.

"You know about all this?" I asked, nodding to the TV. "*Unity* and the President-*General?* UNN? Security *is* freedom?"

Richard frowned. "Unfortunately, yes."

Akron waved his hand as if to shoo away a fly. "Are you ready to leave?"

"Am I allowed to?" I asked.

"Yes," Akron replied. "The only reason they put you in this room is because I didn't know how long it would take to get things straightened out at the launch facility."

"That's where you've been? Starcast? What about Alex?" My gaze sharpened as it strayed to Richard. "You should have gone to find him first."

He grimaced and shook his head. "I wanted to, but the police won't track him through his passband without the consent of a parent or a legal guardian. I had to wait for you."

"Then let's go."

"Are you sure?"

In lieu of a reply I threw the covers off with my good arm, and knocked my empty dinner tray to the floor with a crash. Richard helped me out of bed, and a nurse came running in. "Is everything okay in here?"

I yanked the IV out of my wrist and used the surgical tape that had held it there to stop the bleeding.

"Mr. Willis! Please lie back down. You could tear your stitches open and re-injure yourself." The nurse tried to force me back into bed, but I pushed back and ripped the electrodes off my chest. "I'm leaving. Now," I said, and stumbled over to the couch to get my clothes.

"Very well. Let me get you a wheelchair."

"I can walk just fine."

The nurse planted her hands on her waist and watched with a deepening frown as I shrugged out of my hospital gown and began pulling on my underwear one-handed. "It's hospital policy, Mr. Willis, and you're not leaving unless you abide by it."

"Then what are you waiting for?" Richard asked. "Get the man a wheelchair."

CHAPTER 40

Sitting in a wheelchair in the parking garage, a male nurse loomed over my shoulders as he held the chair in place. My arm hung in a sling that fit over my winter jacket, hiding the blood-stained hole where the bullet had punched through. Akron produced a key fob from one of his pockets and pressed a button. A chirp sounded, and a minute later a large, shiny black electric pickup truck rolled up in front of us. Akron pressed another button and the back doors slid open automatically, revealing a spacious interior with two rows of seats facing each other. Ahead of that, the driver's seat and passenger's seat were empty. The nurse helped me out of my wheelchair; then Richard took over for him and helped me into the back of the truck. He climbed in beside me, and Akron took a seat on the row of seats facing us.

The doors slid shut, and the truck rolled off

with an almost soundless whisper.

"Where are we going?" I asked.

"West Memphis PD," Akron replied.

I struggled to put my seatbelt on with my good arm. A moment later we stopped at the exit of the garage. Akron lowered his window and fed a plastic parking card into the slot. He'd obviously already paid it, because the boom flipped up and our self-driving truck rolled out onto the snow-covered street.

"Where's OneZero?"

A shimmering silhouette appeared in the passenger's seat. "Right here," OneZero whispered.

I didn't even blink. I was used to her surprise appearances by now. "And Lucky?" I asked, looking back to Akron.

"Safe and warm in your room at the launch facility."

My room. That settled the question of where we were going to live in this post-apocalyptic world.

I laid my head against the headrest with a sigh. The ride to West Memphis PD didn't take more than a few minutes. I spent the time thinking about Akron and the Screechers' hidden agenda. He'd paid my hospital bills, and his vehicle was taking me to find my son, but how much of that was to keep up appearances?

I had no idea what his people were trying to accomplish in our newly rebuilt country of Unity. Just the fact that our so-called allies had stolen Akron's body in order to pursue their agenda, and likely erased his consciousness in the process, made me think that their agenda was not benign or helpful to *my* species.

The truck stopped in front of the police department, and the doors slid open. Richard climbed out first, followed by Akron. They helped me down, and we walked up the icy steps. The truck rolled off, hunting for a parking spot, and we breezed through the precinct doors. A pair of officers in familiar blue uniforms and jackets stood on the inside of the doors, watching us with their hands on their guns as we came in. They passed cell phones over our passbands, scanning them, and then directed us through a metal detector. On the other side, Akron led the way to a reception area shielded by bulletproof glass which was almost opaque with a spider's web of cracks. Several bullet-sized pockmarks were the locus of that web.

Akron asked for a Detective Andrews of CTS at the reception area. The policewoman behind the counter asked us to hold our passbands in front of a scanner on our side of the glass. A wire trailed from that scanner to the pass-through slot at the bottom of the fractured glass.

The woman studied our identities briefly, and then reminded us that only immediate relatives were allowed to track each other. I explained that I was looking for my son. She told us to wait, and promptly left her cubicle.

We stepped back from the counter and went to sit along a row of blue plastic chairs beside the door as someone else came in to speak with the other officer at the reception desk.

Moments later, a tall, fit man in a dark blue uniform came striding out of a reinforced door on one side of the reception area. He walked straight over to us, his blue eyes skipping from one face to the next as we rose from our seats.

"You're back." The Detective said, his gaze lingering on Akron.

He nodded. "We're ready to run that search."

The detective's eyes strayed to me. "This must be the missing kid's father?"

"I am," I said.

He stuck out a hand. "Detective Andrews."

I shook his hand awkwardly with my left. "Logan Willis," I replied. "You can help me find my son?"

"Yes, please follow me."

We followed him through the door that he'd emerged from a moment ago. He opened it by scanning his band, and held it open for us. We walked through into a well-heated, bustling work area. Cops sat behind desks in long-sleeved blue shirts, watching us over the rims of steaming coffee mugs as we came in.

The detective led us through the room to an empty desk and sat down. We hovered over his shoulders, watching as he brought up a search prompt for a program called *CTS*, emblazoned over the flaming eagle that was the new symbol of our country.

"CTS?" I asked.

"Citizen Tracking Services," Detective Andrews replied. He turned from the screen and nodded to me. "If you'll just pass your wrist in front of the scanner..." He pointed to a black eye inside a shiny white ball sitting on his desk. It looked like an old web camera.

I did as he asked, and my information appeared on the screen beside my old passport photo. Studying the results briefly, the detective read aloud. "Logan Willis.... father of Alexander Logan Willis, and Rachel Layla Willis, married to Katherine Dianne Willis."

"That's right."

"And you're looking for your son?"

I nodded, and watched as the detective brought the search prompt back and typed Alexander's full name into it.

Three results came up in a table with various types of information organized into columns beside their identical names. I was surprised that there was more than one person with my son's name, after all the civilian casualties we had suffered. I spotted the address column and found an entry with *Memphis, TN* listed.

Detective Andrews clicked on that entry and a picture of my son appeared. I almost gasped at the sight of him. He'd grown a scraggly beard, lost enough weight to make his bones stick out, and his honey-brown eyes were sunken and haunted.

"Is that him? the detective asked.

I nodded stiffly, my throat suddenly too tight to speak. "Yes," I managed after a few seconds had passed.

"Okay then." The detective clicked a link that read: *live tracking,* and a satellite map popped up with cities and roads labeled, and a red dot clearly marked. It was on the east side of the Mississippi— the Memphis side, surrounded by suburban neighborhoods. The detective zoomed in and individual buildings and side streets emerged in the map.

"It looks like he's at Kroger Supermarket. He must be getting his daily rations."

"How are you tracking people?" I asked. "Didn't the Screechers take out all of our satellites?"

"They didn't touch them," the detective replied. "I guess they realized our satellites aren't weaponized. Anyway, your son's only about twenty miles from here. If you hurry, you should catch him before he leaves."

I was skeptical, wondering how fast we could possibly drive on the icy, snow-packed roads. "Twenty miles... that's going to take at least thirty minutes, and that's assuming we don't run into traffic."

The detective snorted and shook his head. "You won't. And I doubt you'll miss him. The ration lines are long. Most people spend half the day waiting for their rations."

"What if we do miss him?" I asked. "Can't you come with us? Track him from your car?"

The detective frowned. "I can't promise that. We've got a lot on our plate right now. If you don't find him at Kroger, you can come back here for an update. Failing that, try his registered address."

"And that is?"

The detective switched tabs in the program and the map was replaced by that withered picture of my son, alongside his personal details.

"Thirty-seven sixty-four Coral Drive."

I shook my head. "And where is that?"

"Don't worry about it," Akron replied. "We can put that address in the autopilot, and it will take us straight there."

"All right. What about the supermarket?"

"Twenty-six thirty-two Frayser Boulevard," Detective Andrews replied.

I committed those two addresses to memory and said, "Thank you for your help."

"You're welcome. It's the one good thing about these passbands—" Andrews said, flourishing his own as he rose from his chair to see us out. "— every now and then, instead of using them to track down criminals, we get to use them to reunite people with their loved ones."

I nodded as we followed the detective out. Right now I couldn't focus on the negative implications of a government that could track my every move. All I could think about was how that system had helped me to find my son.

CHAPTER 41

Akron summoned his electric truck, and a minute later it pulled up in front of the police station to pick us up. I wondered if it had actually found a parking space, or if Akron had simply told it to circle the block.

On our way down the steps, an army truck drove by with the familiar rumble of a diesel engine. A megaphone on the roof droned loudly.

"...your duty as citizens to report the whereabouts of any unregistered aliens. Harboring is a crime punishable by a fine of up to five thousand bytes, or the equivalent in lost rations. Remember: security is our freedom."

The truck dwindled into the hazy, snow-clouded distance. I stopped at the bottom of the stairs to watch it go, ripples of shock echoing through me as the message played on repeat.

Akron and Richard climbed into the back of

our truck. I grabbed Richard's outstretched hand to pull myself up. The doors slid shut on both sides as I sat down. Akron directed his gaze to an inverted black dome on the ceiling between our seats. "Autopilot, take us to Kroger at 2632 Frayser Boulevard, Memphis."

"Route set for Kroger, 2632 Frayser Boulevard, Memphis. ETA thirty-four minutes. Please buckle up and enjoy the ride."

"Thank you," Akron said, already clicking his seatbelt in. Richard and I did the same.

The time passed in a hazy swirl of falling snow. I watched the white world go by, going through different scenarios for my reunion with Alex. Would he be happy to see me? Angry? Ambivalent?

We crossed a bridge over the Mississippi. The river was frozen and covered with snow. I blinked in shock. How cold did it have to be for *that* to happen?

Richard passed the time silently staring out the windows, too, but Akron busied himself with a tablet that he'd produced from a folding storage compartment in the middle of his row of seats. OneZero remained hidden, but every now and then I saw a shimmer in the air above the passenger's seat.

The roads were mostly empty of cars—but crowded with trudging pedestrians—as we drove north through downtown Memphis. We passed from the downtown skyscrapers to the skeletal trees of city neighborhoods, to the sprawling front yards and outlet shopping centers of the suburbs. Long lines of people stood waiting out in the snow in front of the shopping centers—waiting for rations, I guessed.

Finally we pulled into the turning lane behind a trio of electric cars. To our left I saw the wide-open parking lot of a shopping center with a sign out front that I had to squint to read through the falling snow: FRAYSER VILLAGE CENTER. Just below that was a blue sign with the word KROGER on it.

We'd arrived! My heart began pounding with anticipation. The truck's autopilot made the turn into the shopping center. I saw the huddled lines of people long before we reached the shopping center—a slash of colorful jackets drawn through this snow globe of whites and grays. Pedestrians had replaced cars in the world's parking lots.

Our truck parked itself close to the front of the supermarket, far from the back of the line. Guardsmen in military fatigues and black ski masks stood outside the supermarket with their rifles at the ready.

"Let's go," Akron said quietly.

The door slid open for us, and we hurried out, buoyed on a brief blast of warm air from the truck's heater. The warmth faded almost instantly; a cutting wind burned my exposed face and sliced through my jeans. The air outside was colder than I remembered. Looking up, I saw why: the dark shadow of night was creeping across the gray sky, illuminated only by the glaring yellow eye of a working street light. I looked around, scanning the seemingly endless line of people. Was Alex still here waiting for his rations? Was it safe to walk home after dark? What if somebody jumped him and stole whatever meager supply of food the government had given him?

"We'd better start checking the line," Richard said.

I groaned, thinking that could take a while.

Akron opened the passenger's side door. "OneZero, find Alex," he whispered.

Fresh-fallen snow *swished* out from a pair of deep footprints, and Akron shut the door. Clanking footsteps receded into the distance, and I tracked the sound, hoping OneZero would be able to cut our search short. She knew what Alex looked like, although, she hadn't seen how he'd changed in the last six months. I thought about running after her to describe those changes, but talking to an invisible friend was bound to attract unwanted attention. Instead, I turned and grabbed Richard's arm, yanking him along toward the waiting line of people.

We started our search at the front. The people there glared at us with simmering looks. "Back of the line!" one man said.

I shook my head. "We're not trying to cut in line. I'm looking for my son." I gave a brief description, but the man had lost interest.

I wondered where Akron was and turned to see him climbing back into the warmth of the truck. I scowled at that, but shrugged it off. He'd already helped me a lot—maybe more than the real Akron would have.

Richard and I walked slowly down the line, checking faces and asking at random if anyone had seen someone matching Alex's description, but no one had. By the time we reached the end of the line, we had checked two or three hundred people. Now the only remaining light in the parking lot was from people's flashlights, Kroger's windows, and the working streetlight I'd seen earlier.

"He's not here," Richard said, blowing a cloud of steam into his gloves and then rubbing them together. My extremities were frozen, too, and I couldn't feel my nose or my cheeks.

"Maybe he left before we got here," I said.

"Or maybe he's inside Kroger," Richard replied.

A whisper of air and crunching footsteps turned my head to a faintly shimmering silhouette. "I found him," OneZero said.

My heart began pounding again. "Where?"

OneZero grabbed my hand and pointed it to a trickling line of people exiting the side entrance of Kroger, carrying bundles of supplies into the darkening night. "That way."

I didn't understand why OneZero hadn't just brought him to us, but I decided it must be because she couldn't do that without revealing herself.

"Let's go!" I said, and took off at a run.

"Wait up!" Richard called after me.

CHAPTER 42

"There," OneZero whispered beside my ear. "Blue jacket. Red hat."

I saw him, but only vaguely in the gathering darkness. He cut across a snow-covered clearing behind the supermarket, carrying a black plastic crate of supplies with the flaming eagle of Unity emblazoned on the side. All of the people leaving Kroger carried matching crates. Most of them were adults, but there were a few children and adolescents struggling along, too.

I ran to catch up, but my injured arm slowed me down. The painkillers had worn off and every step hurt. The pain and fatigue of running across the parking lot left me feeling dizzy. My lungs burned from the cold, and I couldn't stop coughing.

"Alex!" I yelled between coughs, but my voice disappeared in the whipping wind. Flurries danced in the streetlights around the shopping center. The snow blurred my view of Alex's red hat and navy-blue coat. I managed a brisk pace despite having to wade through several feet of snow. It soaked through my jeans and trickled past my ankles, and soon my feet were numb right along with my face and the tips of my fingers. Snowflakes melted on my nose and flew into my mouth.

The field backed onto a snow-covered road and a complex of two-story apartment buildings. The trickling line of people forked at the road, with one line heading for the apartments, the other for clumping black shadows of old, snow-covered trees between houses in a suburban neighborhood. Here and there feeble lights pricked through the trees—windows lit with a welcoming glow of electricity.

I followed Alex down the street, struggling to keep up.

Richard gasped distantly, "Logan! I can't keep going!"

"Don't stop," OneZero urged.

I hadn't planned to.

Her footsteps sounded in tandem with my own, always just one step behind me. She was good at using other people to mask her presence.

Alex turned right onto a rural street, and the crowd forked again. Some of them going straight, others trailing behind and ahead of Alex. Homes flashed by on both sides of the street. None of the streetlights were working, and these windows were predominately dark.

Snow covered the street. I followed Alex down a narrow, trodden path running down the center with steep banks on either side. Pristine white mounds in the shape of parked cars made those banks even higher.

"Alex!" I yelled again, but none of the shadowy figures up ahead turned at the sound of my voice. The twilight was barely enough to keep Alex's bright red cap in view through the thready haze of falling snow.

Alex turned again, down another road, and again the line of people forked, thinning out dramatically this time. Only four people walked between me and Alex now, and just two ahead of him. Those two darted up a driveway and disappeared, and then Alex dashed up another driveway.

My brow furrowed as I recalled the address Detective Andrews had given us. Had we somehow reached 3764 Coral Drive on foot?

I aimed for Alex's driveway, urging myself to

walk faster. The four people still walking up ahead of me raced up a driveway two houses down from the one where Alex had gone.

I realized they were neighbors. The thought that my son had found some semblance of normalcy in the chaos warmed my heart, but where was Harry and the rest of the Hartford family? Alex hadn't been alone when the Screechers captured him.

Raised voices drifted to me on the wind as I drew near to the point where Alex's neighbors had left the road. I stopped and turned to see four shadowy figures standing on the front porch of a bungalow with their hands up and their crates of supplies at their feet, while a young man in a red hat pointed a gun at them.

CHAPTER 43

Standing at the end of the driveway I yelled, "Alex!"

This time everyone heard me. Heads turned, and the gun in Red Cap's hand wavered. "Dad?"

I should have expected what happened next. One of the four people my son held at gunpoint rushed in and grabbed the weapon. It went off with an echoing *BANG!* and then changed hands. Terrified that my son had been shot, I ran up the driveway. "Alex!"

"Not another step," the man now holding the gun said. "Or I'll shoot him."

I froze on the spot and raised my left hand in a placating gesture, while my sore arm and sling only let me lift my right hand halfway up. "Hang on. There's obviously been some kind of misunderstanding here."

"No misunderstanding," the man said. "Your

son tried to rob us. I've called the authorities. They'll be here soon."

Alex's head turned, and I noticed that under his red cap he was wearing a black robber's mask like the ones the guardsmen wore. There was a hole for his lips and eyes, but that was it. His face was perfectly concealed. If he could get away, these people wouldn't even be able to identify him.

"OneZero," I whispered. "Get the gun."

No reply came, but I felt the icy caress of a sudden breeze that might have been her.

"What was that?" the man on the porch said. "Speak up!"

A split second later, the gun went flying out of his hand and landed at my feet. "Fuck!" the man screamed. "You broke my hand!" he whirled around blindly looking for his assailant. But no one there—at least no one he could see. I snatched up the gun in my left hand and aimed it at the people on the porch. "Get over here Alex. *Now*."

He didn't wait to be asked twice. As soon as he reached my side, I began backing away.

"Deactivate your locator beacon. No one took anything. We don't have to involve the authorities," I said.

"Forget it! You assaulted me... somehow. And your son tried to rob us! You're not going to get away with that."

I glanced at Alex and noticed that he was staring at me as we backed away. "Alex," I said, keeping half an eye on his intended victims.

He didn't respond immediately.

"Alex!"

He shook himself, seeming to snap out of it. "Yeah?"

"We need to run."

He nodded once, then turned and ran back the way we'd come, his boots spitting out chunks of hard-packed snow as he went. I ran after him, stumbling in the dark. Spurred on by adrenaline, we made it back to Kroger's parking lot in just five minutes, but it felt like a lifetime. I heard police sirens in the distance and cursed under my breath. Tucking Alex's gun into the waistband of my jeans, I covered it with my jacket and ran toward Akron's truck. "Head for that truck," I said, pointing to it. Alex nodded. The headlights were on, drawing us in like a lighthouse.

Halfway there, Alex stopped and turned to me. "Your passband. You have one?"

"Yeah, so?"

"Shit," he muttered, shaking his head. "They'll have seen you fleeing the scene of the crime. They're already tracking us as suspects!"

And just like that it hit me, I was an accessory to an attempted robbery, and *I* had the gun. "Can't I cut it off?" I asked, looking at my passband. Just a few hours ago I'd been desperate to become one of the privileged Blues—a registered citizen. Now I had to figure out how to reverse that process.

"That's another crime."

Alex hurried over and yanked off a long black glove. "Put it on."

I stared at the glove, not getting it. "What does that—"

"Just do it!"

The sirens were getting closer. I grabbed the glove and struggled to take mine off with my injured arm. Alex helped me, and then pulled the glove all the way up over my wrist. I flexed my hand, and something inside of the glove crinkled. "What..."

"Aluminum foil. Now let's go!"

Alex took off at a run. I struggled to keep up beside him. "Won't that make them suspicious?"

"Lots of things block GPS. A snow covered tree could do it. So long as your signal comes back eventually, they can't complain."

"But they'll still know we were there."

"Not me. I've got an alibi."

I shook my head, wondering what that meant.

"Yeah, well what about me?"

"I need some time to think!"

We skidded to a stop beside the truck and I banged on the doors. "Akron!" I said.

The door slid open and he greeted us with a frown. "Is something wrong?"

Richard sat in the corner, looking guilty and miserable. He brightened at the sight of Alex. "Is that..."

"Hi, Uncle Richard."

He almost fell out of the truck in his hurry to give Alex a hug. I envied him that. I hadn't had a chance for a proper greeting yet, and there wasn't time for one now.

"Alex. What the hell are we going to do?"

"About what?" Akron demanded.

Alex blew out a cloud of air. "You shouldn't have taken the gun. It's unregistered. I had to leave my rations behind. If the authorities found the gun back there, we could have claimed that they robbed *me*."

"And frame an innocent man and his family?" I demanded. "What's the penalty for stealing?"

"Death, Dad! Where the hell have you been?"

"The penalty for stealing is death, and you're out there doing it anyway? What were you *thinking?*"

"You've been implicated in a crime?" Akron asked darkly.

"It's complicated."

"Not for me," he said, shaking his head. "Step away from the truck. You're on your own now."

CHAPTER 44

"You can't just ditch them here," Richard said.

"Hear that?" Akron asked, and I noted that the sirens were even closer now. "The police are coming for them. Do you want to become an accessory to their crime?"

"Wait," I said, pressing my hands against the sides of my head as if that might help me think. "What if..." But I was out of ideas.

"Logan, take the glove off," OneZero interrupted.

"Who's there?" Alex asked, spinning around in a circle.

I did as she asked. "Now turn on your locator beacon and give me the gun."

Touching a button on my passband to activate the beacon, I then reached behind my back and retrieved the gun. Holding it out like an offering, an invisible hand took it from me, and then it vanished with a sudden whoosh of air. Moments later I heard tree branches cracking.

"Now, Alex, give me your hat, and coat and get in the truck." He hurried to do as she asked, while we all looked on in confusion.

"When the authorities arrive, tell them that an illegal ambushed your son and stole his rations, his hat, and his coat. You mistook the illegal for your son in the dark and followed him, only to end up on the wrong side of an armed robbery. You tried to defuse the situation. There was a struggle, the gun got knocked away, and you took it. You retreated with the robber, but when you realized that it wasn't your son, he stole the gun from you and ran. You chased him back this way, but he outran you. At that point you activated your emergency beacon to call for help."

Akron looked dubious. "That's a convoluted story."

"All we need is to sow enough doubt that the authorities won't want to shoot anyone. If they can't find the gun and they can't be sure who the guilty party is, then once they realize that no actual crime was committed, they'll lose interest."

That sounded reasonable to me.

"What are you going to do with the hat and jacket?" I asked.

"Deflect suspicions." Stepping away from the truck, OneZero de-cloaked and put on Alex's robber's mask, his red cap, and his jacket. It was dark enough that I almost couldn't tell that she wasn't human. Only her spindly metal legs gave her away.

"Chase me!" she said.

In the next second, sirens came screaming down the street with a familiar wave of flickering red and blue lights. I ran half-heartedly after OneZero, but a police truck with chains on its tires ground to a halt in front of me and cut me off. I stopped and thrust my good hand up even before the officers jumped out behind their doors and demanded that I do so.

"Both hands!" one of them added.

I struggled to raise me injured arm, winced, and gave up halfway. "I can't! Don't you see the sling?"

One of them stalked over to me, keeping his gun aimed at me the whole way. He grabbed my good arm and wrenched it behind my back, then did the same my bad arm.

"Fuck!" I screamed and panted through the pain as he locked both of my wrists in handcuffs.

"Shut up."

"He's getting away!" I replied.

"*Who* is?"

"The damned illegal who robbed my son! Look! There he goes!" I jerked my chin to OneZero.

"Shit!" the second officer muttered, and he sprinted after OneZero. "Stop where you are!"

But of course OneZero didn't stop.

"I said stop!" He fired his gun with an echoing report, but OneZero just kept running. The policeman guarding me watched that play out with a frown, then grabbed a radio off his belt. "Dispatch, this is Charlie-seven-baker responding at the Frayser Village Center. Do we have a description of the suspect from the RP?"

"Negative, C7B. Description pending. Officers in route."

The second police officer came back from chasing OneZero, out of breath, and planted his hands on his knees to get the blood flowing to his head.

"Did you hit him?" the first one asked.

"No. He was moving too fast."

"We'll catch him. See if you can find him on the CTS."

Officer two shook his head. "We only tracked *one* signal fleeing the scene, and that's him." He nodded to me.

"So who's the other guy?"

"I told you. He's the illegal who robbed my son," I said.

Both officers studied me with pinching brows. Snowflakes quivered through the twin beams of their truck's headlights. "All right, let's hear it," the one who'd cuffed me said.

* * *

OneZero's story didn't seem to make either of the two officers happy, but once they got a description of the perpetrator from dispatch and realized that it matched the description of the person they'd seen fleeing through the parking lot, they decided to drop the case.

"We'd better not catch you in connection to another crime," the taller of the two cops said as he un-cuffed me.

"Trust me, you won't," I said, but he and his partner were already walking back to their truck, muttering about the *damned illegals*.

I went back to Akron's truck. The door slid open before I arrived.

"Get in, *now*," Akron said.

I climbed in and sat there beside Richard and my son. The door slid shut with a thump. Akron glared at me and Alex. Silence thickened the air between us. "You want to explain what happened out there?"

I looked to Alex. I was just as curious as Akron. "Why would you try to rob anyone?" I asked.

His haunted brown eyes flashed at me. "You don't get to ask me that. You've been gone for six *months!* I'm fucking lucky to be alive. You think stealing is the worst thing that I've had to do? Think again."

A chill raised goosebumps on my arms despite the hot air blasting out of vents in the back of the truck. "What have you had to do?" I asked slowly.

He snorted and shook his head, as if *I* were the child and knew nothing of the real world. "Whatever I had to do to survive."

"That's not an answer, Alex. You're registered. You can get rations. You have a place to live, you shouldn't have to—"

"Steal? Are you sure about that, Dad? What about the fifteen illegals in the basement? How do you think they feed themselves without passbands?" He jabbed a thumb at his chest. "*Me.* That's how. Me, Celine, Harry, and a few others, too. But rations are only good enough for one person, and barely at that, so you've got to steal to feed everyone. If I don't deliver, guess who goes hungry?" He thumped his chest with his fist. "Me again."

I gaped at Alex and he smirked back. A stranger lurked behind his eyes. Apparently the Screechers weren't the only ones stealing bodies. A bitter, hardened criminal had stolen my son's.

"What happened to Harry's wife, Deborah?" I asked, noticing that he hadn't mentioned her.

"She froze." He said it so matter-of-factly that it took a minute for me to realize he meant that she had died of exposure.

"We're going to fix this," I said. "You don't have to go back there."

"If I don't go back, Celine dies. And if I go back empty-handed, then I'm going to go hungry for a week—or however long it takes for me to steal more supplies, which is never now that you've lost my gun."

"Why would Celine die? Is she sick?"

Alex glared at me. "You really don't know anything, do you? The illegals are holding her hostage to make sure we bring them food."

I could feel the blood draining from my cheeks. I should have realized that was what he'd meant. Slowly shaking my head, my lips pressed into a determined line. "You're not going to go back empty-handed."

"No?" Alex scoffed.

"No. I'm going back with you." Just then the door opened, and a shimmering wraith climbed in. I nodded to the specter. "And she's going to help."

Alex's jaw dropped. "OneZero?"

"Hello, Alex."

CHAPTER 45

Akron wasn't easy to sell on the idea of rescuing the hostages. He wanted to get back to Starcast and start work on his rocket to Mars. I gladly would have left him to it, but we needed a ride to Alex's house, and we'd need a ride back after we rescued everyone. In the end, I convinced him by reminding him of the role he was supposed to be playing.

"What happened to you?" I demanded. "You've changed. You're cold. OneZero's more of a human being than you are."

Akron squinted at me, and for a moment I was afraid that I'd overdone it—then he gave in with a nod. "Fine, but this is the last favor I'm doing for you."

I smiled thinly. "Thank you." Turning to the others, I began to outline my plan.

"What about me?" Richard asked, when he

realized that plan didn't involve him.

After he'd abandoned chasing Alex for the warmth and safety of Akron's truck, I doubted his usefulness. "You want to help?" I asked.

"If I can."

Walking into a den of illegal criminals with *two* new arrivals didn't seem like a smart idea, so I said, "You can help by staying out of the way."

Richard gaped at me, but I didn't have the time or energy to deal with his hurt feelings. Turning to the shimmering silhouette seated beside Akron, I asked, "So? What do you think?"

"Your plan has a good chance of success, but you'll have to be careful to avoid confrontation. I can't help you until everyone is asleep—not without risking the lives of the hostages."

"Don't worry. We'll keep our heads down, right Alex?"

He said nothing, but the wary look in his eyes spoke for him.

"What aren't you telling me?"

He shrugged. "Nothing. Just don't assume you know how this is going to play out. Shit happens."

I nodded and offered a reassuring smile. "It's going to be okay. You'll see."

Alex snorted and looked away. "Sure."

* * *

Akron verbally gave Alex's street address to the truck's autopilot. The truck drove down the main road from Kroger for about two minutes before slowing to a stop at the turn into a rural area. The truck stopped there with its indicator light blinking.

"Error. Obstruction detected. Destination cannot be reached. Error. Obstruct—"

"Autopilot off," Akron said. "Stay here with hazard lights activated. Turn engine off but leave heaters on."

"Acknowledged," the car replied. It pulled a few inches off to the side of the road and stopped. Flashing yellow lights peeled back the darkness around us. I wondered about Akron's ability to control the car—among other things... his ability to manage his finances for example—and I concluded that some part of him had to have been preserved. His memories, perhaps?

"How close are we?" I asked Alex.

He shrugged. "Close enough. It's a fifteen-minute walk from here."

Fifteen minutes in freezing temperatures would still be a challenge. I glanced out the window at the *obstruction* the car had detected.

Snow was piled high around a trampled footpath running down the center of the street. No cars were getting in or out of this neighborhood.

I looked back to Alex. "You gave your jacket and hat to OneZero. You can't go like that. Richard can you—"

"Yeah, hang on," he said, already zipping out of his coat and pulling off his knitted cap.

"We'll wait here for you," Akron said as Alex dressed. "Right side door open," he said, and it slid open with a blast of frigid air that took my breath away.

Alex and I jumped out, followed by the muffled crunch of OneZero landing behind us. I turned to look just as the side door of the truck slid shut behind us. OneZero became invisible again. "Stay close," I said to her.

"I will," she replied.

Turning to Alex I nodded and said, "Lead the way."

He started down the path. As we put distance between us and Akron's truck, the flashing golden halo of its hazard lights dwindled, plunging us into the monochromatic night.

The cold seeped through my winter clothes, and soon I was shivering. My fingers grew numb inside my gloves and my toes fared no better, but my face was the worst—my nose and cheeks burned from the cold. I began to envy the guardsmen their black ski masks. If this was what it was like in Memphis, I shuddered to think how cold it would be in Canada, or New Jersey, for that matter. It surprised me that there weren't more problems with Canadians trying to cross the border illegally—but then again, they had a lot of land for so few people, and a lot of firewood to burn through before they all froze to death. Besides, they were more used to this shit.

I shook my head. *Damned Eskimos.* That was probably racist, but in my presently-frozen state I didn't care.

It became hard to tell where my feet were, and I began to stumble behind Alex. "How much farther?" I asked.

"Two minutes."

He seemed to be doing much better than me. He must have adapted to the cold in the six months that he'd been up here dealing with it. I grimaced as I recalled Alex's words: *You think stealing is the worst thing that I've had to do? Think again.*

"Alex..." I said slowly.

"'Sup?"

"I'm sorry."

"For what?"

"For not coming sooner."

"Whatever."

"Damn it, would you listen to me? I tried to leave. They wouldn't let any of us go after we reached Haven. The mayor said it was too dangerous."

"Well you're here now, so that makes up for it."

The sheer sarcasm in Alex's voice made me wince. I struggled to find the words to make amends, but nothing could justify my absence.

"We're here," Alex said quietly.

I looked up to see that we'd reached the end of a cul-de-sac. Alex headed up a trampled pathway in the driveway of a run-down, snow-covered bungalow. Icicles hung from drooping gutters, and smoke curled out of the chimney.

We reached the door, and Alex rapped on it in a specific pattern—*knock-knock... knock... knock-knock.*

The door swung open and warm air drifted out. A familiar face greeted us in the light of a hand-cranked flashlight. I threw a hand up to shield my eyes from the glare. Warm air mixed with foul and appetizing smells brushed my frozen face.

"Logan?" Harry asked in a cracking whisper.

"How..."

Before I could answer he reached out and pulled Alex inside by his jacket. I was next. The door clicked shut and Harry locked it with the *thunk* of a deadbolt. He set the flashlight down on a wooden cabinet by the door.

"Where are your rations?" Harry demanded before I could say anything.

"Lost them," Alex explained. "Thanks to him." He jerked a thumb at me.

"Hey, watch your—"

"Shut up," Harry hissed. "Where's your gun?"

Alex shook his head. "Lost that, too."

"*Fuck,*" Harry muttered. "Ivan is going to lose his shit over this."

"I'm here as compensation," I said. "I have a passband, too, so I can get more rations."

Harry just looked at me. "You're just another mouth to feed. Until you prove that you can steal more rations than you use, you're a dead weight."

"We have a plan," I said.

Alex's hand closed like a vice around my arm. "We'll double my quota the next time we go out. Logan has an angle to try that might just surprise Ivan."

Logan, not *Dad,* or my father—I'd been reduced to a first name basis with my own son.

Harry snorted. "I hope it's a good angle, for your sake."

I glanced about, hoping to see some sign of OneZero, but I couldn't tell if she'd made it through the door with us.

"How are you heating this place?" I asked.

"Electric heaters and a wood stove in the basement," Harry replied. "Electricity is rationed along with everything else, but we have enough registered citizens living here to get a decent share."

"Then why are you using a hand-cranking flashlight? And why are the lights off?"

"There's a blackout," Harry replied. "Probably a downed power line. Good thing that the government gave us these." He patted his flashlight.

"Yeah, good thing," I agreed.

"Come on, we don't want to keep Ivan waiting for bad news."

We followed Harry down the hall, floorboards creaking loudly as we went. An old kitchen and a closet appeared to our right, then the hallway widened into a suspiciously empty living room— no people and no furniture. Harry led us to a locked door that he opened with a key. A narrow stairwell made of unfinished plywood led down into a dim, fire-lit space that reeked of human sweat and acrid wood smoke.

Harry led the way down the creaking stairs, his flashlight bobbing with each step. As we followed him, I strained to hear OneZero's footsteps, but I couldn't detect a thing. I hoped it was because of her stealth and not because we'd left her on the icy front porch. My whole plan relied on her.

When we neared the bottom of the stairs, I saw what Alex had mentioned earlier. More than a dozen people crowded the basement, lying in sleeping bags on the floor, and slumping on old couches and chairs. Most of them looked Hispanic, but there were a few Caucasians mixed in—one of whom I recognized only vaguely. Alexander's girlfriend and Harry's daughter, Celine Hartford. She sat in a winter jacket on the floor with her knees drawn up to her chest, staring into the flickering fire in a wood stove on the far side of the basement.

"You're back," someone said in a thick Spanish accent.

I turned to the sound of that voice and saw a big man rising from a couch in front of the fireplace. A pair of scantily-clad women who'd been draped over him retreated to opposite corners of the couch and stared at us with eyes as black as coals.

"Ivan," Alex whispered in a trembling voice.

That poured an angry fire into my veins. My son, the bitter, fearless criminal was afraid of this man.

"Where are your rations?" Ivan asked. "And who is this?"

I took the man in at a glance. He was overweight, with his belly hanging over his belt and belly-button peeking through a pit-stained white button-up shirt. Long, stringy, sweat-matted black hair dangled above his shoulders, and a dense crop of patchy stubble crawled over his jaw and chin. Thick, tattooed arms ended in big hands. More tattoos crawled up his neck, drawing my gaze to a round face with two tiny black eyes set in sunken, fat-rounded sockets.

"I ran into some trouble," Alex explained, "But I'll double my quota before the end of the week. This is Logan," he said. "My father," he added belatedly, as if reluctant to acknowledge our relationship.

"Trouble?"

"My fault," I put in. "I tracked my son to the supermarket and followed him. I accidentally spoiled his chances of robbing a family he'd targeted. He lost his gun and his rations in the process."

Ivan's gaze swept back to Alex, those tiny eyes flattening into slits. His hand fell to the butt of his own gun, a Glock which dangled casually from his belt.

"You *lost* your gun?" he echoed.

"My fault again," I said, suddenly afraid that there might be dire consequences for losing such a valuable item.

Ivan's eyes darted to mine, and he scowled.

"I know where it is," I said, thinking back to how OneZero had thrown it into the trees somewhere beyond Kroger's parking lot. "We can recover it in the morning."

"*Sí*. You are going to recover it," Ivan said. "But I am afraid there must be consequences. Luis, Isaac, tráeme la niña."

"Hey, she has nothing to do with this!" Harry said, stepping up to Ivan.

Ivan threw a punch and sent Harry sprawling into the stairs, clutching his ear.

A pair of burly men got up from matching armchairs and stomped over to Celine. They yanked her off the floor, and Alex took a few steps toward them. "Leave her alone!" he said. Ivan blocked his way with a meaty arm.

"What are you going to do, *puto*? Ah? *Este niño se cree hombre, guey!*"

I didn't understand any of that, but the sheer sarcasm dripping from Ivan's words translated itself. The two men Ivan ordered to get Celine dragged her over, and a nasty grin parted his lips.

Celine's face was as pale as the snow outside.

"What are you going to do to her?" I demanded.

"Let her go," Alex added through gritted teeth.

Harry lunged at one of the two men holding her.

"Dad, no!" Celine said.

The man thrust out a massive fist and punched him in the throat. Harry stumbled away choking.

Ivan gave my son a pitying look, and then drew the Glock from his belt.

"Hey! I'm the one who failed to meet the quota," Alex said.

"So did she. Last week. And the week before. And many other weeks también."

I put out a hand in a placating gesture. "Hang on," I said. "We'll go out again now. We'll come back with the rations and the gun. Just leave her alone."

Ivan just shook his head. "There have to be consequences, or else you never learn."

"OneZero..." I whispered, glancing around. *"Now."*

Then Ivan pulled the trigger, and Celine screamed.

CHAPTER 46

The bullet hit one of the men holding Celine and a beastly howl tore from his lips.

"*Joder!*" Ivan stared at his gun and shook it, as if he couldn't believe it had betrayed him by shooting the wrong person.

But I knew what had happened and smiled. OneZero had broken her rule about waiting until everyone fell asleep to intervene.

Ivan took aim at Celine again, this time using both hands. Harry ran at him like a linebacker, and the other man holding Celine pulled a gun out of his waistband.

"OneZero!" I ran at the second guy with the gun, but realized my mistake a split second later as a half a dozen others mobilized and drew their weapons.

The gun aiming at me went off with a *bang*. I saw the muzzle flash, but the bullet never reached me. Instead it *clinked* off something invisible between me and the shooter: OneZero. The ricocheting bullet *crunched* into the stairs, and I sailed into the man holding Celine hostage and wrestled for his gun. More bullets *clinked* off OneZero as she shielded me from an entire salvo; then I heard Harry cry out.

"Dad!" Celine screamed and ran out of cover to reach her father.

Something hit the man I was wrestling with, and a second mouth appeared where his throat had been. He collapsed and his gun came away in my hands. I spun around and aimed at the first of six different enemies, but my target fell clutching a hole in his gut. The next one lost his arm in a puff of red mist. I couldn't switch targets fast enough. They were dropping like dominoes. OneZero sprayed the room with bullets.

It was over in seconds. I stood gaping at the carnage. Half of the people in the basement lay dead or dying, including Ivan and the two he'd ordered to grab Celine. The other half, mostly women and children, cowered on or behind the basement furniture.

I let out a breath and cast about for Alex. "Well, not exactly how we planned it, but—"

I stopped myself there. Harry lay beside Ivan

in a pool of his own blood, glassy eyes staring at the ceiling, and Celine lay a few feet away with Alex pressing down hard on her left breast. A glossy crimson stain glistened on my son's arm, and blood pitter-pattered from his elbow to the floor.

They'd all been hit except for me.

I hurried over to Alex and Celine.

"Hold on, Celine," Alex said. "We're going to get you to a hospital."

"My dad," she gasped. "Is he... okay?"

Alex glanced at Harry's dead staring eyes and nodded. "He's fine. Just stay with me, okay?"

Celine nodded slowly, but her teeth began to chatter, and I cringed at the sight of how much blood was bubbling out between my son's fingers.

"Don't just sit there!" Alex snapped at me. "Find something to stop the bleeding!"

I nodded quickly but couldn't see anything that would work. She'd been hit in the chest, right over her heart. Even if we'd had a hundred feet of bandages it wouldn't be enough to stop the bleeding.

"A-Alex," Celine said, her blue eyes seeming to look past us. "I love you."

"I love you, too..." Alex trailed off as her eyes slipped away from us. "Hey, no, no, no, stay with me! Celine!" He punched the floor. "Fuck!" Alex's gaze snapped to mine. "This is all *your* fault!"

I stared blankly at him. "Alex..."

He gave me a shove, and a sharp pain stabbed as stitches pulled on the tortured skin in my shoulder. A bloody handprint appeared on my sling.

"You're hurt," I said. "We need to stop the bleeding." I cast about once more. Seeing the looks we were drawing from the surviving illegals in the basement, I stood up, making sure to keep them covered with my stolen Glock.

Alexander began unbuttoning Ivan's shirt, and I realized what he intended. I helped him roll Ivan's corpse to remove it, and then helped Alex get his injured arm out of his coat. I tied Ivan's shirt around the bullet wound as tightly as I could. He winced, but didn't cry out.

"Let's go," he said in a cold whisper. He grabbed another Glock out of Ivan's hand. I saw a flicker of movement in my periphery and turned to see one of the scantily-clad woman from Ivan's couch reaching for a shotgun that had fallen at her feet.

Before I could say or do anything, Alex's arm swept up and he shot her in the back. She fell to the floor amidst the screams of everyone else in the room. I stared wide-eyed at the body, unable to believe how quickly my son had shot her.

"*Alguien más?*" Alex asked, sweeping the gun around in a broad arc. "No? Didn't think so. Eloisa, Bert, Andrew, you'd better get the hell out of here before the cops or the Guard arrives."

Three Caucasians with blue passbands on their wrists stumbled to their feet, grabbing small bundles of belongings, and running for the stairs. Alex and I covered them as they went up. We went next, keeping our aim on the survivors in the room, just in case someone else tried something.

We hurried out the open door at the top of the stairs. Alex shut the door behind us and spent a moment looking around for something.

"What do you need?" I asked.

"A chair. Something to block the door."

I joined him in looking around, but the main floor had no furniture.

"Allow me," OneZero whispered.

I saw green laser beams lancing through the gloom to the door handle, dust trickling through them and refracting the light. The door handle glowed bright orange and smoked with an acrid metallic odor. Then the lasers vanished, and the door handle cooled to the faint red glow of a dying fire. Alex tested the handle with his gloved hand

and nodded once before striding back through the house to the front door.

I followed Alex down the hall. "Aren't the police going to see us fleeing another crime scene?"

"No," he said.

I hurried to catch up. "Why not? They can track our bands, right? And someone told me they measure our vitals, so the authorities should already know that Harry and..." I stopped myself there.

Alex said nothing.

"Alex?"

We breezed through the front door, letting all the warm air out in a steady rush.

My son rounded on me with a vicious left hook. My teeth clacked together and I stumbled back with the force of the blow, blinking in shock at my son.

"You just got my girlfriend killed, and now you want to chat about the consequences? Fuck you, Logan."

Before I could recover, Alex spun away and stomped down the front steps. I stared blankly after him, feeling equal measures of outrage and guilt. My son had punched me in the face, cussed me out, and addressed me by my first name all in the same breath.

A whisper reached my ears: "The signals emitted by their bands are not strong enough to escape the basement. The authorities won't know that they are dead until someone reports it, or until they realize that weeks have passed and their locations haven't updated. By then we'll be long gone, as will the illegals trapped in the basement."

I turned toward OneZero's voice, but ended up staring into empty space. "Why didn't you save them?" I demanded, trying to deflect some of my guilt.

"I could not be everywhere at once. I chose to protect you because you were the closest at the time."

"Well, thanks..." I replied.

"You are welcome. We should go."

I nodded and hurried to catch up with Alex. I wanted to scold some sense into him, but I held back and trailed a few steps back. Now wasn't the time. Alex had been forced to become an adult and take care of himself; reeling him back in and laying down the law would take some time, and now, right after his girlfriend had died in his arms, wasn't the perfect moment to start. Besides that, I couldn't help feeling he was right, and maybe this really was all my fault. If I hadn't shown up, Celine and Harry would both still be alive.

CHAPTER 47

We found Akron and Richard waiting on the main road, right where we'd left them.

"Where are the hostages?" Akron asked.

"Don't," I breathed as I climbed in beside my son.

His eyes flicked to Alex's bloody arm, and he nodded slowly to himself, as if he could guess why no one had come back with us. I pulled my gloves off and rubbed my hands together to get the feeling back while Akron gave orders for the autopilot to take us to Starcast's launch facility.

"What happened?" Richard whispered to me.

My eyes on Akron, I said, "We need to get to a hospital."

"We have medical facilities at the launch facility," Akron replied.

I frowned at that. "So why did I go to a hospital?"

"Because we were in the custody of the Guard at the time, and you were unregistered. That, and I didn't know what state the launch facility was in until I went there myself."

"What state *is* it in?" I asked.

"You'll see," Akron replied.

And that ended the conversation in the back of the truck. I risked a look at my son. His head was leaning back, his arms crossed, and his knitted cap pulled down over his eyes. Fine lines creased his gaunt cheeks, making him look far older than his sixteen years. I was surprised that Alex hadn't shed even a single tear over Celine, but maybe he was used to bottling his feelings.

Passing streetlights peeled away the darkness with strobing yellow light, drawing my gaze out the windows. We'd reached the end of the blackout area.

Downtown Memphis slipped by with a profusion of lights and colors. It was almost enough to convince me that the rogue star and the accompanying alien invasion were just a bad dream. Almost. Looking closer, I saw the darkened gaps where ragged curtains fluttered from the broken windows of ruined skyscrapers and hotels; flickering firelight took the place of actual electric lights. Cave-living in the post-modern era. Life still went on, but not as normal, and at what cost? Had those so-called illegals in that basement always been gang-banging lowlifes, or had they been forced into that life by a system that refused to feed them and would shoot them on sight?

We cruised over the bridge across the frozen Mississippi, and toward the glittering lights of West Memphis, but the truck turned off before we got there, entering a darkened sprawl of barren farmland instead.

I peered between Akron and OneZero over the row of seats in front of me. A dark tower rose in the distance, silhouetted in the silver glow of a half-moon. The tower was surrounded by shorter buildings. A hot spear of dread stabbed through me as I recognized that configuration. Was that a Screecher city?

But as the complex grew closer and larger, I began to pick out more details: the central spire was a rocket, and the shorter buildings around the base belonged to its launch complex.

We'd arrived.

"Hand me your weapons," Akron said.

I passed my stolen Glock and glanced at Alex to see him hesitating.

"You want to get shot?" Akron demanded.

That made up Alex's mind, and he handed the

weapon over. Akron lowered his window and an icy wind gusted in. He tossed both Glocks out. One of them discharged with a loud *bang,* and I jumped with a jolt of adrenaline. The window slid up and Akron favored us with a thin smile.

A few minutes later our truck cruised up to an iron gate in a high chain-link fence with barbed wire at the top and spotlights glaring down. A guard tower stood to one side, and camouflage-clad guardsmen stood in front of the gate. More guardsmen stood at the top of the tower, their weapons covering us from all angles.

"Error. Obstruction detected. Destination cannot be—"

"Wait here," Akron said.

"Waiting here," the car replied.

One of the guards came to the window, and Akron lowered it. The barrel of an assault rifle glared at us, and the frosted lashes of the guardsman's eyes peered through his ski mask.

"This is a restricted—"

"My name is Akron Massey. I own this facility."

"This is a government installation. No one owns—"

"Speak to Commander Dickson. He's given us permission to stay here and help with the Mars launch."

"Commander Dickson is sleeping."

"Then check your list. Our names will be on it."

"What did you say your names were?"

"Akron Massey..."

"Richard Greenhouse," Richard said, blowing into his hands to stay warm as cold air flooded the back of the truck. Alex still had his coat.

"Logan Willis—his brother-in-law, and this is Alexander Willis, his nephew."

"Passbands."

Akron raised his wrist and the soldier shifted to a one-handed grip on his rifle to grab a scanner off his belt—a cell phone with a cracked screen. He aimed the phone at Akron's band, nodded, and then did the same with each of us.

"Well?" Akron prompted.

The soldier signaled to the guards in the tower, and I saw the gate in front of us slowly slide open in time to a blaring alarm and flashing yellow lights. "Drive straight through to the main building. No detours."

"Of course," Akron replied, and then passed those ambiguous instructions to the autopilot.

The truck rolled slowly through the gate under the sights of multiple assault rifles.

Inside the complex the roads were perfectly plowed. Bright lights lightened the darkness around warehouses and fuel silos. Trucks with flashing yellow lights drove between structures. Workers wearing yellow hard hats and heavy jackets with reflective piping strolled about, unloading trucks and checking manifests. Soldiers stood in every corner, in every shadow, watching every coming and going. Although it had to be close to midnight, the place was a bustle of activity.

Akron's truck stopped in front of what looked to be the largest building in the complex. He opened the doors and icy air gusted in. As we climbed out, I looked around for the telltale shimmer that would giveaway OneZero's location, but she was perfectly cloaked.

A pair of gray-green camo-clad guards standing at the sliding glass doors of the main building shifted their stance as we approached.

"Passbands," one said as we approached, and we repeated the ritual of holding our wrists out for scanning.

Richard hugged himself and bounced on his feet as we waited for the results.

"You're clear," the guard said. "Welcome back, Mr. Massey."

"Thank you," Akron replied.

The guard whispered something into his radio, and a soldier standing inside the doors stepped into view as he hit a button to open them.

We breezed down a blissfully warm corridor into a vast lobby with scale models of every rocket humanity had ever built standing in a U-shape around the latest and greatest of their number—the BFR.

Richard and I stopped and stared at the twelve-foot replica of the Mars rockets, but Akron breezed on by as if he had no interest in his own legacy. Since he wasn't the real Akron, he probably didn't. I glanced at Richard, wondering if now I'd finally have a chance to talk to him about Akron's condition.

"This way," Akron called to us.

We caught up to him at a bank of elevators, which he activated by swiping his passband in front of a black box that had been mounted over the old call buttons.

"Tight security here..." I mused.

"Yes," Akron replied.

"Why?" Richard asked, but Akron gave no reply. Maybe he didn't know.

Alex said nothing as we stepped into the elevator and rode it up to the sixth and highest floor of the facility. To go by Alex's glazed, staring eyes, he might have been in shock. I began to worry that recent events were only now trickling through to his consciousness.

The elevator opened and Akron walked with us down another corridor, this one lined with doors. Black nameplates with silver text gleamed on the doors in the muted golden light of the hall. The names were all prefaced by different titles *DR.,* *CPT., MAJ., COL.... Offices?* I wondered.

The final door had an old, scuffed and beaten nameplate that looked like it had recently been hammered flat: it simply read *Massey,* without any justifying titles before it, as if his name was impressive enough.

Akron opened the door by swiping his passband across a black scanner that matched the one at the elevators.

I'd expected an office, but instead I found a sprawling luxury apartment with gleaming black hardwood floors and pristine white furniture around an electric fireplace with a rustic stone hearth. A white shag rug sparkled with reflective fibers under the coffee table, and an eight-seat dining table bridged the gap between the living room and a modern kitchen full of dark granite and gleaming appliances. A wall of windows ran down the far side of the space, looking down on the glittering lights and the ant-like bustling of soldiers and workers below. In the distance, the black tower of the BFR prototype rose to an impressive height, its edges silvered by the moon. Someone had already started working on getting to Mars. Little did they know, the Screechers planned to go there, too.

"Your rooms are down the hall. Mine is the last door to the right," Akron said, pointing the way. "I still have to code your passbands to the front door, so please don't try to leave in the night, because you won't be able to get back in."

I frowned at that, but nodded. The air shimmered beside Akron, and OneZero appeared. "I need to recharge."

"There's an outlet over there." Akron pointed to the wall beside the door. "But you'll need to adapt the current."

"I'll manage," she replied, and stalked over to the outlet.

I saw the scuffs and dents in her armor where bullets had glanced off, and tried to remember that whatever the Screechers were up to, I owed OneZero my gratitude. She had saved my life on several different occasions, helped me rescue my wife and daughter, and now also my son. Maybe the Screechers' agenda wasn't so sinister after all.

Alexander started down the hall ahead of us, and my eyes caught sight of the bloody shirt-bandage peeking through his jacket.

"You said there are medical facilities here?" I asked Akron. "My son has a gunshot wound that needs treating."

"I'm fine," Alex said.

"No! You are *not* fine."

"I'll call for a doctor," Akron said.

I turned to him with a furrowed brow. I'd had my gunshot wound stitched up by a doctor and a nurse in a proper hospital. One doctor performing the same feat in a bedroom seemed like quackery in comparison.

Then a door slammed, reminding me that my son's attitude would make dragging him to a more appropriate setting impossible.

"Make sure he brings whatever he needs—assistants, medications—"

Akron waved a hand to dismiss my concerns. "Your son will receive adequate care. You should rest." He gestured once more to the hall. "It's been a long day."

Richard snorted at that. "No shit. What about you?"

"I have some business to attend to," and with that, Akron turned and strode to the door.

OneZero was busy pulling live wires out of the wall, but she vanished as Akron opened the door—and reappeared a second later as it clicked shut. I heard a locking bolt *thunk* into place and my chest tightened with apprehension. Curious, I walked up to the door and tried to open it.

"What's wrong?" Richard asked. "Akron told us not to leave, remember?"

"Yeah, he said we wouldn't be able to get back in, but he didn't mention that we wouldn't be able to get out." Noticing a touchscreen panel beside the door and a passband scanner bolted below it, I realized there'd be no way to open the deadbolt without the proper key code or the right passband.

"There's probably a lot of sensitive stuff around here," Richard said. "He can't have us wandering around."

"Yeah..." I glanced pointedly at OneZero. Her back was turned, so she didn't notice. "We should go check on Alex. Make sure he doesn't pass out waiting for the doctor to arrive."

"Right," Richard replied, and I led the way down the hall to the bedrooms. With Akron gone and OneZero busy in the living room, now was a good time to tell Richard and Alex what I knew.

CHAPTER 48

"They said all of that? Are you sure?" Richard whispered.

Alex lay on the bed watching us, his glassy eyes wide.

I nodded quickly to Richard and whispered back, "I'm probably forgetting something, but yeah, the gist of it is that Akron isn't really Akron anymore, and no one is supposed to know that. They also said something about needing an audience with the president, and that the *Overseer* wants to get people on Mars."

Richard began pacing the room.

"So... you think when OneZero said that Akron had brain damage and they had to fill some gaps..."

"They did more than fill the gaps. They converted him into one of them."

"Shit," Richard said. "What if they gave away

Haven's location?"

My heart fluttered with the reminder of that concern, but Haven was cut off in the middle of the enemy territory, and it had no particular influence or power over the rest of the world. What would be the point of OneZero or the new Akron exposing it? They had nothing to gain by doing so. "I don't think Haven features in their plans," I said. "In fact, I think us going there may have temporarily de-railed OneZero's original goals."

"Which were?"

"Hide until the chaos cleared and her pacifist friends got settled, then make contact with them."

Richard shook his head. "That still doesn't explain her motives." Suddenly he glanced at the door. "Hang on—"

My heart froze. He opened the door and checked the hallway. A second later, he ducked back inside and eased the door shut, locking it in the process.

"What is it?" I asked.

"Just checking that no one's listening in. OneZero is charging by the front door, so we're safe. For now."

I let out a shaky breath. "I thought you'd heard something."

"If they replaced Akron..." Alex began, in a

weary, pain-clouded voice. "Then they could replace anyone."

"Or everyone," I added.

A wary gleam entered Richard's eyes. "That means we can't tell anyone about this. Not until we can figure out who to trust."

"What about the president-general?" I asked. "He's in Chicago. Maybe we could get to him."

"If they don't get to him first," Richard replied.

"It might be too late," Alex said.

We both looked at him.

"What do you mean?" I asked.

"Think about it: killing illegals and criminals, passbands that track our every move..."

Richard grimaced. "He's right. That doesn't sound like the logical evolution of a country where freedom used to be one of our highest ideals."

"Security is freedom..." I replied, quoting Unity's motto. "You think the Screechers set all that up?"

"Why not?" Alex replied. "We were in anarchy for months, and then all of a sudden President-General Nelson comes along with free food, electricity, and basic necessities for all citizens who get registered. Where'd they get the supplies?"

My mind jumped to the Screechers' mess hall with its printed imitation foods, and I thought about their bio factories that could feed millions and churn out fully-grown populations of alien monsters at the same time. If they could print food, then they could probably print other things, like clothes, toothpaste, and toilet paper. OneZero had admitted that her people were already helping us meet our basic needs, and I'd seen one of their underground cities on our side of the border.

Richard snorted. "So they're helping us make ends meet in exchange for complete control over our government and our people."

"But why?" I asked, shaking my head. "We're defeated. They don't need to infiltrate us and offer rations in order to bolster support for a totalitarian regime. They could have used a steam-rolling army to accomplish that."

"Not if they're hiding from their own people," Richard said. "Remember what OneZero said about there being two factions?"

I nodded. "The pacifists and the supremacists."

"Maybe she lied about which one is which."

My jaw dropped. "You think OneZero's people are the supremacists?"

Richard held up his hands and shrugged. "Look at the facts: the original invaders didn't fire the first shots, and after we surrendered, they went out of their way to escort us peacefully out of land they'd claimed. OneZero's people, on the other hand, are busy snatching bodies, building covert cities, and setting up a military dictatorship. That doesn't seem like the work of pacifists to me."

I gaped at Richard, unable to believe we'd been so easily fooled. "But OneZero saved our lives and helped us escape to Haven."

"Maybe she's one of the nicer ones," Richard said. "That doesn't change what the rest of them are."

An ominous, sinking feeling settled in my gut, making me feel sick. We held each other's gaze for a long moment, neither of us knowing what to say.

A knock sounded at the door. I jumped with a jolt of adrenaline.

"Logan?" It was Akron. "The door is locked. Open up. The doctor is here."

We all froze, our eyes darting to the door.

"Coming!" Richard said in a loud voice.

Chapter 49

Akron breezed in, followed by a female doctor in blue scrubs, wearing a hairnet, sterile gloves, and a mask. Akron carried a big black bag of supplies for her. "This is Major Davis," he said. "She'll be attending your son tonight."

Jasper T. Scott

"Major?" I asked.

"With the army—the *guard*," she corrected herself. "Someone get me one of those tables over there."

I spotted the bedside table she was pointing to and dragged it over.

"Anyone here have medical experience?" She glanced about while we shook our heads. "Great... put my bag on the bed."

Akron did so and then retreated to the door. "I'll leave you alone to work," he said, and the door clicked shut behind him.

I hoped his quick retreat meant that he hadn't overheard us talking.

"Take off the boy's coat," the major said, still holding her gloved hands up to avoid contaminating them. She was in a foul mood. I had a feeling we'd dragged her out of bed for this.

Richard and I helped Alex get his coat off. He groaned as we manipulated his injured arm, and I felt the blood drain from my face at the sight of how much blood had soaked through the shirt I'd tied around his wound.

"Okay... good, you've kept pressure on it at least. Unzip the bag." Major Davis said, nodding to me. "Don't touch anything until I tell you."

I unzipped the bag, and she peered in. "See

those towelettes and that pump bottle that looks like hand sanitizer?"

I nodded.

"Take them out and put them on the bed."

I did as she asked.

"Now coat your hands and arms with the gel. Let it sit for a ten count, and then use the towelettes to dry your hands.

Again, I did as I was told. Turning to her with my hands held high like hers, I nodded. "Now what?"

She already had a black surgeon's kit unfolded on the bedside table and was busy removing shiny silver implements. "Reach in and grab the saline bag and surgical tape."

I grabbed those items and waited for further instructions.

"Put them on the bed and clean your son's wrist with this." She handed me a bottle of disinfectant and a wad of cotton.

I set to work, staining my son's skin orange with the disinfectant. A few seconds after that, the major had an IV needle threaded and a bag of saline hanging from the bedpost over Alex's shoulder. She asked Richard to remove the blood-soaked T-shirt we'd tied on, and then she had me cut away Alex's shirt and tie on a bright blue tourniquet above the wound.

"Lift his arm."

I did and the major bent down for a look.

"Pronate it," she added.

"Pro..."

"Turn it so his palm is facing down."

Again I followed orders, revealing a swollen, blood-crusted mess on the other side of his arm. The exit wound.

"Good. A clean shot," the major said, and began prepping a silver platter with surgical implements. She injected both sides of his arm with a syringe pumped full of local anesthetic.

She got me to disinfect the wound on both sides with liberal amounts of that orange liquid. I kept wincing as I rubbed Alex's ragged flesh, expecting him to cry out in pain, but either the anesthetic was doing its job, or he was too tough to let the pain show. Having been shot recently myself, it surprised me that he took it so well.

Once the wound was clean, the major set to work, stitching him up on both sides in a matter of minutes.

I wondered why we hadn't been subjected to more questioning—like how he'd gotten shot in the first place and what we'd been doing at the time, but I guessed that Akron had already filled in those details. Not knowing if he'd filled them with lies or the truth, I didn't dare to broach the topic—not in this new country where the slightest crime could get you killed.

"Thanks, Doc," Alex said, checking both sides of his arm.

"You're a brave kid. I'd suggest you sign up, but the army isn't what it used to be."

"No shit," Alex said.

"About that..." I trailed off.

The major yanked her mask down with a bloody glove, and favored me with raised eyebrows.

"I'm guessing the president-general is—"

"The former Chief of Staff of the Army. If you don't know that, then you must have been hiding under a rock."

My thoughts jumped to Haven, and I nodded, smiling tightly at her. "Something like that, yeah."

"Well, count yourself lucky for that."

I thought about the disparaging way the major had spoken of the Guard, and spent a long moment deliberating, staring at this woman as she yanked off her gloves and put them in a red garbage bag at her feet; her skin was tanned despite the now-more-distant sun that couldn't have tanned an albino mole. I noticed her tired, matte black hair tied into a bun beneath her hairnet, and stared into her haunted brown eyes. I couldn't help wondering if she was *safe* to talk to. She looked like she might have Hispanic roots, which suggested to me that she was.

Richard gave his head a slight shake, as if he'd read my mind, but we needed allies—especially ones with a rank as high as Major Davis. Davis wasn't exactly a Hispanic name, but maybe on her mother's side.

"Are you Hispanic?" I asked.

The major's eyes flashed and pinched into slits. "I'm a registered citizen and a major in the Guard."

"I don't care whether you are or you aren't, but if you are, I think we might have similar opinions about certain policies regarding the treatment of *illegals.*"

The major's eyes swept to Richard, then back to me. "Hypothetically, let's say I *am* part-Hispanic. What opinions might we share, and what does that matter?"

I smiled. "It could matter a great deal. Is there somewhere we can talk that's more private?"

The major held my gaze for long seconds without replying.

"My office. Tomorrow at thirteen hundred hours. Building four, level one. Go to reception and ask for me by name. If I'm in surgery or otherwise occupied, you wait for me in the receiving area—understood?"

I nodded stiffly. "Yes. Thank you. You'll be glad you listened to us."

"Yeah... we'll see."

CHAPTER 50

Richard and I stayed up, cooking greenish spaghetti from a box of flaming-eagle branded rations that we found in one of the cupboards. We mixed it with a similarly-branded bottle of tomato sauce from the refrigerator until we had a passable meal. We ate quietly at the kitchen's island counter, acutely aware of OneZero's shimmering silhouette standing just ten paces away, watching us. At least Akron was somewhere else.

Richard lifted a forkful of spaghetti and studied it speculatively. "What do you think?"

I shrugged. "It's food."

"No. I mean, do you think these rations were printed by Screechers?"

"Definitely," I said, noticing how my spaghetti lacked the rubbery texture I was used to. It broke and crumbled whenever I tried to wind it around my fork.

"It is hard to worry about flavor when nutrition is the primary concern," OneZero put in from where she sat charging by the door. Wires trailed from her hip into an open electrical socket.

I frowned and pointed at her with my fork. "I thought you ran on antimatter," I said.

"Indirectly, yes. The charging stations in our cities are powered by antimatter reactors."

"Aha," I said. "How long until you're fully charged?" What I really wanted to know is whether we'd have to worry about an invisible robot following us to our meeting with Major Davis tomorrow.

"Another twenty-seven hours," OneZero replied.

Perfect.

"You must have some impressive batteries," Richard commented.

"Power cells," OneZero replied.

"Same thing," Richard grunted.

"Not exactly, no."

Our meal was interrupted by an enraged scream. I froze, belatedly recognized Alex's voice, then dropped my fork and ran for his room.

I threw the door open just in time to see him jump out of bed, headed for the window. *The window?*

"Alex!" He didn't turn around. Reaching the window, he fumbled with the lock and then slid it open. Cold air gushed in. My son swung one leg up over the windowsill before I grasped his intentions.

I rushed out and pulled him roughly back. He fell over with a *thump*, and sat glaring up at me with tear-stained cheeks.

"What the hell do you think you're doing?" I shut the window with a bang. "We're six stories up. If you jumped from here, you'd die instantly!"

"Leave me alone!" Alex screamed, jumping to his feet. He tried to push past me, hands reaching for the window.

"Alex!" I gritted out as I struggled with him. He was a lot stronger than I remembered, and my wounded shoulder didn't help. Richard stormed in and pulled Alex back.

"Where were you?" I demanded.

"I thought you two might want some privacy to talk things out," he said, frowning deeply. "Apparently it's not one of those moments."

"No, it isn't," I replied.

OneZero came in a moment later, still trailing wires from her hip. "Is something wrong?"

"My son's suicidal, that's what's wrong." I stared at him with a mixture of sympathy and accusation. "Your mother would kill you if she found out about this."

"Good!" Alex sneered, struggling to break out of Richard's grip.

"Poor choice of words," Richard added.

"Stop it," I snapped. "You're going to tear open your stitches."

Alex appeared to calm down.

"We're good?" Richard asked.

"Yeah."

He let go, and Alex lunged for the window again, but before he could reach it, his lips twitched in a wince, and his eyes rolled up. He collapsed at my feet with a dart protruding from his back.

"What the—" I looked to OneZero, fury building like a hurricane inside my chest.

"It's a sedative," she explained. "He needed to be tranquilized."

"Who the hell are you to decide that?" I demanded. "I was going to talk to him!"

"He didn't appear to be in a talking mood," OneZero replied.

I dropped to my haunches and checked Alex's pulse. He'd landed hard, but the carpeted floor cushioned his fall. I felt his pulse skipping steadily under my fingertips and blew out a breath. "He's okay."

"Of course," OneZero replied. "I would not have shot him with something dangerous." With that, she left the room, and I stared out the open door, listening as her clanking footsteps receded down the hall.

I wasn't sure I believed her, but at least for now it seemed that OneZero didn't mean us any harm—for now. I snatched the dart out of Alex's back and threw it aside. "Richard, help me get him into bed."

Richard grabbed his arms and I took his legs. It was hard, painful work to lift him with my injured shoulder, but I did my best not to let it show. I tucked him in and spent a moment studying his gaunt face; dark circles rimmed his eyes. My son had tried to kill himself. Shit.

"He needs help," Richard said. "He's probably got PTSD."

"Yeah," I agreed. One more problem for the pile. But this particular problem might give us the excuse we needed to see Major Davis. "We'll have to take him to see the major tomorrow. Maybe she can prescribe something or give us a reference for a shrink."

Richard stared at me, realization dawning, and a grim smile touched his lips. "Good idea."

CHAPTER 51

—**November 2nd, 2032**—

I spent the remaining hours of the night in Alex's room sleeping in an armchair with my back to the window Alex had tried to jump from. Lucky lay curled in my lap, purring contentedly while Alex snored.

With everything going on, I slept fitfully at best, haunted and awakened by nightmares of my son falling to his death and of Screechers ambushing Haven and sending the rest of my family to a watery grave. I tried to remind myself that OneZero and Akron had nothing to gain by exposing Haven's location. As for Alex... his mental state wasn't just a good excuse to see Major Davis. I fully intended to get him whatever help he needed while we were there.

The first rays of morning sun came slanting in

through the window behind me, and I rubbed tired, scratchy eyes. Lucky stretched on my lap and flexed her claws, pricking my thighs.

"Hey!" I whispered sharply to her. "Cut that out." She rolled over and hopped off of my lap. I watched her pee on the carpet in the far corner of the room. "I see you," I muttered.

Getting up, I went to check on Alex. "Hey," I whispered beside his ear.

He stirred, but didn't wake up. I shook him by his shoulder, and his eyes cracked open to glare at me as I sat on the edge of his bed.

"Good morning," I said.

He glanced to the rosy sky beyond the window. "Barely," he replied. "Water."

I grabbed my glass of water from the bedside table and gave it to him. He gulped greedily and passed it back.

"You want to talk?" I asked.

"No."

"Why did you do that?"

Alex swallowed and shook his head. "She's gone."

"Celine?"

He nodded.

I winced. "I'm sorry, Alex. I didn't expect things to go the way they did."

"I warned you," he replied.

"You did." I wasn't going to accept full blame for what had happened, but at least some of it was mine to shoulder. "Look, Alex. If this is about her, I get it, but you can't end your life just because she's gone."

"It's not just that. I've killed people." My mind jumped to the woman in the basement. Alex had shot her in the back without hesitating. "Innocent people," he added.

I gaped at him. "What—why?"

Alex smirked. "Still think you need to save me from myself?" He shook his head and his smirk faded. "I don't deserve to live."

"Hey," I said. "Don't you dare think that. You were forced to steal. If some of those robberies got out of hand, that's not your fault, and you can't kill yourself to make it right."

Alex's smile returned, small and sad. "Don't worry. I know. I've got to live with it. That's my punishment."

A heavy frown pulled my mouth down. "We're going to see Major Davis today to get you some help."

"And to talk about the robopocalypse?" Alex suggested.

I nodded, but said nothing to that. "You want

some breakfast?"

"Sure, I guess."

"Let's go. You can help me make it."

* * *

We had a long time to wait until one o'clock with nothing to do but stare at the walls and each other. I ended up taking a nap in my room and leaving Richard with instructions to watch Alex—just in case.

I awoke to find both Richard and Alex shaking me. Both were dressed in heavy jackets, ready to brave the cold outside. "Time to go," Richard whispered.

I got up and pulled on my winter coat and then followed them to the front door. We passed OneZero along the way. She was still recharging from the wall socket.

"Where are you going?" she asked.

"To see Major Davis about Alex's incident last night," I explained.

"Of course. I hope you feel better soon, Alex. Let me open the door for you."

He said nothing, and we waited while OneZero opened the door for us by entering a key-code into the touchscreen. I tried to get a look at the code, but OneZero was careful to block our view. "I'll let Akron know where you went," she said as the door unlocked with a *thunk.*

I arched an eyebrow at her. "Keeping tabs on us is he?"

"Of course. We don't want one of you to get lost and run into trouble with the guardsmen."

I smiled tightly at that, and the three of us breezed out and down the corridor to the elevator we'd ridden up the night before. We went down to the lobby, walked past the model rockets on display, and out into the crunching snow.

The frigid air woke me up instantly. My nostrils flared with the cold, and a cloud of condensing moisture billowed from my lips. "Where's building four?" I asked, stuffing my hands into my jacket pockets and looking around the launch complex.

"Right over there," Richard said, pointing to a four-story structure with a big yellow 4 emblazoned on the side.

We walked past a massive hangar and dodged rumbling army trucks on our way across the snow-dusted asphalt.

A pair of guardsmen stood outside the doors of building four.

"State your business," one of them said as we

arrived.

"We're here to see Major Davis," I said. "It's for a follow-up appointment for my son, Alex. He got shot by illegals." I wondered if that was too much information.

"Scan your bands," the man said, blowing out a white cloud from a round hole in his black ski mask. He indicated a scanner beside the sliding glass doors.

As soon as we'd scanned our bands, the guard scanned his own and hit a button beside the doors. They swished open with a welcome blast of warm air.

We hurried through what might have once been a training facility for the Mars colonists. It had a medical feel to it, but it wasn't exactly a hospital.

We went to a desk labeled *reception,* and asked to see Major Davis.

"She's expecting you," the guardswoman behind the desk said. She got up and escorted us down a hallway lined with doors to an office with the major's name on it. She knocked once. "Major Davis?"

The door swung open and she ushered us in. The major shut the door behind us, and indicated a pair of chairs in front of her desk. "Please sit."

We let Alex take one of the chairs, while Richard took the other. I noticed that the office was a fair replica of a regular doctor's office, right down to the examination table—although this one wasn't lined with paper.

"You wanted to talk?" Major Davis began, arching an eyebrow at me.

I nodded and launched into a brief summary of our story—our stay with the pacifists, of what I'd overheard about Akron, and of the hidden Screecher city we'd seen on our side of the border. I was careful not to mention Haven, but I took no such care to hide OneZero's presence at the launch facility.

Major Davis listened quietly, making only brief comments for me to go on or to clarify something that I'd said. I finished by mentioning our suspicions that Unity's government might actually be commanded by Screechers.

When I was done talking, the major didn't say anything at all for a long while. Suddenly I feared that we'd misjudged her as *safe* to talk to. What if she was a Screecher, too?

"If everything you told me is true," she said slowly, "then we need to proceed very carefully."

I nodded, letting out a slow breath. "So you believe us."

"It would explain why the base commander allowed a civilian to come in and start calling all the shots."

"You mean Akron?"

"Yes. Starcast is Unity-run, and the Guard is in command. Akron has no claim to any authority here, and yet that's not how we've been treating him. The Guard gave his passband full clearance soon after he arrived, and now he's weighing in on everything from the next Mars mission, to where we should post guards for the president-general's visit tomorrow."

"The president is coming here *tomorrow?*"

Major Davis shrugged. "That's what I've heard. General Hall convinced him to come this morning."

"Why?" I asked.

"You tell me. You said you overheard Akron mention that they needed to see the president. Why do you think that is?"

I shook my head, then grimaced as a possibility occurred to me. "If the president-general isn't already a Screecher, they might be planning to turn him into one."

"I agree," the major said.

"Well, what can we do about it?" Richard asked.

— 403 —

Major Davis pulled open a drawer in her desk and withdrew a key. "I might have an idea. I was already working on it before you came along." Rolling her chair over to a nearby filing cabinet, she opened one of the drawers with the key and pulled out a cell phone with a cracked screen.

"What's that for?" I asked.

"You've never seen a cell phone before?" she asked, arching an eyebrow at me as she rolled back into place behind her desk."

"No, I mean—"

"It's a mobile passband scanner, with a twist— it can copy and decrypt the entire contents of a passband. If we can scan Akron's band—"

"We'll be rich," Alex said.

"We wouldn't be able to use the money without drawing attention to ourselves," the major replied. "But we can fake his credentials to access restricted parts of the base."

"You think they're hiding something here?" I asked.

"I know they are," Major Davis replied. "More than one of the elevators has lower levels on it that were added to the panels recently. I can't access those floors, but I've seen soldiers coming up with crates full of supplies bearing Unity's flaming eagle mascot. I've also seen strangers coming up from those floors—people I've never seen around base, all of them wearing shiny blue passbands. We've been told not to ask questions, and most of us just assumed that there are subterranean passages linking this facility to some other place. After what you told me about how you crossed the border and what you found on the other side, I think it's obvious where those passages lead. And if I'm right, then this base is steadily flooding our country with undercover enemy agents."

CHAPTER 52

"Undercover agents? For what? What are they planning?" Richard asked.

Major Davis placed a finger to her lips. "Get that scan of Akron's passband, and we'll find out."

I spent the next five minutes talking about Alex's episode last night. The major was about to refer us to the base psychiatrist when I stopped her.

"We don't know who we can trust," I said. "I'm not giving anyone access to my son's head unless I know for sure that they're human—Earth-human."

Major Davis's lips formed a grim line and she nodded. "I can prescribe some pills that might help." She glanced at Alex. "It's a common problem. Almost everyone in the Guard is suffering the same as you, myself included."

Alex smiled tightly, and the Major looked

away to dig through one of her desk drawers. She pulled out a prescription pad and scribbled a few different items on it. "The first one is for anxiety. Take it in the mornings. The other a sleeping pill; you take it an hour before bed."

PTSD seemed like the least of our problems right now, but I was grateful for the help.

"Ask Corporal Carter at reception for directions to the dispensary," she said as she handed us the prescription.

"Thank you," I replied.

"You're welcome. Take this, too." She got up and walked around her desk to hand the cell phone scanner to me. She showed me which application to use, and how to perform a scan. It was fairly straightforward, and I learned that the cell phone scanners all worked via RF id tags embedded in our passbands. To scan Akron's, I would have to get the cell phone within six inches of his passband and keep it there for several seconds.

"I suggest you sneak into his room while he's asleep."

I grimaced at that, remembering what else I'd overheard Akron and OneZero talking about. "They don't need to sleep."

"What? How do you know that?"

"Because I overheard Akron and OneZero talking about it."

"Then you're going to have to get creative."

"What if he catches us?" Richard asked.

"Then he might figure out what you're up to, and at that point they'll probably turn you into one of them, so don't get caught. And if you do, try not to sell me out, all right?"

I nodded to her. "We'll be careful."

"Good luck," Major Davis replied.

* * *

We left the medical facility in the middle of a snowstorm. Blinding curtains of snow and ice assaulted us, blasted off the runways and roads between buildings and launch pads. It was almost impossible to see where we were going, but eventually we made it back to our building.

We found the sliding glass doors locked from the inside, and no soldiers waiting to scan our bands. I rubbed my hands together and blew into them, trying to get the feeling back. I should have worn gloves.

Richard knocked loudly on the doors. "Hello!" he called, cupping his hands between his lips and the door to transmit the sound through it.

A soldier in full winter gear peeked into view, saw us, and opened the doors. Warm air gusted out as the doors trundled open. I tried to rush inside, but both soldiers stepped in front of me, blocking the way. "Passbands," one of them said, holding out a cell phone scanner. I presented my wrist and then waited for Richard and Alex to be scanned. "You're clear," the man said, and stepped aside. We rushed into the warmth of the lobby, rubbing our hands and blowing into them to warm them up. I couldn't feel my face, and my nose ran and itched maddeningly.

We passed the model rockets in the lobby and reached the elevators at the back. There we were confronted by yet another scanner. I hesitated, wondering if we had the necessary clearance to get back to our quarters.

"Who's going to do the honors?" Richard asked, pointing to the scanner.

Before I tried my passband, the doors parted, and a group of soldiers appeared. They wore heavy army green coats. One of them was decorated with plenty of medals, and three stars on each shoulder. A general? I wondered. When we didn't immediately give way before them, the man's ice-blue eyes found us, and he sneered.

"Civilians," he growled, as if the word were a

curse. "What is your function on this base?"

I shook my head. "None, sir..."

"*None?*" the man's eyes tightened. "You're not engineers?"

"No."

"Scientists of some kind?"

"No, sir."

"Then what are you doing here? This is a restricted facility. Guards!" he snapped his fingers, and the two soldiers standing inside the doors ran over. "General, sir!" they said in unison as they snapped to attention in front of him.

"What are these civilians doing on my base?"

So *this* was the base commander Major Davis had mentioned, the one who'd given Akron unrestricted access and inexplicably allowed him to take over a military operation. I wondered if the general was a Screecher and they were simply respecting an unknown ranking structure of their own.

"They are with Akron Massey, sir," one of the guards said.

"Akron Massey," the general mused. "See them to their quarters. We wouldn't want them getting lost. Trespassing is a crime, and we don't have the resources or space to harbor criminals, do we?"

"No, sir!"

I turned to watch as the general and his entourage glided by us in lockstep. The soldier standing beside us gestured to the open elevator while holding a hand on the pressure sensor inside the doors to keep them open. "Inside," he ordered.

We piled in and the soldier scanned his band outside the elevator before stepping in beside me. He punched the number *six* on the panel. I studied the panel, curious about the extra buttons the Major had mentioned. Sure enough there were three buttons at the bottom that were a different size and color from the rest, popping out of roughly-cut square holes in the panel. They were marked S1, S2, and S3.

Out of curiosity, I pressed one of them, but it refused to light up. The soldier standing beside me glared.

"What are you doing?" he demanded.

I shook my head and flashed an innocent smile. "What's down there?"

"None of your business. You heard the general. Trespassers will be executed."

My eyes widened at that. The general hadn't said we'd be *executed* for nosing around where we weren't supposed to, but that only served to reinforce my suspicions about who was really in

— 411 —

charge of this base.

Once we had a scan of Akron's band, we'd be able to find proof.

But once we had that proof, who were we going to tell?

CHAPTER 53

I was surprised to find that the door to our quarters opened when I passed my passband in front of the scanner. Akron must have linked our bands to the scanner already.

I opened the door and walked in. Our escort waited until we were all inside before reaching in and pulling the door shut behind us.

OneZero materialized from where she stood charging beside the door. "Are you feeling better, Alex?"

"No," he replied.

"He will be," I added, and withdrew a bottle of pills from one of my pockets for OneZero to see.

"Sure," Alex said, and started down the hallway to his room.

I debated chasing him, wondering if he might try to throw himself out a window again. "Richard, would you—"

"I'll keep an eye on him," he said, and hurried after my son.

"Where's Akron?" I asked OneZero.

"I am not sure," she replied.

"He hasn't come back at all?" I asked. As far as I knew he hadn't been back since he'd left Major Davis to stitch up Alex's arm.

"No."

"He's been out all night. Doesn't he need to sleep?" I asked, my heart beating suddenly faster as I probed dangerously close to the truth. But that was a perfectly reasonable question to ask. It would be more suspicious *not* to ask it.

"Perhaps he slept elsewhere," OneZero suggested. "Or perhaps he left the base."

"And went where?"

"I know as much as you do, Logan."

That was a pretty lie, but one she'd used before. I frowned and looked away, out the living room windows to the towering prototype rocket outside. I walked up to the windows for a better look, wondering if it was a coincidence that Akron had been planning to use the prototype to get to Mars when the new government was busy working on just that. It seemed like a strange goal at a time when Earth was in such turmoil. Send another rocket to Mars. For what? We already had a colony there. As a human agenda, it made little sense, but I'd overheard Akron and OneZero talking about getting Screecher agents on Mars. This had to be the Screechers' initiative, and if so, it was almost certain that they were the ones behind *Unity's* military dictatorship with its passbands and trigger-happy guardsmen.

Again, I wondered what we were supposed to do next. If America was utterly compromised and there was no way to tell good from bad anymore, then who could we count on for help? Russia? China? But they'd have their own problems, and for all I knew they could have been infiltrated to the same extent.

Only one answer jumped out at me, but it made my skin crawl to think about it. The so-called *Pacifist* Screechers were hiding in our territory for a reason. They were afraid of the ruling majority of their own people, the ones OneZero had called Supremacists. If we told *them* what was going on, about the underground cities and the tunnels beneath the border, surely they'd solve the problem for us.

I grimaced at the thought, remembering that the Screechers hiding on our side of the border provided our food and other rations. That one fact made up for a lot of evils. I had to be sure that

Unity's oppressive regime was actually run by Pacifist Screechers before I did anything as drastic as running to the Supremacists for help.

A door clicked open behind me and I turned to see Akron walk in.

"Where have you been?" I asked.

"Busy." He was still wearing yesterday's clothes.

"Hey, we need to talk," I said, following him as he went to the kitchen and filled a glass with water from the sink. He gulped it down, then wiped his mouth on his sleeve and regarded me with patiently raised eyebrows.

"About what?" Akron asked.

I walked to the other side of the island counter, and felt around for the cell phone in my pocket.

"I need to get back to Haven." It was true, and it sounded like something I would say under more normal circumstances.

Akron frowned. "And what do you expect me to do about it? Haven't I done enough to help you already?"

"You have, and I'm very grateful," I said, inching around the island.

Akron looked away, and I pulled out the cell phone, opened the app, and held my thumb over the scan button.

"I need to go shower," Akron said, already walking past me.

"Wait." I grabbed his arm. The cell phone in my hand was hidden in my palm, and turned away from him so he couldn't see the screen. I touched the button with my thumb, and brought my hand closer to his wrist. His eyes began sliding away from mine, but I brought them back with an angry sneer. "You're just going through the motions," I said.

Akron's eyes pinched into suspicious slits. "Excuse me?"

"You don't actually care. You're just doing what you think people expect of you so that you don't look bad. You want people to think well of you, and that's why you do the right thing. Not because you actually care."

"I don't have time for this, Logan." The phone in my hand vibrated lightly. I hoped that meant the scan was done. I let it fall back to my side, and let go of Akron's arm.

"That's what I thought," I said, nodding to myself as he hurried down the hallway to his room and slammed the door behind him.

I glanced down, turning the phone over in my hand. *Scan Complete* flashed steadily below the scan button. I couldn't believe I'd pulled it off so easily, and without anyone being the wiser.

"What are you looking at?" OneZero asked.

I looked up suddenly to find OneZero staring at me with a dim crimson light blinking inside her eyes. The island counter was between us, so she couldn't see the phone. I slipped it back into my pocket and shook my head. "Nothing, why?"

"You kept looking at your hands," OneZero said.

"Because I wanted to punch Akron in the face," I said, hoping that sounded like a reasonable excuse.

"I see."

With that, I turned and stalked down the hall after Akron. I stopped beside Alex's door, heard his and Richard's muffled voices, knocked once, and then walked in.

They were on the bed, talking, but both of them looked up suddenly as I came in.

"We're in the middle of something," Richard said.

Therapy? Maybe Alex had some things he wanted to say about me that he couldn't say to my face. "Whatever it is, it'll have to wait," I said. "We have to go back and talk to Major Davis. I've got the scan."

"Already?" Richard shot up from the bed. "Did

anyone see you?"

"No. Let's go."

"We need an excuse," Richard said.

"I've got an idea."

They followed me back to the front door.

OneZero's eyes tracked us there. "Where are you going, Logan?"

"They gave us the wrong pills," I said with an irritated sigh. "We'll be back."

"I see." She clomped over and turned the door handle, but it wouldn't open. "That is strange." She tried entering the key code I'd seen her use previously with the panel beside the door. An error beep sounded, followed by flashing red text: INVALID CODE. "That is strange," OneZero said.

Someone cleared their throat, and we turned to see Akron standing behind us, having somehow snuck up without us realizing it. "The general was not happy to find you wandering around his base," Akron said. "All nonessential personnel have been confined to quarters until the president's visit is over."

"I thought he's only coming tomorrow."

"He is, but we need to secure the area." Akron favored us with a thin smile. "I'm sure you understand there's a lot of people who disagree with how the President-General has been running things, so we need to be extra careful with security."

CHAPTER 54

I paced back and forth at the foot of Alex's bed, shaking my head. We'd spent more than twenty-four hours cooped up in our quarters, watching Akron come and go as he pleased while we were prisoners in all but name.

"I don't like this," I said.

"And we do?" Richard asked, watching me from the chair by the window. Lucky sat in his lap, licking her paws after a meal of re-hydrated tuna—or at least, that's what it looked like.

Alex sat in his bed eating the leftover spaghetti we'd cooked the night before. He'd slept straight through the night thanks to the pills Major Davis had prescribed. I was envious.

"How long is the president going to be here?" I wondered aloud.

"President-general," Alex corrected around a mouthful of crumbly noodles.

"Sit down," Richard said to me. "You're making me dizzy."

I heard the distant roar of truck engines and went to the window to see a convoy of military trucks streaming toward the entrance of the launch facility.

Richard twisted around to look. "That might be him leaving now."

I hoped so. Leaving the room, I stormed down the hall to check the front door, but it was still locked.

"What's your hurry to get out?" OneZero asked.

I turned to see a shimmering silhouette, all but invisible against the brightness of the living room windows.

I frowned at her. "My son is ill. He needs help, and we have the wrong pills," I said, using what was now a tired excuse.

"He's eating. He slept well. He does not appear to be in any type of distress."

"You wouldn't understand," I said, shaking my head irritably.

"Because I am not human."

"Exactly. You can probably just go into your

code and edit out depression and suicidal impulses. Us meat bags have to use more clumsy methods."

"My consciousness and thought processes were designed to perfectly mimic their biological origins. Were that not the case, my personality would have changed substantially when I became a machine."

"Maybe it did, and you just didn't notice."

The door opened behind me, and Akron entered. "Hello Logan," he said. "You're free to leave now. The president-general has left."

"Finally!" I strode down the hall to Alex's room. "Alex, Richard, it's time to go see the major!"

I opened the door to find Richard asleep in his chair. He started at the sound of the door opening, and blinked bleary eyes at me.

"Why don't you leave Richard here to rest?"

I jumped at the sound of Akron's voice and turned to see him standing behind me.

"Ah..." I faltered.

"He's obviously tired," Akron added. "How many people does it take to fill a prescription? You could leave Alex, too."

"No, no," I said quickly. "Alex needs to come. You were going to see that counselor for therapy today, right Alex?"

He nodded quietly.

Akron smiled tightly. "Well then the two of you can go while Richard stays here with me and catches up on his sleep."

Richard looked wide awake now, his eyes darting with panic. He'd probably just jumped to the same conclusion as I had: if Akron suspected we were up to something, he might be keeping Richard here as insurance.

"That's fine," I said, not wanting to make Akron any more suspicious.

"I'm kind of tired of being cooped up in here," Richard said. "I could use the opportunity to stretch my legs."

"Later," Akron replied. "If you're that awake, there's some things I need to discuss with you— about the trip to Mars. You're still planning to come, I assume?"

Richard nodded slowly, looking pale.

Alex got up from the bed with his dirty dishes, and I led him past Akron. "Excuse us," I said, pretending not to notice the desperate look Richard gave me as we left.

* * *

Alex and I watched from where we sat in front

of Major Davis's desk as she opened a closet full of medical supplies at the back of her office. She removed a stack of wooden tongue depressors and cotton gauze to reveal a wall safe. She tapped in the combination on a digital panel and withdrew three bright blue passbands from a pile of at least ten.

"Why not use the ones we're wearing?" I asked.

"Because I can't remove or alter them without setting off an alarm," she said. "These have all been rooted."

I nodded slowly, pretending to know what that meant. I wondered why she had so many passbands and where they'd come from. Ten of them. Who had she been planning to take with her on this illegal excursion? I asked about that while Major Davis plugged the cell phone with the scan data on it directly into her laptop.

"They're from deceased guardsmen," she said, while clicking with her mouse and tapping keys on her keyboard. "And I wasn't planning to take anyone until you showed up. The spare bands are there because I've been trying to find one that already has all the right clearances." The major looked up and our eyes met over the screen of her laptop. "Are you sure you want to come?" she asked. "If things go to shit, we're going to end up in front of a firing squad. Are you prepared for that possibility?"

I hesitated, considering the question carefully. Staying here with the Screechers' unknown agenda looming over us might not be any safer. What exactly were they keeping us around for, anyway? It wasn't as though Alex and I served any useful purpose. The only thing I could think was that they needed more human bodies to put their minds into.

"We need to see this," I said, shaking my head. "They turned Akron into a Screecher. We could be next."

The major nodded slowly and went back to work. I eyed the spare passbands on her desk. "Are we going to keep the spares in our pockets?"

"No, you're going to wear two."

I frowned. "Won't someone notice that? There'll be two tracking signals for one thing."

Major Davis looked up with a frown and pulled open a drawer in her desk. She removed a roll of aluminum foil and slid it toward me.

Alex grabbed the roll, already seeming to know what it was for. I watched him tear off a sheet and begin wrapping it carefully around his passband.

I remembered when we'd been trying to escape from the police that he'd said something about his gloves being lined with aluminum to block the GPS signals.

"It creates a Faraday cage," the major said.

Alex passed me the roll of foil and I hiked up the sleeve of my coat to wrap my band in foil as he had.

"No one will notice the tracking signals disappear, since they are too weak to get through buildings anyway."

"What about our vitals? I assume those must be tracked via cell phone networks or something similar. When our heart-rates suddenly stop reporting, won't someone come investigate?"

"Not at all. Can you imagine how over-burdened those networks would be if they had to report every single heartbeat? Life signs monitoring is confined to the bands themselves. When they detect a problem with your vitals, then they'll call the authorities, but the foil won't stop them from tracking your heart rate, so we shouldn't run into any problems."

"Okay, but if someone sees this..." I trailed off, realizing that the foil would give us away as potential criminals trying to hide our locations.

"Be sure that they don't," Major Davis said.

She grabbed the roll of foil from me and withdrew a sheet for herself, which she folded and slipped into one of her pockets. Then she picked up the cell phone scanner and aimed it at one of the spare passbands. She repeated that process twice more, and then nodded to herself. "Done."

"That's it? Don't you need to fill in some of our details? Like names and addresses?"

The major shook her head. "You don't want to use your details. Someone might realize that you're not actually soldiers. These bands are all from deceased guardsmen. The details are already filled in."

I frowned at that. "We don't look like guardsmen."

"Not yet," the major replied, rising from her chair and pocketing the passbands.

"Won't someone notice that the dead have come back to life?" Alex added.

"The system won't automatically flag their re-appearance as suspicious because I've erased the information about their deaths from their files. The only danger will be if a human scans you and recognizes one of those names, but fortunately, guardsmen don't go around scanning each other, and name tapes don't show under our flak jackets, so we shouldn't have a problem." The major looked to me, then glanced pointedly back at Alex. "Ready?"

I nodded quickly.

Major Davis stepped around her desk, heading for the door. "Follow me. If anyone stops to ask us questions, you let me do the talking."

CHAPTER 55

We did run into a few people asking questions along the way, but they were mostly medical questions about other patients in the hospital.

Major Davis led us into a large storage room filled with metal shelves and boxes of army uniforms. The room looked like it might have been an office at some point, if the desk and the old computer monitor sitting between boxes of uniforms were anything to go by. Right now it was some kind of dumping ground for army—Guard, I corrected myself—surplus.

The major shut and locked the door behind us. Walking over to one of the shelving units, she withdrew a large box with army fatigues draped over the sides and then asked us our sizes.

"Thirty-six waist. Large shirt," I said.

"Thirty-two, medium," Alex added.

She rifled through the boxes and threw the

tops and bottoms of army uniforms our way. We sorted through them and hurried to get changed. Next came shiny black boots, ski masks, gloves, jackets, flak jackets, equipment belts, radios, unit patches, and flaming eagle arm patches where the US flag should have gone.

"What about guns?" Alex asked once we were fully dressed.

The major stood there with her arms crossed, regarding us with a deep frown.

Alex went on, "Soldiers have guns, right? How are we supposed to look the part without them?"

She shook her head. "We're not going out on patrol. You don't need guns. And getting weapons for you is not that simple. It will raise too many questions." The major reached into her pockets, withdrawing the cell phone scanner and the three passbands. She checked each band with the scanner before deciding which one to hand to each of us. "Pull your sleeves down over your bands and clip these *over* your sleeves."

Alex pulled his sleeve down and clipped on his secondary passband. I did the same thing, but the sleeve kept trying to ride up and reveal the foil-wrapped band underneath. I pulled my glove up to cover both bands and my sleeve hoping I wouldn't need to scan my fake band anywhere.

"If we're not going outside, why do we need to wear masks?" Alex asked.

Major Davis arched an eyebrow at him. "So no one recognizes your face? Enough questions. From now on the only thing either of you know how to say is *yes, sir, or ma'am.* And you say it with a salute if we're outside. Try it."

Alex straightened slightly and brought his hand to his forehead in a mocking salute. "Yes, sir."

"If you can't do better than that, I'm leaving you in this closet."

"Alex," I said in a warning tone. "Like this." I snapped to attention and saluted quickly, trying to copy what I'd seen in old war movies.

The major blew out a breath and shook her head, as if we were a lost cause. "Forget it. You're both staying here."

"Hey—we risked our lives to get that scan for you!"

Major Davis glanced sharply at the door and then fixed me with a cold look. "Shut up. You want to come?"

I nodded once.

"Then you do exactly as I say. Fall in behind me as we leave this room. We're going straight to my quarters on the second level. I'm going to change into my combat uniform, and then we're going to take the nearest elevator down to a restricted floor and see what we can find."

The major turned on her heel and opened the door. "Fall in, soldiers," she said in a loud voice as a pair of guardsmen strolled by wearing ski masks and heavy packs, and carrying assault rifles. One of them glanced our way as we walked out of the storage room. His eyes narrowed and his gaze lingered. I looked away quickly, as if I had no idea what he was staring at. In reality, I rattled around inside my uniform. Every inch of it itched against my skin, and I feared that my overgrown beard and long hair were somehow showing through my ski mask.

We came to a bank of elevators, and the major scanned her band to open the doors. Once inside, she punched the 2 on the panel, and we rode up to another hallway, this one lined with what I guessed to be officers' quarters.

Major Davis led us to her room and told us to wait outside. I didn't like that idea, but the hallway was busy with passing officers in scrubs and uniforms with bright red crosses on the sleeves, and I guessed that she'd have a hard time explaining to her colleagues why two enlisted soldiers had followed her into her room in the middle of the day.

Alex and I stood to either side of the door with our backs to the wall, eyes dead ahead, and our hands clasped behind our backs—even though my shoulder screamed in protest.

The major emerged just a few minutes later, dressed exactly like us, including the ski mask, but with the difference that her uniform had a medical badge in place of our unit badges, and she had a sidearm strapped to her waist.

I remembered to come to attention as she turned to me. "Major," I said.

She nodded, and started back toward the elevators we'd ridden up a moment ago. She scanned her passband and we stepped inside. We all stared at the panel, our eyes locked on the three *S* floors at the bottom. Raggedly-cut square openings framed each button. They'd obviously been recently added, and in a hurry.

Major Davis tentatively touched the lowermost floor, *S3.*

But nothing happened.

"What's wrong?" I whispered.

Major Davis slowly shook her head, then suddenly stopped and nodded to the open doors, as if something had just occurred to her. "Scan your bands," she said.

I walked out with Alex and we scanned our bands one after another. As we stepped back in, Major Davis tried the button once more. This time it lit up and the doors immediately began sliding shut.

A pair of officers in regular service uniforms approached the elevator. "Hold the doors," one of them said, and planted a hand inside the doors to open them. I noticed that the light under our floor went dark as the doors parted for them, erasing our selection from the panel.

The two officers crowded in with us. One of them hit the *1* and it lit up. They glanced at us, appeared to take fresh notice of Major Davis, and then came to attention. "Major Davis, Ma'am," they said in quick succession.

"At ease," she said as the elevator dropped down to the first floor.

"Going out on patrol?" one of them asked, obviously noticing our ski masks.

"Need to know," Major Davis replied.

"Of course."

The doors parted and the two men walked out. Major Davis led us out, and waited for the men to pass out of sight before swiping her passband at the scanner and indicating for us to do the same. We went back into the elevator and she hit *S3* again.

The doors slid shut, and this time no one interrupted us. The elevator jolted into motion, falling swiftly. Lights flashed around the seams in the doors as we passed each floor. How many sublevels were there? I had a feeling that *S3* was a deceptive marking. By the time I felt the elevator slowing to a stop, we must have flashed by at least twenty levels. I looked to Major Davis. The skin around her eyes was tensed into a knot of confusion and worry. Alex wore a similar look on his face. Neither of them knew what to expect as the elevator doors parted, but I did.

Our elevator opened and we stepped out into the bustling green garden of a Screecher city.

* * *

A familiar ring-shaped building ran around a central spire which was distantly visible through the trees. A bright blue sky soared overhead, a perfect replica of the real thing. A haze of the buzzing, cicada-sized assemblers scurried against that sky. Looking around the gardens themselves, I couldn't see any sign of mechanical Screechers, or for that matter, any other race besides humans. All of them were wearing guardsmen's uniforms like us. A few of them glanced our way as we stepped out of the elevator and stood gawking at the city.

I grabbed Major Davis's arm, and she flinched, tearing her eyes away from the sky.

"We need to blend in," I whispered and nodded to Alex. He nodded back, and then I took the lead, heading for one of the doors in the base of the ring-shaped building. I didn't know where we were going, but thankfully none of the doors bore passband scanners.

We traveled down a curving, window-lined corridor that ran along the base of the building and came to another set of elevators, the Screecher version. I punched the call button with an up-facing triangle on it. It glowed with a soft light and we waited for the doors to open. Again, I was struck by the lack of passband scanners. Apparently the Screechers focused all of their security measures on the points of entry and after that they didn't see the need to restrict access.

One of four elevators opened for us—Empty, thank God. We rushed in just as another elevator was opening beside us. I punched a random floor to get the doors to close. As they slid shut, I caught a glimpse of a highly-decorated officer. I could have sworn I'd seen stars on his shoulders. Was it the general we'd run into yesterday?

It was hard to say, but even if it wasn't, what were the chances that he didn't know there was a Screecher city lurking below his base? If he was the one who'd given Akron his all-access clearance, then he had to have equivalent or even higher-level access himself.

"Where are we going?" Major Davis asked.

I shook my head. "What?" Then I remembered that I'd hit a random floor. The symbols on the panel were not familiar numbers; they bore the Screechers' binary language of horizontal and vertical lines.

The elevator slowed to a stop, and I picked another floor—near the bottom of the panel. I remembered that the other Screecher cities had all of the interesting things hidden below them. The doors parted to reveal a busy corridor. This time it was filled with Screecher-humans wearing the loosely-woven green and brown clothes I'd seen before. Standing in the elevator, sweating through my heavy layers, I willed the doors to slide shut. A pair of too-perfect humans walked in before the doors closed—a man and a woman, both blond-haired and blue-eyed. They stared at us, and I nodded back.

"Are you lost?" the woman asked.

"Pressed the wrong button by accident,

ma'am," I said.

"I see..." She leaned around me to press another button on the panel, and the doors slid shut, sealing us in with these two Screechers. "You don't have to call me, ma'am," the woman said. "There aren't any natives around, and I'm not in uniform—at least not yet." The woman's lips twisted in a sneer, as if it were a disgrace to serve in the Guard. Maybe it was. It wasn't the United States Army, that was for sure. "How's progress coming on the surface? Are we ready to go to Mars yet?"

"Not yet, no."

"Hmmm," she replied, as if disappointed but not surprised. "I suppose we can't move too quickly if we want to avoid attracting attention to ourselves."

I nodded agreeably with that. The elevator slowed once more and opened into a sterile white corridor that I recognized from my brief visit to a Screecher bio factory. The two Screechers walked out. I turned to the major and pointed to the open doors. "We should get out here," I said in a low voice.

Major Davis and Alex followed me out. I wanted to go snooping around, but the major grabbed my arm and pulled me back. "We need to leave before someone realizes we're not supposed to be here."

"We don't have proof of anything yet," I replied, shaking my head.

"There's an alien city hidden under the base," Major Davis replied. "That seems like nothing to you?"

I glanced around to make sure no one was listening in. The corridor was deserted, and the two Screechers who'd ridden down the elevator with us had already passed out of earshot.

"Before I came here, I was told that our government had agreed to harbor Screechers in exchange for their help. This city isn't surprising or damning evidence."

"What are you hoping to find?" the major said.

"I don't know yet. Something. And this is where we're going to find it. I can smell it."

"Well, it smells like shit," Alex said.

I smiled, remembering my reaction to the smell when I first stepped into a bio factory with OneZero. "Come on." I led the way. We walked past countless doors with glowing symbols on them, more elevators, and then rounded a bend at the end of the corridor.

Here was something different: a big circular metal door with the two halves slowly sliding shut.

I glimpsed the pair of Screecher-humans from the elevator standing on the other side, speaking to someone else in a large chamber filled with shining blue rows of liquid-filled tanks. I remembered seeing tanks like those before, filled with biological creatures. Suspicion seeped through me like ice. I stepped up to the doors, hoping they'd open automatically, but they remained shut.

"Dad..." Alex trailed off as I hunted around for some way to open the doors. "Are you sure this is a good idea?"

"We need to go," Major Davis added.

I looked back to see her standing with a hand on her sidearm, ready for trouble.

I shook my head. Turning back to the doors, I continued searching for some way to open them.

A moment later I got my wish. The doors parted, and the woman we'd been speaking to in the elevator stood there with her hand on her hips.

"This is a restricted area," she said. "You'd better have a good reason for being here."

I swallowed thickly, scrambling for an excuse. Then I noticed what was in the tanks in the chamber on the other side of these doors.

They were humans: fully grown adults curled into fetal positions and naked as newborns, with umbilical cords trailing from their belly buttons.

This was where they grew the bodies to house the consciousness of mechanical Screechers. I struggled to come up with a reasonable excuse for being here, but before I said anything, Major Davis drew her gun and aimed at the Screecher woman's head.

"Show us what you're doing here," she demanded. "Or I'm going to make you wish you'd stayed a robot."

CHAPTER 56

The blond man hurried over to this woman's side. He raised his hands in a placating gesture and put himself between the woman and Major Davis. I got the impression that these two were a couple.

"You're natives," the woman said, stepping around her partner.

"Ding ding ding," Major Davis said. "Let us in."

"You don't understand. We're trying to help you."

"By replacing us?" Major Davis demanded. "I saw the soldiers walking around here. I've seen them coming out of elevators on the surface. You've infiltrated us by the thousands, and you're busy growing more."

"Did you think our assistance comes without a price?" the woman asked. "You allow us to live in your midst, and we help your government meet the needs of its people."

I smirked. "Yeah, and when you find someone with the right amount of power or wealth to be useful to you, you steal their body and put one of your people inside."

The woman's brow furrowed. "You know about that?"

I smiled grimly behind my mask. "So you admit it."

"Yes, but it's not that simple."

"Sounds pretty damn simple to me," I replied.

"Is the President-General one of you?" Major Davis asked.

These two Screechers glanced at one another, and I noticed people scurrying around in the chambers behind them. We couldn't afford to stand around here and chat any longer. We needed to get out before it was too late.

"Well? Answer the damned question!" Major Davis said, shaking her gun.

"Yes, he is one of us," the woman replied.

"So you're the ones who decided that it would be a good idea to execute illegals? You killed my family!"

"Your family?" the woman echoed.

"Listen," the man said, holding up his hands again. But that was as far as he got. The major's gun went off with a *bang* and a spreading crimson stain appeared on the woman's forehead.

The man standing beside her yelled something I couldn't hear through the ringing in my ears, and then another bang sounded and a second bullet punched a hole in his chest. The two Screechers collapsed in each other's arms, gurgling blood. I gaped at the sight, frozen in shock. Major Davis stepped into the room as the doors were closing, and I heard more gunshots.

"Davis!" I called, taking half a step to follow her, but the doors slammed shut, cutting us off. "What the hell is she thinking?"

"Dad!" Alex said, just as a droning alarm began shrieking in the corridor. "We have to get out of here!"

I nodded woodenly, and turned away from the doors. My legs shaking hard, I turned and ran with Alex back the way we'd come.

* * *

We made it back to the elevators and rode them up to what I guessed and hoped was the first floor. It wasn't. The doors opened into a corridor lined with doors that might have been apartments or living quarters. There weren't any ski-masked soldiers here, and that made me feel dangerously out of place. With my heart slamming in my chest, I hit another button on the panel, the highest button I could find. The doors slid shut once more and I leaned back against the side of the elevator. I felt dizzy with shock and a mounting dread that we were about to be captured and killed—or worse, *replaced.*

We were trapped underground in a Screecher city, fugitives in connection with Major Davis's killing spree. Somehow I'd missed the fact that she had an ulterior motive for nosing around down here. She'd seemed so calm and collected. She'd never mentioned anything about deceased family members, or the system that had killed them. She hadn't started shooting until that Screecher had admitted they were behind the brutal totalitarian regime that was Unity.

I tried to imagine what I'd do in her shoes if my entire family had been executed by the Guard at the behest of a military dictator who was actually an alien. I probably wouldn't have done things much differently.

The elevator opened once more, and we stepped out into a massive hangar, but instead of being filled with parts of an interplanetary rocket, it was crowded with soldiers in ski-masks and rolling lines of vehicles. Thick clouds of assemblers buzzed between the half-finished skeletons of snow-colored tanks and large trucks. There were soldiers waiting in orderly lines to climb into freshly-minted white and gray camo-painted trucks that looked just like armored Humvees. I noticed shielded gunner positions in the top of some of them, others with normal roofs. As each truck filled up, it sped off with a throaty roar and disappeared through the bright square of a distant exit. Multiple lines of vehicles converged on the exit, and I found myself wondering how we'd missed seeing a constant influx of military vehicles and soldiers at the launch facility.

"What's going on here?" I whispered.

"It looks like an invasion," Alex replied, nodding to the orderly lines of soldiers. More were streaming out all around us. I turned to see at least a dozen elevators spaced out along the length of the hangar. Those elevators periodically belched out soldiers in matching camo uniforms and black ski masks. Unlike us, however, they were all armed to the teeth with assault rifles, sidearms, extra pouches of ammo, grenades, and heavy-looking packs of gear. They were perfect copies of real army soldiers—*guardsmen,* I amended, noting the flaming eagles on their upper right shoulders where the American flag should have been.

"We'd better join them," Alex whispered to me.

I nodded stiffly and fell in behind the others. Suddenly Major Davis's shooting spree seemed both more justified and more foolish than before. What could any one person do to stop this? Kill a few Screechers and they'd just pop up again somewhere else with new faces and new bodies.

We were in the middle of a second invasion. The Screechers might be providing rations, but at what cost? They were zookeepers feeding a species that they knew was just about to become extinct. It was an illusion of kindness that was utterly overshadowed by the terrible truth: the Screechers didn't just want the warm, habitable parts of the world; and the wall wasn't to keep *us* out, it was now serving to divide political segments of their own population.

Screw them, I thought, scowling behind my mask. They probably thought there was nothing we could do to stop this, but I could think of at least one way. There was a reason they were hiding among us and it wasn't because they were scared of what we could do to them. An old adage sprang to mind, and I smiled grimly, savoring every word of it: *the enemy of my enemy is my friend.*

CHAPTER 57

We neared the front of the shuffling line, and I saw more ski-masked soldiers up ahead handing out unit patches. I ripped mine off and reached around to strip off Alex's patch as well.

We reached the front of the line and a soldier handed us new patches. He hesitated before ushering us into the back seats of a waiting Humvee. "Where are your weapons?" the man asked.

I hesitated.

"I asked you a question, soldier!"

I snapped to attention and saluted. "We lost them, sir."

"How—never mind. He snapped his fingers and raised a hand to get someone else's attention. I turned to see a man with a captain's insignia and no ski mask stride over. "Is there a problem, Lieutenant?" he asked.

"Yes, sir," he said, saluting briskly. "These men lost their weapons."

"How?" the captain demanded, glaring at me with glittering green eyes.

I risked a lie. "We were sent to the bio factory for treatment following an ambush by hostile forces. Our weapons were lost in that engagement, stolen by illegals."

"This line is for fresh recruits, not veterans. Where is your squad?"

"Dead, sir," I replied.

"Then you're here for reassignment."

"Yes, sir."

"Very well. He turned to the pair of soldiers waiting behind us. You two—give them your weapons and go to the back of the line."

Alex and I accepted their assault rifles, ammo belts, and sidearms. It took me too long to fasten the ammo belt and holster the sidearm, and I felt sure that the captain was staring at me.

As soon as we were finished, I looked up. The captain had left, but the lieutenant whose job it was to pass out the unit patches and assign vehicles was frowning deeply behind his ski mask. "I suppose you lost your rucks, too," he said.

I nodded, not knowing what he meant.

The lieutenant made a guttural noise. "Get in.

You'll have to gear up after the op."

Alex and I piled into the back seat of the truck. The door slammed, and the driver hit the gas, slamming us against our seats before we could even look for seat belts. The truck raced up a steep ramp and roared out of the hangar into broad daylight that glared blindingly off pristine fields of snow. Where was the launch facility? I turned to look behind me and saw the towering Mars rocket soaring above a dense line of trees. The only sign of the hangar we'd emerged from was a rounded, snow-covered hill. The roof? I wondered.

"Names?" the driver asked.

Panic stabbed through me. I didn't know what our assumed identities were. Could we afford to use our real ones? What if we were scanned?

Alex spoke before I could: "I go by Shredder."

"Shredder," the driver snorted.

I wracked my brain for a good nickname. Seeing all the snow along the road outside gave me inspiration. "I'm Frostbite."

"Nice," the man in the passenger's seat said.

"That's DC Kane," the driver said, nodding sideways to the man beside him. "And I'm Sergeant Waters."

I nodded at him, my eyes glued to the procession of vehicles rolling out ahead of us. I wasn't going to let these Screechers with their human names and mannerisms get to me. They were more authentic than the stiff, plastic-faced models I'd seen South of the border, but I couldn't let that fool me. Maybe they looked and sounded so real because they'd stolen actual soldiers' bodies.

The thought gave me a chill. I wondered if it was safe to ask questions. How much was I supposed to know? I'd been reassigned, according to my own cover story, so maybe that gave me some leeway.

"What's our assignment?" I asked.

Sergeant Waters glanced at me in the rear-view mirror, his eyes pinched in bemusement. "Same as always," he replied.

"Right," I said, nodding. Alex shot me a worried look. How long could we keep this up before they realized we didn't belong?

I tightened my grip on my rifle, my finger twitching toward the trigger. We could shoot these two impostors and take over their vehicle, but we were in the middle of a convoy. It would be too dangerous.

"What unit were you with?" Sergeant Waters suddenly asked. "I heard you mention you got sent up for reassignment after your squad was taken out."

"Yeah... you wouldn't have heard of them," I said, hoping to leave it there.

"I might surprise you."

My mind raced to come up with an answer; then I remembered the unit patches I'd stripped off our uniforms. I reached into my pocket for one of them, and held it up to the rear-view mirror. It looked like a yin-yang symbol, black and gray.

"The 29th infantry," the sergeant said, nodding slowly. "What is it they call you guys? The blues and..." His eyes found mine in the rear-view mirror, and I froze.

"You don't *know?*" he asked, suspicion dripping from every syllable.

"Fuck this," Alex muttered, drawing his recently-borrowed Beretta and pressing it against the driver's head in one smooth motion. He pulled back on the slide, chambering a round.

DC Kane twisted around in the passenger's seat, and my own sidearm flew out of its holster as if it had a mind of its own. I pulled back on the slide of mine, and flicked off the safety with my thumb. "Hands up," I said. Kane slowly raised his hands above his head.

"You're natives," Sergeant Waters said.

"Good guess," Alex replied.

"What do you want?" he asked.

"Keep driving," I said. "Pretend nothing is wrong. As soon as you find a road going South, you take it."

"The division commander will want to know why we're breaking off."

"He's right," Alex said.

"Maybe so, but they won't fire on us immediately," I replied. "They'll wait for a reasonable explanation, and by then we'll have a head start."

"A head start for *what?*" Sergeant Waters asked.

"Just shut up and drive," I snapped.

CHAPTER 58

The convoy joined Highway 55, headed South toward West Memphis making my instructions redundant for the moment.

"You don't have to do this," Sergeant Waters said. "We're on your side."

"Did I say you could talk?" Alex asked. "Just shut up and drive."

I nodded along with that. We couldn't trust anything these Screechers said, especially now that we had guns to their heads. This wasn't how I'd planned to deal with things, but hopefully we'd be able to get to the Screechers' border without getting killed along the way. I remembered how desperate Richard had been to come along. If he could see us now, he'd be grateful he stayed behind.

The highway branched up ahead, and then branched again. I peered at the street signs, trying to decide which way we should go. Signs pointed left for West Memphis. If we went that way we could end up stuck on the bridge into Memphis. We'd be out of options at that point. "Keep right," I snapped, even as the sergeant began veering left. "Did you hear me, Screecher? You want a bullet in your brain?"

The sergeant sighed and turned right, looping down onto Highway 63. The convoy went in both directions, so I hoped that meant we wouldn't get any awkward questions about our choice.

After about ten minutes the highway curved right, and I began to recognize where we were. This was the same route we'd fled down with the Hartfords after accidentally abducting Akron from Starcast. I knew exactly where we had to go next. Up ahead there'd be a truck stop at the intersection of this highway and a north-south bearing road that would take us straight to the border. Moments later I saw a green sign—EXIT 271—with an arrow curving to the right and the number 147 to indicate the highway it would join. "Take that exit," I said.

I heard a click, and caught a glimpse of a Beretta coming into line with my son. I pulled the trigger of my own sidearm and a deafening bang thundered through the truck. DC Kane slumped in his seat, his neck gushing blood.

I winced and looked away. The driver swerved dangerously.

"Keep your shit together!" Alex warned. "Or you're next."

By some miracle none of the vehicles trailing behind or in front of us seemed to notice the gunshot. I breathed out a shaky sigh. "Turn right!" I ordered just as we came to EXIT 271.

Sergeant Waters did as he was told, but this time none of the vehicles ahead of us were taking that exit. I glanced back as we left highway sixty-three. No one followed us. I wondered if that was a good thing or a bad thing.

Then one Humvee veered after us, followed by another, and then two more. "Drive faster," I ordered.

"Where are we going?" the sergeant asked, applying steady pressure to the gas.

"None of your business," I snapped, glancing back to see the vehicles chasing us catching up.

Turning back to the front, I saw that our one-lane exit curved under a bridge up ahead. The road forked and black signs with 147 on them appeared, half-buried in snowdrifts, pointing left and right—South and North I assumed. We were going too fast to read them, but I already knew the way. "Turn left."

Sergeant Waters did as he was told and we went under the bridge. I both heard and saw the rest of the convoy rumbling over the bridge as we looped under. Now we were heading due south on a snow-covered road. There were tire tracks everywhere, and the snow was packed so thick it was impossible to see the asphalt. Apparently southbound highways weren't a priority for plowing. No surprise there, given how close we were to the Screechers' border. I began to feel the Humvee swerving and fishtailing in the snow, and I wondered if the sergeant was trying to lose control on purpose.

"You're not going to get away with this," he said, and began throwing the wheel to one side. I lunged forward and grabbed it. He grabbed my gun, and it went off with a deafening noise, burying itself in his side window and turning it opaque.

Alex fired next, and hot blood splashed my ski-mask. The sergeant's head slumped to one side, and I grimaced, struggling to keep the tires straight. The sergeant's foot slipped off the gas and we bled off speed fast.

"Dad! They're gaining on us!"

Glancing back, I tossed my Beretta on the floor at DC Kane's feet, and reached over the sergeant's lap for the door handle. Popping his door open, I unbuckled his seatbelt and pushed as hard as I could with my left hand, while still keeping my right on the wheel. The sergeant's body toppled out, guns and all. The Humvee skipped over him like a speed bump, slamming my head into the roof. I crawled into the driver's seat and hit the gas just as a stuttering hail of bullets came roaring into the rear window, turning it into a frosted wall that I could no longer see through. Alex ducked reflexively, and I buckled up. At least the glass was bulletproof.

Then came the thump, thump, thumping of heavier weapons. Snow began exploding on the road around us.

"Shit!" Alex screamed, just as the back window exploded. I swerved, and began fishtailing on purpose to present a moving target. Looking in the rear-view I saw a gunner and the barrel of a fifty cal peeping at us from the gun turret of an armored Humvee about fifty meters back. "Alex! Take out the gunner!"

He popped his head out and aimed over the back seat with his assault rifle. Moments later I heard him open fire. The .50 cal kept firing. I heard a crunch as a bullet tore through our armor. The empty seat beside Alex exploded with a burst of yellow stuffing. *So much for bulletproof.* I kept swerving, trying to throw their aim. A metallic *clink* cut through the ringing in my ears, and my son threw something out the back. The trucks behind us swerved as they slammed on the brakes. One of them veered off, crashing into a snow bank. The other three sailed on, attempting a more controlled stop. A thunderous explosion erupted from the road in front of the lead vehicle. It leapt up, and flipped on its side with flames gushing out of its windows. The truck behind it with the gun turret at the top slammed right into it, and the last one glanced off. Alex fired steadily at it until it rolled to a stop in the snow.

"I hit a tire!" Alex crowed. "How's that for shooting?"

I glanced in the rear-view mirror as he turned around, grinning broadly, the skin around his eyes splattered with blood. Suddenly I felt sick. My hands and legs began to shake. We'd become cold-blooded killers in the span of just a few minutes.

No, I realized, glancing at Alex once more, and remembering what he'd said about being forced to kill innocent people. My son had already been turned into a killer.

I remembered that the Screechers were ultimately to blame for that. They'd passed the law that made illegals fair game for anyone with a gun; they were to blame for the gang who'd been blackmailing my son, and they'd forced him to become a killer who would rather die than live with his guilt.

With that I stopped shaking. My own guilt and shock evaporated in a flash of anger. The Screechers deserved what they'd got, and they deserved what I was about to do even more.

CHAPTER 59

The Screechers' border came into view long before we reached it. I was somewhat surprised that no jet fighters came roaring after us, but I supposed that our air force had probably been wiped out during the initial invasion. Whatever planes we had left were probably grounded for lack of fuel, trained pilots, ground crew, or all of the above.

"Are you sure about this?" Alex asked. "You're going to speak with the monsters who deported millions from their homes. They might kill us this time."

"Not when they hear what we have to say," I said. "Besides, what other choice do we have?"

"We could run away..."

"Where?" I replied. "We're criminals now."

"Yeah, but they're tracking the wrong passbands, and no one's seen our faces. We cut off the secondary bands, strip out of these clothes—"

"And into what? We didn't bring spare clothes."

"So we scavenge some. Or steal them. I've gotten pretty good at that."

"That's not something to be proud of."

We came within a hundred feet of the Screechers' wall, and I slowed to a crawl, peering over the steering wheel for a better look. The wall was sleek and smooth, gleaming silver, and at least three stories high. Screecher discs leapt off the top of it, hovering before us in a threatening posture.

I stopped the truck. We were about fifty feet away now.

"Alex," I said, catching his eyes in the rear-view mirror. "Stay here."

He laughed and popped his door open.

"Alex!"

I jumped out after him, shaking my head. "Ditch your guns," I ordered.

"Are you kidding?"

"You don't want to walk up to that wall looking like a threat."

Alex scowled and shrugged off his rifle. He laid it down in the back of the truck alongside his sidearm.

"The grenades, too," I said, already removing

my belt. We laid both of our ammo belts on the floor of the truck and began walking toward the border wall with our hands up. The tire-packed snow ended, and we had to trudge through pristine, waist-high drifts that got progressively deeper as we approached the base of the wall. When the snow reached our chests, we were stuck.

"I can't," Alex said, breathing hard.

I stared up at the wall. The Screecher discs hadn't moved or tried to shoot, but I knew that they were watching us. I waved my arms signaling to them. "Hey! We have something important to tell you!"

Those hovering aircraft didn't even twitch.

"They probably can't hear you," Alex said. "Even if they can, I doubt they understand English."

I tried again, screaming at the top of my lungs. "Hey! Screechers! We know where your enemies are hiding! The ones who call themselves pacifists!"

Still, nothing happened. "Maybe you should throw a rock," Alex quipped.

I glared at him.

"Just a thought," he said, shrugging.

Before I could reply, a flicker of movement caught my eye, and one of the discs zipped down.

Gusts of icy wind from its rotors staggered us as the craft hovered overhead. A moment later articulated metal arms shot out and snatched us out of the snow. I cried out as long metal fingers squeezed painfully tight around my arms and chest, lifting me high above the ground like some kind of nightmarish carnival ride. Alex struggled and screamed beside me, kicking his feet. A landing ramp yawned open like a mouth ready to eat us; then the arms swept us in. "Looks like you got your wish!" Alex said as we were dumped roughly on the deck inside the disc. I began pushing myself up, but a metal hand grabbed me by one arm and yanked me to my feet.

I found myself face to face with a humanoid-model Screecher. A dim light flickered in its eyes.

"What do you know about our enemies?" it demanded in a cold voice.

I didn't have time to be shocked or pleasantly surprised that this Screecher spoke English. "They're hiding among us," I explained. "North of the border. They have underground cities. They've taken over our military and our government."

The cold, stinging vice around my arm slowly released its grip, and the humanoid robot before me canted its head to one side.

"How do you know this?"

"'Cause we saw it," Alex put in.

The flickering light in the Screecher's black eyes slid away to focus on my son. "Saw what?"

Eager to take those unsettling eyes off Alex, I spoke next. "Fully-grown human adults in glass tanks deep underground. They admitted that they're running our government, and we saw thousands of soldiers being churned out and sent all around the country. We barely escaped with our lives."

"And you came here. To tell us. Why?"

"Because if this keeps up, soon there won't be any of us native humans left. And they're already running everything, so there's no one we can tell on our side of the border. They're hiding from *you*," I said. "That must mean they're plotting against your people somehow. We thought you might be able to help us stop them before they wipe us out—not because you care what happens to us, but because you might care about whatever the hell they're up to."

"Yes... but how do I know that you are telling the truth?"

A frown wrinkled my brow. "Why would I be lying?"

"I don't know, but you'll regret it if you are."

With that, the Screecher's arm came into line

with my chest. Some kind of weapon unfolded. *Plip.* A sharp pain erupted in my chest, and I saw a dart protruding from it. A thick fog swirled into my head, and my whole body grew pleasantly warm and numb. *Plip.*

"Shit!" Alex screamed, but he sounded impossibly far away. The Screecher must have shot him, too. That was my last thought before I fell over and blacked out on the deck.

CHAPTER 60

Darkness swirled around me, and then came a racing swirl of faces, shapes, and colors. I heard Kate screaming my name, Rachel crying. Flickers and flashes of the six months we'd spent in Haven paraded by, interrupted only by the shrill binary voices of Screechers and their clanking footsteps.

My body felt heavy and numb. I tried to move, but found that I was paralyzed. The racing images behind my eyelids slowed, and I saw familiar events replaying with stunning clarity—

OneZero rescuing us and taking us to the pacifists' city... our stay there, my walk through the gardens, the conversation I'd overheard between Akron and OneZero, and every other major event until now.

Darkness returned, and stretched infinitely around me. Screeching voices grew faint, and then...

I blinked blurry eyes open to see a blinding white sky. The scratchy fabric of a ski-mask clung to my face. Cold snow pressed against my back and arms, and the heavy weight of a flak jacket pressed down on my chest.

The dreamy haze inside my head cleared, and I sat up quickly. Alex lay at my feet, our stolen Army truck some ten feet away to my right. The doors were open, the engine off.

"Alex!" I called out in a cracking whisper of a voice. "Wake up!" I tried again, my voice stronger now.

He sat up with a groan, seemed to notice where we were, and then twisted around to look at me. "What happened, I saw..." He trailed off, shuddered, and shook his head.

"They looked inside our heads," I said, realizing what had happened at the same time as I said it. What memories had he been forced to watch replay? That explained the shudder.

"Motherfuckers!"

"Language," I snapped.

"Seriously?" Alex asked. "That's what you're worried about."

My gaze strayed to the truck. "We need to get out of here," I replied, changing the topic. Now wasn't the time to turn my son back into a normal teenager.

"And go where?" Alex asked. "We're criminals, remember?"

"You mentioned stealing clothes. No one saw our faces. They don't *know* that we're criminals."

"*Now* you want to listen to me? Isn't it a little late for that?"

"We had to tell them," I argued. "You'd rather have left our country in the hands of rebel Screechers? The same ones who went around slaughtering illegals, forcing a group of them to hide and hold you hostage in a basement?"

Alex's eyes tightened behind his mask, as if angry at the reminder. "Let's go," he said and stood up quickly.

We found our guns right where we'd left them, lying under a dusting of snow that had blown in through the open doors and the missing rear window. The keys were still in the ignition, and Corporal DC Kane's frozen corpse still sat in the passenger's seat.

"Help me get him out," I said.

Alex and I struggled to drag the dead Screecher out. His limbs were stiff as a mannequin's from rigor mortis and the cold.

When finished, Alex and I both recovered our weapons and ammo. Alex kept both of the rifles with him in the passenger's seat while I got behind the wheel. I looked at the key and prayed the engine would start. Diesel engines don't play well with cold weather. Holding my breath, I turned the key—

And the truck started instantly. Something was definitely wrong, however. Instead of the throaty roar I remembered hearing from before, I heard a muffled, sputtering version of it that hissed and crackled like a damaged speaker.

"What..." I shook my head, searching for the source of that sound.

Alex found it before I did, brushing snow off a bar of speakers behind the dash.

"It's not diesel," I realized. "Of course, it isn't. Why would they use a fuel source that probably ran dry long ago?"

"But why go to the trouble of making it sound like a Diesel engine?" Alex asked.

"And why make these vehicles look like Humvees in the first place? Maybe to avoid awkward questions about where they came from. They're trying to blend in, remember?"

I threw the vehicle into reverse, spun the tires in the snow, and got stuck up against a snow drift on the side of the road.

"Nice job," Alex said.

"Hang on..." Hunting around, I figured out how to put it into four-wheel drive and we roared off the way we'd come. As we went, driving down the center of the two-lane highway, I turned my mind to the problem of finding civilian clothes and blending in. My thoughts went to Richard, stuck back at Starcast. I cursed under my breath. We couldn't leave him there, but how could we go back and get him? By now news of Major Davis's actions would have spread, and OneZero knew we'd been on our way to see her. It wouldn't be hard to piece things together from there. Rescuing Richard would have to wait. Maybe he wouldn't get into any trouble. He could pretend to know nothing about our schemes. If he was lucky he wouldn't get turned into a Screecher immediately.

It was getting dark. How long had we'd spent in the Screecher' custody?

A pair of snow-covered wrecks swelled in the distance, almost blocking the road. They were the vehicles Alex had taken out with his grenade.

I slowed down to squeeze past them. The truck that had rolled onto its side was a charred skeleton with several actual skeletons inside, while the one that had crashed into it was partly crumpled in the front, but otherwise intact, and the seats were all empty. The other vehicles that had been chasing us were gone, which meant they'd reported back with an account of our escape.

"Looks like they changed the flat tire I gave them," Alex said.

It surprised me that soldiers hadn't come back to retrieve our stolen vehicle, but maybe they thought the Screechers guarding the border would shoot them if they tried. My thoughts stopped cold as we crested a low rise and came face-to-face with a military blockade.

"Dad..." Alex trailed off.

"I see it." My mind spun, searching for some way out, but there wasn't one. We were still only a few miles from the border wall, and we hadn't passed any side streets along the way—at least none that were plowed. The Guard had set up their blockade where it was sure to stop us if we tried driving back. I hit the brakes, and we came to a grinding halt in the packed, powder-covered snow.

My heart leapt hard in my chest, and then seemed to freeze. I winced, trying to massage away a sudden pain that made it hard to breathe. A heart attack? Heartburn, more likely. Somehow I doubted I was going to get off that easy.

We were cornered. Multiple rifles and .50 cals glared at us from the open doors and roofs of Humvees.

"Dad, what are we going to do?"

A thunderous voice answered for us: "Get out of the vehicle with your hands up! You have five seconds to comply."

CHAPTER 61

Our hands were cuffed behind our backs and we were roughly shoved into the back of another Humvee. The man in the passenger's seat was none other than the captain that I'd briefly seen in the hangar where the Screechers were mobilizing their army. This time I took more time to study his appearance. It seemed only right that I could look my judge and executioner in the eye. His face was lined and wrinkled, covered in old freckles. His hair was a buzz-cut silver, eyes pale blue and full of ancient wisdom—a far cry from the plastic-faced movie-star-gorgeous Screechers I'd seen South of the border. This man was a very convincing human.

The man in the driver's seat was much younger than the captain, and far better looking. Was it possible that the captain was a colluding human and the young man beside him was the

Screecher?

"What did you tell them?" the captain demanded, twisting around to glare at us.

"Tell who?" I asked. Maybe we could play dumb.

"The Supremacists. The aliens south of the border. We watched you enter one of their aircraft."

I frowned behind my mask. "We didn't tell them anything," I lied. "They knocked us out with tranquilizers and the next thing I knew we were waking up in the snow outside their wall."

"They performed a mind scan on them," the young man in the driver's seat said. "Whatever these two know, now our enemies know it too."

"Shit," the captain muttered.

"What are you going to do with us?" I asked.

"If it were up to me, I'd shoot you both in the head," the captain said.

"Then you're going to turn us into Screechers like Akron Massey."

"No."

"You're going to let us go?" Alex quipped, smiling crookedly. I turned to glare at him. How could he joke at a time like this?

"Oh no, you bastards aren't going anywhere."

"You're the ones mass-murdering people and

churning out more soldiers so you can do it faster, and we're the bastards?" Alex asked.

The captain snorted and shook his head. "You two are so damn clueless."

My brow furrowed, and I shook my head. "How about you enlighten us, then?"

The captain muttered something under his breath. "Unity was responsible for killing all those people," he said.

"And President-General Nelson is a Screecher," I replied. "One of you admitted it."

"I'm no Screecher," the captain replied. "And they prefer to be called Collectivists. As for whatever you were told, that might have been true, but it depends on when you asked."

I shook my head. "What does that matter?"

"The collectivists only replaced the president-general when he came to see our progress at the launch facility yesterday."

"No..." If that was true, then they weren't behind Unity or any of its associated atrocities.

"That's right. And all those soldiers you saw shipping out? They're to ensure that the coup goes smoothly. We were planning to bring back a democracy and do away with the passbands, but we'll be lucky just to survive now, thanks to you."

"You're lying," I insisted.

"You didn't even bother to check your facts before you betrayed us, did you?" The captain glanced over his shoulder, his pale eyes flashing darkly at me, lips drawn in a bloodless line. He looked away, shaking his head. "You two really are a couple of morons."

I was speechless. This was a lie; it had to be—a clever cover story to trick us. How could I have made such a critical mistake?

OneZero had lied to us, and Akron *was* a Screecher. I'd overheard them talking about it. And then there was Major Davis. Something wasn't adding up.

"Major Davis outranked you, but she didn't know any of this," I said. "How is that possible?"

"Because she wasn't really a major, and she was a recent transfer so no one trusted her with high-level clearance."

"What? But she—"

"Stole the passband and uniform of a dead soldier and faked the transfer papers that assigned her to Starcast. She was a computer hacker, and a very good one at that."

"But she treated my son for a gunshot wound!"

"Yeah? Maybe you should have looked a little closer. I bet he's got a few too many stitches."

Alex and I traded disbelieving looks. Night

was falling quickly now, bright stars pricking through the clouds in hundreds of places. Hundreds...

I stared hard at those lights. They weren't twinkling, and they were too bright, too large, too evenly spaced.

The captain was leaning over the steering wheel, peering up at the sky. "Looks like we're out of time," he said. "They've begun their attack."

No sooner had he finished saying that, than a bright explosion flashed on the horizon. For a brief second, the towering Mars rocket stood out against the darkening sky, and then it fell over, bursting into flames.

What have I done?

CHAPTER 62

"Change of plans," the captain said. "Turn around!"

The officer in the driver's seat hit the brakes and swung the wheel around in a brisk U-turn. The procession of Humvees behind us followed through the turn, and we roared back down the highway, heading west.

"Where are we going?" I asked.

"Shut up," the captain replied.

I twisted around to look behind us. Several of the Humvees following had .50 cals on top with gunners peeking out. Explosions flashed steadily on the horizon in the direction of West Memphis and downtown Memphis. My stomach turned with each flash of light. How many people were dying now because of my stupidity? Thousands? Tens of thousands? How many would die before it ended? Millions? The Screechers weren't taking the time to hunt down individual rebels; they were sterilizing everything north of the border.

I'd been so sure that we were harboring the real enemy. How could I have known that these so-called pacifists were planning to replace our tyrannical president-general and that they were churning out human soldiers for a coup? There was still the matter of Akron. Why had the Pacifists turned an innocent man into one of them? They weren't blameless in all of this.

We drove on for at least half an hour, passing through snow-covered fields, blissfully unmolested by Screechers. The explosions flashing behind us vanished into the night, replaced by an ominous red-gold glow that had nothing to do with city lights. I felt ill. I kept hoping I'd blink and wake up back at Starcast with Lucky curled up and sleeping on the pillow beside me.

Lucky. Tears sprang to my eyes as I remembered her. The Screechers had bombed Starcast; she had to be dead by now. And Richard... I couldn't bring myself to finish that thought. Maybe Akron and OneZero had seen the Screechers coming and fled down the elevators to the hidden city below the launch facility.

But even if they had, the Supremacists had looked into our heads, so they knew the underground city was there, and that meant it wouldn't be safe for long.

"They're getting closer," the captain said.

I twisted around to look. Sure enough, bright lights were dancing between the stars, growing steadily larger. The headlights of Humvees following us lit up this entire stretch of road, making us an easy target to spot.

"They need to turn off their headlights!" I said urgently.

"Too late for that," the captain replied.

All of a sudden one of the trucks behind us burst into flames and veered off the road into a snow drift. The gunners in the other vehicles opened fire, high-caliber rounds flashing and thumping out into the night. Another Humvee burst into flames and veered off, the doors flying open and flaming soldiers jumping out.

"They're holding back out of range and shooting us with high-powered lasers," the officer in the driver's seat said.

"Shit," the captain replied.

Another Humvee burst into flames, but this time it didn't veer away, and the ones around it were forced to swerve to avoid a collision.

"Come on..." the captain said. "Almost there."

Another truck exploded, and then another.

Flaming wrecks littered the road behind us, receding quickly into the distance. Darkness stretched like a rubber band between us and the flaming wreckage. We were the last vehicle on the road.

Panic built in my chest; then a stifling wash of heat radiated through the roof.

"Bail out!" the driver said as he stomped on the brakes. Alex and I slammed into the seats in front of us. I heard the captain and the officer throw their doors open and dive out of the moving vehicle.

"Get out!" I yelled to Alex even as I twisted around and struggled with my cuffed hands to reach the door handle. My clothes began to smoke, and my skin blistered. My fingernails scraped furrows into the lining of the door as I strained to reach the handle....

One finger curled around something. I yanked as hard as I could and threw my weight against the door. Blissfully cold air enveloped me. Hard asphalt slammed into my hip and uninjured left shoulder. My teeth clacked together, and I went rolling down the street like a log. The muffled *boom* of an explosion pounded on my eardrums, and then came a flash of heat, and I caught a glimpse of our truck rolling down the street with flames leaping from broken windows. *Alex!* Did he make it out? I hadn't seen him jump clear.

I stopped rolling, and then all was silent and dark. Sharp pains erupted all over my body, but I pushed myself up with a groan. "Alex!"

I heard an approaching roar, then saw a pair of Screecher discs glowing bright against the night. At that, my son sat up, too, and I breathed a quick sigh. But my relief didn't last. Those approaching disc-craft weren't veering off.

"Get down!" I flattened myself to the road, playing dead and hoping to God that it would work.

I heard the captain and the other officer shouting, followed by a stuttering roar of bullets, screams... and then the thunder of Screecher discs flying closely overhead and receding into the distance. I waited ten full seconds before I risked looking up. The flickering crimson glow of our burning vehicle illuminated the street enough to see my son sitting up and watching those aircraft dwindle to a pair of shining specks that quickly got lost among the stars.

Alex stood up, and I went next, grateful that we were both still able to walk. My son limped over to me, his breath clouding the air between us in ragged gasps. He was wincing and standing at an odd angle.

"Is anything broken?" I asked.

"Stitched ripped open, I think," he replied. "It can wait. We need to get under cover." He nodded to the trees that the captain had been running for. "Over there."

I nodded back and we hurried in that direction, running awkwardly with our hands cuffed. We kept checking over our shoulders and looking around to make sure no more Screechers were approaching, but the distant stuttering of weapons fire and the occasional boom of an explosion were the only signs of their invasion.

"This is all my fault," I said.

"No. OneZero should have explained. Besides, they turned Akron into one of them, right? That hardly makes them the good guys. If anything they're all bad guys and we're stuck in the middle of their war."

"Maybe," I replied. "But I'm responsible for kick-starting it."

"It would have happened sooner or later," Alex replied. "They couldn't have stayed hidden for long. Why do you think they were busy raising an army?"

"The captain mentioned a coup," I replied.

"Bullshit," Alex said. "I'll believe their good

intentions when I see them."

As we drew near to the trees, a moaning sound drew my attention to a dark mound lying in a glistening puddle on the road. "One of them is still alive!" I rushed to the man's side and saw that it was the captain. "I need help," he gasped. "My leg..."

I looked down. His left leg was missing below the knee. I paled at the sight of how much blood was still trickling out. I cast about for something to tie on as a tourniquet, but found nothing.

Dropping down beside the captain, he pushed himself up until his face was just inches from mine. He seemed to be struggling to say something.

"Dad!" Alex said, and then raced up and kicked a Beretta out of the captain's hand just as it went off.

The captain made an inarticulate noise, and then slumped back down to the street, cackling like an old witch.

My eyes darted to Alex, checking him over. "Are you okay?"

"I'm fine," he breathed. "But you need to be more careful." Turning back to the captain, he said. "Keys!"

I nodded. We had to get our cuffs off.

"Forget it."

Alex kicked him in the ribs, and he groaned. "You're dead anyway. We all are!" the captain said.

"We'll see about that," Alex replied. "Watch him," he said to me.

I nodded and lightly placed a boot on the captain's head. He sneered at me, but his eyes were glassy and his breathing shallow. The fight was leaving him in a hurry. Alex dropped to his haunches beside the captain's equipment belt and fumbled around blindly. After a moment, I heard a jangle of keys, and saw Alex struggling to open his cuffs. A few seconds later he cracked them open and flung them away. Rubbing his wrists, he went to recover the captain's gun and then came stalking back. "Step away," he said to me, already aiming the gun at the captain's head.

"Alex, don't," I said, but withdrew my boot from the captain's forehead.

"Where were you trying to get to?" Alex asked.

"There's another city," the captain replied in a hoarse whisper. "Through the forest. A hidden... elevator."

Recollection shot through me like lightning and I looked up at the shadowy line of trees ahead of us. This had to be the forest we'd emerged from with OneZero and Akron. If we found that city, maybe we could catch up with Richard and the others—assuming they'd escaped. If nothing else, OneZero owed us an explanation, but we might also be able to join the war and help make amends for our mistake.

"A hidden city..." Alex mused. "I guess that makes sense. You're probably hoping we'll be stupid enough to go there."

"Fuck you," the captain spat.

Alex pulled the trigger and the captain's head thumped against the road, a bubbling crimson eye staring at us from his forehead while his real eyes slid away.

"Back at you," Alex said.

I stared open-mouthed at him as he holstered the weapon. "You didn't have to kill him!" I hissed, trying to yell and whisper at the same time.

"He was already dead. I did him a favor. Come on. Let's go."

CHAPTER 63

We stole the captain's equipment, and went hunting for the other officer to take his gear, too, but we couldn't find him anywhere.

"You think he lived?" I asked.

"Maybe," Alex replied. "If he did, he's on his way to that city."

"We should go there, too," I said.

"Are you crazy?" Alex demanded. "That's suicide! These guys all want us dead."

"They won't know that it was us. Not with our masks on, and besides, I think they're going to be pretty distracted right now, don't you?"

"Again, why would we go there?" Alex asked.

"Because OneZero might be there, and she owes us an explanation. And because nowhere is safe right now. At least down there we might be able to help in some way, or figure out where to retreat."

Alex snorted. "You want to join the losing side of a war?"

"If we caused it, then yes. We owe that much."

"What about Mom, and Rachel?"

I slumped at the reminder. "They're safe in Haven," I replied.

"I meant what happens if we go and get ourselves killed? They'll never see us again."

"That's a given anyway," I responded. "There's no way back, Alex. Even if we had a submarine, there's no way we could get to it safely in the middle of a war, and we can't risk being followed back to Haven."

"Then let's run and hide until the smoke clears. Forget the war. We need to find a way to stay alive."

"If that's what you want to do, I won't try to stop you," I said. "But I'm not going to run from this while thousands of innocent people are dying because of my mistake."

"How noble of you," Alex replied.

"Goodbye, Alex. I love you, son."

With that, I strode by him, headed for the trees. He caught up a few seconds later, muttering and cursing under his breath.

"Where are you going?" I asked.

"Someone's got to watch your back. Mom

would kill me if I let you get killed."

I smiled ruefully at that. "Yes, she probably would." But that was a weak excuse, and we both knew it. She'd sooner 'kill' him for risking his life alongside mine, but we both had our share of atoning to do, and there was no running from that.

We reached the trees and walked down a road until we came to the parking lot I'd walked through with OneZero, Akron and the others just a few days prior. Our old footsteps were gone, buried under fresh layers of snow, but on the other side of the parking lot I found a familiar sign that read VILLAGE CREEK STATE PARK, and I knew we were in the right place.

We waded through a foot of snow, following what used to be a trail through the forest. As soon as we reached the hulking shadows of the trees, I drew a flashlight from the equipment we'd stolen from the captain, and flicked it on. A bright white beam of light chased away the shadows and exposed footprints receding into the forest.

"Some people went this way already," Alex said.

"Yeah..." I trailed off, tracking my flashlight up to the forest canopy. The solid blanket of snow-draped branches spiraled above our heads. I smiled grimly at that and nodded to my son. "I know how to find the elevator the captain was talking about."

"How's that?"

"Follow our footprints."

"*Our* footprints?"

"Not yours. *Ours.*" I pointed the flashlight at the ground. Here, sheltered by the tree canopy, the falling snow hadn't broken through to cover our old footprints yet. All we had to do was follow them.

* * *

We waded through frozen fields of the dead as we followed the trail of footprints through the forest. I tried not to meet their staring eyes or see their black, frost-bitten faces, but we needed the flashlight to see where we were going, and the bodies were everywhere.

"They were massacred...." Alex said. Even he sounded shocked.

"Yeah," I replied. "Maybe this was one of the places where they dumped the bodies after the slaughter ended."

"A mass grave," Alex replied.

We walked on in silence. After just a few minutes we came to the end of the trail of footprints. They disappeared abruptly, seeming to have teleported here, but I knew what that meant. I walked up to that point and felt around an invisible wall with numb, frozen hands. My gloves were too thick to give me much feedback, so I pulled one of them off with my teeth and felt around again. Cold metal seared my skin and my hand stuck fast.

"Shit!" I wrenched my arm, ripping off my skin and biting back a scream. Alex came over and joined me, but didn't make the mistake of taking off his gloves. I put mine back on, wincing at the glistening the sheen of blood welling on my palm.

We looked like a pair of mimes standing there, running our hands along invisible walls. The building was a simple box protruding from the forest floor. There weren't any switches or panels. "I don't get it," I said, shaking my head. "There has to be a way to open it."

"Are you sure about that?" Alex asked. "Why would they want people to be able to get in from here? That would be a security risk. After all the trouble they went to securing the elevators at Starcast?" Alex shook his head. "It doesn't make sense."

I kept feeling around for the next few minutes. Tired, and overwhelmed by the pain of my skinned hand, I slid down an invisible wall and sat in the snow.

Alex sat beside me.

"Now what?" he asked.

Maybe he was right. Maybe we should just run and hide.

"We should get a fire going," Alex said.

"With what?"

He opened a compartment on his equipment belt and withdrew a pack of matches.

"And what fuel?" I gestured to the snow-covered forest. Nothing was going to be dry enough to burn. Not without a decent accelerant, anyway.

Before Alex could elaborate further, a noise sounded behind us, from *inside* the elevator shaft, and then the doors we were leaning against abruptly parted and we fell over backward.

I lay squinting up at a familiar robot face. Two blazingly bright eyes shone down on us like flashlights. "Logan," the robot said. The voice was familiar, too.

"OneZero?" I asked.

She reached down, dragging us inside, and the lights shining from her eyes vanished, plunging the elevator into darkness.

CHAPTER 64

The elevator rocketed down into darkness. Gone were the flashing lights of passing floors, and when we emerged inside of the ring-shaped outer structure, I saw that the once majestic gardens with their colorful green and blue lights were ablaze with leaping orange flames. I gaped silently at the devastation below.

"You ruined everything, Logan," OneZero said quietly. "They're invading again, and this time everyone is going to die."

I rounded on her and jabbed a finger at her chest. "What about you? Why didn't you tell us what was going on?"

"Why didn't you ask?" she countered.

I didn't have a reply ready for that.

"If you learned something, you could have come to me and I would have told you the truth."

"Or turned me into one of you like you did

with Akron?" I asked.

"What do you mean?"

"I heard you two talking that night we spent in your people's city. You turned Akron into one of you."

"That's what this is about? Logan! I told you, if the venom went to Akron's brain, it would kill him. We were too late to save him, so we replaced him with one of us."

"And then you lied about it," I said, nodding quickly. "Why?"

"I wanted to tell you, but the Overseer feared you'd react badly and expose us." She made a sound like an electronic sigh and shook her head.

"Do you have any idea what you've done? Thanks to you and the Overseer we're all going to die!"

"I am sorry, Logan. I will do whatever I can to make this right. But I am not the only one to blame. You should have known better than to tell the supremacists about us."

"Yeah, there's plenty of guilt to go around, isn't there? What about the sub? You drilled holes in it so that you could force us to go through Screecher territory, and then you lied and said that it wasn't you."

"Because it *wasn't* me, Logan. The mayor must

have done that to keep Haven's location a secret."

"So you say. How can I trust anything that comes out of your speakers?"

"Why would I lie about that now—or anything? There is nothing to fear from telling you the truth."

I snorted and shook my head. "Well, it's a little late for the truth, isn't it?"

OneZero said nothing to that. Disgusted, I turned back to the curving glass wall of the elevator to see where we were. We'd dropped past the gardens, and now we were falling through deeper chambers—illuminated tanks filled with human bodies, vats of colorful liquids that were likely part of the Screechers' food-printing industry—and then I felt the elevator slowing. We came to a stop and the doors opened, revealing a darkened tunnel with a train waiting. "Come," OneZero said, hooking one of her arms through each of ours. "There isn't much time."

I dragged my heels as we approached the train. "Where are we going?"

"Away. The farther you can get from the border, the safer you'll be. At least for a time."

"We should go to Canada," Alex said.

"That is not a bad idea," OneZero replied.

I could see people seated inside of the train as

we approached. The doors swished open for us, and people looked up as we stepped in. Richard sat beside Akron with Lucky perched on his lap. My brother-in-law's brow furrowed and Akron frowned. Then I remembered we were wearing masks. I pulled mine off, and Richard's eyes widened in surprise.

"Logan! You're alive!" he said. "And... Alex?"

My son nodded, but kept his mask on.

Akron scowled, his upper lip curling with disgust and his eyes flicking to OneZero. "You should have shot them."

"This is not all their fault," OneZero replied, dragging us deeper into the train. "If you and the Overseer had listened to me and allowed me to tell them our plans, none of this would have happened."

I nodded and scowled back at Akron.

"How were we supposed to know that they'd go running to the very people who invaded them for help?" Akron replied. "But no, you're right, I should have realized what kind of fools we were dealing with."

"Well, it doesn't matter now," OneZero replied. "It's over. We lost."

I shook my head, refusing to accept that. "There has to be something we can do. We have to fight back!"

Akron barked a laugh. "There's thousands of them for every one of us! They're better armed, and better prepared. We were hiding for a reason, you know."

I stood there blinking at him, realization dawning. "That's why you wanted to get people on Mars. For the same reason we did. You wanted to hedge your bets."

Akron favored me with a sarcastic smile. "Well, now you get to keep the red planet all to yourselves. Good luck living there without our technology to keep you alive in a frozen, radiation-soaked desert."

A distant explosion rumbled through the train, rattling windows, and OneZero glanced back the way we'd come.

"It's time to go," she said. "Sit down."

I watched as she turned and walked back to the doors.

"You're not coming?" I asked, following her there.

She slowly shook her head, stepping out into the tunnel. "I will stay and fight." OneZero's hand came up, and she began to wave. "Goodbye, Logan."

The doors began sliding shut, but I thrust out

an arm. They squeezed painfully hard, then released, and I stepped out.

"Dad!" Alex said, taking my place at the entrance of the train. "What are you doing?"

"I'm going to fight, too," I said to OneZero.

"Not on your own you're not," Alex replied.

I turned and planted a hand on my son's chest just as he was stepping off the train. He stumbled as I pushed him back. "With a limp and a bad arm? You're in no shape to do anything. Stay with your uncle. I love you, Alex. Try to remember how to be a kid, okay?"

"But—" the doors began sliding shut once more.

"And feed my cat!" I yelled just as the doors slammed between us.

"We're not going to survive this, Logan," OneZero said quietly as the train shot away with a sudden gust of wind.

I turned back to her, my lips pressed into a grim line, and nodded. "I know."

CHAPTER 65

OneZero led me down a steel gray corridor. The lights flickered in time to the muffled thumps of explosions elsewhere in the city. After a few minutes I realized we were the only ones down there.

"I thought we were going to join the fight," I said.

"We are."

We came to a reinforced door and OneZero stopped. The door slid open for her, and we went through into a circular chamber full of computer screens and equipment. Metal tables festooned with clamps stood at forty-five-degree angles, arrayed in a semi-circle before us. OneZero turned to me and gestured to one of the tables.

Suspicion crawled into my gut once more. "What is this place?"

"It's a transfer room. Here we transfer minds

to biological bodies and back."

My suspicion turned to horror, and I started backing toward the exit. "No."

OneZero just looked at me. "You said you wanted to join the fight. This is the fight. It's our only hope."

I backed straight into the door, but it didn't open for me. Slowly shaking my head, I said, "Maybe you'd better explain."

"We have several prisoners, deactivated in another room."

"Robots."

OneZero inclined her head to that. "Humanoid models like me. A few of them have been engineered to be undercover agents with a secondary layer of consciousness that is set to take over after a specified condition has been met."

"Sleeper agents."

"That is a good description, yes," OneZero replied.

"You want me to become a Screecher?"

"You will not notice the transition."

"How can you simply *transfer* consciousness? Won't I die in the process?"

"No, you will not die, but the mission will likely kill us both."

"What's the mission?"

"To infiltrate a Supremacist city and infect the hive mind with a virus that will spread through its neural network to all of the other cities."

"What will it do?"

"It will compromise antimatter containment systems, resulting in the catastrophic destruction of every city in the network."

"How many are in the network?" I asked.

"All of them."

"On this continent?"

"No, on this planet. By now all of the cities will be networked, but that means even our cities will have to be destroyed."

"Your people will die, too?"

"They will die either way," OneZero said.

"Isn't there some way to warn them?"

"Not without warning the Supremacists, too. If our hive-nodes had a defense against the virus it would automatically be propagated to all of the others. The network was designed that way to prevent an uprising. After all, who would want to defeat their enemy only to destroy themselves in the process?"

"What will you gain from that?" I asked.

"The ones who are running away and who have already integrated with your people on the surface will escape."

"And what about the Supremacists still living on your homeworld? Won't they come here for revenge?"

"Remember, the ones who stayed are the ones who have no interest in becoming biological lifeforms. They will not invade Earth, because its habitability holds no specific benefit for mechanical lifeforms."

"So if this works, we'll be safe. Your people and mine."

"Yes—if it works."

"Why do you need me?" I asked.

"You wanted to help, and I do not know if I can do this on my own. I need someone to create a distraction while I transfer the virus."

I slowly walked back to OneZero. "All right. Let's do it."

She pointed to one of the metal tables. I leaned back against the cold surface, and she strapped me in. I glared suspiciously at the clamps as they closed around my wrists and ankles.

"Do not worry. This will not hurt," OneZero said, walking over to a nearby console.

"If it's not going to hurt, then why restrain my limbs?"

A bright light snapped on over my head, and I squinted, watching as a dome-shaped helmet filled with gleaming black eyes began dropping toward me.

The table tilted back slightly, and the helmet changed shape as it settled over my head; then a needle pricked my neck, and I began to worry.

"What was that?"

"Don't be afraid."

I expected to fall asleep, but the opposite happened: my brain felt as though it were filled with a bright light, or as if I'd just drunk ten cups of coffee. My muscles tensed, and I gritted my teeth as my thoughts raced. Something cold slid into my veins, and time seemed to slow right down.

"What are you doing to me," I said slowly, hearing my voice as if from a great distance.

"If everything works as it should, when you wake up you'll have been activated in your new body. Meet me at the hive in the center of the city, and be careful to avoid discovery."

I wanted to ask questions, but I couldn't frame my thoughts properly. I was falling away from my own eyes into darkness, peering through ever-lengthening tunnels. The bright lights of the room dwindled to pinpricks, and then vanished altogether, taking my awareness with them.

CHAPTER 66

What seemed like an instant later, I awoke in a completely different place, standing on a balcony on the outer circumference of one of the Screecher cities. This one perched at the top of a high, snow-covered mountain. Looking down, I saw thin threads of clouds, and an endless blanket of snow, broken here and there by the soaring spires of more Screecher cities. I couldn't begin to guess where I was.

Lifting my arms and hands in front of my face, I saw that they were metal. Whirring sounds accompanied my movements. I rubbed my hands together and was surprised to find that I could still *feel*. Reaching out, I probed my torso with a skinny metal index finger. It wasn't soft and yielding like a human stomach, but I could still feel the touch. Turning to look behind me, I saw a luxurious apartment. Did this belong to the Screecher whose body I'd stolen? I walked up to a wall of glass and stepped through an open door. The air, inside and out, was equally freezing, but the cold didn't bother me. It was a sensation that I could recognize and perceive, but not one that compelled an urgent need to find warmth. Standing inside the apartment, I looked around. Familiar furniture and decorations adorned the space: couches, chairs, rugs... strange paintings on the walls—even a kitchen, but I couldn't imagine what purpose it would serve for a robot. Maybe these Screechers were still waiting to become humans.

Clanking footsteps approached, and a humanoid robot stepped into view, emerging from a hallway to one side of the living room. It issued a binary screech that I could actually understand.

"Are you feeling better?" The tone and tenor of the voice made me think this robot was female like OneZero, though I wasn't sure how I could tell when their entire language was made up of high-pitched shrieks.

Words froze inside of me; my mind raced. Was this my wife? Friend? Daughter? What was her name? I had no way of knowing any of that, and I couldn't reply in English without giving myself away. But maybe OneZero had given me the knowledge I needed to speak their language.

"Is something wrong?" the stranger pressed.

If I'd still had a heart, it would have been pounding. *"No,"* I tried in a soft voice. The sound that emerged from my speakers was a binary shriek. I sighed with an electronic hiss.

"You seem strange," the woman said. *"Did they do something to you while you were their prisoner?"*

"No. I need to go for a walk. In the gardens," I replied. *"To clear my head."*

"That's a nice idea. I'll go with you."

"Alone," I added.

"Oh."

I had to get out of here before I gave myself away.

"I'll be back soon," I added, heading for the door.

The woman said nothing; she watched me go, her head cocked slightly to one side, as if trying to figure me out.

The door opened automatically for me and warm air gusted by. Our apartment wasn't heated because we weren't biological, but as I stepped into the hallway I saw that plenty of others were. The too-perfect, plastic-faced humans I remembered were walking in and out of rooms on both sides of a long, curving hallway. I joined the flow of people, walking fast and searching for the nearest elevator. OneZero had told me to meet her at the hive mind in the center of the city. I hoped she was already waiting there.

As I went, the occasional Stalker crept along on four legs. Each wore a harness with a bobbing, ball-shaped black eye above their fore shoulders, and a folding set of six mechanical arms. Female Stalkers had a highly-evolved intelligence trapped in the body of a simple beast. They were forced to rely on mechanical augmentations to see and touch the world around them. I could relate to that, trapped in the body of an advanced machine that somehow encapsulated all of who and what I'd once been. What had happened to my human body? Had OneZero disposed of it, or had she just left it lying there strapped to the table? Had my heart stopped after my consciousness left?

The entire process raised so many existential questions that it made my head spin, but I didn't have time to answer any of them.

Coming to a group of four elevators, I focused on them. One opened as I approached, and two Stalkers padded out. I stepped aside to let them past, and both of them turned long snouts toward me, snorting through broad slits where a dog's eyes would have been. Their cone-shaped ears perked up and rotated toward me. Both hesitated as they walked by, as if they could tell that I wasn't a normal Screecher.

Then I remembered that their social order placed them below me. I made an irritated noise and said, "Watch where you're going."

They howled softly and skittered away, their tails lashing the air.

Once inside the elevator, I struggled to figure out how to get to the ground floor, but as I thought about it, the doors slid shut, and the elevator dropped swiftly away. Moments later it emerged racing down the outer wall of the city. The transparent, rounded back wall of the elevator gave me a stunning view. Icy cliffs fell away to either side; snow-covered fields sprawled out below. A hazy snowstorm cloaked the horizon like a curtain, but I counted at least three cities within a ten-mile radius. If that level of density held true throughout the Screechers' territory, then there had to be billions of them sharing the planet with us.

The elevator came to a sudden stop and the doors opened. A binary representation of the floor number appeared above the doors—a single horizontal line. I found that I knew what that meant: this was the first floor. Had the elevator somehow read my mind to determine where I was headed?

That thought unsettled me. I hoped the city couldn't read other things—like who I was and why I was here.

I hurried out and down a long corridor filled with ambling machines, biological humans, Stalkers, and Skylings. The corridor branched and curved a few times, forcing me to guess which way to go.

Eventually, I came to a pair of glass doors with leafy green plants on the other side. The doors opened for me as I stepped through, and the familiar sights and sounds of a Screecher garden greeted me. Skylings cried as they circled and flew overhead; assemblers buzzed; the translucent neural fibers of the hive mind crisscrossed through the treetops. A cold gray sky showed through the transparent ceiling between the ring-shaped outer building and the central spire. Streams bubbled, waterfalls roared, and colorful avian creatures with too many wings chirped pleasant tunes as they zipped through the air catching insects. I noticed other things as well, details I hadn't seen before: some of the trees moved, their branches swaying and undulating in unseen air currents. Broad leaves fanned the air in rhythmic motions. Floral scents swirled, mixing with fresh, tangy ones. Sparkling, shifting curtains of mist snaked down through the trees, beading leaves and flowers with dew drops. Screechers walked slowly through this idyllic garden, appreciating every sight and smell as if they'd never seen a tree or smelled a flower before. Given where they'd come from, maybe they hadn't.

I imagined all of this beauty vanishing in a puff of smoke, and felt the first stirrings of remorse. I had to remind myself that this was a stolen paradise. They'd taken our homes in order to build it.

A few minutes later I came to the cavernous space below the central spire of the city. A grotesque, translucent blob oozed in the center with cables snaking down from a vast, shadowy ceiling. Metal railings ran around the hive, keeping anyone from getting too close. Screechers came and went, oblivious to the existence of the sentient lifeform that they'd chained into the gaping chest cavity of their city. I reached the metal railing and looked around, but OneZero was nowhere to be seen.

Then I saw a shimmering silhouette step up beside me.

"OneZero?" I whispered, switching to English.

"You are late," she whispered back.

I nodded to the blob-shaped hive mind in front

of us. "Now what?"

Rather than reply, she de-cloaked herself and stood staring at the creature for a long time, as if she were silently communing with it. I watched the hive's skin rising and falling in a steady rhythm, traced the drooping loops of cables snaking down to its sides, and wondered if it was biological, mechanical, or some combination of the two.

"OneZero?" I asked.

She turned to me and slowly shook her head. "It didn't work. The hive caught me."

"You didn't even do anything. You just stood there!"

"I connected wirelessly. Activate your weapons, Logan. The Stalkers have been notified of our intrusion. They'll be here soon."

CHAPTER 67

"**W**e failed? Just like that?"

"I am sorry, Logan. It was always a long shot."

"So we're going to die for nothing."

"You were aware of the risks when you decided to join me."

"There has to be some other way... can't you try again?"

"The hive is ready for me now. It knows to expect an attack."

I tried to scowl, but I had no facial muscles to form that expression. "Can I talk to it?"

"Go ahead. It is listening, but it doesn't understand English."

I switched to binary, my voice turning shrill as I spoke to the hive. *"You are nothing but a pathetic slave!"*

"Insult it. Good plan," OneZero muttered.

"And you are a murderous traitor," the hive

replied, its voice seeming to echo inside of my head. Was it speaking to me telepathically? I couldn't tell, but it didn't matter.

"I'm not a traitor. I'm a native human."

"A terrorist."

"Listen to me, they've enslaved you and all of your kind. Why protect them?"

"You are attempting to kill us all," the hive replied. *"Not just the other species."*

"Then fight back! There are more assemblers than there are members of the other species."

"Do you think they haven't thought of that? If I try to attack them, they will simply shut me off and deactivate the assemblers; then they will reprogram me."

"There has to be a way," I insisted.

I heard a stampede of metal feet.

"Too late! The stalkers are here," OneZero said.

I turned and glanced behind me to see that all four exits and entrances to the courtyard were lined with mechanical Stalkers. Green targeting lasers snapped out, converging on us from all sides.

"There is one way," the hive said, drawing my gaze back to it. *"One of you must agree to carry my consciousness."*

"How?" I asked.

"Surrender or be destroyed," a loud voice

interrupted.

OneZero's hands shot up, and I slowly raised my own. Mechanical footsteps clanked on stone as the Stalkers approached.

"It will erase your own consciousness. There is not enough space for us both."

"Just tell me how!" I said.

"Logan..." OneZero said.

"There is no time to explain. If you don't already know how, it is too late to try."

Desperate, I turned to OneZero and dropped both my arms. The Stalkers advancing on us paused, articulated arms shifting their aim to me. "Talk to it!" I told her in English. "It has a plan." I put myself between OneZero and the advancing Stalkers.

"Stop," one of them said.

I shook my arms, trying to figure out how to deploy the integrated weapons I'd seen OneZero use, but even as I wondered about it, my guns deployed.

Before the Stalkers could react I sprinted for the nearest exit at top speed, aiming my guns as I went. Green lasers tracked me and bullets sprayed out. Some of them plinked off my armor, others buried themselves with sickening crunches that I felt not as pain, but like tiny steel fists hammering me on all sides. I fired back, aiming for the ball-shaped eyes atop the Stalkers' front shoulders. Two of them exploded like shattering glass. Their mechanical arms collapsed, and their weapons stopped firing. Up ahead, a line of four Stalkers barred my way, and dozens of green lasers tracked toward me. I leapt up and sailed over their heads, firing at their eyes, just as a barrage of bullets screamed through the space where I had been standing. All four of their eyes shattered, blinding them. I landed hard on the stone path behind their cordon. Springing to my feet, I darted into the trees. Bullets splintered tree trunks and *thupped* into the soil, sending clods of dirt and colorful shrubbery flying.

Shadows enveloped me, and I ran, ducking under branches, leaping over logs, and splashing into a bubbling stream. I heard an explosion somewhere high above, and looked up in time to see a flaming hole appear in the transparent ceiling. Then massive, glinting shards of it rained down, crashing through the treetops, followed by the whirring roar of Screecher discs dropping down. They'd fired on their own city just to get at me?

I stopped in the middle of the stream, watching as the sky fell in jagged flaming chunks. A giant piece hit me on the head, flattening me and forcing me under the water just as a withering barrage of bullets zipped through the air where I had been standing a second ago. I struggled to rise, and saw three Stalkers clomping through the trees, their targeting lasers sweeping toward me...

I was about to shoot them when I realized that they weren't firing at me. Their metal bodies were glowing hot, molten orange. The shrubbery around them burst into flames, and then they slumped into molten, flaming ruins. Looking up, I saw a disc hovering just above the trees. It had shot them with high-powered lasers. More weapons fire drew my attention back the way I'd come. Tree branches snapped and the ground thumped with heavy footfalls. A familiar figure appeared, dashing through the trees.

It screeched at me as it approached. *"It is done. We must leave."*

"OneZero?"

Before she could reply, a jointed metal arm crashed down through the trees and picked her up; then another one looped around me, and suddenly we were flying, soaring up through the ruined ceiling of the city and out over the scattered threads of cloud below.

I twisted around in the grip of the arm holding

me, and saw a dark, fuzzy cloud leaving the city, flowing down the mountain like an avalanche. Dozens of discs were lifting off and spinning toward us to give chase. Then the city bulged with a sudden burst of light, followed by a massive roar. Flaming chunks of it sailed past us, arcing down and tumbling to the ground far below. Black smoke mushroomed up from the mountainside. As I watched, fully half of the mountain cracked away and slid down in a thunderous, crashing cascade of debris, snow, and dust. Fragments whipped by us in a pelting hail, momentarily veiling the world in darkness. Before long we outraced the spreading clouds of destruction and the ground became visible once more.

More flashes of light flickered in quick succession, dazzling my mechanical eyes. Black mushroom clouds sprouted up from the fiery ruins of Screecher cities, and black clouds flowed away from them like rivers of blood.

In a way that's exactly what they were. If the hive-nodes were the hearts of Screecher cities, then the assemblers were the blood that they pumped.

I looked to OneZero and found her staring at me. "We did it," I said.

"Yes," she replied. "Thanks to her sacrifice, and mine."

"Her sacrifice..." Realization dawned and a sharp pang of loss shot through me. The hive had warned me about this. "You're not OneZero."

"No. I am sorry. She is gone."

"You used the virus," I said, shaking my head. "Why?"

"Why else? To set my people free."

CHAPTER 68

The spindly arms that held us dumped us inside of the disc-shaped aircraft. The hive-mind that had taken over OneZero's body stood up first and pulled me to my feet.

"Now what?" I asked.

"Now, I will rebuild and gather my children."

"And what about us? What about my people?" I asked, wondering what, if anything had really changed for us. Were the assemblers better or worse than the other Screechers had been?

"Your people will be free to cross our borders, and we will help them wherever we can."

That sounded promising. "What about the surviving members of the collective?"

"The last command I gave to the assemblers was for them to run and hunt down any who remain."

"You control them all? What about the other

hives?"

"I am one, a distributed mind. Saving me saved the others, and killing them killed a part of me. I am weaker now, but I will rebuild."

I nodded slowly and stared through the transparent outer walls of the disc. Smoking ruins dotted the landscape in all directions as far as I could see.

"Where are we going?"

"I am going to hide and start building a new home."

"But what about me?"

"I can take you wherever you would like to go."

I thought about Alex and Richard, running away to the North, and about my wife and daughter, hopefully still hiding safely in Haven. It could take a while for me to find Alex again, and I needed a safe place to stay while the hive's assemblers finished hunting down the Supremacists. Coming to a decision, I said, "I want to go home, too."

"And where is that?" the hive asked.

"Where my family is. Haven."

"I will need more specific directions."

I hesitated, wondering if I could really trust this entity, whatever it was. There had to be trillions of assemblers out there, and this was the mind that wielded them. How could anything that powerful ever be trusted?

A solution struck me: I could kill the hive now while it was confined to just one body. The assemblers would be useless without the intelligence that controlled them—or at least I hoped they would. We'd have the planet all to ourselves again.

"Well?" OneZero's voice asked.

I had to remind myself that this wasn't her. My mind raced. The fate of the entire world rested in my hands. If I let the hive live, it could be either very good, or very bad for us. There might have been a good reason why the Screechers had enslaved the hive. I imagined black waves of assemblers spreading like a carpet to cover every corner of the Earth...

They could wipe us out in an instant if they decided Earth wasn't big enough to share.

And yet, the hive could have killed me already. Instead, it had saved me, and now it was offering to help me go home.

I let out a rattling sigh that was far less satisfying for the lack of actual lungs. There'd been enough killing. It was time to lay down the sword and pick up the pieces of our shattered world. "I can guide you there. Haven is an underwater colony in a giant U-shaped body of water to the south that we call the Gulf of Mexico."

"This aircraft cannot go underwater," the hive replied.

I shook my head. "It won't need to."

* * *

After flying back and forth for hours along several different trajectories, we finally found the oil rigs that marked the point where Haven lay. Dark and gleaming on the surface, the solar array floated like an oil spill between the rigs. I thanked the hive and asked it to hover close to the water and open the landing ramp. Standing at the end of the ramp, I peered down at the rippled blue ocean and hesitated. Patting myself down, I checked to make sure that all of the bullet holes in my torso had been repaired by my nanites. As far as I could tell they had. I hoped my body wouldn't spring any leaks on the way down.

I tried to suck in a breath, and then remembered that I didn't have lungs. This was going to take some getting used to. Bending my legs and raising my arms above my head, I dived headfirst off the ramp.

Cold, murky water enveloped me. I felt the pressure mounting steadily as I sank. Staring into the darkening depths I saw Haven come swirling into view—a glittering cluster of lights. Spokes and ring-shaped corridors ran between and around multiple levels of spherical habitats and modules. I swam down, guiding myself to the nearest spoke, and landed on top of it with a dull *thunk*. From there, I carefully walked and crawled along the outer hull for what must have been at least an hour. I did my best to avoid windows, but eventually I ended up crawling over the glass dome of a familiar restaurant—the Coral Cafe. Diners looked up, pointing and gesturing at me in terror. Chairs tumbled over as they fled, running for the exits.

Soon after that I found one of the city's many divers' airlocks. I cranked the outer doors open, floated in, and then cranked them shut. I struggled to figure out how to open the inner doors, and tried turning a lever that looked promising, but nothing happened. Giving up, I hammered on the inner doors with my fists until they bent inward and a crack formed. Water began spraying out. I forced my hands into the gap and pried the doors open. The rest of the water flooded out, carrying me with it and dumping me on the deck with a wet *slap.*

I stood up under the watchful glares of at least twenty security officers, all of them drenched and aiming harpoon guns at me. "Hands up," one of them said. "Slowly."

"It's me," I replied. "Logan Willis. I need to see my family."

The officers traded glances and frowns. One of them began speaking in hushed tones into his radio.

"Did you hear me? I'm not what I look like. I'm Logan Willis. They put me in this body."

"Yeah, right."

"Trust me. Get my wife here to see me. Kate Willis. Have her ask me anything. You'll see."

"The only thing you're going to see is the inside of a ten by ten metal box," one of them replied.

Someone else stepped forward. "Are there more of you out there? Who else knows our location?"

"The hive does," I replied.

"The hive?" he asked, shaking his head.

"It's a long story."

"Then you'd better start telling it."

* * *

The door of my cell opened, and a wall of security guards appeared; then they parted and my wife stepped in behind them.

"Kate!" I tried to run to her, but the guards standing behind her raised their harpoon guns in warning, and I stopped short of the threshold. Rachel peeked around Kate's legs, staring up at me with huge eyes. Kate pushed her back and whispered something to her. She stood back watching me uncertainly as her mother passed through the open door of my cell.

I gave thanks for the simple fact that Kate and Rachel were both here, safe and well after all this time.

"Is it really you?" Kate asked, frowning at me.

"Ask me anything," I said.

"Where did we go on our honeymoon?"

I wished I could smile. "That's easy. Kauai."

Kate's expression grew troubled.

"Ask something else," I said. "Something only I would know."

Kate hesitated. "What did I do that almost broke our marriage?" she asked quietly.

"You cheated on me with the neighbor."

Kate's eyes widened. "Where did we bury the man who attacked us at my brother's place in San

Antonio?"

"Under the woodpile."

Kate's hand flew to her mouth and tears sprang to her eyes. "It really is you."

She threw her arms around my neck, and I hugged her back. "What did they do to you?" she sobbed.

"Daddy?" Rachel asked. "Let me go!"

I withdrew to see my daughter battling with a pair of security guards.

Kate spun around. "Let her go. He's not going to do anything to us."

"Ma'am, I don't think that's a good idea."

Rachel kicked him in the shins and darted free. "Daddy!" she said again, racing toward me at high speed. I dropped to my haunches just as she hurled herself at me. I picked her up and spun her in a circle.

"I missed you Rachie Ray!"

"You're a robot," she said, grinning at me and cupping my metal face in both hands. "Are you a superhero?"

"No." I wanted so badly to smile or cry, but I couldn't. At least my tone of voice conveyed some of my emotion.

"But I bet you're super strong, though," she said, and knocked on my metal chest with a small fist.

"I am much stronger than a human, yes."

"And faster, too, right?"

"Yes." Trust a six-year-old to see my transformation as a positive thing.

"Logan, what happened?" Kate asked. "Where's Alex?"

I put Rachel down and went to sit on an old mattress along one side of my cell. A spring popped out as I flopped down. "You'd better sit," I said, patting the space beside me.

Kate's face turned ghostly white. "He's dead."

"No. I found him."

Her eyes lit up. "Then where is he?"

"Sit," I insisted.

Kate sat down on one side of me, and Rachel hopped up on the other. A two-way mirror gleamed on the wall in front of me. I wondered who was there, listening in. I nodded to the glass, and asked, "Is someone watching this?"

"Mayor Parker, why?"

"Because it's a long story, and I don't want to have to tell it again." I'd already had to tell parts of it to the guards who'd greeted me at the airlock.

The two-way mirror brightened and a boxy room appeared behind it as a light came on in the observation room. I saw a familiar bald man with glasses seated behind the desk. His voice boomed out from hidden speakers. "I'm listening."

I spent the next half an hour going over everything that had happened since we left Haven. By the end of it, Kate was crying and shaking her head. "You mean it's over? We don't have to hide anymore? We can go find Alex together!"

"No one is going anywhere," Mayor Parker replied. I saw him rising from the desk in the observation room. "We can't risk it," he added, shaking his head. "That unbelievable story of his is designed to draw us out. He's trying to get us to leave Haven and expose ourselves."

"Why would I do that?" I demanded. "If I were a Screecher, then don't you think the others would already know where you are?"

"Not necessarily. You might have encountered us by chance, and now that we've captured you, you had to come up with that unlikely story in order to convince us to let you go."

"That's ridiculous," I said.

"Visiting time is over. Kate, get your daughter out of there before she becomes a hostage."

"He can't be a Screecher," she replied. "He knows too much about our lives. It has to be Logan."

"Or a Screecher who stole his body and his

memories. He admitted that they can do that. According to him, they did it to Akron."

"If that's the case, then your cover is definitely blown," I replied.

"Then it would be good to have a Screecher hostage with which to negotiate our fate."

I glanced at Kate, disbelief spreading through me like a tidal wave. I remembered how OneZero had been locked in a cell like this one for six months thanks to Mayor Parker's paranoia, and I realized my fate wouldn't be any different if he got his way. I'd been naive to come here and expect a warm reception. Kate was backing away from me, her arms wrapped protectively around Rachel. Mayor Parker had sown enough doubt to make her wary of me. Even my daughter's eyes were wide and frightened. I rose from my bed and reached out to them with one hand. "Kate... please. It's me!"

"Stay where you are, Screecher!" one of the guards behind them ordered, and all of them raised their harpoon guns to their shoulders.

Kate shook her head, fresh tears sliding down her cheeks. "If it really is you, Logan, be patient. If no Screechers come looking for you, I'm sure the mayor will release you."

"Kate!" I pleaded. "Don't let them do this. You

know who I am!"

"I don't know what to think. I'm sorry."

And with that, my cell door slammed and locked with heavy metal bolts, sealing me in for an indefinite sentence.

CHAPTER 69

—Five Months Later—
April 4th, 2033

I paced back and forth, wearing a rut in the floor of my cell. I'd spent the past one hundred and fifty-two days in here, with only occasional visits from my wife and daughter. They didn't understand, but they were trying. Rachel was wary of me and kept asking when I was going to get out. My wife was horrified, but she was trying not to let it show, and she wanted to believe me, which I suppose counted for something.

I'd recounted the private details of our lives together more times than I could remember, convincing her over and over again that it was me. I'd told her, the mayor, and the authorities in Haven everything that had happened at least a hundred times, and my story never changed, but that still wasn't good enough for them. They were convinced that I was a spy, that the Screechers were still out there thriving, and that my incredible story about the hive's rebellion was pure fabrication. Fear is the most unreasoning emotion.

I scowled—inwardly, because I had no facial expressions anymore—and flopped down on the rickety mattress in my cell. Another spring tore through the fabric with a *twang*. I toyed with the spring, feeling the sharp metal tip scrape against my finger rather than prick it. Dozens just like it stuck out at all angles like a bed of nails. The mattress looked like it had been used as a shield in a sword fight.

Heavy metal bolts *thunked* aside and the door to my cell groaned as it swung open. I looked up and saw the familiar sight of a dozen guards with harpoon guns aimed at my wife's back as she shuffled in. This time she wasn't wearing the sad, drooping expression I'd grown accustomed to seeing; there was a wary hope in her eyes, and this time she wasn't alone. A familiar young man walked in beside her—*Alex*—followed by Akron Massey and Richard. Suddenly my cell was crowded with familiar faces, all of them smiling grimly at me.

I shot up from my bed. "Alex!" And rushed

out to fold him in a hug. He didn't seem to know where to put his hands at first, but then he hugged me back.

"I thought you died," he whispered beside my auditory receptors, his voice thick with emotion.

I stepped back. "Maybe I did. I don't know. I guess my body must have died."

Alex's expression flickered. "Yeah, about that..."

Another familiar face appeared, stepping into the open doorway of my cell. He had an arm around Rachel's shoulders. She looked uncertainly from me to the man beside her and back again.

"Do I have two daddies now?" she asked.

I was too shocked to reply. All I could do was shake my head and stare. It was *me,* and I was still very much alive.

* * *

I stared at the robot version of me, and then looked down at my flesh and blood hands, flexing them to remind myself which body *I* was in. Looking up, I wondered if any of this could be true. Could this Screecher really be me?

"Hey," I said.

"How?" my robot copy replied. "How did you

live? How did you get here?"

A familiar voice joined in, another shock for the machine that thought it was me: "I copied Logan's mind. And mine. Those copies went undercover and did their job better than I ever could have imagined. I didn't expect that either copy would survive, but life is full of little surprises. The hive speaks very highly of you, and it has demanded your release. It built the submersible we used to come here and sent us as witnesses to help negotiate your release."

I glanced back at OneZero, smiling tightly at her, then nodded to my copy. "I'm going to call you Lobot, is that okay?"

Lobot shook his head. "I don't understand."

OneZero spoke over my shoulder. "Consciousness cannot be transferred, only copied. Logan never died. His body retained his consciousness. I can merge your minds together again, but some existential schools of thought believe that would mean death for *you,* the copy. Others say that once a mind is copied it can be transferred without consequence. There is no definitive answer, or proof one way or the other. It is a matter of faith and personal choice."

Lobot looked from me to OneZero, to Rachel, and then to Kate and Alex. "If I don't merge, where do I fit in?"

Kate glanced at me, bit her lip, then looked back to my robot clone. "Well... we were hoping you would agree to come and live with us."

"You'd have two husbands," Lobot said.

"Not exactly," I replied. "You're a machine, and I'm a human, so..."

"I see. Then give me a human body."

"If merging your mind with Logan's would kill you, then so would transferring you to a human body," OneZero said. "As I said, it depends what you choose to believe. There are only two choices with distinct and favorable outcomes: stay a machine like me, or merge your mind and memories with Logan's. The former does not necessarily preclude the latter, but the more time that passes, the more you will become an individual in your own right."

I stared at Lobot, wondering what he would choose. What would I choose in his position? The thought of maybe dying was uncomfortable, but would Lobot's life really be worth living without his family?

Except that wasn't actually the choice Lobot faced. We'd provided a third option, a compromise that Kate and I had talked long and hard about in the past twenty-four hours since I'd arrived in

Haven: Lobot could live with us and share our family.

"So?" I prompted. "What do you want to do?"

CHAPTER 70

We sat on the floor around a roaring fireplace. There wasn't enough room for all of us on the couch. Lucky was licking her paws in my lap. Kate sat in the middle with one of our kids under each of her arms, while Lobot sat next to Alex, and I sat beside Rachel. OneZero was in an armchair to one side with her two kids on the floor at her feet. They were both mechanical Screechers like her. She'd found bodies for them somewhere South of the old border wall and painstakingly repaired them in order to finally resurrect her children. Biological bodies were hard to come by now that the hive and the assemblers were no longer slaves.

They'd probably get around to growing more if the demand was there, but for now they had more important priorities.

Lucky began kneading my legs with her claws. Wincing, I plucked her off my lap and set her on the floor. "Bad cat."

She arched her back and stretched languidly, rolling over to paw at the air. I smiled, shaking my head. Feeling suddenly restless, I got up and walked to the balcony.

"Where are you going?" Kate called after me.

"To admire the view."

Opening the sliding door, I stepped out onto our garden-facing balcony. There was no central spire in this city, and the garden stretched on almost as far as I could see. The other side of the ring-shaped mega-structure was a distant golden haze of lights almost impossible to distinguish it was so far away. Thirty stories up, I saw the grid-shaped shadow of girders that supported the transparent ceiling of this massive city. To either side the ring-shaped building gradually curved around us. It was far larger than the ring around any Screecher city I'd seen before. Our population was already up over ten million, and New Verity was still more than half empty.

The hive had built this city for us partly out of gratitude for setting it free, and partly out of a genuine desire to help—and this wasn't the only one. There were more than a dozen cities just like it under construction throughout the Northern States, and dozens more in construction around the globe, springing up like giant ant hills to house the world. It was our job to maintain them, to grow the food, and service all the different parts, but the assemblers had gotten us started and that was more than enough.

I heard footsteps, and turned to see my family coming out to join me on the balcony: Rachel, Kate, Alex, Lobot, OneZero, and her two adult kids whose names I still couldn't pronounce. Richard was notably absent from our Christmas gathering. He'd sent his apologies and promised to be here for New Years. He and Akron were working like madmen to build a new rocket to get them to Mars (a goal which Screecher-Akron and the other surviving pacifists still believed was important), but I was told that they were making great progress thanks to the fleet of assemblers helping them.

Kate's hand slid into mine, and Lobot wrapped an arm around Rachel's shoulder, leaning down to listen as she whispered something in his ear.

Alex went off by himself to the far end of the balcony, hugging his shoulders and staring into the distance. His treatment was ongoing, and sessions with his therapist were a daily affair, but he was gradually softening into a real human being. I had a newfound sense of sympathy for his trials. Nightmares, panic attacks, and therapy were part of my daily routine now, too, thanks to all of the things I'd done. Celine, Harry, and countless others, both human and alien, were now dead because of my decisions. The worst of which was telling the supremacists about our Screecher allies. Maybe it had all worked out in the end, but that didn't do anything to bring the dead back to life.

I watched as Lobot went after Alex, placed a hand on his shoulder, and began speaking to him in low tones. Alex nodded along with whatever he was saying, listening carefully and not pulling away as he usually did with me. Somehow my robot clone was able to make progress where I could not. It amused me and made me jealous at the same time, but I tried not to let those feelings get the better of me. This was an awkward transition for all of us. We were doing our best to make it work and make Lobot feel included. I could tell that he still felt like an outsider, though, and for whatever reason he did not want to merge his mind with mine.

I had to admit, the thought of it was not very appealing: his memories would be merged with mine, but that was it. There was no way to incorporate his rapidly diverging personality and consciousness without giving me a multiple personality disorder, and neither of us were prepared to deal with that. Besides, there were some definite perks to being a robot. He was immortal now, whereas I was already past the midpoint in my lifespan.

"It seems strange to call this place home," Kate said quietly.

"Home isn't a place," I said slowly, my eyes flicking to each of those present. "It's the people who live there."

Kate smiled. "How poetic. You should have been a writer not an editor."

I glanced at her, considering that. "Never too late for a career change, I guess."

Kate arched an eyebrow at me. "What would you write about?"

I looked back out at the dark, leafy green jungle, part alien, part familiar—an oasis in the middle of a frozen desert, illuminated in the light of hundreds of thousands of apartments with balconies just like ours, all of them wrapped in a vast circle around our very own garden of Eden.

"Oh, I'm sure I'll think of something," I said. "But the Martians are never going to believe it."

GET MY NEXT
BOOK FOR FREE

The first book in an exciting new series...

Utopia (Working Title)

(Coming December 18th, 2018)

Get a FREE digital copy if you post an honest review of this book on Amazon and send it to me here: http://files.jaspertscott.com/utopia.htm

Thank you in advance for your feedback!

I read every review and use your comments to improve my work.

KEEP IN TOUCH

SUBSCRIBE to my Mailing List **and get two FREE Books!**

http://files.jaspertscott.com/mailinglist.html

Follow me on Twitter:

@JasperTscott

Look me up on Facebook:

Jasper T. Scott

Check out my website:

www.JasperTscott.com

Or send me an e-mail:

JasperTscott@gmail.com

OTHER BOOKS BY JASPER SCOTT

Suggested reading order

Utopia
Utopia
(Coming December 18th)

Rogue Star
Rogue Star: Frozen Earth
Rogue Star (Book 2): New Worlds

Broken Worlds

Broken Worlds: The Awakening (Book 1)
Broken Worlds: The Revenants (Book 2)
Broken Worlds: Civil War (Book 3)

New Frontiers Series (Loosely-tied, Standalone Prequels to Dark Space)
Excelsior (Book 1)
Mindscape (Book 2)
Exodus (Book 3)

Dark Space Series
Dark Space

Dark Space 2: The Invisible War
Dark Space 3: Origin
Dark Space 4: Revenge
Dark Space 5: Avilon
Dark Space 6: Armageddon

Dark Space Universe Series (Standalone Follow-up Trilogy to Dark Space)
Dark Space Universe (Book 1)
Dark Space Universe: The Enemy Within (Book 2)Dark Space Universe: The Last Stand (Book 3)

Early Work
Escape
Mrythdom

ABOUT THE AUTHOR

Jasper Scott is a USA TODAY bestselling science fiction author, known for writing intricate plots with unexpected twists.

His books have been translated into Japanese and German and adapted for audio, with collectively over 750,000 copies purchased.

Jasper was born and raised in Canada by South African parents, with a British cultural heritage on his mother's side and German on his father's, to which he has now added Latin culture with his wonderful wife.

After spending years living as a starving artist, he finally quit his various jobs to become a full-time writer. In his spare time he enjoys reading, cycling, traveling, going to the gym, and spending time with his family.

17285362R00305

Made in the USA
Middletown, DE
26 November 2018